Australian Sh

Kerryn Goldsworthy was born in South Australia in 1953. She is a graduate of the University of Adelaide, has taught in several Australian universities since 1977, and is currently a senior lecturer at the University of Melbourne where she teaches Australian literature, women's studies and creative writing. She edited *Australian Book Review* in 1986-87, and is a regular book reviewer for newspapers, literary journals and radio. A collection of her own short stories, *North of the Moonlight Sonata*, was published by McPhee Gribble in 1989.

Australian Short Stories

Selected by
Kerryn Goldsworthy

Jacaranda

This edition published 1992 by
JACARANDA WILEY LTD
33 Park Road, Milton, Qld 4064

Offices also in Sydney and Melbourne

First published 1983 by J. M. Dent Pty Ltd
Reprinted 1986

Re-issued 1989 by Houghton Mifflin Australia
Reprinted 1990

Collection © Kerryn Goldsworthy 1983
Introduction © Kerryn Goldsworthy 1983
Copyright © of stories retained by individual authors

National Library of Australia
Cataloguing-in-Publication data

Australian short stories.

ISBN 0 7016 3064 7.

1. Short stories, Australian, I. Goldsworthy, Kerryn, 1953–..

A823.0108

All rights reserved. No part of this publication
may be reproduced, stored in a retrieval system,
or transmitted in any form or by any means,
electronic, mechanical, photocopying, recording,
or otherwise, without the prior permission of
the publisher.

Cover: **Tom ROBERTS**
Australia 1856-1931
A break away!
1891, oil on canvas,
137.0 × 168.0 cm.
Art Gallery of South Australia, Adelaide
Elder Bequest Fund 1895

Printed and bound in Australia by
Australian Print Group, Maryborough, Vic.

10 9 8 7 6 5

Contents

Introduction	IX
CATHERINE HELEN SPENCE (1825-1910) Like All First Chapters — Introductory	1
MARCUS CLARKE (1846-1881) An Up-Country Township	9
"PRICE WARUNG" (1855-1911) The Crime of Convict Cunliffe	15
BARBARA BAYNTON (1857-1929) The Chosen Vessel	22
HENRY LAWSON (1867-1922) The Union Buries Its Dead Telling Mrs Baker	29 34
HENRY HANDEL RICHARDSON (1870-1946) Two Hanged Women	48
ETHEL ANDERSON (1883-1958) Miss Aminta Wirraway and the Sin of Lust Juliet McCree is Accused of Gluttony	53 61
KATHERINE SUSANNAH PRICHARD (1883-1969) Flight	77
FRANK DALBY DAVISON (1893-1970) The Woman at the Mill	91

CHRISTINA STEAD (1902-1983)
Guest of the Redshields — 104
Sappho — 109

ALAN MARSHALL (1902-1984)
The Three-Legged Bitch — 114

JOHN MORRISON (b. 1904)
Christ, the Devil and the Lunatic — 130
The Incense Burner — 155

E.O. SCHLUNKE (1906-1960)
The Man Who Liked Music — 168

GAVIN CASEY (1907-1964)
The Last Night — 180

HAL PORTER (1911-1984)
Say to me Ronald! — 188
Brett — 202

DAL STIVENS (b. 1911)
Warrigal — 220

PATRICK WHITE (1912-1991)
Down at the Dump — 230

PETER COWAN (b. 1914)
The Voice — 260

THELMA FORSHAW (b. 1923)
On Our Safari — 267

ELIZABETH JOLLEY (b. 1923)
Poppy Seed and Sesame Rings — 279

ELIZABETH HARROWER (b. 1928)
The Cost of Things — 287

MORRIS LURIE (b. 1938)
Africa Wall — 301

FRANK MOORHOUSE (b. 1938)
A Person of Accomplishment — 325
Audition for Male Voice — 338

MURRAY BAIL (b. 1941)
A,B,C,D,E,F,G,H,I,J,K,L,M,
N,O,P,Q,R,S,T,U,V,W,X,Y,Z   342

MICHAEL WILDING (b. 1942)
The Man of Slow Feeling   350

PETER CAREY (b. 1943)
American Dreams   357

Biographical Notes   369

Acknowledgements   374

Introduction

If the short story has always held a prominent place in Australian literature, it is partly because writers of short fiction have usually had the support, in one form or another, of various editors and publishers. Apart from the *Bulletin* magazine, which put the Australian short story on its feet at the beginning of this century (and is now a well-preserved 103 years old), the long-running anthology series *Coast to Coast* and its virtual successor *Tabloid Story* have provided opportunities for publishing which might otherwise have been denied to many short-story writers.

Coast to Coast, whose total life-span was 32 years, was established in 1941 through the combined efforts of Beatrice Davis and Douglas Stewart; published by Angus and Robertson, it appeared annually between 1941 and 1948, biennially between 1949 and 1970, and once more in 1973, with a different editor each time. Meanwhile, in 1972, the first two issues of *Tabloid Story* had appeared. 'We came up with the idea,' says Michael Wilding, one of the original editors, 'of producing a packaged short story magazine as a supplement to other host journals . . .' Eleven years later *Tabloid Story* has appeared in numerous newspapers and journals, and is still in operation. While other publications have played their part in the care and maintenance of the Australian short story, these three stand out as the most significant; most of the authors whose work is represented in this anthology have had stories published in at least one of them, and a few authors in all three.

Any reader familiar with Australian literature may, on looking through the titles included in this anthology, be struck by the absence of certain stories widely regarded as classics of Australian literature. He or she may be even more struck by the inclusion of stories, and authors, comparatively obscure. The choices made — choices to exclude as well as to include — have been made with much deliberation and, in one or two cases, some trepidation; and they have been made for reasons which perhaps require some explanation here. I don't believe that it is possible to represent adequately the 'best' of all Australian short stories in anthologies such as this; that such a 'best' comprises an agreed-upon and static canon; or, indeed, that such a 'best' exists at all. Widespread changes in the critical perception and judgement of literature, and the rapid growth and development of Australian writing, have made such beliefs highly questionable, and have certainly made it impossible for anthologists of Australian literature to go on needlessly re-canonising its classics without questioning the motives behind, or the effects resulting from, such choices.

One of the aims of this anthology, then, is to sidestep this attitude: to avoid presenting a 'Best Of . . .' selection which would tell the reader nothing except which Australian stories are most frequently reprinted and which ones the editor likes best. I have tried instead to steer a middle course between the idiosyncratic and the predictable; while most of the well-known Australian writers of short fiction are represented here, many of the stories themselves have been chosen not so much for their critical reputation as for the relation they bear in form or content, or both, to each other. In choosing the stories I have tried to establish and maintain certain kinds of continuity, and, in doing so, to illustrate some general ideas and observations about the Australian short story.

The stories have been arranged in chronological order according to the birthdates of the authors; they have been chosen partly to reflect the three roughly identifiable short-story 'booms' in Australia. In the 1890's and early 1900's the immensely popular *Bulletin* magazine, based in Sydney, fostered and encouraged a number of short-story writers who came to be known, loosely and collectively, as the '*Bulletin* school', and of whom the two most widely read today are Henry Lawson and Barbara Baynton. Both are represented here by stories which, while not their standard anthology pieces, are fairly typical of the respective authors' styles and attitudes, and which bear some relation in form or content to the other stories in this collection.

In the 1940's the short story again began to dominate Australian fiction and flourished through into the 1950's; as with the *Bulletin* period, the comparative scarcity of novels published in the 1940's highlighted the predominance of the short-story form, which was favoured in any case by many of the social realist writers who dominated the period. John Morrison in particular became, and has remained, one of the best-known writers of short fiction in Australia.

The emergence in the 1970's of a new generation of short-story writers was the result of several different developments. Government support for the arts in the early seventies made writing more of an economically attractive proposition than it had ever been in Australia; the lifting of censorship restrictions meant that writers like Frank Moorhouse and Michael Wilding, much of whose work is sexually oriented, could find a more respectable and less limited readership than was constituted by the devotees of the soft-porn magazines in which much of their early work was originally published. Novelists also enjoyed the benefits of these two developments, so the new interest in the short-story form did not, this time, emerge at the expense or in the absence of interest in the novel.

Michael Wilding, also a publisher, critic, and university teacher, sees in recent Australian fiction a reaction away from what he calls the 'Lawson tradition' — away, that is, from the dominant critical attitude to Australian short stories rather than from Lawson himself. (Wilding is quick to clarify his meaning here, and adds 'Not that we had anything against Lawson'; and, as critic Elizabeth Webby points out, Lawson's stories actually have much in common with those of recent writers.) This 'reaction' manifested itself chiefly as a new interest in formal and stylistic experiment; stories by Wilding, Moorhouse, Peter Carey and Murray Bail — as well as by Dal Stivens, a writer from an earlier generation — all indicated a departure from the predominantly realist, 'well-made' short stories of the 1940's and 1950's. Fantasy, surrealism, experiments with the nature of narrative in general and the short-story form in particular all marked an increasing self-consciousness and sophistication in Australian writing.

Such experimentation demands of the reader, among other things, a readjustment of his or her own expectations; most readers of fiction unconsciously anticipate realism, a certain number of 'believable' characters, and a plot with a beginning, a middle and an end. According to those criteria, this collection contains a number of pieces — not all of them recent — which could not be called 'short stories' at all. Seen in conjunction with the other stories, however, they raise questions as to just where the boundaries of definition lie.

The first piece in the anthology is actually the first chapter of a novel — Catherine Helen Spence's *Clara Morison* (1854), the first novel by a woman to be published in Australia. Marcus Clarke's 'An Up-Country Township' is a sketch with no discernible plot; Price Warung's 'The Crime of Convict Cunliffe' is a piece of impassioned polemic in which one of the characters is a real historical figure. The two fantasies by Christina Stead, one of Australia's most extraordinary and highly regarded writers, are from her first book *The Salzburg Tales;* an exuberant extravaganza of short fiction, this book is constructed along *Decameron* lines, with a large number of tales — displaying an astonishing variety of style and subject — told by different characters and loosely held together by an overarching narrative continuity. Frank Moorhouse's 'A Person of Accomplishment' is from *The Americans, Baby*, which like most of Moorhouse's collections is a series of semi-detached stories; while there is little narrative continuity between them, many of the characters, settings and themes reappear from story to story, weaving in and out of the overall structure of each book. Moorhouse calls his books 'discontinuous narratives', a term which has passed into Australian literary parlance and can now be retrospectively applied to Ethel Anderson's *At Parramatta*, from which those of her stories included here are taken. Published more than ten years before Moorhouse's first collection, and written by a woman born 55 years before him, *At Parramatta* displays exactly the same technique — albeit with very different results.

Some of these 'outsider' pieces are self-consciously original or deliberately experimental; others were never intended to be read as individual stories. But all have been chosen to demonstrate that the genre labelled 'short story' is not an easily definable one.

The term 'Australian' is not an easily definable one either,

Introduction

and, as with all new cultures, it has been largely the task of artists to define it; these stories have been chosen partly to reflect the changing images of Australia produced by its writers since the mid-nineteenth century. The first piece in the collection — the chapter from *Clara Morison* — seemed not only to have a narrative self-containment which gave it a certain structural resemblance to the 'short story' proper, but also to serve as an ideal introduction to the stories which follow. The anxiety and apprehension felt by the heroine Clara at the prospect of migrating to Australia — and shared by most of her counterparts in both fiction and history — are shown to have been amply justified in the pieces by Clarke, Warung, Baynton and Lawson, who all paint vivid and almost unrelievedly negative pictures of Australian life in the nineteenth century.

But from around the turn of the century — the heyday of the *Bulletin* — there is a discernible shift in emphasis. The *Bulletin*, and hence the kind of short fiction it published and encouraged, was characterised by a spirit of nationalism that often bordered on the aggressive, if not the truculent; the short fiction which flourished around the turn of the century was of a kind which insisted on its own 'Australian-ness'. And while Lawson in particular maintained in his stories an attitude to the Australian landscape which is dour at best, he depicts the Australian national character as formed by the adversity of the circumstances in which it found itself. More often than not his characters score at least some kind of victory over the conditions in which they live by the exercise of virtues represented, implicitly or explicitly, as characteristically Australian — hardihood, the 'mateship' variety of loyalty, a more or less rough kindliness, and courage.

Although recognisably 'Australian' characters and settings, deliberately constructed as such, still predominate in the fiction of the next few decades — Katharine Susannah Prichard's story 'Flight' is a case in point — the note of nationalistic stridency sometimes sounded by the *Bulletin* school all but disappears. The increasing influence, formal and stylistic, of British, American and European literature on Australian writers was accompanied by the retreat of Australia's landscape into the background of its short fiction. Urban life, personal dilemmas and social conditions moved into the foreground of the post-Lawson short story; while writers remained — and still remain — concerned with the question of what is 'Australian', their mode of dealing with it began to change. Stories like Frank Dalby Davison's 'The Woman at the Mill', Alan Marshall's 'The Three-Legged Bitch' and Gavin Casey's 'The Last Night' are not 'about' Australia in the way that Clarke's, Warung's and Lawson's almost ostentatiously are; but Australian settings, characters, ways of life and habits of mind and speech are mimetically represented in them with equal amounts of unobtrusiveness and care.

The number of stories in this anthology which deal with specifically non-Australian characters or settings may seem, in this context, disproportionately large; but it is possible to trace in Australian fiction — especially since World War II — a trend towards the use of contrasts between Australian and non-Australian characters and settings. Writers began to cease dealing with their increasingly difficult task of defining a national culture and identity by saying what we *are*, and began to point to what we are *not* — to define Australia by contrast with what was, or seemed, alien to it. One disquieting variation on this theme is Prichard's 'Flight', in which the contrast is between black Australians and white ones. Prichard avoids the conventional *mea culpa* stance of the white observer — although the story manifests a kind of muted outrage at the treatment of blacks by whites, most of the individual white characters in it are treated sympathetically — and concentrates instead on the mutual incomprehension between the two races.

The influx of European immigrants to Australia which began during the war years not only produced a kind of delayed-action literary sub-culture of migrants' writing which is beginning to make itself more and more keenly felt — *Alien Son* (1952) by novelist Judah Waten is one of the earliest and best-known examples — but it also gave Australian writers a new and fertile field of subject matter and a renewed awareness of what 'being Australian' might or might not mean. Two of the three stories here which deal specifically with Europeans in Australia are lighthearted if not downright comic, but 'lighthearted' should not be confused with 'lightweight'; both E.O. Schlunke's 'The Man Who Liked Music' and Thelma Forshaw's 'On Our Safari' barely conceal beneath their comic surfaces some very careful thinking about the messages they convey. Forshaw in particular uses her laconic first-person narrator — whose own view of the situation is gently satirised by the author, through the things she has him see and say — to direct some light but double-handed irony at her fellow Australians. The third of these stories, Elizabeth Jolley's 'Poppy Seed and Sesame Rings', is a delicately understated comment on the situation of immigrant families whose older generation is backward-looking, homesick, death-bound, while the younger is forward-looking, assimilation-bent, and moving away from the European culture which produced it.

Other writers in this collection also measure 'alien' characters and settings against their Australian ones. John Morrison looks at the other side of the homesickness coin in 'The Incense Burner'; the narrator's absence from and nostalgia for Australia make him see the country with a new clarity, and force him to articulate and define just what it is that he is homesick for:

Some building close by had a clock that chimed the hours, and whenever I heard it I would think carefully and call up a scene in Australia that I knew was true and exact of that very moment.

At midnight I would say to myself: it's ten o'clock in the morning, and the hotels down Flinders Street are just opening . . . And there's a white sky and a smell of dust, and trembling pavements which by noon will be hot enough to fry eggs on. And down at St. Kilda Beach lazy little waves are lapping in . . . And there's a place down there in the heath country where my mates and I used to go rabbiting on Sunday afternoons . . .

Hal Porter, like Schlunke and Forshaw, exploits the comic possibilities of the cultural shock sustained by Australians in the presence of exotic foreigners (and, of course, vice versa) in 'Say to me Ronald!'; like Forshaw, Porter treats his first-person narrator ironically, exposing the inadequacies of his Australian hero's response to the unfamiliar. Porter's 'Brett' is a quieter and more reflective story of, this time, Australians abroad; 'Brett' is an ambiguous portrait of an attractively brash young Australian girl who gradually reveals herself as a nervy, brittle stranger in a strange land — as does the main character of Morris Lurie's 'Africa Wall', increasingly alienated by and finally driven to escape from the encroaching, invading strangeness of Tangier. Peter Carey's 'American Dreams', obliquely exploring the misplaced, naive dissatisfactions of an Australian small-town community, deals with invasion rather than escape; the reality of crass, nosy American tourists replaces the town's 'American dreams' of 'the big city, of wealth, of modern houses, of big motor cars.' And in all these stories, the presentation of Australia as the norm — the known quantity being measured and redefined against alien geography or alien humanity — is emphasised by contrast with Spence's 'Introductory' chapter, where Australia is depicted as a mysterious, inchoate, looming threat.

The deliberately large number of such stories included here demonstrates that the so-called 'Lawson tradition' of what Michael Wilding calls 'formula bush tales' has not — even though such stories were for a long time generally preferred by publishers — had the stranglehold over Australian short fiction that some critics have attributed to it or tried to give it; and another deliberate emphasis has been made in this selection for th same kind of reason. The dominant figures of Australian social mythology are all male — the bushman, the Anzac, the sporting hero (all, of course, sun-bronzed) — yet a survey of Australian short fiction reveals that its writers, both male and female, have always been equally concerned with female experience of Australian life, or, indeed, female experience in general. One of the purposes of this anthology is to demonstrate that concern: to attempt to redress the balance of a popular imagination which sees male figures and male experience as predominant in Australian life.

Hence a large number of stories about, or partly about, women have been included here; and while most though not all of these depict women as the passive objects or victims of male decisions and actions, the focus of many of the stories is nevertheless on the female character — who is almost always depicted in a sympathetic light.

In several stories, particularly some of the early ones, the odium of this socially enforced passivity is exacerbated by the conditions of Australian life. Spence's 'Introductory' chapter depicts a woman of spirit and intelligence who is totally at the mercy of her uncle's decision to send her away to a place she fears. Baynton's 'The Chosen Vessel' portrays, with the savage irony of the title, a woman caught and destroyed in a complex

Introduction

web of masculine machinations largely determined by the environment: the isolation of her home is rendered complete by the absence of the hostile husband and exploited by the predatory drifter, and her chance of rescue is lost in a small-town maze of politics and religion — both male-dominated. The very title of Lawson's 'Telling Mrs. Baker' hints at the position of the woman in the story; Mrs. Baker has been left at home, beyond the peripheries of the events of which she must be 'told'. These events occur in the masculine landscape of droving, drinking, and the 'flash barmaids' of outback towns; and Mrs. Baker is successfully deceived by virtue of her absence from it, first by her husband and then by the well-meaning 'mates' who come back to tell her a touching but inaccurate tale about the circumstances of her husband's death. Frank Dalby Davison's 'woman at the mill' is another victim of her own isolated circumstances, emotionally at the mercy of the lover who is free to come and go as he pleases.

The wives in John Morrison's 'Christ, the Devil and the Lunatic' and Gavin Casey's 'The Last Night' bear a resemblance to these other women; although not geographically isolated in the same way, they are obliged by the conventions of marriage to follow — for better or worse — in the wake of their husbands' experience, and their lives are determined by their husbands' actions.

Henry Handel Richardson in 'Two Hanged Women' and Ethel Anderson in 'Miss Aminta Wirraway and the Sin of Lust' arrive from opposite directions at the same subject; these two stories present what seem at first to be totally dissimilar views of young women contemplating the prospect of sex and marriage — although a closer look at the Anderson story reveals a shimmer of irony which brings it closer to Richardson's brooding, negative tone. In 'Juliet McCree is Accused of Gluttony', Anderson maintains the blithe tone and conscious anti-realism of 'Miss Aminta Wirraway', but in this second story the whimsy has a nasty sting; one of the blacker aspects of paternalistic authority is revealed in the smug, hypocritical brutality of Dr. Boisragon towards the children in general and Juliet in particular. Prichard's story 'Flight' — although its central male character is far more sympathetically portrayed — makes the same kind of point; power and authority, personified in one man, are extended (in a way which has brutal effects) over a group of human beings rendered doubly helpless by virtue of being female as well as children.

As might be expected, the more recent stories by male writers portray women as complex creatures with powers and motives, as well as sorrows and virtues, of their own; Patrick White's 'Down at the Dump', for instance, concentrates — like so many of his novels — on different kinds of female sensibility, behaviour and experience. The changing attitude to women in society is reflected in Frank Moorhouse's 'Audition for Male Voice', where the absence of female characters — far from seeming natural or being taken for granted — is, as the title hints, largely the point of the story.

These are some of the considerations, then, which directed my choice of the stories included here: the desire for some kind of chronological coherence in showing the development of the Australian short story; the necessity of presenting as wide a spectrum, in form, style and content, as possible; the way that the terms 'Australian' and 'short story' are defined in practice by writers; and the dominant presence in so many stories of 'outsiders' like children, females and foreigners. If, in the selection of stories, some dark horses have been included at the expense of favourites, it is partly because such a race is always more interesting than one in which the outcome is predictable, and partly because of some recent and significant changes in the condition of the track.

* * * * *

I owe thanks for their help to several people: Jeff Prentice, who is partly responsible for the choice of authors; Paul Salzman, who found so many of the books; and, especially, Ian Reid and Sneja Gunew, whose ideas have been as useful as always.

Kerryn Goldsworthy

Introduction

References: Elizabeth Webby, 'Australian Short Fiction from *While the Billy Boils* to *The Everlasting Secret Family*,' *Australian Literary Studies*, 10 (1981), 147-156.

Michael Wilding, 'The *Tabloid Story* Story,' in Wilding (ed.), *The Tabloid Story Pocket Book* (Sydney: Wild and Woolley, 1978), pp.295-316.

Like All First Chapters — Introductory

Catherine Helen Spence

Mr. Morison had been sitting in his study for half an hour one morning, neither reading nor writing, but apparently settling the pros and cons of some new resolution which he had just formed, or perhaps trying to make it appear as graceful as it was convenient. At the end of his half hour's deliberation he rung the bell, and desired the servant to let Miss Susan and Miss Clara Morison know that he particularly requested their presence in his study immediately. They soon appeared, obedient to their uncle's summons; and while he is clearing his throat and making a few preliminary observations not much to the point, we will take a glance at the parties, and briefly explain their relative positions.

Mr. Morison was a grave, respectable looking man, between forty and fifty, who had a handsome house, and saw a good deal of company, in a fashionable street in Edinburgh. He had a delicate and rather *exigeante* wife and seven children, to whom he was as much attached as he could be to anything; but living up to his income, he felt that the recent death of his brother, leaving him two penniless girls to provide for, was a dreadful calamity; and it was in order, as he thought, to do the best for them with the least possible inconvenience to himself, that he sent for his nieces on this memorable morning. He did not like to be opposed in any-thing, and both of the young ladies knew it.

Susan was about one-and-twenty, with a plain face, and a figure barely tolerable; but her voice was exquisitely musical, her manners graceful and refined, and every accomplishment which she had cultivated was thoroughly acquired; she was a skilful musician, she drew admirably, and she understood more than one foreign language. Mr. Morison felt that she would be an excellent governess for his family, and rejoiced in the idea that he was able to do all his duty by her. But with poor Clara, what was to be done? There she stood, with her soft grey eyes, sunny brown hair, radiant smile, and graceful figure, formed to delight her father's eyes and to gladden his heart, but without one accomplishment that had any marketable value. She neither played, nor sung, nor drew, but she read aloud with exquisite taste; her memory was stored with old ballads and new poems; she understood French, and was familiar with its literature, but could not speak the language; she could write short-hand, and construe Caesar's Commentaries; she played whist and backgammon remarkably well, but she hated crochet and despised worsted-work. In her father's lifetime, Clara had been the general referee at home on all miscellaneous subjects. She knew what book such a thing was in, what part of the book, and almost at what page. But alas! no one cared now for such accomplishments, and she hung her head before her matter-of-fact uncle.

'My dear girls,' said he, 'you are aware that I am not rich, and I hope that neither of you have any objections to doing something for yourselves. I think, Susan, that you could make yourself useful in instructing my three girls, for your education has been a long and expensive one, and must now be turned to account. You will be treated by me and by your aunt exactly as a daughter of our own, and visit and receive visitors with us. And, my dear Susan, as you know your poor aunt's delicate state of health, I hope you will relieve her as much as you can from the fatigue and worry of looking after servants and ordering dinner. You have, since your mother's death, three years ago, had the whole management of your father's establishment, and I am sure you take sufficient interest in us to do your utmost in mine. Now I hope, Susan, that you have no objection to make to this arrangement.'

Susan murmured, 'None whatever; but what shall Clara do?'

'Clara, unfortunately, has not made the same use of the advantages she had,' replied Mr. Morison. 'I do not see how I

Like All First Chapters — Introductory

could get a situation for her, except perhaps as a nursery governess, with some eight or ten pounds a-year, which I am afraid Clara might think too small, and her employer too large, a remuneration for her services. My idea for Clara is, that she should emigrate to Australia.'

'Australia! sixteen thousand miles off!' cried both sisters, bursting into tears.

'What matter for distance?' said Mr. Morison. 'If Clara were to take a situation at all, you must be separated; and if you would look on the thing rationally, you would see that the greater the distance the better for her. In Australia they cannot want accomplished governesses; Clara might get fifty or sixty pounds a-year, and take a good position in society besides. And Clara, you are a pretty and a good girl; you will be sure to marry well in a country where young ladies are so scarce, and where nobody looks for a fortune with his wife; and then you can write for Susan, if you like, to join you.'

'But am I to go alone?' said Clara. 'I am only nineteen, and it is a dreadful thing to go through that long voyage without a friend.'

'I have spoken to Captain Whitby, of the *Magnificent*,' said her uncle, 'and he says that his wife will be a mother to you during the voyage. You will probably make friends among your fellow-passengers in a four months' voyage; and I will give you a strong letter of recommendation to my old friend Campbell, who is a rising merchant in Adelaide, and whose wife will give you a home till you get a situation. And I hope, my dear girl, that you will hold fast by your religious principles even in such a distant land, for that is my only anxiety about you; and write to us by every opportunity that offers. I am confident that you will make a capital colonist. I have spoken to Captain Whitby about an intermediate berth for you; the accommodation between decks is of a very superior description — very superior, indeed. But, my dear child, if you do not like to go, say the word.'

Clara gasped, and felt nearly choked; but managed to say —

'What does my aunt say about my going so far?'

'She thinks it highly advisable, particularly as the climate is so fine, and she does not think the long, cold Scotch winters agree with you.'

'If I am to go, when does the vessel_____'

Clara could say no more.

'Oh, no hurry—not for six weeks yet. You will have to get your things in order, and I will see that your outfit is complete; but you will tell me to-morrow morning if you have any reasonable objection to make. You had better sleep upon it, Clara, and tell me to-morrow.'

The sisters withdrew into their own room—not to consult, but to weep. They had never been separated in their lives. The loss of both their parents had made them all in all to each other; and though a vague and alarming idea had crossed each of their minds that their poverty might prevent them from living together in future, it had never been expressed in words, and it was only intimated by the frequency and tenderness of their caresses, and by long silent gazes into each other's eyes, that they felt a time might come when they could neither caress nor look at one another.

Susan's tears were of unmingled sadness; but there was some indignant bitterness in Clara's. Susan felt that her uncle was kind to her, and that for Clara he was doing the best he could. But Clara, more clear-sighted, saw that her uncle wished to be spared the mortification of seeing so near a relative reduced to be a nursery governess in his neighbourhood. But this feeling she did not communicate to Susan, when she saw that her sister did not herself perceive it; but said, she dared to say it was all for the best, but it was very sad.

They did not think of making any objection or of pleading for any delay, but prepared for the worst by fresh bursts of tears; and when they did at last speak on the subject, it was about the long letters they would write, and the prayers they would offer up to God for each other.

'I shall be comfortable,' said Susan; 'but what troubles you may have to go through, and I not near to help or comfort you! But yet, my darling, you are not appreciated here. You have finer abilities than I have; but because I make a noise on a piano, and scratch figures on Bristol board, I am extolled, and you are disparaged. They will judge better in Adelaide, I hope; and you will be marrying some rich man, and keeping your carriage; for you are very lovely, at least in my eyes. And when you are rich, and I would be no burden to you, send for me; for though my

Like All First Chapters — Introductory

uncle and aunt are very kind, I am yours and you are mine, till death.'

'Till death,' said Clara. 'But I can form no hopes of anything brilliant in the prospect before me. I feel so helpless, so useless, as if I might perish, and no man regard it. Only in your heart would I leave a void.'

Thus all that day did the sisters grieve together; and, after a sleepless night, rose at their usual hour, and went in to breakfast. Mrs. Morison was up, and dispensing coffee, which they scarcely expected, for she had been confined to her bedroom all the preceding dreadful day.

'Well, Susan,' said she, 'this is the last day I mean to get breakfast for the family. You will, as my eldest daughter would do if she were old enough, preside at the breakfast-table in future, I hope. The effort is really too much for me. I feel now quite exhausted, and I think I caught a chill this morning. Clara, will you ring the bell for me, my dear? What a treasure you will be in any Australian family; you are so obliging and so fond of children. Your domestic virtues are quite undervalued in this country: every one looks to show and flourish here; but I believe that a truer taste pervades the communities of our colonies. I expect to hear of your being domiciled in some nice Scotch family in Adelaide, or near it. I would not like you to go far in the bush. The natives and bushrangers make it unsafe; and I have heard, too, that snakes are numerous and dangerous in the thinly-settled districts; so, for our sakes, as well as your own, do not venture far out. But every one says that the climate is delightful, and that is a grand consideration; and people are so simple and unsophisticated: the state of society is very charming. Governesses of every kind are so much wanted, that I have heard of people going in quest of them on board every newly-arrived ship, and engaging them before they put foot on shore. But, Clara, you must follow Mr. Campbell's advice, and not take the first situation that offers. You should prefer forty pounds a-year, with a comfortable home, to sixty, where everything is not *comme il faut.* We hear of servants and distressed needle-women making brilliant marriages in Australia. So, Clara, who knows how long you may continue teaching? But let your choice fall on a man of sound principles and religious feelings, if you mean to be happy.'

5

Mrs. Morison had gone on, without looking at Clara's red eyes, or Susan's woe-begone face; but, in presenting to them both the idea that Clara would be appreciated in the far land they destined for her home, she had done something to comfort and encourage her. So that when, after breakfast, her uncle asked her how she felt on the subject of emigration, she replied, in a firmer voice than she could have thought possible the day before —

'I have no objection to make. I will go to Australia.'

Her uncle and aunt encouraged and indulged Clara during the short time she had still to remain with them. Every one was busied with her outfit, which was a very good one, though principally adapted for summer wearing; for English and Scotch people never reckon on Australia having a winter at all. All Mr. Morison's children gave Clara a little present to keep for their sakes. A great proportion of her friends gave her books, chiefly religious ones, with good wishes for her temporal, and especially her spiritual, prosperity, written in a bold hand on the fly-leaf.

Susan wished Clara to take all her books, as she herself did not care so much about reading as Clara did, and, besides, she would always have access to her uncle's library, and the circulating libraries in town, whereas Clara might not be able to meet with books in that distant land.

Clara accepted her sister's generous offer, leaving her only a few keep-sakes. Everything that Susan had she would have given to her sister; but, except in the matter of the books, Clara would not consent to such robbery.

Captain and Mrs. Whitby were invited several times to Mr. Morison's, that Clara might become acquainted with them.

The host and hostess thought them most excellent and delightful people; but Clara could not admire them. They took too much notice of her, and made her feel uncomfortable. They talked of the colony of South Australia with raptures, which encouraged her at first; but when she discovered that this was their first voyage thither, she felt that their praises were no recommendation. Clara read every book that she could procure about the colony she was bound for; but the accounts were so contradictory, that she came to no satisfactory conclusion.

She felt nervous when she heard that a young lady, named Miss Waterstone, was to share her cabin, and must, necessarily, be her intimate companion during the long dreary voyage. Mrs.

Like All First Chapters — Introductory

Whitby was to be a mother to Miss Waterstone likewise. Clara begged her uncle to invite this young lady to spend a few days with her before undertaking the voyage together. And Miss Waterstone accepted the invitation for the last week but one of her remaining in Edinburgh.

Miss Waterstone was apparently about twenty-five. Her charms were fully developed, her complexion florid, her voice loud, and her manner imposing. She took so much notice of Mrs. Morison's children, that this lady was fully convinced of Miss Waterstone's amiability; and, as she behaved with great deference to both her host and hostess — never allowing herself to contradict them in the slightest point — they thought her a young woman of good judgment, with very correct principles. Mr. Morison earnestly recommended his young niece to her care, and presented her with a handsome workbox, which raised her opinion of his virtues to an extravagant pitch. Miss Waterstone's final destination was Melbourne; so that, as she sometimes regretfully said, she could do nothing for Clara at the end of the voyage; though, every now and then, she forgot it, and, with singular irrationality, proposed entering into partnership and commencing a school, in which she would take all the higher branches, while Clara would look after the house, and teach the junior members of the establishment. Mrs. Morison could not see that there was much to choose between Melbourne and Adelaide, and thought it would be as well for Clara to change her destination, to secure so valuable a friend; but her husband, not knowing anybody in the colony of Victoria, but an unmarried sheep-farmer, who lived a hundred-and-fifty miles up the country, was obliged to give up the idea of the partnership, which would have been, indeed, an excellent arrangement for Clara. A few friends gave her letters of introduction to their Australian acquaintances; of which more hereafter.

Miss Waterstone had no doubt of her success: she was thoroughly competent to undertake anything in the way of education, though, as yet, she had had no experience; and she trusted to her letters of introduction bringing her at once into the best society in Melbourne. Clara tried hard to get up her confidence as well, but could not. She saw a thousand difficulties from within and from without, which no one else seemed to see for her. And when her friends wished her a safe and pleasant voyage, as if all would go smoothly if she were once landed in Australia, she felt that worse might follow, and that dangers by sea were the least of the risks she ran.

An Up-Country Township

Marcus Clarke

Bullocktown is situated, like all up-country townships, on the banks of something that is a flood in winter and a mud hole in summer. For general purposes the inhabitants of the city called the something a river, and those intelligent land surveyors that mark 'agricultural areas' on the tops of lofty mountains, had given the river a very grand name indeed.

The Pollywog Creek, or as it was marked on the maps, the Great Glimmera, took its rise somewhere about Bowlby Gap, and after constructing a natural sheepwash for Bowlby, terminated in swamp, which was courteously termed Lake Landowne. No man had ever seen Lake Landowne but once, and that was during a flood, but Lake Landowne the place was called, and Lake Landowne it remained; reeds, tussocks, and brindled bullocks' backs to the contrary notwithstanding. There was a legend afloat in Bullocktown, that an unhappy new comer from Little Britain had once purchased Lake Landowne from the Government, with the intention of building a summer residence on its banks, and becoming a landed proprietor. The first view of his estate, however, as seen from the hood of a partially submerged buggy, diverted his ambition to brandy and water, and having drunk hard for a week at the Three Posts, he returned into his original obscurity by the first Cobb's coach driver that could be prevailed upon to receive him.

I do not vouch for the truth of the story, I only know that a peculiarly soapy part on the edge of the 'lake' was known as 'Smuggins's hole', by reason of Smuggins, the landed proprietor, having been fished therefrom at an early period of his aforesaid landed proprietorship.

However, any impartial observer in the summer months could see Spot and Toby and Punch, and the rest of the station bullocks, feeding hard in the middle of the lake, and if after that he chose to make observations nobody minded him. Mr. Rapersole, the bootmaker and correspondent of the *Quartzborough Chronicle*, had a map in his back parlour, with Lake Landowne in the biggest of possible print on it, and that was quite enough for Bullocktown. Impertinent strangers are — locally speaking — the ruin of a township.

There was a church in Bullocktown, and there were also three public-houses. It is not for me to make unpleasant comments, but I know for a fact that the minister vowed the place wasn't worth buggy-hire, and that the publicans were making fortunes. Perhaps this was owing to the unsettled state of the district — in up-country townships most evils (including floods) are said to arise from this cause — and could in time have been remedied. I am afraid that religion, as an art, was not cultivated much in Bullocktown. The seed sown there was a little mixed in character. One week you had a Primitive Methodist, and the next a Hardshell Baptist, and the next an Irvingite or a Southcotian. To do the inhabitants justice, they endeavoured very hard to learn the ins and outs of the business, but I do not believe that they ever succeeded. As Wallaby Dick observed one day, 'When you run a lot of paddocked sheep into a race, what's the good o' sticking half-a-dozen fellers at the gate? The poor beggars don't know which way to run!' The township being on a main road, and not owning a resident parson, all sorts of strange preachers set up their tents there. It was considered a point of honour for all travelling clergymen ('bush parsons', the Bullocktownians called them) to give an evening at the 'brick edifice'. Indeed, Tom Trowbridge, the publican (who owned the land on which the 'edifice' was built,) said that it was 'only fair to take turn about, one down t'other come on, a clear stage and no favour', but, then, Tom was a heathen, and had been a prize-fighter. I think that of all the many 'preachments' the inhabitants suffered, the teetotal abstinence was received with the greatest favour. The 'edifice' was crowded, and Trowbridge, vowing

An Up-Country Township

that the teetotaler was a trump, and had during the two hours he had been in his house drunk gingerbeer enough to burst a gasometer, occupied the front pew in all the heroic agony of a clean shirt and collar. The lecture was most impressive. Tom wept with mingled remorse and whiskey, and they say that the carouse which took place in his back-bar after the pledge was signed was the biggest that had been known in Bullocktown since the diggings. The lecturer invited everybody to sign, and I believe that everybody did. 'Roll up, you poor lost lambs,' he cried, 'and seal your blessed souls to abstinence!' He did not explain what 'abstinence' meant, and I have reason to believe that the majority of his hearers thought it a peculiar sort of peppermint-bitters, invigorating and stimulating beyond the average of such concoctions.

The effect, however, was immense. The lambs signed to a wether, and where they could not sign, made their mark. The display of ignorance of the miserable art of writing nearly rivalled that shown at a general election. As the lecturer said afterwards, over a pint of warm orange-water in the bar-parlour, 'It was a blessed time,' and Mrs. Mumford, of the Pound, volunteered to take her 'dying oath' (whatever that might be) that Jerry had never been so 'loving drunk' in all his life before. Billy, the blackfellow, came up to the homestead two days afterwards, gaping like a black earthquake, and informed us that he had taken 'big fellow pledge, big one square-bottle that feller', and felt 'berry bad'. M'Killop, the overseer, gave him three packets of Epsom salts, and sent him down to the creek with a pannikin. Strange to say, he recovered.

It was not often that we had amusement of this sort in Bullocktown. Except at shearing time, when the 'hands' knocked down their cheques (and never picked them up again), gaiety was scarce. Steady drinking at the Royal Cobb, and a dance at Trowbridge's, were the two excitements. The latter soon palled upon the palate, for, at the time of which I write, there were but five women in the township, three of whom were aged, or as Wallaby said, 'broken-mouthed crawlers, not worth the trouble of culling'. The other two were daughters of old Trowbridge, and could cut out a refractory bullock with the best stockman on the plains. But what were two among so many? I have seen fifteen couples stand up in Trowbridge's to the 'Cruiskeen Lawn', and dance a mild polka, gyrating round each other like intelligent weathercocks.

The stationary dance of the bush hand is a fearful and wonderful thing. Two sheepish, grinning, blushing stockmen grip each other's elbows, and solemnly twirl to the music of their loose spurs. They don't 'dance', they simply twirl, with a rocking motion like that of an intoxicated teetotum, and occasionally shout to relieve their feelings. If the Cruiskeen Lawn had been the Old Hundredth, they could not have looked more melancholy. Moreover, I think that to treat a hornpipe as a religious ceremony is a mistake. The entertainment was varied with a free fight for the hands of the Misses Trowbridge. One of these liberal measures was passed every ten minutes or so, Trowbridge standing in the background, waiting to pick up the man with the most money. As a study of human nature the scene was interesting, as a provocative to reckless hilarity it was not eminently successful.

The other public-houses were much of the same stamp. The township was a sort of rule of three sum in alcohol. As the Royal Cobb was to Trowbridge's, so was Trowbridge's to the Three Posts, or you might work it the other way. As the Three Posts was to Trowbridge's, so was Trowbridge's to the Royal Cobb. The result was always the same — a shilling a nobbler. True, that Trowbridge's did not 'lamb down' so well as the Three Posts, but then the Three Posts put fig tobacco in its brandy casks, and Trowbridge's did not do that. True, that the coach stopped at the Royal Cobb, but then the Royal Cobb had no daughters, and some passengers preferred to take their cut of the joint at Trowbridge's. Providence — mindful of Mr. Emerson's doctrine of compensation — equalized conditions even in Bullocktown.

The Royal Cobb was perhaps the best house. Before Coppinger bought the place, it was kept by Mr. Longbow, a tall, thin, one-eyed, and eminently genteel man, who was always smoking. He was a capital host, a shrewd man of the world, and a handy shot with a duck gun. No one knew what he had been, and no one could with any certainty predict what he might be. He shot birds, stuffed beasts, discovered mines, set legs, played the violin, and was 'up' in the Land Act. He was a universal genius, in fact, and had but one fault. His veracity was too small for his imagination.

An Up-Country Township

It was useless to argue with Longbow. *He* was 'all there', no matter where you might be. The Derby! He had lost fifty thou in Musjid's year. The interior of Africa! He had lived there for months, and spoke gorillese like a native. Dr. Livingstone! They had slept all night with but an ant-hill between them. The Duke of Wellington! He had been his most intimate friend, and called him 'Arthur' for years. I shall never forget one pathetic evening, when, after much unlimited loo, and some considerably hot whiskey, Longbow told me of his troubles. 'Beastly colony!' he said, 'beastly! Why, my dear boy, when I was leaving; but there, never mind, Buckingham and Chandos was right. Never mind what they may say, Sir, Buckingham and Chandos was right as the mail.' I replied that from the reports I had heard of Buckingham and Chandos, I had no doubt whatever that he was all that could be desired by the most fastidious. Upon which Longbow favoured me with a history of B. and C. lending him £20,000 on his note of hand, and borrowing his dress waistcoat to dance at Rosherville Gardens. Before I left he volunteered to produce — some day when I wasn't busy — the Duke of Wellington's autograph letter, containing the celebrated recipe for devilled mushrooms, with a plan of the lines of Torres Vedras drawn on the back of it, and he would not allow me to leave him until he told me how Her Majesty had said, 'Longbow, old man, sorry to lose you, but Australia's a fine place. Go in and win, my boy, and chance the ducks!' This last story was quite impressive, more especially as Longbow acted the scene between himself and Her Majesty, and — making the whiskey-bottle take the place of the Duchess of Sutherland — alternated parts with himself as poor Jack Longbow, and himself as the first lord-in-waiting, crying 'Damme, Jack, come out o' that; she's going to cry, you villain!' I listened with approving patience, and never smiled until the very end of the story, where Longbow rushed frantically from the Presence, and knocked A. Saxe Gotha head over heels into the brand new coal scuttle on the landing! 'Oh! those were the days! D — the colony, and pass the whiskey!'

Opposite to the Royal Cobb was the school-house. It had four scholars, and the master was paid by results. He used to drink a large quantity of rum (to settle any symptoms of indigestion, arising from his plethora of funds, I suppose,) and was always appealed to on matters of quotation. He was a very old man with a very red nose, and 'had been a gentleman'. There was never an up-country township yet that had not some such melancholy waif and stray in it.

When the schoolmaster got very drunk indeed, he would quote Aristophanes, and on one memorable occasion put Flash Harry's song

> Oh Sally, she went up the stairs, and I went up to find her, And as she stopped to buckle her shoe, I tumbled down behind her!

into Horatian alcaics. He quarrelled with the Visiting Inspector because he (the V.I.) said that wigs were not worn by the ancients, and our broken-down gentleman put him to his purgation with the case of Astyages as given by Xenophon. He confessed afterwards that setting your superiors right on matters of quotation is not politic, and that he wished he had let it alone. He was from Dublin University. How is it that the wittiest talkers, the most brilliant classics, and the most irreclaimable drunkards, all used to come from Dublin University?

There was a Post-office in Bullocktown, kept, if a Post-office can be kept, by Mr. Rapersole aforesaid, who was regarded as quite a literary genius by the bullock drivers. Mr. R. 'corresponded for the paper' — *the* paper — and would loftily crush anybody who gave him cause of offence. If Rapersole lost a chicken or missed a pig, the world was sure to hear of it in the Paper. Rapersole, however, did not affect writing so much as speaking. 'The platform for me!' he would say, as though the platform was a sort of untamed fiery steed, and he a rough rider. However, nobody came forward with the article, and he did not show. It was generally believed in Bullocktown, however, that if Rapersole once got his platform, the universe might consider itself reformed without further trouble.

The Crime of Convict Cunliffe

Price Warung

I

Dawn at Norfolk Island. As the night sped away before the early greyness, the terraced forestry of Mount Pitt took upon itself a sheen of splendour. The upper heights were the first to catch the glory and resplendence which heralded the day; and as they, no less than the lower levels of the hill, the vales and dells at its base, and the charming, artificially arranged gardens surrounding Government House and some of the outlying tenements, had been bathed in delicious dew, once the sun's rays caught the pinnacles of the stately pines and the feathery crowns of noble king-ferns, every dewdrop became a miniature sun and shot forth its peculiar iridescence. Then, as the sun in full majesty rose over the margin of ocean and swept, with all-embracing light, the illimitable waste of water, the great hill, in all its lower ranges also, shivered and shone with a blazing radiance till it seemed a very mount of fire. The very purples and sapphires that marked the undulations and curves of the roads and valleys added strength to the illusion; they acted but as additional facets of the prism. With this mount of light rising from the land, and ecompassed as it was with a crystalline sea, an observer from a vessel's deck, supposing one had been in the neighbourhood of the island, might well have been pardoned for assuming that his craft had voyaged to some isle of dreams, or to paradise itself.

In one of the vales of smaller area, which was linked by umbrageous arcades to the exquisitely beautiful valley, where once stood the famous cluster of eight fern trees, in the stems and garniture of which reposed every form of arboreal grace and elegance, the dew lingered long after the new day had driven away with its heat the sparkling moisture of the hill-crest; and at ten o'clock there was still visible in that beautiful glen the cool softness and delicacy of the early morn. It was such a glen as might have been hidden in green Illyrian hills — taken as a playground for Fauns or Naiads; and so sweet and virginal was it, that it would seem as though earth could be cursed by no creature so base or rude as to intrude upon it with the coarsest machinery of human punishment.

Yet, this lovely spot upon which both heaven and earth had showered grace and beauty had been chosen by Mr. Scragge, the Civil Commandant of Norfolk Island, as the scene of a unique penalty.

For, in the heart of the glen stood a wooden post with supporting stay-pieces. And to this post there had been attached, during the long chilliness of the night, Convict Cunliffe.

II

The crime of Convict Cunliffe was one which at this en-lightened day has been excused by pope, and cardinal, and bishops, and statesmen; nevertheless, in the early forties, Commandant Scragge denounced it, and punished it as heinous. There is this much to be said for Scragge — the offence was one rigorously denounced by regulation. And regulations, it will be understood, had to be obeyed at all costs and all hazards; except when — it suited the convenience of an official in authority to disobey them.

The offence of which Convict Cunliffe was undoubtedly guilty, was one committed under dire personal necessity; but that is nothing to the point. The regulations had been framed by the authorities in Sydney, under the sanction and by direction of the supreme powers of the System in England; therefore, they had embodied in them all the vital principles of law-abidingness which have made the British nation great and lawless. They had, moreover, in the form in which they were finally approved by the colonial authority, that higher sanction that would be granted to them by the consecration of a prelate's presence; for had not the first Bishop of Australia

The Crime of Convict Cunliffe

himself attached his signature to the proclamation of enforcement?

Therefore, everything considered, when so heinous an offence had been perpetrated, it was only right and proper, according to the regulations, and the blessed precedents, and the holy traditions of the System, that the criminal should be visited with penalty sufficient and singular, and of a character to reform himself and to inspire horror of the like crime in the minds of other transports.

Convict Cunliffe belonged to that class of criminals which Great Britain, with a fine impartiality that was not to be swayed by any national prejudices, bred in England, Scotland, and Ireland indifferently, the city Gutter-snipe. Born in the gutter, he had been suckled in the gutter, spent his early youth in the gutter, and, but for the philanthropy of British law, would possibly have died in the gutter. The law, however, took him by the scruff of the neck, and, when the necessary formalities before the judge and jury had been completed, had thrown him on to the shores of the new land of Australia, as 'splendid colonising material'. There was always underlying the System a beneficent regard for 'our new and thriving dependencies under the Southern Cross'. Seldom indeed, from 1787 till the early sixties, did England despatch a convict-ship without some titled nincompoop or idiot of a lesser grade, expressing his delight at the magnanimity of the Motherland in thus contributing some more of her bone and sinew to Australia 'as splendid colonising material'. 'Our colonies', declared a noble lord — it pains us to have to record that he was shortly afterwards cast in heavy damages in a case of *crim. con.* — 'can never repay us for the contribution to its population that we have made through our Transportation System'. The noble speaker came, for an aristocrat of the time, uncommonly near the truth. Australia will never be able to repay the debt it incurred to England through the Transportation System: unless it ships home every soul of its living and nascent politicians. But this is by the way.

Cunliffe was a gutter-brat of a great seaport city. Deformed in body, yet his outward appearance was the only semblance he possessed to humanity. Utterly lacking in any perception of right or wrong, he had no conception of honesty or dishonesty, save that acquired by the rough tutorship of punishment. Needless to say, therefore, the finer elements of gratitude and thankfulness had no part in him, even in the most rudimentary state; and this being so, it will not be surprising to learn that he was utterly deaf and blind to the advantages the penal establishment of Norfolk Island conferred upon him. Not all the monitions of scourgers, or the sympathetic tuition of the gentlemen who flourished whips over the tramway 'Team', of which he formed one, could persuade him into a proper attitude of humility and appreciation. Even the softening influences of Mr. Scragge's Monday morning lectures at the 'police court' had failed to bring him to a due sense of respect to the high powers, and consequently Mr. Scragge had decided that so recalcitrant a customer should, for his latest offence, be honoured by special treatment.

And the manner of his treatment was, that he should be 'spread-eagled' to a punishment-post in Guava Glen; and the spread-eagling was to continue from the noon of one day to the noon of the next.

No one could say surely that Convict Cunliffe's crime merited more merciful treatment. As to duration, it was not long — only a day of twenty-four hours; and as to variation of temperature with its attendant discomforts, when all is said and done, the difference between forty degrees at midnight and eighty degrees at midday is not very much.

And if it could be objected that even eighty degrees of heat might prove excessive when the sun was vertical in the heavens, and the subject was unable to escape into shelter, you must not overlook the fact that the mean temperature of the twenty-four hours was only sixty degrees. The circumstance that the mid-hour of the night in a Norfolk valley, where the dew fell as plenteously as the manna of the Israelites in the desert, was of almost a freezing bitterness, need not be considered. It is always wise to take the average of things — when extremes lead to the drawing of unpleasant inferences.

III

Notwithstanding the beauty of the place, Convict Cunliffe was not an agreeable object to look upon as the morning radiance filled the glen. His mittened hands had been fastened to the stay-pieces — and they were numb. His feet, in like manner, had been tied to the post, and they, too, were sensationless. A leathern brace held his shoulders firmly to the upright, and a broad girdle of the same unbending material encircled his body and the post in the one affectionate loop. His head — the considerate System had left him a peakless cap — lolled now on one shoulder and now on the other; sometimes it varied its grotesque movements by drooping forward. It could not well fall backwards, the square of timber blocked its movement in that way.

And yet, with all these appliances for his comfort, the look on Convict Cunliffe's face was that of a tortured animal.

Weazened, every line on the scarred and wrinkled face had been cut in by the knives of starvation and physical misery. Shapeless lips edged the drawn mouth, and protruding cheekbones tightened the skinny surface to bursting point. And the eyes! From between the puckering eyelids peered the look of terror and an inarticulate appeal — for what or to whom, no human being can say — that you may see in the eyes of a dog or rabbit upon the table where the vivisectionist gluts the greed of his red-fanged science. And in the circumstances, it would have been rather surprising had any other look been visible in the windows through which Convict Cunliffe's soul would have looked on the world, had he only possessed a soul. He was only an animal, after all, under the dissecting weapon of the experimenter. 'Norfolk Island', declared a right hon. gentleman in the House of Commons, when the administration of the island was attacked, 'is only an experiment'.

There was no sound in the glen save the breath of a morning breeze as it stirred fern-fronds and other foliage. The countless birds were silent — possibly waiting the issue of the experiment; all hesitating to disturb the hallowed silence. Not even when Convict Cunliffe, shortly after the second bell — 'muster for work' — had sounded in the distance, had taken it into his rebellious head to utter a cry, did the birds twitter or shriek in response. Possibly, if they had, they might in their musical clamour have overborne Convict Cunliffe's cry.

As it was, that cry, to the eternal glory of the hearer, and to the everlasting condemnation of the System, was heard by a passerby — one who had no right to be there; that is, according to all orders and regulations in that case made and provided, he should have been elsewhere.

It was a soldier of Garrison Company B who heard Cunliffe's cry for help, or for water, or for food, or Whatever it was. He had absented himself, not without *quasi*-permission from Sargeant Dines, from first parade, with a very singular purpose in view. This private soldier was a Protestant, and he was searching for a Roman Catholic priest — not the resident chaplain, but a visitor. He had heard, had Private Smithers, that the young priest who had visited the island fifteen years before from Sydney, in order to shrive eight men who lay under sentence of death, prior to their formal despatch into another world, had again arrived — this time from Hobart Town. There were traditions lingering in the island of the priest's former visit, and it was now the private's intention to tell the ecclesiastic, if he could only meet with him, what the views were of the soldiery as to the state of things that existed in the Establishment. It was a courageous determination, and one not altogether lacking in a certain high-principled consideration for the class between whom and the common soldier there was a natural and formidable enmity. If, so he and others of his company thought, the visiting ecclesiastic could but be informed of what the soldiers saw every day, and every hour of the day, it would have an effect different, but none the less instructive, to that which would be conveyed by the evidence of men of superior official position. The private soldier saw, and knew of things done, that the commissioned officers of a garrison must necessarily remain in ignorance of. Smithers had been told that the priest was fond of early morning exercise, and also that very likely he would make his way to the valley of the Eight Fern Trees. His desire, therefore, was to waylay him in his morning's stroll.

But — he overheard Cunliffe.

Smithers took in the situation in a glance.

The Crime of Convict Cunliffe

'Spread-eagled all night! what devils! What can I do for you, covey?'

Through the shapeless lips a mumble of something or other was projected. The soldier bent to hear, and then bethought himself of the purling stream running along the gully he had crossed to approach the glen. Seizing the convict's cap, he ran and filled it with water, which Cunliffe, like the animal to which Society had reduced him, lapped.

Then the mumble became more distinct.

'Can't yer-cut-m'-down?'

Smithers instinctively pulled out his jack-knife as though to cut the withes which bound the mittened hands to the stay-pieces. But then a thought, a very inspiration, came into his mind.

'No,' he cried, 'I will leave you as you are for a bit, I am off to find the priest,' and he put up his knife.

The bright hope which had struggled for life for a moment in the animal's consciousness faded away. What cared he for priest or parson? What knew he of God, or Church, or Devil?

So he fell back into mumbling once more — into imprecations and curses this time, as he saw the soldier disappear into the undergrowth.

Nevertheless, Convict Cunliffe, that morning by that very cry of his, had set into motion waves of influence and forces of sympathy which were to destroy the System. That cry, seemingly, had reached heaven; when the prayers of noble men like Mr. Taylor, and the imprecations of ten thousand damned souls had brought no response.

For Private Smithers found the priest, and the priest turned out to be no other than Bishop Willson, one of the heroes of Australian heroes. But what the Bishop did as a consequence of being thus encountered is a story in itself.

The Chosen Vessel

Barbara Baynton

She laid the stick and her baby on the grass while she untied the rope that tethered the calf. The length of the rope separated them. The cow was near the calf, and both were lying down. Feed along the creek was plentiful, and every day she found a fresh place to tether it, since tether it she must, for if she did not, it would stray with the cow out on the plain. She had plenty of time to go after it, but then there was her baby; and if the cow turned on her out on the plain, and she with her baby, — she had been a town girl and was afraid of the cow, but she did not want the cow to know it. She used to run at first when it bellowed its protest against the penning up of its calf. This satisfied the cow, also the calf, but the woman's husband was angry, and called her — the noun was cur. It was he who forced her to run and meet the advancing cow, brandishing a stick, and uttering threatening words till the enemy turned and ran. 'That's the way!' the man said, laughing at her white face. In many things he was worse than the cow, and she wondered if the same rule would apply to the man, but she was not one to provoke skirmishes even with the cow.

It was early for the calf to go to 'bed' — nearly an hour earlier than usual; but she had felt so restless all day. Partly because it was Monday, and the end of the week that would bring her and the baby the companionship of his father, was so far off. He was a shearer, and had gone to his shed before daylight that morning. Fifteen miles as the crow flies separated them.

There was a track in front of the house, for it had once been a

The Chosen Vessel

wine shanty, and a few travellers passed along at intervals. She was not afraid of horsemen; but swagmen, going to, or worse coming from, the dismal, drunken little township, a day's journey beyond, terrified her. One had called at the house to-day, and asked for tucker.

That was why she had penned up the calf so early. She feared more from the look of his eyes, and the gleam of his teeth, as he watched her newly awakened baby beat its impatient fists upon her covered breasts, than from the knife that was sheathed in the belt at his waist.

She had given him bread and meat. Her husband she told him was sick. She always said that when she was alone and a swagman came; and she had gone in from the kitchen to the bedroom, and asked questions and replied to them in the best man's voice she could assume. Then he had asked to go into the kitchen to boil his billy, but instead she gave him tea, and he drank it on the wood heap. He had walked round and round the house, and there were cracks in some places, and after the last time he had asked for tobacco. She had none to give him, and he had grinned, because there was a broken clay pipe near the wood heap where he stood, and if there were a man inside, there ought to have been tobacco. Then he asked for money, but women in the bush never have money.

At last he had gone, and she, watching through the cracks, saw him when about a quarter of a mile away, turn and look back at the house. He had stood so for some moments with a pretence of fixing his swag, and then, apparently satisfied, moved to the left towards the creek. The creek made a bow round the house, and when he came to the bend she lost sight of him. Hours after, watching intently for signs of smoke, she saw the man's dog chasing some sheep that had gone to the creek for water, and saw it slink back suddenly, as if it had been called by some one.

More than once she thought of taking her baby and going to her husband. But in the past, when she had dared to speak of the dangers to which her loneliness exposed her, he had taunted and sneered at her. 'Needn't flatter yerself,' he had told her, 'nobody 'ud want ter run away with yew.'

Long before nightfall she placed food on the kitchen table, and beside it laid the big brooch that had been her mother's. It was the only thing of value that she had. And she left the kitchen door wide open.

The doors inside she securely fastened. Beside the bolt in the back one she drove in the steel and scissors; against it she piled the table and the stools. Underneath the lock of the front door she forced the handle of the spade, and the blade between the cracks in the flooring boards. Then the prop-stick, cut into lengths, held the top, as the spade held the middle. The windows were little more than portholes; she had nothing to fear through them.

She ate a few mouthfuls of food and drank a cup of milk. But she lighted no fire, and when night came, no candle, but crept with her baby to bed.

What woke her? The wonder was that she had slept — she had not meant to. But she was young, very young. Perhaps the shrinking of the galvanized roof — hardly though, since that was so usual. Yet something had set her heart beating wildly; but she lay quite still, only she put her arm over her baby. Then she had both round it, and she prayed, 'Little baby, little baby, don't wake!'

The moon's rays shone on the front of the house, and she saw one of the open cracks, quite close to where she lay, darken with a shadow. Then a protesting growl reached her; and she could fancy she heard the man turn hastily. She plainly heard the thud of something striking the dog's ribs, and the long flying strides of the animal as it howled and ran. Still watching, she saw the shadow darken every crack along the wall. She knew by the sounds that the man was trying every standpoint that might help him to see in; but how much he saw she could not tell. She thought of many things she might do to deceive him into the idea that she was not alone. But the sound of her voice would wake baby, and she dreaded that as though it were the only danger that threatened her. So she prayed, 'Little baby, don't wake, don't cry!'

Stealthily the man crept about. She knew he had his boots off, because of the vibration that his feet caused as he walked along the verandah to gauge the width of the little window in her room, and the resistance of the front door.

Then he went to the other end, and the uncertainty of what he was doing became unendurable. She had felt safer, far safer,

The Chosen Vessel

while he was close, and she could watch and listen. She felt she must watch, but the great fear of wakening her baby again assailed her. She suddenly recalled that one of the slabs on that side of the house had shrunk in length as well as in width, and had once fallen out. It was held in position only by a wedge of wood underneath. What if he should discover that? The uncertainty increased her terror. She prayed as she gently raised herself with her little one in her arms, held tightly to her breast.

She thought of the knife, and shielded its body with her hands and arms. Even the little feet she covered with its white gown, and the baby never murmured — it liked to be held so. Noiselessly she crossed to the other side, and stood where she could see and hear, but not be seen. He was trying every slab, and was very near to that with the wedge under it. Then she saw him find it; and heard the sound of the knife as bit by bit he began to cut away the wooden support.

She waited motionless, with her baby pressed tightly to her, though she knew that in another few minutes this man with the cruel eyes, lascivious mouth, and gleaming knife, would enter. One side of the slab tilted; he had only to cut away the remaining little end, when the slab, unless he held it, would fall outside.

She heard his jerked breathing as it kept time with the cuts of the knife, and the brush of his clothes as he rubbed the wall in his movements, for she was so still and quiet, that she did not even tremble. She knew when he ceased, and wondered why, being so well concealed; for he could not see her, and would not fear if he did, yet she heard him move cautiously away. Perhaps he expected the slab to fall — his motive puzzled her, and she moved even closer, and bent her body the better to listen. Ah! what sound was that? 'Listen! Listen!' she bade her heart — her heart that had kept so still, but now bounded with tumultuous throbs that dulled her ears. Nearer and nearer came the sounds, till the welcome thud of a horse's hoof rang out clearly.

'O God! O God! O God!' she panted, for they were very close before she could make sure. She rushed to the door, and with her baby in her arms tore frantically at its bolts and bars.

Out she darted at last, and running madly along, saw the horseman beyond her in the distance. She called to him in Christ's Name, in her babe's name, still flying like the wind with the speed that deadly peril gives. But the distance grew greater

Australian Short Stories

and greater between them, and when she reached the creek her prayers turned to wild shrieks, for there crouched the man she feared, with outstretched arms that caught her as she fell. She knew he was offering terms if she ceased to struggle and cry for help, though louder and louder did she cry for it, but it was only when the man's hand gripped her throat, that the cry of 'Murder' came from her lips. And when she ceased, the startled curlews took up the awful sound, and flew wailing 'Murder! Murder!' over the horseman's head.

'By God!' said the boundary rider, 'it's been a dingo right enough! Eight killed up here, and there's more down in the creek — a ewe and a lamb, I'll bet; and the lamb's alive!' He shut out the sky with his hand, and watched the crows that were circling round and round, nearing the earth one moment, and the next shooting skywards. By that he knew the lamb must be alive; even a dingo will spare a lamb sometimes.

Yes, the lamb was alive, and after the manner of lambs of its kind did not know its mother when the light came. It had sucked the still warm breasts, and laid its little head on her bosom, and slept till the morn. Then, when it looked at the swollen disfigured face, it wept and would have crept away, but for the hand that still clutched its little gown. Sleep was nodding its golden head and swaying its small body, and the crows were close, so close to the mother's wide-open eyes, when the boundary rider galloped down.

'Jesus Christ!' he said, covering his eyes. He told afterwards how the little child held out its arms to him, and how he was forced to cut its gown that the dead hand held.

*

It was election time, and as usual the priest had selected a candidate. His choice was so obviously in the interests of the squatter, that Peter Hennessey's reason, for once in his life, had over-ridden superstition, and he had dared promise his vote to another. Yet he was uneasy, and every time he woke in the night (and it was often), he heard the murmur of his mother's voice. It came through the partition, or under the door. If through the partition, he knew she was praying in her bed; but when the

The Chosen Vessel

sounds came under the door, she was on her knees before the little Altar in the corner that enshrined the statue of the Blessed Virgin and Child.

'Mary, Mother of Christ! save my son! Save him!' prayed she in the dairy as she strained and set the evening's milking. 'Sweet Mary! for the love of Christ, save him!' The grief in her old face made the morning meal so bitter, that to avoid her he came late to his dinner. It made him so cowardly, that he could not say good-bye to her, and when night fell on the eve of the election day, he rode off secretly.

He had thirty miles to ride to the township to record his vote. He cantered briskly along the great stretch of plain that had nothing but stunted cotton bush to play shadow to the full moon, which glorified a sky of earliest spring. The bruised incense of the flowering clover rose up to him, and the glory of the night appealed vaguely to his imagination, but he was preoccupied with his present act of revolt.

Vividly he saw his mother's agony when she would find him gone. Even at that moment, he felt sure, she was praying.

'Mary! Mother of Christ!' He repeated the invocation, half unconsciously, when suddenly to him, out of the stillness, came Christ's Name — called loudly in despairing accents.

'For Christ's sake! Christ's sake! Christ's sake!' called the voice. Good Catholic that he had been, he crossed himself before he dared to look back. Gliding across a ghostly patch of pipe-clay, he saw a white-robed figure with a babe clasped to her bosom.

All the superstitious awe of his race and religion swayed his brain. The moonlight on the gleaming clay was a 'heavenly light' to him, and he knew the white figure not for flesh and blood, but for the Virgin and Child of his mother's prayers. Then, good Catholic that once more he was, he put spurs to his horse's sides and galloped madly away.

His mother's prayers were answered, for Hennessey was the first to record his vote — for the priest's candidate. Then he sought the priest at home, but found that he was out rallying the voters. Still, under the influence of his blessed vision, Hennessey would not go near the public-houses, but wandered about the outskirts of the town for hours, keeping apart from the townspeople, and fasting as penance. He was subdued and mildly ecstatic, feeling as a repentant chastened child, who awaits only the kiss of peace.

And at last, as he stood in the graveyard crossing himself with reverent awe, he heard in the gathering twilight the roar of many voices crying the name of the victor at the election. It was well with the priest.

Again Hennessey sought him. He was at home, the housekeeper said, and led him into the dimly lighted study. His seat was immediately opposite a large picture, and as the housekeeper turned up the lamp, once more the face of the Madonna and Child looked down on him, but this time silently, peacefully. The half-parted lips of the Virgin were smiling with compassionate tenderness; her eyes seemed to beam with the forgiveness of an earthly mother for her erring but beloved child.

He fell on his knees in adoration. Transfixed, the wondering priest stood, for mingled with the adoration, 'My Lord and my God!' was the exaltation, 'And hast Thou chosen me?'

'What is it, Peter?' said the priest.

'Father,' he answered reverently; and with loosened tongue he poured forth the story of his vision.

'Great God!' shouted the priest, 'and you did not stop to save her! Do you not know? Have you not heard?'

*

Many miles further down the creek a man kept throwing an old cap into a water-hole. The dog would bring it out and lay it on the opposite side to where the man stood, but would not allow the man to catch him, though it was only to wash the blood of the sheep from his mouth and throat, for the sight of blood made the man tremble. But the dog also was guilty.

The Union Buries Its Dead

'You remember when we were in the boat yesterday, we saw a man driving some horses along the bank?'

'Yes.'

He nodded at the hearse and said:

'Well, that's him.'

I thought awhile.

'I didn't take any particular notice of him,' I said. 'He said something, didn't he?'

'Yes; said it was a fine day. You'd have taken more notice if you'd known that he was doomed to die in the hour, and that those were the last words he would say to any man in this world.'

'To be sure,' said a full voice from the rear. 'If ye'd known that, ye'd have prolonged the conversation.'

We plodded on across the railway line and along the hot, dusty road which ran to the cemetery, some of us talking about the accident, and lying about the narrow escapes we had had ourselves. Presently someone said:

'There's the Devil.'

I looked up and saw a priest standing in the shade of the tree by the cemetery gate.

The hearse was drawn up and the tail-boards were opened. The funeral extinguished its right ear with its hat as four men lifted the coffin out and laid it over the grave. The priest — a pale, quiet young fellow — stood under the shade of a sapling which grew at the head of the grave. He took off his hat, dropped it carelessly on the ground, and proceeded to business. I noticed that one or two heathens winced slightly when the holy water was sprinkled on the coffin. The drops quickly evaporated, and the little round black spots they left were soon dusted over; but the spots showed, by contrast, the cheapness and shabbiness of the cloth with which the coffin was covered. It seemed black before; now it looked a dusky grey.

Just here man's ignorance and vanity made a farce of the funeral. A big, bull-necked publican, with heavy, blotchy features, and a supremely ignorant expression, picked up the priest's straw hat and held it about two inches over the head of his reverence during the whole of the service. The father, be it remembered, was standing in the shade. A few shoved their hats on and off uneasily, struggling between their disgust for the living and their respect for the dead. The hat had a conical crown and a brim sloping down all round like a sunshade, and the publican held it with his great red claw spread over the crown. To do the priest justice, perhaps he didn't notice the incident. A stage priest or parson in the same position might have said, 'Put the hat down, my friend; is not the memory of our departed brother worth more than my complexion?' A wattle-bark layman might have expressed himself in stronger language, none the less to the point. But my priest seemed unconscious of what was going on. Besides, the publican was a great and important pillar of the church. He couldn't, as an ignorant and conceited ass, lose such a good opportunity of asserting his faithfulness and importance to his church.

The grave looked very narrow under the coffin, and I drew a breath of relief when the box slid easily down. I saw a coffin get stuck once, at Rookwood, and it had to be yanked out with difficulty, and laid on the sods at the feet of the heart-broken relations, who howled dismally while the grave-diggers widened the hole. But they don't cut contracts so fine in the West. Our grave-digger was not altogether bowelless, and, out of respect for that human quality described as 'feelin's', he scraped up some light and dusty soil and threw it down to deaden the fall of the clay lumps on the coffin. He also tried to steer the first few shovelfuls gently down against the end of the grave with the back of the shovel turned outwards, but the hard dry Darling River clods rebounded and knocked all the same. It didn't matter much — nothing does. The fall of lumps of clay on a stranger's coffin doesn't sound any different from the fall of the same things on an ordinary wooden box — at least I didn't notice anything awesome or unusual in the sound; but, perhaps, one of us — the most sensitive — might have been impressed by being reminded of a burial of long ago, when the thump of every sod jolted his heart.

I have left out the wattle — because it wasn't there. I have also neglected to mention the heart-broken old mate, with his grizzled head bowed and great pearly drops streaming down his rugged cheeks. He was absent — he was probably 'out back'. For similar reasons I have omitted reference to the suspicious moisture in the eyes of a bearded bush ruffian named Bill. Bill failed to turn up, and the only moisture was that which was induced by the heat. I have left out the 'sad Australian sunset',

The Union Buries Its Dead

because the sun was not going down at the time. The burial took place exactly at midday.

The dead bushman's name was Jim, apparently; but they found no portraits, nor locks of hair, nor any love letters, nor anything of that kind in his swag — not even a reference to his mother; only some papers relating to Union matters. Most of us didn't know the name till we saw it on the coffin; we knew him as 'that poor chap that got drowned yesterday'.

'So his name's James Tyson,' said my drover acquaintance, looking at the plate.

'Why! Didn't you know that before?' I asked.

'No; but I knew he was a Union man.'

It turned out, afterwards, that J.T. wasn't his real name — only 'the name he went by'.

Anyhow he was buried by it, and most of the 'Great Australian Dailies' have mentioned in their brevity columns that a young man named James John Tyson was drowned in a billabong of the Darling last Sunday.

We did hear, later on, what his real name was; but if we ever chance to read it in the 'Missing Friends Column', we shall not be able to give any information to heart-broken mother or sister or wife, nor to anyone who could let him hear something to his advantage — for we have already forgotten the name.

Telling Mrs. Baker

Henry Lawson

Most bushmen who hadn't 'known Bob Baker to speak to', had 'heard tell of him'. He'd been a squatter, not many years before, on the Macquarie River in New South Wales, and had made money in the good seasons, and had gone in for horse-racing and racehorse-breeding, and long trips to Sydney, where he put up at swell hotels and went the pace. So after a pretty severe drought, when the sheep died by thousands on his runs, Bob Baker went under, and the bank took over his station and put a manager in charge.

He'd been a jolly, open-handed, popular man, which means that he'd been a selfish man as far as his wife and children were concerned, for they had to suffer for it in the end. Such generosity is often born of vanity, or moral cowardice, or both mixed. It's very nice to hear the chaps sing 'For he's a jolly good fellow,' but you've mostly got to pay for it twice — first in company, and afterwards alone. I once heard the chaps singing that I was a jolly good fellow, when I was leaving a place and they were giving me a send-off. It thrilled me, and brought a warm gush to my eyes; but, all the same, I wished I had half the money I'd lent them, and spent on 'em, and I wished I'd used the time I'd wasted to be a jolly good fellow.

When I first met Bob Baker he was a boss drover on the great north-western route, and his wife lived at the township of Solong on the Sydney side. He was going north to new country round by the Gulf of Carpentaria with a big mob of cattle, on a two years' trip; and I and my mate, Andy M'Culloch, engaged to go with him. We wanted to have a look at the Gulf Country.

Telling Mrs Baker

After we had crossed the Queensland border it seemed to me that the boss was too fond of going into wayside shanties and town pubs. Andy had been with him on another trip, and he told me that the boss was only going this way lately. Andy knew Mrs. Baker well, and seemed to think a deal of her. 'She's a good little woman,' said Andy. 'One of the right stuff. I worked on their station for a while when I was a nipper, and I know. She was always a damned sight too good for the boss, but she believed in him. When I was coming away this time she says to me, "Look here, Andy, I am afraid Robert is drinking again. Now I want you to look after him for me, as much as you can — you seem to have as much influence with him as anyone. I want you to promise me that you'll never have a drink with him."

'And I promised,' said Andy, 'and I'll keep my word.' Andy was a chap who could keep his word, and nothing else. And, no matter how the boss persuaded, or sneered, or swore at him, Andy would never drink with him.

It got worse and worse: the boss would ride on ahead and get drunk at a shanty, and sometimes he'd be days behind us; and when he'd catch up to us his temper would be just about as much as we could stand. At last he went on a howling spree at Mulgatown, about a hundred and fifty miles north of the border, and, what was worse, he got in tow with a flash barmaid there — one of those girls who are engaged, by the publicans up-country, as baits for chequemen.

He went mad over that girl. He drew an advance cheque from the stock-owner's agent there, and knocked that down; then he raised some more money somehow, and spent that — mostly on the girl.

We did all we could. Andy got him along the track for a couple of stages, and just when we thought he was all right, he slipped us in the night and went back.

We had two other men with us, but had the devil's own bother on account of the cattle. It was a mixed-up job all round. You see it was all big runs round there, and we had to keep the bullocks moving along the route all the time, or else get into trouble for trespass. The agent wasn't going to go to the expense of putting the cattle in a paddock until the boss sobered up; there was very little grass on the route or the travelling-stock reserves or camps, so we had to keep travelling for grass.

The world might wobble and all the banks go bung, but the cattle have to go through — that's the law of the stock-routes. So the agent wired to the owners, and, when he got their reply, he sacked the boss and sent the cattle on in charge of another man. The new boss was a drover coming south after a trip; he had his two brothers with him, so he didn't want me and Andy; but, anyway, we were full up of this trip, so we arranged, between the agent and the new boss, to get most of the wages due to us — the boss had drawn some of our stuff and spent it.

We could have started on the back track at once, but, drunk or sober, mad or sane, good or bad, it isn't bush religion to desert a mate in a hole; and the boss was a mate of ours; so we stuck to him.

We camped on the creek outside the town, and kept him in the camp with us as much as possible, and did all we could for him.

'How could I face his wife if I went home without him?' asked Andy, 'or any of his old mates?'

The boss got himself turned out of the pub where the barmaid was, and then he'd hang round the other pubs, and get drink somehow, and fight, and get knocked about. He was an awful object by this time, wild-eyed and gaunt, and he hadn't washed or shaved for days.

Andy got the constable in charge of the police station to lock him up for a night, but it only made him worse: we took him back to the camp next morning, and while our eyes were off him for a few minutes he slipped away into the scrub, stripped himself naked, and started to hang himself to a leaning tree with a piece of clothes-line rope. We got to him just in time.

Then Andy wired to the boss's brother Ned, who was fighting the drought, the rabbit pest, and the banks, on a small station back on the border. Andy reckoned it was about time to do something.

Perhaps the boss hadn't been quite right in his head before he started drinking — he had acted queer sometimes, now we came to think of it; maybe he'd got a touch of sunstroke or got brooding over his troubles — anyway he died in the horrors within the week.

His brother Ned turned up on the last day, and Bob thought he was the devil, and grappled with him. It took the three of us to

Telling Mrs Baker

hold the boss down sometimes.

Sometimes, towards the end, he'd be sensible for a few minutes and talk about his 'poor wife and children'; and immediately afterwards he'd fall a-cursing me, and Andy, and Ned, and calling us devils. He cursed everything; he cursed his wife and children, and yelled that they were dragging him down to hell. He died raving mad. It was the worst case of death in the horrors of drink that I ever saw or heard of in the bush.

Ned saw to the funeral: it was very hot weather, and men have to be buried quick who die out there in the hot weather — especially men who die in the state the boss was in. Then Ned went to the public-house where the barmaid was and called the landlord out. It was a desperate fight: the publican was a big man, and a bit of a fighting man; but Ned was one of those quiet, simple-minded chaps who will carry a thing through to death when they make up their minds. He gave that publican nearly as good a thrashing as he deserved. The constable in charge of the station backed Ned, while another policeman picked up the publican. Sounds queer to you city people, doesn't it?

Next morning we three started south. We stayed a couple of days at Ned Baker's station on the border, and then started on our three-hundred-mile ride down-country. The weather was still very hot, so we decided to travel at night for a while, and left Ned's place at dusk. He parted from us at the homestead gate. He gave Andy a small packet, done up in canvas, for Mrs. Baker, which Andy told me contained Bob's pocket-book, letters, and papers. We looked back, after we'd gone a piece along the dusty road, and saw Ned still standing by the gate; and a very lonely figure he looked. Ned was a bachelor. 'Poor old Ned,' said Andy to me. 'He was in love with Mrs. Bob Baker before she got married, but she picked the wrong man — girls mostly do. Ned and Bob were together on the Macquarie, but Ned left when his brother married, and he's been up in these God-forsaken scrubs ever since. Look, I want to tell you something, Jack: Ned has written to Mrs. Bob to tell her that Bob died of fever, and everything was done for him that could be done, and that he died easy — and all that sort of thing. Ned sent her some money, and she is to think that it was the money due to Bob when he died. Now I'll have to go and see her when we get to Solong; there's no getting out of it, I'll have to face her — and you'll have to come with me.'

'Damned if I will!' I said.

'But you'll have to,' said Andy. 'You'll have to stick to me; you're surely not crawler enough to desert a mate in a case like this? I'll have to lie like hell — I'll have to lie as I never lied to a woman before; and you'll have to back me and corroborate every lie.'

I'd never seen Andy show so much emotion.

'There's plenty of time to fix up a good yarn,' said Andy. He said no more about Mrs. Baker, and we only mentioned the boss's name casually, until we were within about a day's ride of Solong; then Andy told me the yarn he'd made up about the boss's death.

'And I want you to listen, Jack,' he said, 'and remember every word — and if you can fix up a better yarn you can tell me afterwards. Now it was like this: the boss wasn't too well when he crossed the border. He complained of pains in his back and head and a stinging pain in the back of his neck, and he had dysentery bad — but that doesn't matter; it's lucky I ain't supposed to tell a woman all the symptoms. The boss stuck to the job as long as he could, but we managed the cattle and made it as easy as we could for him. He'd just take it easy, and ride on from camp to camp, and rest. One night I rode to a town off the route (or you did, if you like) and got some medicine for him; that made him better for a while, but at last, a day or two this side of Mulgatown, he had to give up. A squatter there drove him into town in his buggy and put him up at the best hotel. The publican knew the boss and did all he could for him — put him in the best room and wired for another doctor. We wired for Ned as soon as we saw how bad the boss was, and Ned rode night and day and got there three days before the boss died. The boss was a bit off his head some of the time with the fever, but was calm and quiet towards the end and died easy. He talked a lot about his wife and children, and told us to tell the wife not to fret but to cheer up for the children's sake. How does that sound?'

I'd been thinking while I listened, and an idea struck me.

'Why not let her know the truth?' I asked. 'She's sure to hear of it sooner or later; and if she knew he was only a selfish, drunken blackguard she might get over it all the sooner.'

Telling Mrs Baker

'You don't know women, Jack,' said Andy quietly. 'And, anyway, even if she is a sensible woman, we've got a dead mate to consider as well as a living woman.'

'But she's sure to hear the truth sooner or later,' I said. 'The boss was so well known.'

'And that's just the reason why the truth might be kept from her,' said Andy. 'If he wasn't well known — and nobody could help liking him, after all, when he was straight — if he wasn't so well known the truth might leak out unawares. She won't know if I can help it, or at least not yet a while. If I see any chaps that come from the north I'll put them up to it. I'll tell M'Grath, the publican at Solong, too: he's a straight man — he'll keep his ears open and warn chaps. One of Mrs. Baker's sisters is staying with her, and I'll give her a hint so that she can warn off any women that might get hold of a yarn. Besides, Mrs. Baker is sure to go and live in Sydney, where all her people are — she was a Sydney girl; and she's not likely to meet anyone there that will tell her the truth. I can tell her that it was the last wish of the boss that she should shift to Sydney.'

We smoked and thought a while, and by and by Andy had what he called a 'happy thought'. He went to his saddlebags and got out the small canvas packet that Ned had given him: it was sewn up with packing-thread, and Andy ripped it open with his pocket-knife.

'What are you doing, Andy?' I asked.

'Ned's an innocent old fool, as far as sin is concerned,' said Andy. 'I guess he hasn't looked through the boss's letters, and I'm just going to see that there's nothing here that will make liars of us.'

He looked through the letters and papers by the light of the fire. There were some letters from Mrs. Baker to her husband, also a portrait of her and the children; these Andy put aside. But there were other letters from barmaids and women who were not fit to be seen in the same street with the boss's wife; and there were portraits — one or two flash ones. There were two letters from other men's wives too.

'And one of those men, at least, was an old mate of his!' said Andy, in a tone of disgust.

He threw the lot into the fire; then he went through the boss's pocket-book and tore out some leaves that had notes and addresses on them, and burnt them too. Then he sewed up the packet again and put it away in his saddle-bag.

'Such is life!' said Andy, with a yawn that might have been half a sigh.

We rode into Solong early in the day, turned our horses out in a paddock, and put up at M'Grath's pub until such time as we made up our minds as to what we'd do or where we'd go. We had an idea of waiting until the shearing season started and then making out back to the big sheds.

Neither of us was in a hurry to go and face Mrs. Baker. 'We'll go after dinner,' said Andy at first; then after dinner we had a drink, and felt sleepy — we weren't used to big dinners of roast-beef and vegetables and pudding, and, besides, it was drowsy weather — so we decided to have a snooze and then go. When we woke up it was late in the afternoon, so we thought we'd put it off until after tea. 'It wouldn't be manners to walk in while they're at tea,' said Andy — 'it would look as if we only came for some grub.'

But while we were at tea a little girl came with a message that Mrs. Baker wanted to see us, and would be very much obliged if we'd call up as soon as possible. You see, in those small towns you can't move without the thing getting round inside of half an hour.

'We'll have to face the music now!' said Andy, 'and no get out of it.' He seemed to hang back more than I did. There was another pub opposite where Mrs. Baker lived, and when we got up the street a bit I said to Andy:

'Suppose we go and have another drink first, Andy? We might be kept in there an hour or two.'

'You don't want another drink,' said Andy, rather short. 'Why, you seem to be going the same way as the boss!' But it was Andy who edged off towards the pub when we got near Mrs. Baker's place. 'All right!' he said. 'Come on! We'll have this other drink, since you want it so bad.'

We had the drink, then we buttoned up our coats and started across the road — we'd bought new shirts and collars, and spruced up a bit. Half-way across Andy grabbed my arm and asked:

'How do you feel now, Jack?'

'Oh, *I'm* all right,' I said.

Telling Mrs Baker

'For God's sake,' said Andy, 'don't put your foot in it and make a mess of it.'

'I won't, if you don't.'

Mrs. Baker's cottage was a little weather-board box affair back in a garden. When we went in through the gate Andy gripped my arm again and whispered:

'For God's sake, stick to me now, Jack!'

'I'll stick all right,' I said — 'you've been having too much beer, Andy.'

I had seen Mrs. Baker before, and remembered her as a cheerful, contented sort of woman, bustling about the house and getting the boss's shirts and things ready when we started north. Just the sort of woman that is contented with housework and the children, and with nothing particular about her in the way of brains. But now she sat by the fire looking like the ghost of herself. I wouldn't have recognized her at first. I never saw such a change in a woman, and it came like a shock to me.

Her sister let us in, and after a first glance at Mrs. Baker I had eyes for the sister and no one else. She was a Sydney girl, about twenty-four or twenty-five, and fresh and fair — not like the sun-browned women we were used to see. She was a pretty, bright-eyed girl, and seemed quick to understand, and very sympathetic. She had been educated, Andy had told me, and wrote stories for the Sydney *Bulletin* and other Sydney papers. She had her hair done and was dressed in the city style, and that took us back a bit at first.

'It's very good of you to come,' said Mrs. Baker in a weak, weary voice, when we first went in. 'I heard you were in town.'

'We were just coming when we got your message,' said Andy. 'We'd have come before, only we had to see to the horses.'

'It's very kind of you, I'm sure,' said Mrs. Baker.

They wanted us to have tea, but we said we'd just had it. Then Miss Standish (the sister) wanted us to have tea and cake; but we didn't feel as if we could handle cups and saucers and pieces of cake successfully just then.

There was something the matter with one of the children in a back room, and the sister went to see to it. Mrs. Baker cried a little quietly.

'You mustn't mind me,' she said. 'I'll be all right presently, and then I want you to tell me all about poor Bob. It's seeing you, that saw the last of him, that set me off.'

Andy and I sat stiff and straight, on two chairs against the wall, and held our hats tight, and stared at a picture of Wellington meeting Blücher on the opposite wall. I thought it was lucky that that picture was there.

The child was calling 'mumma', and Mrs. Baker went in to it, and her sister came out. 'Best tell her all about it and get it over,' she whispered to Andy. 'She'll never be content until she hears all about poor Bob from someone who was with him when he died. Let me take your hats. Make yourselves comfortable.'

She took the hats and put them on the sewing-machine. I wished she'd let us keep them, for now we had nothing to hold on to, and nothing to do with our hands; and as for being comfortable, we were just about as comfortable as two cats on wet bricks.

When Mrs. Baker came into the room she brought little Bobby Baker, about four years old; he wanted to see Andy. He ran to Andy at once, and Andy took him up on his knee. He was a pretty child, but he reminded me too much of his father.

'I'm so glad you've come, Andy!' said Bobby.

'Are you, Bobby?'

'Yes. I wants to ask you about daddy. You saw him go away, didn't you?' and he fixed his great wondering eyes on Andy's face.

'Yes,' said Andy.

'He went up among the stars, didn't he?'

'Yes,' said Andy.

'And he isn't coming back to Bobby any more?'

'No,' said Andy. 'But Bobby's going to him by and by.'

Mrs. Baker had been leaning back in her chair, resting her head on her hand, tears glistening in her eyes; now she began to sob, and her sister took her out of the room.

Andy looked miserable. 'I wish to God I was off this job!' he whispered to me.

'Is that the girl that writes the stories?' I asked.

'Yes,' he said, staring at me in a hopeless sort of way, 'and poems too.'

'Is Bobby going up among the stars?' asked Bobby.

'Yes,' said Andy — 'if Bobby's good.'

'And auntie?'

'Yes.'
'And mumma?'
'Yes.'
'Are you going, Andy?'
'Yes,' said Andy, hopelessly.
'Did you see daddy go up among the stars, Andy?'
'Yes,' said Andy, 'I saw him go up.'
'And he isn't coming down again any more?'
'No,' said Andy.
'Why isn't he?'
'Because he's going to wait up there for you and mumma, Bobby.'

There was a long pause, and then Bobby asked:

'Are you going to give me a shilling, Andy?' with the same expression of innocent wonder in his eyes.

Andy slipped half a crown into his hand. 'Auntie' came in and told him he'd see Andy in the morning and took him away to bed, after he'd kissed us both solemnly; and presently she and Mrs. Baker settled down to hear Andy's story.

'Brace up now, Jack, and keep your wits about you,' whispered Andy to me just before they came in.

'Poor Bob's brother Ned wrote to me,' said Mrs. Baker, 'but he scarcely told me anything. Ned's a good fellow, but he's very simple, and never thinks of anything.'

Andy told her about the boss not being well after he crossed the border.

'I knew he was not well,' said Mrs. Baker, 'before he left. I didn't want him to go. I tried hard to persuade him not to go this trip. I had a feeling that I oughtn't to let him go. But he'd never think of anything but me and the children. He promised he'd give up droving after this trip, and get something to do near home. The life was too much for him — riding in all weathers and camping out in the rain, and living like a dog. But he was never content at home. It was all for the sake of me and the children. He wanted to make money and start on a station again. I shouldn't have let him go. He only thought of me and the children! Oh! my poor, dear, kind, dead husband!' She broke down again and sobbed, and her sister comforted her, while Andy and I stared at Wellington meeting Blücher on the field at Waterloo. I thought the artist had heaped up the dead a bit extra,

Australian Short Stories

and I thought that I wouldn't like to be trod on by horses, even if I was dead.

'Don't you mind,' said Miss Standish, 'she'll be all right presently,' and she handed us the *Illustrated Sydney Journal*. This was a great relief — we bumped our heads over the pictures.

Mrs. Baker made Andy go on again, and he told her how the boss broke down near Mulgatown. Mrs. Baker was opposite him and Miss Standish opposite me. Both of them kept their eyes on Andy's face: he sat, with his hair straight up like a brush as usual, and kept his big innocent grey eyes fixed on Mrs. Baker's face all the time he was speaking. I watched Miss Standish. I thought she was the prettiest girl I'd ever seen; it was a bad case of love at first sight; but she was far and away above me, and the case was hopeless. I began to feel pretty miserable, and to think back into the past; I just heard Andy droning away by my side.

'So we fixed him up comfortable in the wagonette with the blankets and coats and things,' Andy was saying, 'and the squatter started into Mulgatown . . . It was about thirty miles, Jack, wasn't it?' he asked, turning suddenly to me. He always looked so innocent that there were times when I itched to knock him down.

'More like thirty-five,' I said, waking up.

Miss Standish fixed her eyes on me, and I had another look at Wellington and Blücher.

'They were all very good and kind to the boss,' said Andy. 'They thought a lot of him up there. Everybody was fond of him.'

'I know it,' said Mrs. Baker. 'Nobody could help liking him. He was one of the kindest men that ever lived.'

'Tanner, the publican, couldn't have been kinder to his own brother,' said Andy. 'The local doctor was a decent chap, but he was only a young fellow, and Tanner hadn't much faith in him, so he wired for an older doctor at Mackintyre, and he even sent out fresh horses to meet the doctor's buggy. Everything was done that could be done, I assure you, Mrs. Baker.'

'I believe it,' said Mrs. Baker. 'And you don't know how it relieves me to hear it. And did the publican do all this at his own expense?'

'He wouldn't take a penny, Mrs. Baker.'

'He must have been a good true man. I wish I could thank him.'

Telling Mrs Baker

'Oh, Ned thanked him for you,' said Andy, though without meaning more than he said.

'I wouldn't have fancied that Ned would have thought of that,' said Mrs. Baker. 'When I first heard of my poor husband's death, I thought perhaps he'd been drinking again — that worried me a bit.'

'He never touched a drop after he left Solong, I can assure you, Mrs. Baker,' said Andy quickly.

Now I noticed that Miss Standish seemed surprised or puzzled, once or twice, while Andy was speaking, and leaned forward to listen to him; then she leaned back in her chair and clasped her hands behind her head and looked at him, with half-shut eyes, in a way I didn't like. Once or twice she looked at me as if she was going to ask me a question, but I always looked away quick and stared at Blücher and Wellington, or into the empty fireplace, till I felt her eyes were off me. Then she asked Andy a question or two, in all innocence I believe now, but it scared him, and at last he watched his chance and winked at her sharp. Then she gave a little gasp and shut up like a steel trap.

The sick child in the bedroom coughed and cried again. Mrs. Baker went to it. We three sat like a deaf-and-dumb institution, Andy and I staring all over the place: presently Miss Standish excused herself, and went out of the room after her sister. She looked hard at Andy as she left the room, but he kept his eyes away.

'Brace up now, Jack,' whispered Andy to me, 'the worst is coming.'

When they came in again Mrs. Baker made Andy go on with his story.

'He — he died very quietly,' said Andy, hitching round, and resting his elbows on his knees, and looking into the fireplace so as to have his face away from the light. Miss Standish put her arm round her sister. 'He died very easy,' said Andy. 'He was a bit off his head at times, but that was while the fever was on him. He didn't suffer much towards the end — I don't think he suffered at all . . . He talked a lot about you and the children.' (Andy was speaking very softly now.) 'He said that you were not to fret, but to cheer up for the children's sake . . . It was the biggest funeral ever seen round there.'

45

Mrs. Baker was crying softly. Andy got the packet half-out of his pocket, but shoved it back again.

'The only thing that hurts me now,' said Mrs. Baker presently, 'is to think of my poor husband buried out there in the lonely bush, so far from home. It's — cruel!' and she was sobbing again.

'Oh, that's all right, Mrs. Baker,' said Andy, losing his head a little. 'Ned will see to that. Ned is going to arrange to have him brought down and buried in Sydney.' Which was about the first thing Andy had told her that evening that wasn't a lie. Ned had said he would do it as soon as he sold his wool.

'It's very kind indeed of Ned,' sobbed Mrs. Baker. 'I'd never have dreamed he was so kind-hearted and thoughtful. I misjudged him all along. And that is all you have to tell me about poor Robert?'

'Yes,' said Andy — then one of his 'happy thoughts' struck him. 'Except that he hoped you'd shift to Sydney, Mrs. Baker, where you've got friends and relations. He thought it would be better for you and the children. He told me to tell you that.'

'He was thoughtful up the end,' said Mrs. Baker. 'It was just like poor Robert — always thinking of me and the children. We are going to Sydney next week.'

Andy looked relieved. We talked a little more, and Miss Standish wanted to make coffee for us, but we had to go and see to our horses. We got up and bumped against each other, and got each other's hats, and promised Mrs. Baker we'd come again.

'Thank you very much for coming,' she said, shaking hands with us. 'I feel much better now. You don't know how much you have relieved me. Now, mind, you have promised to come and see me again for the last time.'

Andy caught her sister's eye and jerked his head towards the door to let her know he wanted to speak to her outside.

'Good-bye, Mrs. Baker,' he said, holding on to her hand. 'And don't you fret. You've — you've got the children yet. It's — it's all for the best; and, besides, the boss said you weren't to fret.' And he blundered out after me and Miss Standish.

She came out to the gate with us, and Andy gave her the packet.

'I want you to give that to her,' he said: 'it's his letters and papers. I hadn't the heart to give it to her, somehow.'

Telling Mrs Baker

'Tell me, Mr. M'Culloch,' she said. 'You've kept something back — you haven't told her the truth. It would be better and safer for me to know. Was it an accident — or the drink?'

'It was the drink,' said Andy. 'I was going to tell you — I thought it would be best to tell you. I had made up my mind to do it, but, somehow, I couldn't have done it if you hadn't asked me.'

'Tell me all,' she said. 'It would be better for me to know.'

'Come a little farther away from the house,' said Andy. She came along the fence a piece with us, and Andy told her as much of the truth as he could.

'I'll hurry her off to Sydney,' she said. 'We can get away this week as well as next.' Then she stood for a minute before us, breathing quickly, her hands behind her back and her eyes shining in the moonlight. She looked splendid.

'I want to thank you for her sake,' she said quickly. 'You are good men! I like the bushmen! They are grand men — they are noble. I'll probably never see either of you again, so it doesn't matter,' and she put her white hand on Andy's shoulder and kissed him fair and square on the mouth. 'And you, too!' she said to me. I was taller than Andy, and had to stoop. 'Good-bye!' she said, and ran to the gate and in, waving her hand to us. We lifted our hats again and turned down the road.

I don't think it did either of us any harm.

Two Hanged Women

Henry Handel Richardson

Hand in hand the youthful lovers sauntered along the esplanade. It was a night in midsummer; a wispy moon had set, and the stars glittered. The dark mass of the sea, at flood, lay tranquil, slothfully lapping the shingle.

'Come on, let's make for the usual,' said the boy.

But on nearing their favourite seat they found it occupied. In the velvety shade of the overhanging sea-wall, the outlines of two figures were visible.

'Oh, blast!' said the lad. 'That's torn it. What now, Baby?'

'Why, let's stop here, Pincher, right close up, till we frighten 'em off.'

And very soon loud, smacking kisses, amatory pinches and ticklings, and skittish squeals of pleasure did their work. Silently the intruders rose and moved away.

But the boy stood gaping after them, open-mouthed.

'Well, I'm *damned*! If it wasn't just two hanged women!'

Retreating before a salvo of derisive laughter, the elder of the girls said: 'We'll go out on the breakwater.' She was tall and thin, and walked with a long stride.

Her companion, shorter than she by a bobbed head of straight flaxen hair, was hard put to it to keep pace. As she pegged along she said doubtfully, as if in self-excuse: 'Though I really ought to go home. It's getting late. Mother will be angry.'

They walked with finger-tips lightly in contact; and at her words she felt what was like an attempt to get free, on the part of the fingers crooked in hers. But she was prepared for this, and

Two Hanged Women

held fast, gradually working her own up till she had a good half of the other hand in her grip.

For a moment neither spoke. Then, in a low, muffled voice, came the question: 'Was she angry last night, too?'

The little fair girl's reply had an unlooked-for vehemence. 'You know she wasn't!' And, mildly despairing: 'But you never *will* understand. Oh, what's the good of . . . of anything!'

And on sitting down she let the prisoned hand go, even putting it from her with a kind of push. There it lay, palm upwards, the fingers still curved from her hold, looking like a thing with a separate life of its own; but a life that was ebbing.

On this remote seat, with their backs turned on lovers, lights, the town, the two girls sat and gazed wordlessly at the dark sea, over which great Jupiter was flinging a thin gold line. There was no sound but the lapping, sucking, sighing, of the ripples at the edge of the breakwater, and the occasional screech of an owl in the tall trees on the hillside.

But after a time, having stolen more than one side-glance at her companion, the younger seemed to take heart of grace. With a childish toss of the head that set her loose hair swaying, she said, in a tone of meaning emphasis: 'I like Fred.'

The only answer was a faint, contemptuous shrug.

'I tell you I *like* him!'

'Fred? Rats!'

'No it isn't . . . that's just where you're wrong, Betty. But you think you're so wise. Always.'

'I know what I know.'

'Or imagine you do! But it doesn't matter. Nothing you can say makes any difference. I like him, and always shall. In heaps of ways. He's so big and strong, for one thing: it gives you such a safe sort of feeling to be with him . . . as if nothing could happen while you were. Yes, it's . . . it's . . . well, I can't help it, Betty, there's something *comfy* in having a boy to go about with — like other girls do. One they'd eat their hats to get, too! I can see it in their eyes when we pass; Fred with his great long legs and broad shoulders — I don't nearly come up to them — and his blue eyes with the black lashes, and his shiny black hair. And I like his tweeds, the Harris smell of them, and his dirty old pipe, and the way he shows his teeth — he's got *topping* teeth — when he laughs and says "ra-*ther!*" And other people, when they see us, look . . .

49

well I don't quite know how to say it, but they look sort of pleased; and they make room for us and let us into the dark corner-seats at the pictures, just as if we'd a right to them. And they never laugh. (Oh, I can't *stick* being laughed at! — and that's the truth.) Yes, it's so comfy, Betty darling . . . such a warm cosy comfy feeling. Oh, *won't* you understand?'

'Gawd! why not make a song of it?' But a moment later, very fiercely: 'And who is it's taught you to think all this? Who's hinted it and suggested it till you've come to believe it? . . . believe it's what you really feel.'

'She hasn't! Mother's never said a word . . . about Fred.'

'Words? — why waste words? . . . when she can do it with a cock of the eye. For your Fred, that!' and the girl called Betty held her fingers aloft and snapped them viciously. 'But your mother's a different proposition.'

'I think you're simply horrid.'

To this there was no reply.

'*Why* have you such a down on her? What's she ever done to you? . . . except not get ratty when I stay out late with Fred. And I don't see how you can expect . . . being what she is . . . and with nobody but me — after all she *is* my mother . . . you can't alter that. I know very well — and you know, too — I'm not *too* putrid-looking. But' — beseechingly — 'I'm *nearly* twenty-five now, Betty. And other girls . . . well, she sees them, every one of them, with a boy of their own, even though they're ugly, or fat, or have legs like sausages — they've only got to ogle them a bit — the girls, I mean . . . and there they are. And Fred's a good sort — he is, really! — and he dances well, and doesn't drink, and so . . . so why *shouldn't* I like him? . . . and off my own bat . . . without it having to be all Mother's fault, and me nothing but a parrot, and without any will of my own?'

'Why? Because I know her too well, my child! I can read her as you'd never dare to . . . even if you could. She's sly, your mother is, so sly there's no coming to grips with her . . . one might as well try to fill one's hand with cobwebs. But she's got a hold on you, a stranglehold, that nothing'll loosen. Oh! mothers aren't fair — I mean it's not fair of nature to weigh us down with them and yet expect us to be our own true selves. The handicap's too great. All those months, when the same blood's running through two sets of veins — there's no getting away from that, ever after. Take yours. As I say, does she need to open her mouth? Not she! She's only got to let it hang at the corners, and you reek, you drip with guilt.'

Something in these words seemed to sting the younger girl. She hit back. 'I know what it is, you're jealous, that's what you are! . . . and you've no other way of letting it out. But I tell you this. If ever I marry — yes, *marry!* — it'll be to please myself, and nobody else. Can you imagine me doing it to oblige her?'

Again silence.

'If I only think what it would be like to be fixed up and settled, and able to live in peace, without this eternal dragging two ways . . . just as if I was being torn in half. And see Mother smiling and happy again, like she used to be. Between the two of you I'm nothing but a punch-ball. Oh, I'm fed up with it! . . . fed up to the neck. As for you . . . And yet you can sit there as if you were made of stone! Why don't you *say* something? *Betty!* Why won't you speak?'

But no words came.

'I can *feel* you sneering. And when you sneer I hate you more than any one on earth. If only I'd never seen you!'

'Marry your Fred, and you'll never need to again.'

'I will, too! I'll marry him, and have a proper wedding like other girls, with a veil and bridesmaids and bushels of flowers. And I'll live in a house of my own, where I can do as I like, and be left in peace, and there'll be no one to badger and bully me — Fred wouldn't . . . ever! Besides, he'll be away all day. And when he came back at night, he'd . . . I'd . . . I mean I'd___' But here the flying words gave out; there came a stormy breath and a cry of: 'Oh, Betty, Betty! . . . I couldn't, no, I couldn't! It's when I think of *that* . . . Yes, it's quite true! I like him all right, I do indeed, but only as long as he doesn't come too near. If he even sits too close, I have to screw myself up to bear it' — and flinging herself down over her companion's lap, she hid her face. 'And if he tries to touch me, Betty, or even takes my arm or puts his round me . . . And then his face . . . when it looks like it does sometimes . . . all wrong . . . as if it had gone all wrong — oh! then I feel I shall have to scream — out loud. I'm afraid of him . . . when he looks like that. Once . . . when he kissed me . . . I could have died with the horror of it. His breath . . . his breath . . . and his mouth — like fruit pulp — and the black hairs on his wrists . . . and the way he looked — and . . . and everything! No, I can't, I can't . . . nothing will make me . . . I'd rather die twice over. But what am I to do? Mother'll *never* understand. Oh, why has it got to be like this? I want to be happy, like other girls, and to make her happy, too . . . and everything's all wrong. You tell me, Betty darling, you help me, you're older . . . you *know* . . . and you can help me, if you will . . . if you only will!' And locking her arms round her friend she drove her face deeper into the warmth and darkness, as if, from the very fervour of her clasp, she could draw the aid and strength she needed.

Betty had sat silent, unyielding, her sole movement being to loosen her own arms from her sides and point her elbows outwards, to hinder them touching the arms that lay round her. But at this last appeal she melted; and gathering the young girl to her breast, she held her fast. — And so for long she continued to sit, her chin resting lightly on the fair hair, that was silky and downy as an infant's, and gazing with sombre eyes over the stealthily heaving sea.

Miss Aminta Wirraway and the Sin of Lust

Ethel Anderson

The weather, in the summer following the Bishop's visit, was hardly less beneficent than the autumn had been. The days were cloudless. A picnic was to celebrate Miss Aminta Wirraway's seventeenth birthday, chiefly because it was the one form of entertainment likely to be eschewed by the 'agéd'.

'Though I do not call people really old till they take their baths with the door open,' Victoria McMurthie had observed, 'people begin to be elderly when they look thoughtful after eating apple-dumplings —'

'Or when they refuse toffee —'

'Speak when you are spoken to, Alberteena McMurthie!' Victoria silenced her younger sister, and continued: 'But though we are not old, we will leave our bathing dresses behind. Why should we suddenly become stand-offish with each other when we have shared a hot tub every Saturday night until just lately?'

'And when Donalblain (who is four) thinks nothing of coming into the Nursery to borrow the soap?'

'Alberteena! How often must I tell you that speech is silver, silence is gold?' Victoria again quenched her younger sister. 'So why be squeamish?' she added, and before climbing into her place in the buckboard, she hid nine voluminous sets of garments, made of many yards of serge, and decorated with white vandyked braid, behind the hedge.

The Vicarage buckboard, an unwired aviary of chirping girls, and drawn with cloppy animation by 'old' Ruby, who was rising two, then set off, to creak, to hesitate, to side-slip in the ruts of the sandy track that led from Mallow's Marsh to Lanterloo Bay.

The road was often repaired with bridgings of wattle saplings laced together with rope or vines, yet over the creeks there were no bridges; these had to be forded with a great splashing of water and many shrieks of excitement.

However, Juliet McCree was a dashing whip — she brought her gay passengers safely to the harbour's rim.

And in Lanterloo Bay the sand's golden half moon, the calm yet mettlesome hiss of the placid sea, the entirely conventional sky.

Lying after her dip to dry her pliant body in the warm, down-soft sand, each girl paid her tribute to its beauty.

'Such a blue sky, such a radiant sea, not a cloud, not a wave, not a wrinkle on the water!' Alberteena, for once, was allowed her say.

'The sea is darker than the sky.'

'Where we lie, above high tide mark, the sand is as fine as icing-sugar, and it is never covered with seaweed or sea-shells.'

'What I like best is the smell of the umbrella fern coming from that creek.'

'The sea smells of lobster.' Juliet McCree, as usual, was seeking after truth. She sniffed, with a scientific expression of her glowing face, the hardly stirring waves that lapped her sunlit body, which, from top to toe, rivalled a ripe apricot in colour.

'Juliet!' Aminta felt it necessary to assert her age. Shielding her flawless complexion with a minute, hinged parasol (its ivory stick was chaperoned by a tell-tale silver bell) she lay, more beautiful than any Venus known to art, among the castles of sand Alberteena, Gussie and Octavia had built round her. 'Juliet! Come out! You have been in the water long enough!'

'Oh, no! I can't come out yet! The water is so delicious! I want to find out exactly what it really smells of! Sometimes it has a queer reek, almost like a noise, and at other times it has a whiff like Grandmama McCree's white Camellia —'

'Whose pink lawn handkerchief is this?'

'Mine, dear.'

'Tie it round your wrist.'

'Across the harbour Sydney begins to look like a real city,

Miss Aminta Wirraway and the Sin of Lust

doesn't it? There's St. James' spire — such an elegant candle-snuffer.'

'So many lovely sailing ships, too! I like them best like that, with all their sails set, drying in the sun, and all reflected in the water, as they just swing with the tide.'

'Dr. Phantom does not really care for women.'

Gussie Wirraway had a younger sister's uncomfortable habit of introducing an unwanted subject.

'What a pity!' Victoria McMurthie became worldly. 'He's the only eligible bachelor between Mallow's Marsh and Hornsby Junction.'

'His three brothers all made such good matches.' Gussie was not to be outdone. Sitting on a sand-castle she searched, like 'The Spinario', for a thorn in a pink toe.

'Simeon married ten thousand pounds in bonds,' Victoria remarked, still in her role of woman of the world.

'And the handsomest set of buck teeth this side of the equator.'

'Ninian, the second boy, married twenty thousand acres —'

'What! More teeth, dear?'

'No. Goosie-Gussie! A-C-R-E-S! Of land! Covered in sheep, in Victoria.'

'And three sets of twins.'

'Septimus, the third brother — (what a cheat Mrs. Phantom was, to call her third son Septimus) — well — he married a line of South Sea Whalers!'

'And a whale of a wife!'

'No, dear, she was a minnow — a gold fish, merely. I was a bridesmaid at the wedding.' Aminta sadly roused herself from a reverie.

'My dears!' Victoria evaded contact with a flowering wattle branch which Alberteena was using to brush off sand. 'They all married Prosperity.'

'Yes! And look at them! Ninian at thirty with a barouche, a gig, five saddle horses, a Crown Derby dinner service with covers for forty, a tolerably handsome residence at Point Piper — right in the bush, really —'

'And the intolerable bathos of three sets of twins!'

'And Simeon, dear man! I'm very fond of Simeon! He's *so* rich, *such* a handsome property. Two thousand Merinos, a thousand head of cattle, all within a day's ride —'

'Of the nearest glass of rum.'

'And with a shambling progeny of fourteen daughters, and a face pockmarked with hen-pecks —'

'Dr. Phantom cares for nothing but sport.'

'Yes! The minute he's free, off he goes on that sawney sorrel brute of his, and surrounded by all those curs, pariahs, dingoes, collies, kelpies! Yap, yap, yap! Bow-wow-wow! Oh, the din! Oh, the clatter! They woke me up at four o'clock this morning.'

'Where does he go?'

'Most often to that old Inn, "The Devil's Tail", at Doggett's Patch, about fourteen miles past Windsor, out by the Hawkesbury River.'

'He goes to shoot wallabies or dingoes.'

'No one really believes he goes simply to shoot.'

'Oh, keep away, Juliet! Keep away! If you shake yourself so near us you'll make us all wet again, and we are just drying nicely.'

Such was the chorus that greeted Juliet, who ran out of the water at last, to pirouette, to stamp, to squeeze the moisture out of her auburn hair, now black and sticky.

'All right, all right! I'll sit here on this hillock of sand with the mimosa tree to keep the sun off! Poor Dr. Phantom says he has not the slightest wish to marry, much less to become a father —'

'Who told you that, pray?'

'He did. In Church. Of course we were sitting right at the back. No human being could sit silent through Grandpapa's sermon on the Hittites, the Jebusites and the Ammonites! It's too learned!'

'What! Dr. Phantom a bachelor? He'll fall in love and marry just like any other man.'

'No. He says not. The trouble is, he says, that one is allowed no choice! And, really, it does seem to be so. My dear Papa used to say, "Sweet or dry?" or "Say when, old chap", and Mama says, "Milk and sugar?" Grandpapa asks anyone who goes into the Snuggery, "Do you prefer the window open or shut?" And that old waiter out at The Devil's Tail breathes over your shoulder and says, "Thick or Thin?" And we always think we are being asked to make our choice between things that do not matter in the least, which makes us think we are actually somebody with a will of our own, but God does not ask "Boy or Girl?" when we are

Miss Aminta Wirraway and the Sin of Lust

waiting to be born — which is important, really. He knows we would all say "Boy", and then where would posterity be?'

'There should have been a third sex,' Victoria agreed, 'with the vices of neither men nor women and the virtues of both.'

'And without the bore of having to live like men and women.' Juliet was emphatic.

'Of course there are the saints. They refuse to be men and women, but do they enjoy it? Look at St. Lawrence with his gridiron, and St. Catherine with her wheel, and St. Sebastian with his arrows and St. Stephen with his stones! They are always painted with calm, holy expressions on their faces, but I doubt if they enjoyed themselves. As things are, Dr. Phantom says, nothing would induce him to marry.'

'Why, dearest Aminta! Tears! Oh, that scrap of pink lawn is useless! Take my handkerchief.' Even Victoria was concerned to see such grief.

'Yes,' went on Juliet, who was turned the other way, 'all Dr. Phantom wants is to be free to go to Burragorang or to cross the Wollondilly, or explore the Nepean, or the Diamantina, or to go to the hills to shoot pigeons, or shovellers on the lakes, or to the Limestone Plains, he says, to shoot plovers and wild turkeys — there are flocks of them there, he says, and he wants to go to the Snowy River, to fish for trout — rainbow trout — that's the life for him, he says, and he's making a collection —'

'Of women?'

'No, silly! Of goannas! He has four beauties already.'

'Why — *whatever is the matter with Aminta?*'

'Oh, poor darling! Doesn't she look unhappy!'

'She's getting so thin, too! I can count all her ribs.'

'Why,' Juliet exclaimed, looking round, 'her backbone looks just like an oxtail, with all those knobs.'

'Oh, my dear! Tell us all your sorrows. A sorrow told is a sorrow halved, they say.'

'Oh, I'm in love!' Aminta's tone was desperate. 'Oh, love is a terrible thing, so sweet when it begins, and then, ah — the ache, the yearning, the longing! I get no rest. I toss and turn. I can't get *him* out of my thoughts, and oh! he doesn't care a rap for me!'

'Take up woolwork; it's so fascinating.'

'Knit him a smoking-cap, in double Berlin wool, and line it

with plush. With *that* on his head he could not help thinking of you!'

'Embroider him a set of the new braces — like the curate's.'

'Don't tease her, girls. Can't you see this is serious?'

'I'm so restless. I can't concentrate. The world seems quite unreal! I wanted above all things to come to this lovely picnic, but now I'm here I keep thinking — "suppose *he* passed our gate and I was not there to see". Oh, and I lie awake all night making up conversations with him!'

'Do please tell us what you talk about. I've never been in love.'

'Nor I.'

'Neither have I.'

'Of course we haven't, yet.'

'I should never dream of falling in love, myself.'

'Let me rest my head on your shoulder, Juliet dear, then I'll tell you. I'm so weary, I suffer, oh, how I suffer! I have no strength left. Look at my arm. It's so weak that I could not even support the weight of my bracelet —'

'You mean that silver filigree bangle?'

'Yes. I left it at home.'

Aminta's was, apparently, a classic case! Her every symptom of hopeless love matched poor Phaedra's, who, through weakness, discarded her cumbrous ornaments, and let her auburn tresses fall over her shoulders — as Aminta's then were doing, for she had freed her chignon of its net — it seemed to ease her.

'I found its weight insupportable. I did not eat a bit of breakfast.'

'Do tell us, dear Aminta, about those conversations.'

'I imagine we are riding together on two most beautiful horses (a roan and a dapple-grey) and we talk about the flowering trees and the swiftly moving clouds —'

'Trees and clouds, dear? You are going quite the wrong way about it. *He* cares to discuss nothing but the price of hay.'

'Or I pretend we are sailing in a little yacht (such a pet of a boat with tan sails) and we glide across the water, and the sun shines and the breeze is as soft as silk on one's cheek —'

'Just like this! What could be lovelier than it is today?'

'But he is not here. *He* is not with me! Oh, I shall die! I know I shall! I cannot endure this nag, nag, nag at the very marrow of

Miss Aminta Wirraway and the Sin of Lust

my heart one moment longer. I can't, I can't.'

'Oh, isn't it sad?'

'Oh, poor, poor girl!'

'Oh, it's agony, agony!'

'Have you tried getting Granny Smith to read your fortune in the dregs of your cup?'

'I did. She said she could not see a ray of hope.'

'I always think Granny Smith has such an amused expression on her face, don't you, Gussie?'

'Hush! I want to hear what Aminta is saying.'

'I bowed three times to the new moon and wished. I slept with a stocking full of apples under my pillow. Oh, such a dreadful thing I did! I stuck a flail up the chimney! Nothing was the least use!'

'Stuck a flail up the chimney! Aminta! What a dreadful thing to do! But that's Black Magic. Oh, you naughty girl!'

'The terrible thing is, I have grown quite shameless. I shock myself. Sometimes I have to get out of bed and say my prayers, however cold it is, and however bad my chilblains are! And that's not the worst! I saw *him* go into the chemist's! I did not want to buy anything but in I went! Just to see him smile — I felt my reputation was of no consequence! And he gave me such a cool nod. Such a respectful salute — just with two fingers.'

'Better get her dressed.'

'Better harness Ruby and take her home.'

'Juliet, you slip your clothes on and run and harness Ruby.'

'Yes, yes, I will, immediately! Someone come and hold the shafts. Ruby is so immense, it's a squeeze to get her between them. She's a pure-bred brewer's dray horse from Marseilles, and she's much bigger than any Flanders mare.'

'Get dressed, Aminta darling, and come home. And when we're all nine of us in the buckboard, and the hot sun is shining, and old Ruby is going at a brisk trot, with all her brasses clinking, and her hairy hooves clapping the stones, and all of us are chattering like jays, oh, darling, it might cheer you up, indeed it might.'

'Nothing could! Oh, dear! Oh, dear! Abigail has put too much starch in my chemise, and the frills are as sharp as knives round my armpits, and they cut my flesh to ribbons —'

'There, there, darling girl, dry your eyes, my pet, and come home.'

'A liberal dose of hartshorn, that will pull her round.'

Victoria, laden with the luncheon basket, paused. 'What about this doll, dear, that you made of milk and bread while we were all eating our sandwiches?'

'Shall we bring it?'

'It's not a doll. It's Venus. A votive offering. After all, you never know, do you? I'd like to leave it by the sea's edge — just in case!'

'Paganism, too!'

Even Juliet McCree was shocked, and she was almost a freethinker.

'Miss Loveday Boisragon,' Gussie Wirraway volunteered, to change the subject, 'sometimes goes to stay at The Devil's Tail. The landlord's daughter was one of her Sunday school pupils. Yes, she drives over and stays a few nights sometimes.'

'My dear!' Victoria whispered to Octavia, who was next to Aminta in age, 'do look at Aminta. Directly she heard *that* she dried her eyes! If a kitten could look calculating — well! Just look at her! She has suddenly got quite a scheming air, hasn't she? I think she is far less innocent than she appears to be.'

'Nonsense! She is the dearest thing! I suppose you mean to infer that she will try to get Miss Loveday to take her with her next time she goes to The Devil's Tail?'

'What!' Overhearing, Alberteena, who was precocious for ten, exclaimed, 'Aminta go with Miss Loveday to The Devil's Tail at Doggett's Patch! What would she do in Doggett's Patch?'

'Why, Dr. Phantom goes there sometimes, Goose!'

In the haste of departure the bevy of girls trooped through the flowering wattles and stiff, aromatic umbrella ferns in the creek bed, and nothing was left of the picnic but a great many footprints and dimples in the sand, a branch or two of mimosa, lying golden in the sun, and the small image of Venus, made of milk and bread, which (the beach once deserted) soon attracted the sea-gulls and poddymoddies, who, knowing no better, ate her up to the last crumb.

Juliet McCree is Accused of Gluttony

Ethel Anderson

Dr. Phantom did not really care for children. It is doubtful whether any child had ever been invited to ride beside him in the dashing Hyde Park in which he made his daily rounds. This was a canopied and curtained vehicle, its four wheels rimmed with iron, and it was drawn by a piebald Waler, and driven by a white-gloved, personable murderer.

It was usual in those days for citizens of Sydney who applied for convict servants to ask for a murderer if any should happen to be available. They were in great demand, for, though apt to be impulsive on occasions of emotion, killers had generally been found to have warmer-hearted and more likeable dispositions than criminals of other persuasions. Dr. Phantom, caring little for thieves, sheepstealers, pickpockets, lags, or the abductors of heiresses, employed, when he could do so, only murderers. Though he drew the line at poisoners (his dispensary being, he felt, a temptation) he was at this period particularly lucky; he was rich in the possession of 'First and Second Murderers' — as he designated them — and his servants' hall, in the neat red-brick Georgian house, some twenty miles from the capital, had never been more cheery.

On this energetic afternoon in early autumn, when a mellowing sun shone obliquely down on a humming and triumphing world, 'First Murderer' was on the box, a check-string with its wide band attached to his right arm, that had, on some earlier occasion, presumably wielded a lethal weapon (an axe was at that time the most popular tool), and Dr. Phantom, sitting directly behind him, would jerk the cord to ensure attention before issuing directions as to which track should be followed, or at which house, shack, shanty, hovel or mansion he should stop.

In this beneficent district the fruit had never been finer.

The grapes growing in the direction of Dural had recalled to Dr. Phantom a Tuscan summer.

The peach harvest, he noted, had never been more luscious. Lying at his feet two large baskets testified to an almost Olympian abundance; one was an Ossa of Jargonells, orange Bergamots, and 'Williams'; from a second willow-ark rose a perfect Pelion of grapes, apricots and plums (blue perdrigons), the first fruits of several orchards.

As Dr. Phantom bowled along in his nicely shaded carriage his eyes lingered on the signs of an earlier optimism, on many a phalanx of raspberries, on plantations of gooseberries, and ordered battalions of strawberries. A particularly fine crop of these delectable berries punctuated the Undertaker's neatly kept plot with bright red nodules nestling on straw. It was an age when straw laid down on a roadway paid its sympathetic tribute to the difficulty of producing the coming generation, and discreetly muffled the departure of age; and straw was plentiful.

On this garlanded highway, where even the hedges were bright with rose-haws, the good doctor experienced the pleasure afforded to a reasoning man by the contemplation of a Universe based on reason.

He passed the chain-gang knocking sparks out of flint.

'They are dressing stone for the repair of the bridge,' he (rightly) concluded.

He skirted the milkman's trotting cart which pleasantly recalled to him the hip-waddles of a Zulu belle. The cart was painted yellow and a scarlet scroll was ciphered with the words 'Families supplied twice daily'.

'He is delivering the late afternoon milk,' Dr. Phantom instinctively realised.

That, too, was a reasonable conjecture, though the statement on the cart was, perhaps, cryptic to the uninitiated.

Just outside Parramatta he observed the Rector entering Mrs. Furbelow's lean-to. 'The latest addition to that poor widow's family of twenty is about to pass, non-stop, through this vale of tears,' was his natural inference; he was right.

Juliet McCree is Accused of Gluttony

But a sight that baffled his intelligence as his Hyde Park clattered to a standstill by the kerb outside his partner's brass-plated, two-storied yellowstone house beside the bridge in Parramatta, was the apparition of seven little boys and girls, of ages ranging from four to, perhaps, ten or eleven years, each holding in their trembling hands a black papier-mâché basin; each standing on a separate step of the stone stairway that led down to the slowly-meandering waters of the Lane Cove River.

His first thought had been 'Whooping-cough', but 'No', he reminded himself, 'I should have been the first to be informed of any such epidemic'.

He found his partner Dr. Boisragon (pronounced Borrygan) standing on the top step of the flight.

He looked grave.

He looked even more stern than usual, and his handsome face wore an expression that might almost have been called 'pained'. Though he was dressed with his customary ceremony in a full-skirted marine blue frogged coat, with yellow Nankin breeches, nicely moulded over Wellington boots and his own (almost famous) legs, with a thick, gold bemedalled watchchain caressing a buff waistcoat, a black satin stock meticulously folded under white linen points, and with a stovepipe hat, cocked sideways, as he always wore it, he might have been going to a funeral; to the obsequies of the victim of someone else's rapacity and incompetence.

'The grapes,' Dr. Phantom explained, handing him the larger of the two baskets which he had carried from the Hyde Park, 'are from Widow Plunkett. The pears are selected from a basket given to me by Mr. Jarvey in recognition of the pretty compliments I paid him on his wall-fruit. The greenish apples are from Granny Smith, whose cottage near Castle Hill I passed in pursuit of a ruined stomach and a case of mumps out at Hornsby Junction.'

Accepting the basket Dr. Boisragon touched the grapes reverently with his sensitive hands — he had a surgeon's hands — 'The bloom!' he marvelled, 'How does Nature do it? Is it an efflorescence? Is it a quintessential patina?'

He set the heavy basket down on the parapet beside him and broke off a sizeable bunch of Muscatels.

'I must confess my ignorance.' Meditatively Dr. Phantom

peeled with his equally sensitive fingers a Yellow Monday peach of august proportions. 'No-one, to my knowledge, has conducted research into the mysteries of the bloom on fruit. It may be a sort of attar of perfection, like the fragrant scum one skims off a tank of rosewater. It may be a fructuous halo, or nimbus, like that bright manifestation of Holiness which (we are informed) accumulates round the heads of saints.'

He savoured his golden-fleshed peach.

'These,' Dr. Boisragon murmured, converting another grape to a corporate Christianity, 'are gifts from the Gods of Plenty! What a country is ours! Begging the question of the scientific nature of bloom, I can rejoice in the luxuriance that showers on us such a prodigality of gifts.'

He took a bunch of white muscadines from the diminishing heap.

'But I am a sad man! I have a heavy heart! I am too conscious of the serpent that lurks in our Eden, of the wickedness of the almost irreclaimable YOUNG!'

He sighed heavily and with an asbent mind voiced the opinion that 'The muscadine is, perhaps, the best white grape. Its juice is so pleasantly insinuating in texture, its flavour is so ethereal — a mixture of sharp and sweet — its bouquet (if one might call it so) is of so subtle an aroma.'

Dr. Phantom chose an apricot. (It was an *abricot persique*.)

'Yes. In this glorious Eden of ours, I am confronted by sin in its most loathsome aspect, by error in its most leprous form.'

'Dear me,' Dr. Phantom agreed, easily, and without much due attention. 'You are having, I gather, a party, a jollification, a romp-a-way for these children? Who are all these visitors?'

Dr. Boisragon was eating a plum — a White Nutmeg.

Dr. Phantom took a bunch of Black Frontignacs, and put them back.

'The three immature females in tartans and plaits are the indigent McMurthies, my poor sister Téméraire's brood. Her husband, as you know, is Captain of the brig *Rose*. The boy and girl standing on the step below them, whom I have heard referred to as 'the Coppertops', are my unfortunate eldest sister Jessica's grandchildren, Juliet and Donalblain McCree. With my own hopefuls, James and Grizel, you have been acquainted from their birth — surely you recognised them all?'

Juliet McCree is Accused of Gluttony

The glances Dr. Boisragon cast on the children were dour in the extreme. Dr. Phantom excused himself, saying, 'Their colour is unusual. Are they not unnaturally pale?'

A douce sea-breeze, a zephyr faintly tinged and tinctured with ozone, and spiced with salt, which daily about this hour found its way up the estuary from Sydney harbour and the Heads and the Pacific beyond, stirred the hitherto placid waters of the river into infinitesimal wavelets, and blew the little girls' skirts about, flapping them like wings against their ankle-length *culottes*.

A number of seagulls, their presence so far inland perhaps presaging storm, were dipping and wheeling about the surface of a patch of ruffled water which, in the deeper reaches, hinted at a shoal of fish.

A group of saplings that dotted the sloping lawn right down to the water's edge also swayed and rustled, and their lively branches reminded Dr. Phantom to enquire after — 'The nectarine? Is it ripe? Did your poor wife enjoy it as much as you hoped? I see it has gone.'

An expression of deeper suffering clouded Dr. Boisragon's already gloomy face.

'My wife did not have the pleasure of putting one toothmark on it. It was stolen.' He looked desolate. 'It was a Red Roman.'

It occurred to Dr. Phantom that the group of children hugging their black basins looked, if possible, even greener about the gills, and, though he did not care for children, he averted his gaze from the rows of suffering upturned faces.

'Stolen? A bat? A parrot? Mr. Jarvey told me of the depredations of many flocks of rosellas, or parakeets — or was it lorikeets?'

Half-sated Dr. Phantom ventured on a jargonelle.

'It was stolen,' Dr. Boisragon reiterated simply, dropping a handful of pips into a garden urn. 'I inspected it at three o'clock, when we first assembled on the lawn for our festivity. I decided to allow it one more hour of sunshine before giving it to my wife. Noticing how warm the sun had become, I went, an hour later, to pluck it — it had gone. It had vanished. Under the tree — not a sign of it. Down the slope? Not a vestige of it!'

He sternly regarded the flinching rows of upturned faces.

'I questioned the children closely. They all denied having

stolen it.'

Dr. Phantom ran a physician's discerning eye over the greening faces.

'Are the children sickening for something, do you think?'

'They are.' Dr. Boisragon's tone was succinct. 'I gave them all an emetic. Nature never lies. I shall soon find out who stole and ate my nectarine.'

'Surely, by observation, you might have detected the culprit? Children are transparent enough. I once met a fraudulent financier. What struck me at the time was the complete absence of all experience in his blue eyes. Knowing nothing about his defalcations, I said at the time, "That young gentleman has got something to hide. He has obliterated his past from his expression." And he had, too! Look at those faces! The girls in plaits and tartans have eyes as black as sloes, without even a highlight in the pupils. I know that type. To learn how they feel — look at their mouths.'

The two doctors looked at the three tremulous mouths.

'I should say those girls were innocent.'

'Deduction is well enough in its way. I prefer the certainty of the scientific method.'

'Your boy James is like you. Is he six?'

'Yes.'

'Rule him out. By this time he should have learnt not to risk displeasing you.'

Though glad of this opinion on his son's probable innocence, Dr. Boisragon was not certain he liked the inference.

'As for the coppertops, they are both suffering so acutely that their queasiness must soon take an active turn.'

It did.

Their breakdown was the signal, it seemed, for which everyone had been waiting. Seven black basins bore witness to the efficacy of Dr. Boisragon's emetic.

Dr. Phantom was just remarking, 'It strikes me that there is a guilty knowledge, a hint of a hidden appeal to one's sympathy, in the squirrel-like eyes of the girl coppertop,' when her basin demonstrated her guilt.

The regurgitation of the skin of a Red Roman was proof of it.

'Juliet McCree! You are both a thief and a liar.'

Dr. Boisragon had never been more impressive.

Juliet McCree is Accused of Gluttony

'You wicked child! What have you to say to explain away your downright lie?'

He was forced to wait till she was capable of answering.

'What excuse do you offer for your felony?'

'Felony, Uncle Peter?'

'How do you excuse your theft of my nectarine?'

'I didn't steal it.'

Even Dr. Phantom was shocked by such depravity.

'What — do you deny it? In the face of such evidence as that basin holds?'

'I just took it. I didn't steal it.'

'To take what is not your own is stealing.'

'But I didn't think it was not —' she retched — 'was not —' she was violently ill — 'was not —' she had scarcely got her breath when another paroxysm overtook her — 'was not —' Dr. Phantom turned away his eyes — 'was not mine.'

That innocence was no shield from suffering was being aptly demonstrated by the six other children who were noisily and liberally contributing to their basins.

'Wicked sinner! Look about you! Through your obstinate denial of your guilt you have caused great suffering to your young relatives — poor innocent children! Does that not shame you? Does that not soften you?'

Dr. Boisragon grew more angry.

'Do you persist in saying that you did *not* lie to me?'

He took his pocket-book out of his buff waistcoat pocket.

'I will run through the notes I made when questioning you. Here they are.' He flicked a page. 'Juliet McCree — my question — "Did you steal that nectarine? My Red Roman?" *"No, Uncle Peter"* — That was your answer!'

He snapped the elastic band back and put the book away.

'I said, "Remember, child, your hope of Heaven hangs on your answer. Speak the truth! *Did you speak the truth?*" You again answered, "Yes, Uncle Peter!" What perfidy! To rob your dear Aunt of my gift! The fruit I had watched from the bud up! What do you mean, wretched liar, in saying you did not know it was my nectarine. It grew on my tree.'

'There are so many things everywhere, and I don't quite know who owns everything. It's all so puzzling, Uncle Peter, because when I filled my bucket with sand no one said I had

Australian Short Stories

stolen it, and when I dipped my mug in the river, no one said I was not to steal the Lane Cove River, Uncle Peter, and when we pick blackberries, and mushrooms along the roads or in the paddocks, no one calls us thieves, and I'm only a little girl, Uncle Peter, and I don't rightly know the way to get things that don't belong to me for nothing, Uncle Peter, the way you and Dr. Phantom do, and I don't know whose sea-gulls those are, neither.'

She again had recourse to her basin.

'What! Dreadful child! Do you accuse *us* of theft!'

'Oh, no, Uncle Peter, it's not quite like that. But you can get the things you want without stealing them, and you know what things belong to other people, and I don't yet! But I will try to learn, indeed I will.'

'What a depraved mind.'

'But you see, you know what is free and I don't! And you know what you must *pay* for, and I don't! I did hear the sound you were making with your words, Uncle Peter, but I did not understand what the noise you made really meant; and if you could please explain to me how you got the fruit in the baskets and didn't pay for it, and didn't really steal it, I mean, if it was someone else's, and you did not have to pay for it? Will you teach me how to get things that are someone else's and not pay?'

She suffered an attack of dry retching that was quite spectacular.

The six other children had filled their black basins and waited, white of face and wet of eye.

'Empty your basins in the river, my bairns, and then wash your hands and faces and go into the dining-room for tea. Since you have been proved to be innocent you may each have two pieces of the birthday cake Cook Jane has made for James. But, before you go, take leave of your cousin, Juliet McCree, for this is the last time that — with my approval or permission — you will ever speak to her. If God spares me, she shall never darken my doors again. Wicked, wicked child!'

'Good-bye, Juliet,' the children murmured, awe-struck, walking uncertainly past her, their black papier-mâché basins carefully carried in their weak hands; they had all been very sick — the emetic had been a powerful one, though perhaps slow in starting.

Juliet went dutifully down to the water's edge and emptied her

Juliet McCree is Accused of Gluttony

basin into the Lane Cover River, and, in going up to the house to wash, she lagged well behind her cousins, not that she suffered any sense of guilt, but because she appreciated the drama of the occasion.

While awaiting Juliet's return, Dr. Boisragon remarked genially to his companion: 'It is an extraordinary thing that the expulsion of food — with us — should require so much effort. I believe that the Romans, before they had a banquet, tickled the backs of their throats and emptied their stomachs. They must certainly have practised regurgitation as an art, for they were a civilised people and I imagine that the hall of Augustus, the house of Maecenas, the villas of Horace and Cicero, could hardly have presented such unbridled scenes as those we have just witnessed! They must have had some nicer system of their own in the method of vomiting!'

Dr. Phantom ran an eye over the row of lace curtains that draped the windows of the square, yellowstone house behind them.

'The ladies of your household?' he enquired, 'How is it they were not present?'

As a matter of fact he had several times noticed the agonised faces of Dr. Bosiragon's younger step-sisters, Miss Loveday, Miss Tabitha, and Miss Matilda, peeping through the lace of upstairs windows.

'I can't understand,' he mused, 'why his womenkind left those unhappy children to my friend's untender mercies! They must, by this time, know what he is like!'

He said this to himself, but as if replying to him Dr. Boisragon broke off from his classical conjectures to say, 'My dear wife was prostrate! She was inclined to be hysterical, so I ordered her off to her room to lie down for an hour or two. My sisters, too, attempted to gloss over an incident they regarded as trivial. Poor, silly women! I ordered them indoors, and I will thresh out the question with them tonight after dinner.'

Juliet here came back, her face shining with tears and soap, her red hair, so wet that it looked dark, drawn off her forehead with two combs; she had tried to hide the stains on her apron by rolling it up round her elbows, with the result that the unfaded patch on her green cotton checked dress showed how old and worn it was.

The child looked peaked and hungry.

She had left her brother, Donalblain (who was four), happily eating bread and butter masked with 'hundreds and thousands', and she could see the glow of the candles, round the birthday cake, and the six other children laughing and talking round the table, with its sweets and bon-bons, crackers and toys, and sugar animals, while the three aunts, having, as it were, come into their own, were busy 'making it up' to the infant martyrs.

Juliet's straw hat (from China) was swinging from her arm by a green ribbon, and her reddening curls, which, as they dried resumed their gloss, were seen against a background of pale river-water and the brackish hillside of the further bank; the salt seemed to have cured the hanging leaves of the grey-boled trees; and it encrusted, too, the pool-brightened rocks. The sky was purely Tuscan as Dr. Phantom had already noted.

Dr. Boisragon, as Juliet joined them, at once returned to the pursuit of Truth.

'Do you not realise, Juliet, that if I had not hit on the expedient of interrogating Nature herself, six innocent children might, all their lives, have lived under the stigma of theft — of being *thieves*! And *this* for your crime. Do you not realise the enormity of your crime against society?'

'But, don't you see, Uncle Peter, it is only *you* who see anything wrong in it? When Papa used to go shooting duck — whose ducks did he shoot? And when you go catching fish — whose fish do you catch? And you know perfectly well that when God gave Adam the earth — as for all I can learn He did — He gave him every blessed thing! And I have never heard anyone say that what belonged to Adam does not belong to me. And whether I took a Red Roman, or whether any of my cousins, or my brother Donalblain (who is four) took a Red Roman, it is only a person like you, who thinks so much of owning a thing, who makes a sin of it. It is just the natural thing to do.'

'Then, being naturally a thief, you are, naturally, a liar?'

'Oh, no, Uncle Peter, I did not think I was a thief. So, of course, I was not a liar. Don't you see, there is no such thing as sin, it is only that some men, who don't understand God or what God said, begin to make their own rules to suit themselves, and they invent sin, Uncle Peter. I expect, if you thought a little about it, you would soon grow to see that this is the truth. It is

Juliet McCree is Accused of Gluttony

just grown-ups who invent wickedness, and then accuse innocent children of it.'

'Hopelessly casuist. Irreclaimably evil. A dangerous liar, a thief! I see, Juliet, that no Christian teaching I can give is likely to reclaim you! I shall write a letter for you to take back to your mama and grandmama — what sort of home life you have at Mallow's Marsh Vicarage, I tremble to think! It baffles my imagination. Wait, wicked girl, wait! Phantom, watch her, if you please! Be careful to allow her no intercourse with any member of my family.'

Dr. Boisragon walked majestically up the tree-dotted slope to his four-square yellowstone house, where a shaded lamp in Mrs. Boisragon's bedroom showed that she was still 'resting', and where flickering candles in the dining-room, reddening still more gaily the crimson rep of the curtains, showed that the birthday party was still in full swing.

As soon as Dr. Boisragon's back was turned Juliet slapped her flat stomach and said, conversationally, 'I'm like a tympanum! I'm as empty as a drum — just you listen!'

She twanged her thin body again. It certainly gave out a hollow moaning sound.

Dr. Phantom gave her a very cool, direct look from eyes that hitherto avoided any direct encounter with her own brightly sparkling copper-coloured glance. It was, perhaps, rather the squirrel's tanny coat than its wildwood eye that (as he had at first considered) her lively regard had evoked.

'Not quite hollow,' Dr. Phantom rejoined with meaning.

Juliet blushed. She really looked quite lovely, her small, Titian-bright head set trimly against a skyey nimbus of Tuscan gold.

'What do you mean?' she asked cautiously.

Dr. Phantom leant towards her and took, from a fold in her bib, two or three carraway seeds and a few cake crumbs.

'Dry,' he explained. 'They were not there when you went up to the house to wash.'

'Oh, those? Oh, I just asked Cook Jane for a piece of cake! I was simply starving!' After considering her companion for a few minutes in silence she asked, 'Don't you think I took the best line with Uncle Peter?'

'I thought it clever enough.'

71

Looking relieved, Juliet drew closer.

'I just didn't have a chance of thinking it out! We were playing at murdering the Duke, when James suddenly caught sight of the nectarine we'd been hearing so much about, and called out — "First in gets the Holy Globe!" And we all started running down the slope and shouting out, "Bags I the Holy Globe!" It was a great lark, really, and I got there first; I only beat Victoria McMurthie by the edge of a hair-ribbon as you might say; so I had it, but of course we all shared it. Everyone had a bite! But I had the skin, mostly, and of course that showed more.'

'Then all the children were equally guilty?'

'But, don't you see, we don't think it guilty!'

'The fact remains that since you stole something — took what did not belong to you — you have committed a sin against society, and you will have the whole world against you. People think theft the meanest of crimes.'

'But Mama brings back a few hairpins every time she goes to her Club, and Papa used to carry home some envelopes and notepaper every time he visited *his* Club, in Sydney, and I wouldn't mind betting, Dr. Phantom, that I could catch you out in a theft of some sort if I gave my mind to it.'

A mere flutter of dismay, a fraction of alarm, passing across his face as swiftly as the shadows made by the sea-gull's wings on the darkening waters (for the sun was now due west and as red as an apple) told Juliet that she might, as she put it, 'be on to something'.

Jumping up and down and clapping her hands, the dreadful child pressed home her advantage.

'Will you let me search you? That would be a perfectly fair test!'

She sprang towards him.

He kept her at bay with a grip of iron.

'No! No! I never heard of such a thing! What cheek!'

Dr. Phantom shed ten years of his assumed dignity at least, as, laughing and red in the face, he struggled with the lively Juliet.

'A prize! A prize!' shouted that exasperating child, wild with excitement. 'I shall find a spoon! One of Lady Mary's salt-cellars!'

The tussle was really incredibly brisk! Juliet's darting attacks,

Juliet McCree is Accused of Gluttony

first at one pocket, then at another, were quite spectacular in their success.

'A case book!'

'Mine!'

'A purse!'

'Mine!'

'A pencil!'

'Mine!'

'Bitten at the end!' gasped Juliet, breathlessly, putting it back as she whirled, wriggled, twirled.

'A key! Two keys! Three keys!'

'Mine! Mine! Mine!'

'A love letter!'

'No! No! *A bill!*' He clutched it.

'Ah, ha!' Juliet wrenched herself free, doubled up with laughter, 'A prize! A prize! Whose pocket handkerchief is this, you wicked thief?'

As Dr. Phantom rushed after her she doubled and dodged round the saplings.

'Whose? Whose?'

'You dreadful child! Give me that handkerchief this instant!'

Catching a moment when her hardly less agile opponent had side-slipped in skimming too quickly round a juniper, Juliet read the name embroidered on the bit of scented lawn, her treasure.

'"Aminta Wirraway"! Oh! Dr. Phantom. Oh, you wicked thief! Bad, bad man! I shall tell your mother! Does that poor girl know you have stolen her new Irish linen?'

'Do I understand,' asked Dr. Boisragon, joining the struggling pair and judging as usual by appearances, 'that this depraved child has actually stolen your handkerchief?'

Silence.

Dr. Phantom pulled down his waistcoat and re-buttoned his hip-pocket. He looked blankly at Juliet.

'No, of course she hasn't,' he blurted out, getting back his breath.

He looked appealingly at Juliet.

She sniffed at the scented square of pink lawn.

'I was just guessing what kind of scent Dr. Phantom uses,' she said, meekly, 'I think it must be Opopomax or Alderman's Bouquet.'

'The only perfumes allowable for male use are Florida Water and Eau de Cologne. I myself use Florida Water.' He addressed himself entirely to Dr. Phantom, ignoring Juliet. 'As a bachelor, you might conceivably be permitted a sprinkling of Verbena; it is slightly astringent and not too tropical.'

Juliet put the handkerchief back in Dr. Phantom's breast pocket.

'Over your heart,' she whispered.

Dr. Boisragon turned his attention to her.

'Juliet McCree,' he announced, portentously, 'I have in this letter informed your widowed mother and grandparents of your incredible perfidy. That you, a girl of eleven or twelve, should steal in a house where your lightest request, if not granted, would at least have been sympathetically considered, that you should, when detected in that theft, lie, and that, having lied in the most bare-faced manner, in the plain proof of your falsehood, that you should persist in the most Jesuitical casuistry, in asserting your *innocence*, has so shocked me, so outraged my feelings, that I feel compelled to forbid you ever to enter my house again. My house, or my *grounds*,' he looked meaningly at Juliet.

With a humble and gentle expression his niece stepped forward and took the letter he extended to her, at an arm's length.

'Good-bye, Uncle Peter,' she said, sadly, and she dropped him a curtsey, the charity bob she had been taught to use when greeting or saying good-bye to her elders.

'If Dr. Phantom would be so kind as to send you home in his Hyde Park — should the murderer not object to your company — I should be much obliged to him.'

'Oh, certainly, certainly.' Dr. Phantom was all complaisance. 'I will remove everything of value and give my coachman due warning of her weakness. There is a second basket of fruit — '

The trio walked across the shadowed lawn to the Hyde Park which drooped by the kerb in the warm, windless air, for the sea-breeze had expended its energy and a glowing sun, cut across the middle by the twin towers of the church, was pouring its hot rays through the valance and neatly tied-back curtains. Juliet was surprised to find 'First Murderer' asleep in the driving seat; she had hardly expected that murderers could sleep, but it was still

Juliet McCree is Accused of Gluttony

oppressively warm, and even the piebald Waler in his straw hat snuffled his nostrils and stamped his hooves and whisked his cream tail with less than his usual verve.

'I am sending a duplicate letter by post,' Dr. Boisragon mentioned to Dr. Phantom, intending Juliet to hear. 'Should anything happen to my first missive, her poor relatives will hear of her wicked conduct by the first post on Monday morning.'

'I think you are so wise,' Dr. Phantom rejoined, also intending Juliet to hear. 'What a disaster it would be for her family if they did not learn what a hardened criminal the child is!'

And in the most ostentatious manner he removed the basket of pears from the vehicle. Their aroma was almost as heady as wine, the heat had brought out their delicious, yet not cloying, fragrance.

'A pear, perhaps, is the most delicate of all fruits.' Dr. Boisragon's elegant hand hovered. 'A *Beurre du Roi?*' He tasted. 'Yes, I thought I could not be mistaken! The skin paler than the finest champagne! The shape, symmetrical, but slightly squat, if one could apply so bald a word to so desirable a form! Pipless! Indeed the faultless fruit.'

With a grave propriety, settling her green checked skirts and folding her hands in her lap, Juliet crossed her neat ankles, in the white culottes, and, at last assuming her straw hat (from China), she settled herself on the box beside 'First Murderer', in the Hyde Park, while he, having saluted his master with two fingers, and flicked the piebald Waler's back with his whip, urged that animal to the pace which was, in those days, described as 'a spanking trot'.

As they were moving off Dr. Phantom heard Juliet saying in an easy and conversational manner to 'First Murderer': 'I am not quite in your class, of course, but this afternoon I have been proved to be both a thief and a liar, and, as one criminal to another, I should very much like your advice, as a more experienced — ' He heard no more. He was, however (since he did not care for children), rather surprised to find himself envying 'First Murderer'.

'At this time of the evening,' Dr. Boisragon took Dr. Phantom's arm, 'it is pleasant to sit on the steps facing the water, where one occasionally gets a puff of sea air, and since the children's party is in full swing in the house, let us linger here for an hour before going indoors.'

The partners took their places on the step where the basket of mixed fruits still adorned the parapet. Dr. Phantom, having set down his own basket of pears by his side, made an incision in a Golden Pear of Xaintonge with thirty-two sharp white teeth.

'I have been thinking over that depraved girl's case,' Dr. Boisragon murmured, having embarked on a second pear. 'I see that her first sin — *theft* — was the cause of her second sin — *lying* — but, delving more deeply into the cause of her crimes, I am of the considered opinion that the child's inability to control her carnal appetite was the primal reason for her downfall. *That girl is a glutton*! Did you notice the way she kept eyeing these grapes?'

'Yes, I did,' Dr. Phantom rejoined, averting his eyes.

Flight

Katharine Susannah Prichard

Constable John O'Shea was an angry man as he rode away from Movingunda with three little half-caste girls strapped on behind him.

The only three white men on the station had watched, laughing and slinging off as he mounted and set out, a horde of aboriginal mothers and dogs yelping after him. Most of the native men were out mustering — thank God, O'Shea reflected — or there might have been more trouble.

For miles the women and dogs ran behind him, yelling and screaming; the children yelled and screamed to them. The women fell back at last, but the children kept on snivelling and wailing.

Constable O'Shea was glad to reach the cover of the scrub and follow the track over rough, drought-stricken country to Lorgans.

It was a clear day, cold and sunshiny. From the station tableland, he could see the plains stretching away, grey-blue as the sea in winter, a wedge of hills darker blue against the distant horizon. Near by, the mulga looked dead or dying, although recent rains had left pools beside the track. Fresh green was streaking the red earth near them, making vivid patches against its mail of black ironstone pebbles.

Constable O'Shea resented having to pick up half-caste girls and send them down to government institutions at the request of the Aborigines Department. He considered it no job for a man who had to maintain the prestige of the force and uphold law and order in an outlying district.

But he had received instructions that three half-caste female children on Movingunda were to be sent down by the train which passed through Lorgans on the eighth of the month. So there was nothing for it but to collect the children, and hand them over to the officer who would be on the train.

A rotten business, it had been, removing the youngsters from their mothers. What a shrieking and howling, jabbering and imploring, with attempts to hide the children and run away with them into the bush! One of the gins and her terror-stricken kid had climbed a tree near the creek. It was not until after dark he had got that one, when mother and child crept back and were sleeping by the camp-fire.

Constable O'Shea sweated and swore as he thought of it, and the laughing-stock he had been to the white men on Movingunda, not one of whom would lend a hand to help him. He knew better than to try to make them. Murphy kept the fun going, a father of one of the kids — but not game to admit it. You couldn't blame him. There was a penalty, these days, for cohabiting with native women. But Fitz Murphy had been living with a gin for years, and had several children by her, everybody knew.

McEacharn, at least, made his position clear.

'No,' he said, 'they're not my kids. If they were, you wouldn't get them, O'Shea.'

There had been all the writing to do for official purposes also, giving the kids' names, without reference to their parents, black or white — just labels to differentiate them by. Waste of time, O'Shea told himself, since the object of the drive was to separate the children from their aboriginal parents and environment.

Constable O'Shea was at his wits' end inventing names for half-caste brats. This was not the first lot he had had to register. The name a girl was known by in the camp or on the station might be used, but a surname had to be attached. O'Shea cursed the regulations.

This time he had got the native names of the children — Mynie, Nanja and Coorin. Molly, Polly and Dolly were easier to remember, so he put them down as Molly, Polly and Dolly. But surnames — he racked his brains about surnames for the bunch. A girl's father could not afford to be implicated, although occasionally the name of a station or locality might be adopted

Flight

with certain satisfaction.

'What does Movingunda mean in the blacks' lingo?' he asked McEacharn.

'Ant-hill.'

'That'll do,' O'Shea grinned, and wrote 'Anthill' beside 'Molly'. 'How about you chaps,' he continued, 'any of you willing to lend a kid a name?'

'Not on your life,' Murphy blustered.

'Anything you say may be used in evidence against you, eh, Murphy?' O'Shea remarked dryly.

The men guffawed.

'You can name the whole damned lot after me, if you like,' McEacharn growled, 'though God knows I've left the gins alone.'

'Right!'

O'Shea scrawled McEacharn for the next child.

'And the youngest?'

Mick Donovan, the old prospector, who had come into the station for stores, chuckled: 'She's the one gave you such a run for your money, Sarge.'

'Call her Small and be done with,' McEacharn advised.

O'Shea was grateful for the suggestion.

'There,' he said, folding up his report and packing it away with a wad of papers in the breast-pocket of his tunic. 'This batch will start life as young ladies with real classy names.'

The worst of it was, he could not remember which was which, and the kids didn't know which of them was supposed to be Molly, Polly, or Dolly. They would only answer to their native names. But, Hell, a man could not be worried about that! The Department would have to sort them out somehow.

Constable O'Shea's temper did not improve as he rode. His charger, a nervous, powerful brute, took some handling at the best of times, and those three stinking kids on his back irritated him. They didn't weigh much more than a bunch of wild pigeons; but their dangling legs and bony little behinds chafed and upset Chief. He had tried to shift them, more than once, shying and pig-rooting whenever he got a chance. The kids stuck like leeches, strapped together though they were. The eldest hung on to O'Shea's belt, the rest to her.

It was hot at midday, the sky bare blue overhead and the sunlight dazzling. When he was thirsty himself, O'Shea gave the

Australian Short Stories

kids a drink from his water-bag, and a piece of bread and meat from the crib the station cook had put up for him.

The kids were so scared, they stared, goggle-eyed, when he spoke to them. Not a word would they say. There would be another meal to provide, O'Shea realized, so he rationed supplies carefully.

He had not anticipated this picnic. He had expected that McEacharn would make his car available and drive the kids into Lorgans. McEacharn had intimated, with specious regrets, that he could do nothing of the sort. He had an important engagement on Ethel Creek, a hundred miles in the opposite direction, and the station buggy was out on the mustering camp.

Constable O'Shea understood that if the children were to be dispatched by the train in three days' time, he must be responsible for their means of transport himself. There was no other way but to hoist them up behind him. He would have to sleep out for the night too.

Of course, he could call in at Sandy Gap station and require the manager to put him and his passengers up for the night. But stand another round of laughter and chiacking — not if he knew it! It would be awkward, camping by the track, and keeping an eye on the brats. He had no blankets. They would have to sleep by the fire. He had his rain-coat for a ground-sheet and covering, his saddle for pillow.

At sunset, when he lifted the children down from the big, bay horse, he would have liked to unfasten the straps knotted round their waists; but he knew very well what would happen if they found themselves free. They would be off and away like greased lightning. They knew this country better than he did, young as they were, and would make their way back to Movingunda. Then what sort of a fool would he look, going back after them, with all the business of catching and getting away with them again?

Ordinarily, he would have had his black tracker, Charley Ten, to look after the kids and make the fire; but Charley was giving evidence at a native trial in Meekatharra. There was nothing for it but to keep the kids tied up and make the fire himself.

O'Shea cursed his luck as he hauled a couple of mulga logs together and set them alight. He cursed the hopes of promotion

Flight

which had brought him to the back-country; cursed Murphy, and every man in the nor'-west, who begot half-castes; cursed McEacharn for making it obvious that he did not intend to facilitate arrangements for removing youngsters from his station: cursed the Protector of Aborigines and the Department for their penurious habit of pushing on to the police in out-of-the-way places, work that should be done by officers of the Aborigines Department: cursed every well-meaning man and woman who believed that the Government ought to 'do something' for half-caste girls, without proper consideration of what that 'something' ought to be.

The three small girls sat on the ground watching him. Three pairs of beautiful dark eyes followed his every movement, alert and apprehensive. The eldest of the children, he had put down as nine years old, the other two at eight and seven.

Part of Constable O'Shea's grouch, though he would not have admitted it, was due to the way the children looked at him. He could not endure children to look at him as if he were an ogre who might devour them at any moment. A good-looking, kindly young man, he prided himself on carrying out his duties conscientiously but without harshness.

A man had to be considered a good sort to get anywhere in a district like this, where he was the only policeman for nearly a hundred miles in any direction, and had to depend on assistance from station-owners and mine-managers in an emergency. This job made him unpopular on the stations and he loathed it. He would rather wade in and clean up a dozen fighting drunks, he said, than go round collecting half-caste girls on behalf of the Aborigines Department. Why didn't the Department do its own dirty work?

O'Shea was disturbed by the thought that it was dirty work he had been forced to take part in. How would any woman like her kids being yanked away from her, knowing quite well the chances were she would never see them again? His own wife, for example?

Constable O'Shea smiled, trying to imagine any man separating his Nancy from her three linty-haired little girls and small son. But after he had fed the aboriginal children and given them each a drink of water, he took the precaution of tying their hands together with strips of rawhide in case they might try to

Australian Short Stories

unfasten the strap round their middles and run away. The children huddled together and fell asleep, wailing a little, but evidently with no hope of escape. Constable O'Shea stretched and dozed uncomfortably on the far side of the fire.

It was evening of the second day when he rode over the ridge by a back track into Lorgans. He had taken care not to arrive until dusk so that no one would see him.

For several years Lorgans had been one of those deserted mining townships, with only the dump and poppet-legs of an old mine, a pub and the ruins of a row of shops to testify to its former prosperity. But the railway still ran about a mile away, and with re-opening of the mine, the township took a new lease of life. Gold was bringing a good price.

Constable O'Shea's appointment followed a rush on the flat below the ridge. New shafts were sunk, shops sprouted among the ruins. Lorgans acquired a population of three or four hundred in a few months, and O'Shea had brought his wife and family to live in the smart, new police-station put up for him at the entrance to the town.

When he reached the gate of the yard behind his house, O'Shea dismounted, and lifted Mynie, Nanja and Coorin down from his horse. He did not want his wife to see him with those kids stuck up behind, and start laughing, as she surely would. She laughed so easily. Her sense of humour kept her fat and content in this god-forsaken hole, she said; but O'Shea was not going to have her laughing at him if he could help it.

A dog started barking at the sight of him. Mrs. O'Shea hurried out of the house as soon as she heard the dog. Her children swarmed about her. A big, fair-haired, youngish woman, she was, Mrs. O'Shea, full-bosomed and sonsy. The children were like her, with fair hair and clear rosy skins. All excitement and delight, they ran to meet their father. He swung his son into his arms and the little girls hung onto him.

It was Mrs. O'Shea who discovered the three small half-castes, crouched together and staring at her, wide-eyed and woebegone.

'Oh, Jack,' she exclaimed, 'the poor little things! What are you going to do with them?'

'What do you think?' O'Shea asked impatiently. 'Keep them for pets?'

Flight

His daughters guessed just what had happened. They queried maddeningly.

'Did you give them a ride on your horse, Daddy?'

'Why can't we have a ride on your horse, Daddy?'

'Want to sit up behind you on Chief, too, Daddy!'

'Want a ride . . .'

'Can't I have a ride, too, Daddy?'

The half-castes gazed at these other children with amazement. How was it possible for them to talk to the policeman so cheekily and light-heartedly?

'But you can't keep them tied up like that,' Mrs. O'Shea protested, still concerned about those wretched little figures.

'They're as wild as birds,' Constable O'Shea declared testily. 'If I gave them a chance, they'd be off back to Movingunda like a shot. And I wouldn't go through all I have had to, to get them again, for quids!'

He put his son on the ground, and walked over to a shed of corrugated iron with barbed wire across a small, square window, unlocked the door and flung it back.

'Come along, you feller,' he called. 'Nothing hurt'm. Missus bring'm tucker, d'reckly.'

Mynie, Nanja and Coorin moved slowly, reluctantly, towards the door, their eyes searching desperately for some way to save them from that dark shed.

It served as a lock-up, but was rarely used except for an unruly drunk or a native prisoner.

'Don't put them there, Jack,' his wife begged. 'They'll be scared stiff — and it's freezing cold these nights.'

'You can't take them into the house,' O'Shea objected.

'What about the room at the end of the veranda?' Mrs. O'Shea persisted. 'They can't do any harm there. I'll take them along while you feed Chief.'

'Have it your own way. They'll have to be scrubbed and disinfected tomorrow.'

O'Shea unbuttoned the navy tunic of his uniform, hung it on a post and turned to unsaddle.

'Come on, children,' his wife called cheerily to the half-castes. They trailed behind her as she trundled across the yard. Her own offspring followed curiously.

'Go and finish your tea,' their mother said. 'And Phyll, see that Bobbie doesn't spill his cocoa on the table-cloth.'

Constable O'Shea snapped back the surcingle and girths of his saddle, heaved it on to one arm, and the big bay followed him into the stable. He gave his horse a good hard feed, rubbed him down and ran water into the trough by the stable door before going into the house.

His son was sitting in his high chair, and the three little girls, just about the same age as those half-caste children, chattering gleefully as they finished their meal. Very fresh and pretty they looked, with their hair in neat pig-tails and print aprons over their frocks. Nancy was a wonderful mother; always contrived to have the children looking clean and bonny for the evening meal, and everything bright and pleasant when he came back from one of these long trips across country.

But tonight, as she stood by the fire grilling his steak, Nancy seemed vaguely troubled. Her easy-going, good-natured tolerance of life at Lorgans was overcast.

'I'll be glad when we get a move,' she said, putting a large plate of steak, poached eggs and fried potatoes before her husband. 'It's getting on my nerves — this kidnapping of children.'

'You're not more fed-up with it than I am,' O'Shea replied irritably. 'If the Department wants me to do this job, they'll have to provide me with a car, or a buggy at least.'

'It's a rotten shame, the way these kids are taken from their mothers,' Mrs. O'Shea exclaimed. 'The gins will be trailing in from Movingunda for months to ask me what's happened to the children. And what can I say?'

'Tell them they've gone south to be made into young ladies — like you've done before.'

'They don't believe me. You can't lie to an abo. All I know is, they'll never see their children again. The kids won't remember their mothers and the mothers'll lose all trace of them.'

'The great idea,' O'Shea reminded her, 'is that the kids are being saved from leading immoral lives in the native camps.'

'That's all very well,' his wife cried indignantly. 'But how does it work out? The girls learn to read and write, become domestic servants; but more than half of them lead immoral lives in the towns, just the same. Only it's worse for them down there, because they're among strangers. If a half-caste girl has a baby up here, it's taken as a matter of course. But down south, it's a disgrace. And anyhow, why can't the girls be given a chance to come back, work on the stations — and marry? It's because women are so scarce in the back-country that there are half-castes in the first place.'

'It's not my fault.' Her husband swung over and sprawled in an easy chair by the fire. He hauled off his riding-boots and stretched his long legs, with thick home-knitted socks pulled up to the end of his breeches.

'You remember Emmalina from Koolija station,' Mrs.O'Shea continued. 'She just sat down by the fence of our yard and wailed for days, after her little girl was sent down. If ever a woman died of a broken heart, she did, Jack.'

'For Christ's sake, Nancy,' O'Shea protested, 'stop fussing about those kids. I've just about had enough of them, and being made to look a fool, hiking across country with the little brutes hanging on to me.'

Mynie, Nanja and Coorin, sitting on the floor of the room nearby, heard the talking: heard for the first time something of the fate before them. They listened intently, staring at the square of window, crossed by barbed wire.

Their quick senses, following every sound of movement and voices, constructed vivid pictures of what was happening in the fire-lit kitchen they had glimpsed as they passed along the veranda. They could see Constable O'Shea having his meal and his woman, standing near, talking to him.

When one of the girls asked for more bread and jam, they could hear the mother cutting the bread, and the small boy get a slap for putting his fingers in the jam. He bawled and his father lifted him out of the high chair and took him to sit on his knee by the fire. The little girls clamoured to sit on their father's knee, too; but he threatened to send them to bed at once if they did not keep quiet and behave themselves.

When her own family had eaten and was satisfied, Mrs. O'Shea announced that she was going to take 'those poor little things' something to eat. She turned the key in the lock of the room at the end of the veranda a moment later, and appeared with a plate of bread and jam and mugs of tea on a tray.

Mynie, Nanja and Coorin watched her as she put an enamel mug before each of them and the plate of bread and jam in the middle. No need to share out the portions. They would do that themselves scrupulously, Mrs.O'Shea knew.

Each little girl was strapped one to the other. Their wrists were tied together. Mrs.O'Shea hovered over them, smiling and motherly, trying to reassure them. She could not bear to see these children so scared and dumb. Such skinny little things, they were, with great brown eyes and curling lashes, blackish-brown tousled hair, and gina-ginas, no more than scraps of faded blue cotton stuff, on their meagre bodies.

The room was a lock-up cell in all but name, kept for more respectable prisoners. There was a chair and table in it and a bed covered with blue-grey blankets. The window had no glass, but was double-crossed with barbed wire.

There was no way the half-castes could get out when the door was locked, Mrs.O'Shea told herself. So she took the law into her own hands: knelt down, and with firm white teeth unfastened the leather thongs which bound them: undid the strips of raw-hide biting into those slim brown wrists.

Jack would be furious, she knew, if he found out what she had done. She intended to tie the children up again in the morning, and gambled on no one being the wiser except herself and the children. They could be trusted not to tell.

Anyhow, Mrs.O'Shea assured herself, she would not sleep a wink if she thought of those poor little scarecrows sitting there tied up, cold and miserable. She pulled a blanket from the bed and threw it on the floor for them.

'There, now,' she said cheerily, 'you'll be good girls, won't you? You won't try to run away? The Boss'd kill me if you did.'

When she went away, locking the door behind her, Mynie, Nanja and Coorin grabbed the thick slices of bread and jam she had brought them, and guzzled down the warm, sweet tea made with condensed milk.

The room was in darkness, except for that square of starlit sky framed by the window and crossed with barbed wire. When she had eaten her bread and jam and drunk all the tea in her mug, Mynie sidled over to the window.

Stealthily she looked out. Across the yard behind the policeman's house, the stables and the horse-paddock, there was the black wall of the ridge. Mynie could see the track Constable O'Shea had come in by, winding past the mine and the old township until it was swallowed up by a dark mass of trees. One

Flight

sniff and a quiver of instinctive decision sufficed to inform her companions. The brown eyes communicated, wise and wary.

Leaning against the wall, in the shadow, Mynie began fiddling with the barbed wire. She tried each row where it was held by nails driven into the wooden framework. Her brown fingers curled and twisted, crawled on. It was not until Mynie had tried several rows of wire that she turned to look at Nanja and Coorin with a gleam in her eyes. They crept over, and saw a couple of nails loose in their sockets. The red wood had shrunk, so that the nails could be worked out, and the wire turned back to leave a gap through which a child's body might squeeze.

The three slunk back to their place on the floor and sat watching and waiting. Coorin fell asleep. Her head drooped on Nanja's shoulder; but Nanja and Mynie listened, tense and alert, to all that was going on in the kitchen.

Mrs. O'Shea put the boy to bed. She shooed the little girls off to wash and brush their hair. They didn't want to go to bed. The policeman told them a story about three pigs. Then they kissed him, saying, 'Goodnight, Daddy!' over and over again, and ran away laughing and chattering.

'Don't forget your prayers,' Mrs. O'Shea called.

One after the other, the little white girls talked as if they were remembering the words of a corroboree song:

Gentle Jesus, meek and mild,
Look upon a little child;
Pity my simplicity,
Suffer me to come to Thee.

Mrs. O'Shea trotted into their bedroom, kissed the girls and put out the light. Then there was the washing up to do. She bustled about, clearing away dishes and chatting to her husband in a brisk, jolly way. He yawned and stretched a good deal.

At last, he exclaimed:

'Cripes, I'm dead tired! How about a bit of shut-eye?'

They went to a room at the front of the house. Mynie and Nanja heard them moving about as they undressed. The bed creaked as they got into it. For a while, the policeman and his wife talked softly together. Now and then Mrs. O'Shea's little laugh flew out. Then all was quiet.

Nothing more than the sound of regular breathing vibrated through the thin partitions, the sound of two people sleeping heavily, tranquilly, with an occasional puffing sigh or long-drawn snore.

Mynie and Nanja did not need to talk. They wakened Coorin. She understood immediately why they had done so. One passion dominated all three. They did not know whether to believe the policeman would kill his woman if he found out she had untied their hands and unfastened the strap. They could not think of that.

Their only instinct was to escape, to make their way back over the hills and plains to the miahs of their own people. It was rough, strange country they would have to pass through. They were on the far side of the hills which had been the boundary of their world. Those mysterious blue hills where, Wonkena said, the gnarlu lived, the gnarlu who came hopping out of the darkness like a frog when there was a corroboree on Movingunda.

They had heard the women singing to scare him away, and seen old Nardadu herself, stand up and hurl a burning stick at him when he came too near the camp-fire. They were terrified at the thought of having to cross the gnarlu's territory at night; but they were so little and insignificant, Mynie thought, they might find their way back to Movingunda without being noticed. Anyhow their fear had to be overcome if they were not to be taken away, never to see their mothers or the back-country again.

Mynie slid over to the window and worked on the nails. She drew them out. Her eyes searched the yard. There was nothing moving. She turned back the wire where she had untwisted it. The hole in the barbed screen was just big enough for her to squeeze through. Nanja lifted Coorin. Mynie pulled her through and put her on the ground. Nanja stuck and struggled before she joined them.

For a moment they clung to the shadow of the house, afraid to stir in case the dog might fly at them, his barking arouse Constable O'Shea and his woman. Then they crawled under the veranda to the far side. Stepping carefully, they crossed the shingly ground to the road, scarcely stirring a pebble.

Swiftly, silently, on bare hard feet, they streaked along the track to the ridge. In a few minutes the township lay behind. As they climbed the ridge, trees closed round them; mulga, dark

Flight

and creaking, whispering with strange voices, thorn-bush and minnereechi casting black shadows, shadows that sprawled and clutched, sliding away with dry cackling laughter.

Nanja and Coorin kept close to Mynie as they went on. All three shrank together when the gaunt arms of a dead tree swayed out towards them. They scudded off through the scrub. The scrub became denser. Writhing shapes peered and leered at them from every bush. Thin, bony fingers grabbed at and scratched their legs, tore their gina-ginas. They ran on, coming at last to a gorge between two great hills.

A pool lay at the bottom of the hills, but Mynie steered away from it, knowing the worst jinkies lurk beside shadowy water. A sinister '*wauk, wauk!*' came from the pool, and sent them scrambling up the hill. The great weather-beaten rocks were less fearsome than the trees; but they crept from the shadow of one rock to another, stopping with wildly beating hearts to listen and gaze about them before stealing on.

Then the moon rose, a worn silvery plate, thrusting itself up behind the back of the hillside. It had scarcely risen half-way when a squat, unwieldy shape moved across it, hopping and flopping towards them.

It was the gnarlu, Mynie, Nanja and Coorin were sure — the dreaded evil spirit they had seen hopping and flopping, just like that, up to the camp-fire in a corroboree. They did not wait to see whether this gnarlu had the same white markings. There was no Nardadu, now, to scare him away with her fire-stick. Mynie turned and fled, with Nanja and Coorin after her, back along the way they had come, through the gorge and the dark scrub again, coming at last to the track that led to the mines, the township, and the police-station.'

The sky was dimming in the false dawn before they got there, slipped under the fence, crossed the shingly ground beside the house and crawled under the veranda to the further side. The barbed wire gaped over the window, just as they had left it. Mynie squirmed through. Nanja lifted Coorin, then hoisted herself through the window.

When they were sitting huddled up on the floor again, their eyes met and conferred. Without a word spoken, they agreed that their fear of the future was nothing to the terrors they had passed through. It was a comfort even to hear the policeman and his wife sleeping peacefully, with a puffing sigh and a long-drawn snore now and then.

Mynie stole over to the window, found the nails on the ledge where she had left them, fitted them into place and twisted the wire round. That done she went back to Nanja and Coorin, stretched on the floor, and drew the blanket over them.

When Mrs.O'Shea brought in some porridge and milk a few hours later, they were still asleep, lying curled up like chrysalids in the dingy blanket.

'That's good girls,' she said, gaily. 'I knew I could trust you. You feller only little bit blackfeller. Little bit white feller, too.'

'Yukki!' Mynie breathed, wondering if that was why they had come back to the white man's house.

Mrs.O'Shea found the strap and fastened it round their waists again. Painstakingly, a little apologetically, she knotted the strips of raw-hide round their wrists.

The Woman at the Mill

Frank Dalby Davison

In the kitchen of the dwelling at the mill the little yellow-faced alarm-clock, ticking loudly on the shelf above the stove recess, marked the hour at noon. At the table, Irene Lawrence, in a wine-red dress that looked rather inappropriate to the hour and place, was sitting staring straight before her. In her ears were ringing the sound of a horse's hoof-beats, receding at a canter, dwindling into silence along the track leading to the township.

The mill was unwontedly quiet. Generally it was a noisy little mill, its saw splitting the air every few seconds with a hungry shriek as it tore its way through the green cypress-pine logs and loosed the scent of their sap on the air. At other times there would be heard the clatter of planks being stacked for seasoning, the shouts of Dick Skinner, and the cracking of his whip, as his team drew a load of logs in from the bush, muffled trampling of hooves, the thud of logs being let slip from the chains, and the jingle of shaken harness.

Today there were none of these sounds. Mat Lawrence, the owner of the mill, was in Wilgatown, arranging the disposal of sawn timber; Skinner had taken the day off to attend to some jobs on his selection, and Eric, the youth who helped Mat on the saw-bench, was with him.

Irene, Mat's wife, had spent the morning awaiting the arrival of Bert Caswell. She had heard that he had returned from the droving trip that had taken him out beyond Cunnamulla, and that he was staying with his relations, the Warburtons, in the township.

Her reasons for supposing that he might come were that he

would be almost sure to know of Lawrence's departure on the Wilgatown train and being, she hoped, as eager to see her as she was to see him, he would ride out toward the mill. Its inactivity would surely draw him to complete the journey.

Her suppositions were not in themselves of great strength, but they were supported in her mind by her urgent wish toward their fulfilment. Since hearing of Caswell's return to the settlement, three days ago, she had lived in a secret welter of doubts and longings, resolutions and their immediate retractions. She had thought of seeking a meeting with him in the township under cover of a visit to the store, but had been deterred by two considerations. First, the fear of observing eyes—people were quick to put two and two together, particularly if the total promised a scandal; second, the torturing conviction that for proof that what had happened between them meant the same thing to them both she must wait upon his seeking her.

Mat had gone off with the children in the old sulky in which they travelled between home and school. As soon as he was well on his way she had begun making preparations for Caswell's coming; tidying up the house, and changing her dress. The speed of her movements had varied. At one moment she hurried as if his arrival were imminent, at another she lingered over brushing down the stove, or smoothing a coverlet, as if hope ceased temporarily to sustain her, or she feared running out of occupations with which to fill the time of waiting. Impossibly soon after Mat's departure—it took three-quarters of an hour to reach the railhead—she fancied she heard the mutter of approaching hooves. More than once, as if wishing conjured up a picture, she had glanced, in passing the kitchen door, to where the track appeared through the grass, on the ridge, under the solitary silver-leafed ironbark.

She had put on an afternoon frock, old enough that wearing it of a morning seemed justifiable, and long enough in temporary disuse that it had regained freshness in her own eyes. Its colour, wine-red, was the same as that she had worn the night she danced with Caswell. Its hue supported her gipsyish colouring.

While changing, before taking the frock down from its hanger, she had stood with bare arms before her mirror, taking stock of herself, fortifying herself with a brief survey of her

The Woman at the Mill

charms. Full-figured in youth, the grossness that seemed likely to be her portion in later life had begun to overtake her at thirty-five. The almost waistless body, the large loose bust and thick shoulders, could scarcely have been overlooked except by eyes filled to satisfaction with her more attractive qualities. It was on these that her attention was concentrated.

The fine texture and creamy-whiteness of her skin was a consolation for the increasing quantity of flesh it covered. A well-shaped mouth, large dark eyes under a broad, smooth forehead, and brows that arched naturally, compensated for crow's-feet, sunburn, cheeks that were no longer firm, and a throat that had begun to sag. To further the love she made to herself, she put her hands to her head and shook out her dark mane. It fell about her shoulders, giving a gleam to their whiteness, and framed her face, seeming to focus attention on its good features. The act was one that Bert Caswell might be imagined performing. She clung to the thought a moment, embarrassed by it, yet tasting its sweetness. With a few swift strokes she brushed out her hair and re-coiled it, studying her reflection appreciatively the while.

Her toilet was completed when she produced a stick of carmine from the back of the dressing-table drawer and applied it to her lips. She had used it before only experimentally, briefly and in secret. The shrewd look she believed the sight of it would have brought to Mat's eyes would have embarrassed her. She had her doubts about Mat, when he was in Wilgatown. There were those girls at the Western Star. But Mat wasn't one to tolerate any romantic longings in a wife—and he would have taken the lipstick as a sure advertisement. Not that he seemed to mind the sight of it on other men's wives. She was slightly tremulous now, in using it; and exultant, too. On her unaccustomed lips she found its effect pleasingly dramatic. It heightened the tone values of natural colouring.

She returned to the kitchen, experiencing a quickening of her heart-beats when she saw that the clock, at a quarter past ten, confirmed her thoughts that Bert might possibly now be on his way. She glanced at the little blistered mirror on the wall by the roller-towel, then stood for a while by the window, looking out along the track.

She had no qualms—scarcely even a thought—about the part she was playing toward Mat, with his compact nuggety body; his gingery head, round and hard like quandong nut; his green eyes, flecked with brown, bright but opaque, like glass marbles, and the little hard bulge in his cheek where he carried his chew of tobacco. For more years than she could accurately number she had cherished a grudge against him, a quiet secret grudge.

There were times when she remembered with exasperation the girl she thought she must have been when she married him. She couldn't recall her motive. Good nature, simplicity, and no clear idea of what she was committing herself to, was how she explained it to herself. Hers, as she remembered it, had been a singularly vacant girlhood. The mentality of childhood seemed to have carried over into adolescence, and that of adolescence into maturity. She couldn't recall a wide-awake state of being such as she observed — or seemed to observe — and envied in so many of the young girls she now saw about her.

Mat was a cattle dealer at that time, and a fairly frequent caller at her father's farm on the Darling Downs. She had a — nowadays — displeasing recollection of him, on Sundays and holidays, flashily dressed and driving in a polished and twinkling sulky behind a smart-stepping pony. He was five years her senior. She had a feeling that in spirit, if not in fact, she had been part of a deal arranged between Mat and her father; a feeling that Mat had led her from her father's farm as he might have led a well-grown and promising heifer. It angered her to recall that she had once been pleased and flattered to go driving with him in his twinkling sulky.

He had got three children by her. That was how she thought of it — in terms of the paddock. The first was the child of her complete inexperience; the bearing of the second and third she had faced with the accommodating good humour with which she met circumstances she felt incapable of combating. Three, Mat had decided, would do. Toward them she was affectionate, but not with any depths of tenderness; a good humour came in again here. They didn't expect a great deal from her beyond feeding and clothing. They were tough like Mat; as toddlers they had looked upon the world with his eyes.

Awakening — maturity of outlook — seemed to have begun between the coming of the first and second child. It gained with the years. Generally she was able to get a twisted humour out of the contemplation of her lot; but from it fell a fine accumulating

The Woman at the Mill

sediment of resentment. On this her thoughts fed during those times when cheerfulness failed her. She thought about things over the cooking stove and the sewing-machine, over the wash-tubs, lying beside Mat, and even in moments of greater intimacy.

She suspected herself of being a fool, in the sense of having capacity to feel, to experience, without being able to wrest from these things an ability to cope with life. Mat made her feel like that. His mentality was the dominant one; it undermined her, making her feel that in secret he estimated her exactly, marked her limitations, and valued her for what she was worth to him; that he thought of her, behind those unrevealing eyes, as a man might think of a docile and profitable cow. It wasn't quite like that, really, but that was how, in her discontent, she dramatized it.

She turned from the window with a deep-drawn sigh. Its prospect was not absorbing for long. There was just a partial view of the iron roof of the mill, silent now, and of the track running up the slope between the tall yellow grass to where, under a solitary, leaning silver-leaf ironbark, it sidled over the low ridge; above these a blue void.

From a shelf she lifted an armful of old magazines, weeklies and department store catalogues, and flopped them on the table. Seating herself, she drew them to her one by one — as she had done a hundred times before in leaden-footed hours — and turned the pages, glancing at the illustrations with inattentive eyes.

Bert Caswell was not the first man who had engaged her notice. Since she first suspected that she had started married life on the wrong foot she had, without fully acknowledging it to herself, been keeping covert watch for someone with whom she might find consolation. She had no clear idea of what she would do with such a person when found; it was just a groping for something with which to ease a dissatisfaction.

During the years a changing acquaintanceship had brought a number of candidates into view, but fastidiousness, caution, and points of principle had caused each to be rejected, often without their knowing they had been objects of consideration. There had been Larry Matheson, a distant relation of Mat's, who used to stay with them sometimes. She had been friendly with Larry, big, slow and kindly, but she had never become unaware of his neglected teeth and warty hands. There had been Alec Withers, with whom Mat had been in partnership for a short while in a carrying business in Toowoomba. She liked looking at Alec, but that was as far as it got. Other things aside, she feared Mat's sharpness. Then there had been Tom Wallace, a stock and station agent. Here had arisen the consideration of her friendly regard for his wife; though *he* had been willing enough — unexpectedly, embarrassingly so, on one occasion.

On the new settlement, before Bert Caswell's arrival, and just after the establishment of the police station, she had found herself thinking sometimes of the sergeant of police. At dances and bush races, and when he called at the mill on patrol, she was able, by a special show of friendliness, to gain his attention. The sergeant was interested, and the consideration of going back on a fellow-woman didn't arise here, for she and Mrs. Fitzpatrick were unfriendly; but there was the counter-consideration that the unfriendliness was rooted in Mrs. Fitzpatrick's sense of social superiority. In the circumstances wouldn't Irene be degrading herself? While these matters were under review by her the affair slipped from her hands. By a subtle change of behaviour the sergeant indicated that his capacity as a gallant, his moral or immoral predilections, his sense of marital fidelity — or sense of caution or whatever it was — must all remain for ever unriddled beneath the cloak of his official dignity.

Within ten minutes of meeting Bert Caswell she was happy in the thought that none of these previous fancies had come to flower. They met at the Murdochs', whose homestead lay just a hundred yards through the bush at the back of the township. They were friends of hers and also of the Warburtons, who had offered him, following the death of his parents, the right to make their home his during the intervals of his bush wanderings. Two of the younger Warburtons had brought him to the Murdochs' on the afternoon of her call.

In his late twenties, upstanding, jauntily confident of himself, friendly facing the world, and with a ready laugh, he had filled her eyes at once. It had been no more than a polite social occasion, but they had exchanged a little one-to-one cross-room conversation, and she had found it easy to catch his eye between times. She had driven home thinking about him, and had

The Woman at the Mill

continued to do so during the two days that elapsed before they met again. Thought of him fed a glow within her. Two things caused her a pang each time they came to mind. He was six or seven years her junior and he was — she thought — better-looking than any man had a right to be. The first she assuaged by the thought that sometimes such differences didn't matter, the second was cancelled out as often as it cropped up by the reflection that she wouldn't have him any different if she could.

At the end of two days she had driven into the township armed with a list of errands sufficient to keep her there for the afternoon. Whether she was making the journey really to do errands or in hope of seeing Bert she would decide on the drive home, in the light of whether she ran into him or not.

As if in answer to her anxious hope, Bert had come from the store just as she drove up to it. Before he went on his way, and before she entered the store to begin a list of errands whose nature had miraculously changed from dubious to gladsome, they had a short but pregnant conversation under the store veranda. She had almost gulped when he, obviously daring a little, had called her Irene, but she was glad of it and instantly called him Bert.

They didn't meet again till the night of the dance.

As the evening wore on there had been a certain amount of coming and going between the Murdochs' — where wraps and sleeping children were left — and the School of Arts. They met on the track in the darkness under the boughs.

'It's you, is it?'

'Yes.'

And a little later at the sound of approaching voices:

'There's someone coming.'

They withdrew among the trees to one side, and there she had both encouraged and yielded to Caswell's ardour. She wasn't sure whether she was doing the best thing. She felt she hadn't meant to come so quickly to this part of it, but she couldn't bring herself to say no to him, and she wanted to herself, anyway.

On the next morning but one Caswell left for the job for which he had engaged, at Charleville.

For a while, afterwards, Irene was lost in her feelings between being something aghast at what she had done, and taking pride in that she had gone, daring worthily, where most women

Australian Short Stories

ventured only in guarded excursions of the imagination.

From her thoughts of the future relationship of herself and Caswell she was not able to draw comfort. During the months he was away she lived over and over again, in smallest detail, every memory she had of him, from the first moment she had seen him, finding a significance in the recollection of a look, a gesture, a movement of his head, the readiness or unreadiness of a reply to something she had said to him.

From those that were pleasing to recall she built a happy dwelling-place for her spirit. While the mood of optimism was on her it sufficed her need. She didn't begrudge him his absence — he had his living to earn. Even the lack of a letter was immaterial — he was unhandy with the pen; he feared making trouble for her. There had been the consolation of a message contained in a single scrawled page to the Warburtons, 'Remember me especially to Mrs. Lawrence.' She had built a lot around that.

But there were times when doubt tortured her; when she felt she had nothing of his in her keeping. She had given too much and too readily. From so many of the remembered things there might be drawn a disturbing significance. Perhaps in finding assurance in her memories, she was deluding herself. There was the word he might have given, but hadn't; the touch she might have had but didn't receive. He had scarcely thought of her since he went away! In the pain of it she built a hell for herself. She could have hated him — with a hate that would have melted at the sight of him.

Looking always at the same set of facts she would swing, like that, from one extreme of feeling to another. She was being foolish in hoping that there was some lasting bond between them. Heaven was witness to the strength of their attachment. He hadn't given her another thought. He was being careful out of fear for her. She would never see him again. When he came he would take her away with him. Perhaps, at the last, she wouldn't be able to leave the children. But there must be some way past all difficulties for feeling such as theirs.

Through these alternating fears and hopes she passed in quick succession as she sat turning the pages of the magazines. At one moment warming to the thought of his nearness. At worst he was no further away than the township. At another moment cold in the stomach and shaking in the limbs. He had returned

The Woman at the Mill

three days ago! He should have come to her, if only to give her the comfort of a word. He wasn't coming.

At the sound of hooves on the track she went paper-white. For a few seconds she couldn't move, feared she was going to faint; then she raised herself and looked through the window.

It was he. He had dropped his horse's reins at the edge of the grass and was coming toward the house.

'Good day!' His tall figure was in the doorway, blocking the light.

'Hullo, Bert . . . Come in and sit down.'

She was standing by the table. Her colour had returned. Her heart was thumping so violently that it pained her. Her eyes were idolatrous.

Caswell did as he was bidden, taking a seat on the bench by the wall. She — physically lost to consciousness of herself — remained standing. They were both nervous, uncertain of their ground.

'You're back again, Bert!'

'Yes, Irene. For a little while.'

'Why?' In his reply there had been an inflection of voice that she didn't understand and which gave her a stab of fear. 'You're not going away again soon?' It seemed incredible to her that he should come to her talking of going away.

'I might.' The question — it seemed — had touched the quick of his pride of calling. He swung one leg across the other. 'There's a man after me now to go with him to pick up a mob of cattle out from Quilpie. Never have much trouble about getting a job!'

She caught the note of vainglory, and a short laugh that was almost a sob expressed the relief to her feelings. Men, Bert included, were just like big boys. She saw how it was; because Bert was just as nervous as herself. Their opening exchanges had taken on an unfortunate turn, run off into an irrelevancy. She could see now, by the way he was smiling, that that was how it was.

They went on to talk of the trip he had just finished. She inquiring and he replying. Their talk continued for some time.

But this was only conversation. They were looking at each other all the time with questioning eyes.

Caswell rose and came over to her. He was thinking how nice she looked, and was wondering how soon he could come to the point. His uncertainty vanished when he went to take her in his arms and found with what eagerness she accepted.

The yellow-faced alarm-clock had the room to itself for an hour before the door leading to the rest of the house opened and Bert and Irene re-entered the kitchen. He took a cigarette from his pocket and stood tapping the end on the back of his hand.

'I'll put the kettle on for a cup of tea.' Irene went to the stove, shook up the embers and put fresh wood on.

Caswell glanced at her back, then walked across the room and sat down on the bench. He was uneasy again, not nervously, this time, but thoughtfully.

He had ridden out from the township in some doubt as to his reception. What had taken place between them had been a good deal in his thoughts during his months on the stock route. He felt genuinely attracted to Irene. When he had called her by her name that day under the store veranda it had been a spontaneous act, an act of momentary daring. It had gratified him, quite innocently, when she responded. He had been a rather surprised as well as a much elated young man, that night of the dance, when he had found his amorous advances being welcomed. Hitherto his experiences had been confined to the girls at fourth-rate country pubs; housemaids whose employers expected them not to be above entertaining guests on terms to be arranged between them. This matter of his encounter with a very desirable married woman was in a different class. Life was opening out! At the same time their contact with each other had been so brief as to be rather insubstantial in recollection. By the campfires of the west a doubt as to the probable reception awaiting him when he next saw Irene had, in consequence, developed in him. He needed the reassurance of repetition.

Events since coming to the mill had set his mind at rest in that connection, but something fresh had come to his notice. He had become aware of a difference between himself and her; a difference of intention. She didn't want just occasional adventure. She wanted all of him. Things she had said, questions she had asked him while they were in the bedroom, had apprised him of that. He had concealed the effect on him, but it had come as a bit of a jolt. She had possessed his body

The Woman at the Mill

with a passion that exceeded his own, a soft abandonment that at once gratified and daunted him.

Irene was setting out the cups and saucers. Though she had yielded to his request as if will were a thing apart from herself, and having yielded had done so without reserve, she had been, for a moment, a little hurt that he should have come at her so soon after his arrival. However, that moment of regret was past now; its memory deeply overlaid by the memory of their intimacy; the memory of the joy of yielding without an inward core of resentment against her partner. She recalled the directness of his approach that night under the trees; perhaps it was part of his nature. She didn't mind if it was; so long as he had other feelings for her. They had touched on these while in the bedroom, but she hoped to hear more fully. A good part of the day — before he need go — was still before them. She wasn't quite reassured as yet, but she had enough warrant for belief, for — as now — imagining his tenderness when she told him how much she had thought of him while he was away.

Caswell was looking out the door as if he was concerned about his horse. He was thinking how, by half-truths, evasions and direct lies, by both feigning to answer, and stifling questions with caresses, he had misled her in the bedroom. But what else could he have done? He didn't mean to be unkind — you couldn't think unkindly of a woman who had taken you to bed with her — but she really was a bit of a mug!

'I'll have to be getting along as soon as we've drunk our tea,' he said. He had one thought now — escape.

'Not right away?' she asked.

His ear caught the expected note of surprise and pain in her voice, and from the tail of his eye he saw her movements cease.

'Yes, I'll have to be pushing along.'

'I thought you'd stay a while with me, Bert.' She spoke with a tremor.

He was still pretending to concentrate on the scene outside, and was intensely conscious of her watching him. She had a right to expect that he would stay awhile, he knew that. He wasn't treating her with even common politeness. But he couldn't help that; couldn't bring himself to meet what he felt sure would come if he waited.

She had come a few paces toward him, and was standing

there with the tea-pot in her hand. Just standing there. Why didn't she put the tea-pot down?

'I thought you'd want us to have a nice long talk together,' she was saying. 'We could. We've got all day.'

He could no longer avoid looking at her. Their eyes met and held; his like one trapped, hers bright with pain.

'You see, Irene,' he explained, 'I've got to see that man about lifting those cattle. I wouldn't like to miss that job.'

Her eyes searched his. Why had the matter suddenly become urgent?

He smiled defensively as he returned her glance, but his eyes were hard.

'I've got to see that man,' he repeated.

She searched his face for a little while, her own pale, and showing the full tally of her years. She realised now the extent of her past pretences; her house of make-belief had vanished. Neither in the months of his absence nor in the recent hour of their clipped bodies had they shared a thought. What to her had been a blind groping for something of which life had cheated her had been for him just a cheap sexual success, something to bolster his conceit of himself.

Her mind told her this, but she couldn't quite bring her feelings to acquiesce. There was still a little hope. She would go and sit beside him and tell her story. At least he would sympathise and understand. She put the tea-pot down and took a step toward him, but that was as far as she got. She saw him flinch, and move as if he were about to get up. He was afraid of a scene. Well, she'd spare him that.

She had sunk into the chair by the table, scarcely aware of having moved. She had a feeling that she wasn't a fool any more, but that it was going to be a long time before she could bring herself to accept this sudden accretion of wisdom. There was a long silence in which the ticking of the clock sounded like a gong.

'When do you think you'll be back this way, Bert?' Her voice was scarcely above a whisper. There was something guilty about her question, as if the words were torn out of her by her feelings, against the command of her mind.

He knew instinctively that she was clutching at straws. 'Not for some time, I suppose, Irene,' he answered firmly. 'We're

The Woman at the Mill

taking cattle out to Windorah and then I understand there's a chance of picking up another mob at Bedourie.'

Again silence fell. He saw that she had forgotten about the tea. He might be able to get away.

He scuffled uncertainly in the doorway.

'Well, so-long, Irene.'

'Good-bye, Bert,' she answered, 'and the best of luck!' She looked up at him in speaking and smiled. She must appear to take what had happened between them in the spirit in which he had intended — at any rate until he was gone.

For a moment his eyes were held unwillingly by hers. He saw in them pain, and resignation to pain that was yet to be endured; he caught a glimpse of reaches of human feeling that he hadn't known to exist. He looked away hurriedly. He was half-angry that this light enterprise should have brought him to this.

He went down the steps. With his foot in the stirrup he looked back at the house; then swung into the saddle and moved off. The sooner he saw that man about the cattle the better.

Guest Of The Redshields

Christina Stead

On the second of January, when I was wondering how I should stave off my creditors on the fifteenth, Mr. James Redshield visited me and acquainted himself with my home. It is a studio on the eighth floor, furnished with casement-cloth curtains, grass mats, a typewriter, a chair, a stove, and a lawyer's filing cabinet. Shortly after, I was invited to the castle of the Redshields for the weekend. In the afternoon we rode, with a small party, through the beech and chestnut forest, where deer abound, and over the pastures of the estate. The weather was showery, with gleams of sunshine; and so that we should not be encumbered with waterproofs, our host ordered out two small donkey-carts, which followed us at a strategic distance, with rugs, mackintoshes, galoshes and umbrellas. Outriders, discreetly passing behind distant clumps of trees, warned off picnickers, poachers and billposters; with them, a small band of waiters carried provisions hot and cold, which were prepared for us in a small clearing, when the sun shone, around four o'clock. A small cloud driving over the scene, caused a band of footmen in livery to rise modestly from behind bushes and hold in readiness umbrellas and a waterproof canopy to cover the trestle tables. Our ride terminated and we encountered no untoward accident.

After a peaceful evening with my cultivated hosts, I retired to my room, one large and compendious. The curtains and wall covering were of the same silk and same design. When the door was closed I found myself in a floral bower, mossy and perfumed. In a cabinet at my bedside was an exhaustive collection of cigarettes of the strength and provenance I am used

Guest of the Redshields

to. A bookcase contained the English poets bound in shagrin, the French poets in morocco, the Arabian Nights, with augmentations, in oasis goat, a private edition of the journals of the most famous prose-writers and poets in parchment, and the secret annals of the Papacy, the Quai d'Orsay, Scotland Yard and the lost archives of Gortchakov bound in sharkskin. A universal dictionary, a rhyming dictionary, a thesaurus, an illustrated bestiary, inks of various colours and consistencies, pencils of all hardnesses, penhandles of many shapes, and pens of steel, quill and gold, were all fitted into a combination lectern and writing desk, which held also a dictaphone, an improved pantograph for writing by hand, and a stenotype machine. The modern poet could desire no more.

A small handbook on the table explained that by pressing buttons in the entry I could change the wallpaper and curtains, or cause a series of spot, flood, and footlights to play, so that the aspect, perspective and size of the room would alter entirely. If I wished, the walls would slide back, leaving me enclosed in a pavilion of glass, transparent from within but not from without, so that I might ruminate in privacy on the rich and rolling demesne.

In a small glass-and-metal bar, fruits, soft and alcoholic drinks, coffee and mineral waters, cakes and comfits, bromides and sedatives, and bouillons in hot flasks stayed to comfort the wakeful guest. But I will not attempt to indicate the infinite advantages of this room: time can destroy but cannot compass them.

I sat in an easy chair with adjustable back and foot and placed one dangling foot on a small brass knob planted in the dais on which the bed stood. The platform immediately rose and the bed, all in a moment, sank into the ceiling without a trace, while the floor, perfectly carpeted and unencumbered permitted me to stretch my legs, when I felt kinaesthetic. On reading in the book of directions that the walls were soundproof, I took up a violin which lay on a table of calamander wood and silver, and began to play the Chaconne of Bach. A moment after finishing, I heard a light tap, which, I imagined, was on the shutters. I loosened these, but only the tempered wind was there. I looked forth. A rolled-up ladder was attached to the balcony, and at a careless tap of my cigarette, it unwound and invited me to descend directly into the park. The full but cloudy moon shone irregularly on the cockscombed glades, rounded knolls, ideal vistas, terraces and wildernesses sweetly artificed, which appeared momently along the serpentine paths; and here fountains, a well of dark sound, a jet of snow, and there watercourses, dulcet with pools, resonant with pebbles, with flute and lyre, descanted in the woods. In an hour I returned, wound up my ladder, closed the shutters and thought of sleeping. I had begun to undress, meditating lazily, when again I heard a soft rapping, louder than before. 'Surely,' said I, 'that is something within the wall, a click-beetle, or death-watch, a rat running over the beams, the hot-water pipes vibrating.' But I said: 'Come in.'

A maître d'hôtel immediately entered the room through an invisible door in the wall, served by a secret passage. This mode of access was to avoid the embarrassment a guest feels at hearing a *passe-partout* turned in his lock: moreover, since the passage was overheated, aliments could be conveyed along it without turning cold. The man had a silver-backed tablet in his hand, and, addressing me with a mathematically modulated courtesy, he asked if I would take anything on waking in the morning, and whether it should be tea, coffee, cocoa, or some other thing I might suggest. I said I would take tea.

'Ceylon, China, Russian or Indian tea?' he asked delicately, with pencil poised.

'China tea,' said I.

'Black or green?' he asked.

'Black,' said I.

'And of what flavour: Pekoe, Orange Pekoe, Congou, Oolong, Soochong, Pekoe-Soochong, Poochong or Bohea?'

'My mother liked Soochong,' said I.

'With, or without, an admixture of dried tea-flowers, or jasmine flowers?' he continued.

Said I: 'With jasmine flowers.'

'Now may I trouble you,' he said politely, 'to know whether you like it hot or cold, and with or without lemon, or milk or cream, and sugar?'

'With milk and sugar.'

'As to the milk,' said he, 'will you have whole milk, skim milk, condensed milk, buttermilk, cream or whey?'

Guest of the Redshields

'Whole milk,' I said, much taken aback.

'Should it be, sir,' he said, 'from the Guernsey or the Jersey herd?'

'Guernsey,' I cried.

'Then as to the sugar,' he said, 'will you have cane sugar (white or brown), beet sugar, palm, maple or sorghum sugar?'

And when I replied: 'White cane,' he inclined and inquired: 'From Cuba, the Philippines, Queensland or Natal?'

'Cuba, then,' I said, thinking that no more discrimination could be required, even of a guest of the Redshields.

Sensing my fatigue, he asked softly: 'May I suggest the Province of Camaguey?'

'Even so.'

'Good, and as to form, loaf, granulated, crystallised, or soft?' he asked; and I replied: 'Loaf!'

'Now sir,' he said, in a firmer tone, 'what will you eat?' In haste I replied, ere he could begin his inexorable enumeration: 'Bread and butter.' But the words had not left my mouth before his ingeniously insinuating vocables were upon me with, Wheaten bread, corn, oats, barley or rye bread, gluten or protein bread, and if wheaten, as he took the liberty to suppose, whether that made from spring patent (high protein), ordinary spring patents, clears (first spring), soft winter straights, hard winter straights, hard winter patents or hard winter clears, and whether new baked, or old, hot or cold, and whether crumb or crust, and in what form, whether Danish, Swedish, German, French or English (for example), and, my choice being made, whether aërated or salt-rising bread, and in what shape, plain or fancy, tin, cottage, twist, roll or crescent?

But now I arose quietly from my thrice-sprung seat and said in a soft voice: 'Nothing it is to me, if maître d'hôtel you be, or fiend or dream, or the three: but take my word, I am only a poet, and I cannot cope with the verbal resources of your universal larder. Let me only not starve! Thank you, good night!'

At these words, the butler, flitting, gave a soft submissive smile, like one, too courteous, that has not been well understood: he bowed himself to the wall and suddenly disappeared. I shut my eyes and drew a bottle at random from the automatic bar, and soon after falling asleep, dreamed I saw Gargantua pouring from an ever-running bottle the active ferments of a monstrous digestion.

You can well imagine that when I reached home again, and my mother asked me: 'Well, did you eat well at the Redshields? At least, I suppose they have pure food, if their servants are not thieves,' I was in a position to rejoice her heart.

Sappho

Christina Stead

The sea froths, the coroneted swans cover the cliff with their feathers, a groan bursts from the belly of the sea, black as blood. Sappho has sung to the sea-king's daughter, who steals the keys of jasper and opens the prison gates for her to pass out. The waters divide, and Sappho, with shut eyes, her white amorous body asleep, and still and pale as a sandy beach under the last embraces of regreful seas, passes upward, drawn by the desires of the hosts of heavenly virgins. With the sound of the surge, the swans burst from the cliff, leaving it sable, and, closing round Sappho, bear upward in their flight, a sweep of long wings into heaven. The misty beam of the moonlit night strikes on the swan's plume as it shoulders away the dark, and glistens on the dark eyeball: left and right, the line re-forms as they rise and fall along the dewy uplands of air. Ever they climb precipitously up the steep of night, spirally as a Babylonian tower. The sinuous waves have long ago been calmed beneath them, and sleep like frost: the forests and lakes are dark, like the secret locks of young women. They pass out of the cone of night, and they see the earth struck by sunlight, smiling as it imperceptibly rolls over the twilight strand into the surf of dawn.

The Swans pass through the groaning meteors and the yelping winds and tempests of the upper air: their wings, wearing, drop feathers and down, which, a month after, come to earth, as the snow that falls in white climes. They cross the red, blue, green, yellow and white rivers which shine in the rainbow, they cross without danger the blue burning plains and the rivers of corrosive gold which show when the pavilions of air are rent

Australian Short Stories

by thunder: they hear the growling of the bears, escape the hoofs of the charioteer who treads the tails of comets to dust, and make signs to all the impudent Zodiac. As they pass by the Maiden, Sappho stirs in her sleep, and her nostrils, hitherto obstructed by the bad cold she caught two days ago falling into the Mediterranean, expand. The first flush of blood gushes into her cheek as they pass swift as light through the palaces of Perihelion and Aphelion, cleaving the bowing and murmuring company of astral mandarins, with coloured topknots according to their magnitudes.

But now the solar system is past, and they are in the pathless waste. Only the instinct of the coroneted swans, who are fed on dragon-flies every morning at the heavenly gate, can guide her over the steppes of the Middle Distance. It is past: the heavenly light begins, as the dawn with us, only with all those known delights heightened in their transcendental way to delights inconceivable: this I say, who relate it, for I cannot conceive what they may be. Now the hosts of virgins and all the saints of the calendar, even the full tale of saints of these latter days, sing faintly as sings the morning star to the lover who has watched all night in the shrubbery: the noise grows louder, as surf to tempest-tossed ears: it sings about them as sings the drenching summer rain: and Sappho wakes.

'Where are we, O dearest Swan?' says she to the nearest crowned head, resting so lightly on its long stalk of pleasing form.

'We approach the gates of pearl,' said the Swan, singing now, as do the heaven-born Swans.

'Who is there to receive us?'

'The Virgin, the Lords of Heaven, Buddha, Confucius, the hosts of martyrs and saints, Venus, Diana and other celebrities, the Muses with elegantly-poised feet, the Graces in their naked chastity, all, all you knew on earth and under sea.'

'What will I wear? I am naked!'

'The future director of the Moscow Art Theatre, yet unborn, will study your type and tell you!'

'Whom shall I have to love me?'

'The Lord, the saints _____'

'Hm! Hm!'

'_____ the nymphs and oreads _____'

110

'Pallid souls!'
'_____Ariadne, Andromeda, Cassiopeia_____'
'Too sentimental!'
'_____Lilith, Dalila, Potiphar's wife, Cleopatra, Thaïs, Ninon, Catherine the Great, Ste. Thérèse_____'
'Too religious!'
'_____all the daughters of Eve!'
'But Eve?'
'On Wednesdays and Sundays,' said the Swan, 'she vists Heaven to see her numerous descendants, but at other times she stays on earth, refusing to give up her little notions.'
'Is to-day Wednesday?'
'Alas, there is a wretched innovation here, the Gregorian Calendar,' said the Swan, 'I never know what day it is, now.'
'Give me a mirror,' said Sappho.
'There are no mirrors in heaven, for no one can make reflections there,' said the Swan, shaking his head.

Sappho pouted, but she reached for an asphodel floating past in the air, and twined this in her hair, shaking from it as she did so seaweeds and pearls put there secretly by the sea-king's daughter. 'Lend me a pen,' said Sappho, and the Swan made haste to do so. Sappho began frowning and counting on her fingers: 'This sapphic metre is the very dickens,' she said. Presently she said to the Swan, 'Do you know a rhyme for Leda?'

'Certainly not,' said the Swan coldly: 'and I hope you were not taken in by that very tall story of Leda's, none of us swans was. But it was generally believed by a population ignorant of biology, and we have been much annoyed by those forward water-nymphs ever since.'

'Don't take on so,' said Sappho: 'but I admit a girl is lucky who lives in antiquity, a taradiddle is as good as coin of the realm.'

'There you have it,' said the Swan indignantly. 'Take Semele: she had a happy conceit: she bothered no one.'

They now arrived at the gates of pearl on the crystal shore. St. Peter pulled aside a little shutter and looked out through a grille, a razor in his hand and his face covered with suds. 'You are very early,' he observed amiably, 'but do come in. I took you for a gentleman who has been too much with us lately. He contributed to the rebuilding of the Delphic oracle, and has always treated the cloth honourably; and then, that loafer

Mercury slept late and permitted him to be caught short on the stock exchange. Most unfortunate; and he positively insists that we cover his losses!'

'Very reasonable,' said the Swan, ruffling his feathers. 'There is a good deal too much *dolce far niente* in this place: look at yourself, not shaved at this time of day!'

'I've a good mind to grow a beard,' said St. Peter ruefully. 'Beatitudes are so frequent now that I have no time to dress for dinner: and here, as you know, we still feel that manna maketh man.'

They entered. Tents of silk covered endless lawns, harps twanged of themselves in the air, so that the blessed should not have to work, for it was an honourable society living entirely on its capital of faith and good works. The Lord, an old-timer, conscious of his rustic origins, sat and listened valiantly to the Earl of Chesterfield, Brillat-Savarin and Vedius Pollio, but he could not keep his eye from glazing, nor his foot from idly waggling.

An angel bore down on Sappho, and politely but firmly took from her fist her pen.

'I can't write here?' said Sappho, surprised, knowing that the holy are addicted to the Word.

'No,' said the angel, 'it is a very old regulation, first imposed by the Lord (God bless him!), who is a writer himself, as you have probably guessed from the number of his writings, both attested and apocryphal, scattered about the earth. The day after Heaven opened, two journalists came here and immediately started rival journals: the interpretations they gave of the Gospels and their disputes under the heads of theophany, theogony and theopathy were so ridiculous and bitter, that the Lord himself was assailed by religious doubt: but he was wisely advised, and since then there has been no literature in heaven.'

'This is very painful to hear,' said Sappho.

'You will get used to it,' said the angel putting the pen back in the Swan's wing. 'Besides, you will soon be perfect, therefore your interpretation of celestial phenomena will be the same as everyone's, so you will have nothing to say.'

'And I will be perfect!'

'Naturally!'

'I won't feel any more hunger, toothache, suffocation,

Sappho

ambition, love, the wind, the sun or the sea?'

'Your questions are typically sentimental,' said the angel shrugging his wing.

'But, goodness me, I want to see Eve and love her!'

'This is Thursday,' said the angel. 'By Sunday you will be too perfect to love her.'

'Where is she, O, where is she?' cried Sappho, much agitated.

'How do I know?' said the angel. 'She earns her living by snake-charming: she is at present, hm, let's see, in Lesbos. Yes, look through the terrestrial telescope over there on the ramparts, and you'll see her in Lesbos.'

'In Lesbos!' cried Sappho. 'A malediction! And I in heaven! But I must see her for whose charms the whole world was eternally damned by a jealous god.'

Sappho leapt to the platinum wall of heaven, and plunging her glance through the variegated universe, she found the earth's surface. There, as in a silver mirror, she saw a beautiful and holy face, fair as Psyche's, passionate as Medea's, terrible as the Medusa's, calm as Hera's, in which the forces of love and self-love, as of life and death, perpetually made war.

'What divinity! What frailty!' said Sappho. The beautiful face seemed to her to cloud. 'Something annoys her, some regret her brow, some gnat her bosom, some worm her heel,' said Sappho: 'I must go! At that sight a storm of passions so bitter and burning has risen in my breast, that I cannot stay any longer from her side.' And spreading her arms like the albatross as he takes off, she leaped towards the far sea's polished mirror, into which, in error, she had been gazing.

'There she goes,' said St. Peter with self-possession, putting away his razor. 'So much the better. The housing problem is really getting acute here.' He fed to the swans their dragon-flies. 'Besides,' he said to the chief Swan, 'she would have had no luck with Eve: Eve and Adam are a most devoted couple, they say.'

The Three-legged Bitch

Alan Marshall

Tim Sullivan was seventy-five years of age. He was a thickset, powerful man with a crown of grey hair. His face had weathered wind and sun and rain, and now bore the character of an old rock. He had calm blue eyes and spoke slowly, gathering words from a mind that had been given few opportunities to express itself in speech.

He lived in Jindabyne at the foothills of the Australian Alps. Everybody knew him. He had been a dogger, a dingo trapper, and the years of his youth and manhood had been spent with packhorses and dog traps among the mountains and high plains.

He had lived by killing. The death of dingoes brought him prestige, friendship, praise and sufficient money to live on. With the scalps of those he killed bagged on his packhorse, he would come down from the mountains to collect the bounties and replenish stores. He would ride down the main street of Jindabyne, his traps clinking from the back of the packhorse following him. Men standing at the hotel doorway would wave to him as he passed.

'How are ya, Tim?'

The station-owners, with their broad-brimmed hats and Harris tweed sports coats, shouted for him in pubs, threw him a fiver when some notorious dingo fell victim to his traps. They listened to his stories with interest, an interest born of an involvement with his successes and his failures. When on mustering rides they met him on lonely mountain tracks, they reined in their horses to yarn with him.

They vied with each other in offers of hospitality should he

The Three-Legged Bitch

visit them to trap the dingoes that harassed their sheep.

'Spend a few weeks with me at Geehi, Tim.'

'There's always a room for you at Khancoban, Tim.'

He was a good fellow, an honest bloke, a chap you could rely on.

Upon the attitude of these men towards him, Tim Sullivan built a framework of confidence and pride in himself.

He had never known praise in his childhood. Now, as a man, his fame as a dogger brought him self-respect. It pleased him that educated and wealthy men spoke to him as an equal. It was his great achievement. It gave some meaning to his life, supported him in lonely moments when the howl of a dingo at night made him look up from his camp fire.

For fifty years he hunted dingoes. He followed them into remote valleys, along ridges few men had trod. He knew every cattle and sheep pad that bound the hills. He drove the few remaining dingoes back to the inaccessible places where they lived on wallabies and from where they were afraid to venture down to the sheep country. He acquired great skill and knowledge.

When Tim was sixty-five his wife died. She had been a placid, stout woman with a friendly manner. She wore aprons upon which she wiped her hands before offering one to your grasp. She would then bustle round the kitchen making tea, anxious to please his guest. The glance she sometimes gave her husband affirmed what he was saying.

He had always felt young when she was alive. He could lead his packhorse into the mountains and stay away a month tracking some elusive dingo. But he thought of his wife a lot. He was always happy to return, and felt a reluctance to leave again, to subject his stiffening joints to the sway of a saddle over miles of mountain tracks.

When she died he suddenly felt old. It was as if a cloak had been removed from him and he felt the coldness of the wind. His movements became slower, and from thinking ahead he began recalling the past.

'I can never sleep on Sunday nights. I keep thinking about when Nell was alive. Every Sunday we had a roast.'

He sold his horses and his traps. He became an old-age pensioner and hunted dingoes no longer. The attention of those people who noticed him walking up the street carrying a sugar-bag was momentarily arrested by his carriage.

'See that old bloke! He carries his head like he was somebody. I forget his name but he used to trap dingoes or something. They say he was famous at it. He keeps clean, doesn't he?'

He had been confident in the continuation of his friendships. But he was of no value to the station-owners now. He was finished, out, done . . . He was an old-age pensioner who bored you with tales of your past losses. Gradually the men he had once served began to avoid him. They passed him on the street without a greeting. He began to realise where he now stood in the complex of the district's social structure.

'It sort of hurt me, him not recognising me. I spent a month at his place once. I was going to say to him, "Look, I'm not going to bite you for a couple of bob or the price of a drink. I just want to say 'hullo', that's all." But he just kept going.'

So it was — until the Three-legged Bitch came over from the Snakey Plains to harry the flocks in the Snowy River area.

For eight years the Three-legged Bitch roamed the ranges around the Snow Leases of the Kosciusko country. From the Grey Mare Range to the Pinch River men spoke of her. Her howl had been heard on the Big Boggy and they knew her tracks on the Thredbo. The bones of sheep she had slain lay along the banks of the Swampy Plains River on the Victorian side of the Snowy Mountains. She had crossed the Monaro Range, some sheepmen said.

The Three-legged Bitch was an outsize dingo with a thick rusty-red coat and a short bushy tail. When she was young and inexperienced she had been caught in a trap and one of her forepaws had been partly severed. Only one toe was left on this disfigured foot and the track it made was the brand by which she was known to those who hunted her.

She ran with a slight limp, her shoulder dropping a little when the leg she favoured took her weight. It had long since ceased to be the limp of pain or defective action; now it suggested a sinister development of style and her speed and strength seemed to stem from it.

She worked alone. Sometimes her howl brought a trotting male dog to a sudden halt on a valley track and he would stand

The Three-Legged Bitch

a moment with lifted nose then turn and make up through the wooden spurs to the treeless uplands where she made her home.

But those wandering dogs who answered and went to her never possessed her cunning and they either fell victim to doggers or failed to survive long periods of hunger when the snow came.

On the crown lands above the timber where the tussocky grass grows thick and gentian flowers come in the Spring, sheepmen drive their flocks up from the valleys during the Summer months and leave them to graze on areas they have leased from the government — Snow Leases, they are marked on the maps that define them.

When the first horsemen appeared on the high plains the Three-legged Bitch would retire into the remote parts where they could not follow her. From here she came out to kill.

In March, before Winter begins, the sheepmen go in and bring their flocks down to the snow-free valleys round the homesteads where the wild dogs never go.

There are no sheep on top in the Winter and then the snow lies in heavy drifts on the Snowy Plains and the dingoes and wild dogs grow lean with hunger. Yet the Three-legged Bitch always retained her strength. Some said she raided the rubbish dumps of the tourist chalets on those wild nights when her tracks would be covered by morning. A few doggers — those who delayed leaving the high valleys until snow forced them out — suspected she lived on sheep missed in the annual muster. These animals are often buried in the snow and here the Three-legged Bitch would scent them as she trotted through the still, white world of the surface. When the warm breath of them came to her through the snow she burrowed down until she reached them huddled together in terror. Then she tore the living flesh from their backs.

In the Summer she came in about every third night, favouring boisterous nights when terrified bleating would be lost in the wind and her panting was just another sound. She had been known to slaughter fifty sheep in one run when there was a gale and a full moon was whipped by clouds. She had killed for a week at Thompson's when Thompson was away.

All the sheepmen knew her work. She always revealed her

identity in the method of her killing. She was the criminal betrayed by 'fingerprints'. Long before she became known as 'The Three-legged Bitch' tales were told of sheep with mangled throats lying in lines on the snow leases of the high country. The unknown dog that slew them ran on the offside of each panic-stricken victim until, in that stumbling moment of weakness for which it awaited, it leapt for the throat, jerking the head backward as its teeth sank deep, and breaking the animal's neck as it came down.

Sheep still alive but gasping horribly through torn windpipes were brought in at the muster. Many sheep were never found. Their torn bodies lay in ravines and among rocks where their last frantic run had taken them.

Angry men held quick musters and swore at the count. In the bars of mountain pubs, with the froth of beer on their stubbly lips, they slew the Three-legged Bitch with fury.

'I'll fix her once I get hold of her.'

'If she gets amongst my ewes I'll follow her to the Murray.'

She robbed them of money and for this they hated her. Each murderous raid she made, each new killing, created in the minds of those whose sheep had died from her teeth a picture of a new and more ferocious dog, an animal governed by human passions of revenge and hate, one that for some strange personal reason had selected them as victims of her vendetta.

The kill of minor dingoes was blamed on her; kills twenty miles apart did not save her from a double accusation.

'She killed at Groggin's Gap on Wednesday.'

'She came in to Big Boggy on Wednesday.'

All slaughtered sheep were hers; the kill of every dog was hers.

She killed for sport, they said. She was blood-hungry, blood-mad . . . She snarled and drove in, she ripped down then back, she leaped like a shadow, whipped round and in again, on to another one. Snarl and rip and slash and on again. This was how they saw her, flecked with blood, her snarling mouth dripping. This was how they described her one to another, from man to man, across bar counters, in sheds and homes. The instinct that drove her to kill as many sheep as she could in a run seemed to them evidence of a creature with the mind of a murderer.

The Three-Legged Bitch

Before sheep had come to this country kangaroos and wallabies had been the dingoes' food. These animals could outrun the hunting dogs. It was only when an unsuspecting mob of wallabies was quietly feeding near trees or sheltering rocks that they were in danger. The hiding dingo suddenly burst into view fully extended and was among them with ripping teeth before they had time to gather speed. Two or three would die before the mob bounded away.

Food was life. Survival demanded the seizing of every opportunity to kill, for such opportunities did not come every day. Two slain wallabies were food for days.

Then sheep came to the mountains, helpless animals that could not escape by running. So the dingoes killed until they were tired, driven to slaughter one after another, not by a mind finding a savage joy in killing but by an instinct born thousands of years before when the animals they hunted had the speed to escape them.

The Three-legged Bitch had survived because of her skill in obtaining food, by her skill in avoiding the guns and traps and poisons of man.

She was afraid of men but there lingered in her some allegiance to them handed down from remote times when her domesticated ancestors had reached Australia with the first dark man. Sometimes from a safe distance she followed the cattle-drovers or a solitary musterer. She stood far back from the light of campfires, howling quaveringly as she watched them.

She was the last of her kind in those parts, the only pure-bred dingo that had survived the hunting of men. Yet she was incapable of feelings of revenge. That feeling marked the attitude of men towards her, the men from whose vast flocks she had taken her food.

For eight years the trappers hunted her. First for the price of her hide, then for the value of her scalp, then for twenty pounds reward . . . fifty . . . a hundred . . . They came up from the farms and the towns and the cities. There were young men with brown faces and strong arms and old men with beards. They came leading packhorses or tramping up through the woolly-butt and snow-gums carrying guns. Solitary riders with the stock of a cocked gun resting on their thigh walked their horses through the timber, across plains of snow-grass, down long ravines, their heads turning from side to side in an eager seeking. Packs of dogs, noses to the ground, followed in the confident steps of owners seeking a final payment. From some of the laden horses stumbling along the high tracks huge dog-traps clanked and swung. Men came with poison, with pellets of dough and ground glass, with stakes and snares. They shot brumbies and with bloodstained gloves upon their hands thrust poisonous crystals into the gashes made in the flanks. They poisoned the carcasses of sheep, cattle . . . Groups of sheepmen rode in lines, shouting through the scrub. On the far side their companions waited with guns.

She watched them come and go.

The defeated men came down from the mountains with tales that made minor triumphs of their failures. They lied to save their pride, they boasted to impress.

'I bowled her over with my second shot,' Ted Arthur said. 'She was staggering when she got up. I reckon she'd toss it in somewhere round by Little Twynam.'

He didn't say how he came upon her at a kill on the Grey Mare Range, how he fired and missed. She went down that slope in long bounds, hugging the cover, with his kangaroo-dog at her heels, then shot into a clump of wattle. When Ted's spurred horse reached the clump the Three-legged Bitch glided out on the far side and disappeared into the scrub. It was then he found his dog thrashing in a circle on the bloody leaves.

She had thrown up three of Bluey Taylor's baits, and Jack Bailey always swore she lost another toe in one of his traps.

But they all came down — Ted and Bluey and Jack and scores of others. They all left the snow leases, left the mountains.

Five men visited Tim one day. They left their cars at the gate and stood in a group before his door, waiting for it to be opened to their knock. Tim invited them in. He knew them all. Once he had imagined they were his friends. They still were, it seemed, by the warmth of their handshakes and the tone of their voices.

'We want to talk to you about the Three-legged Bitch, Tim,' said one. 'She killed seven of my ewes last night and Jack here

The Three-Legged Bitch

lost five on Friday night. We've got to do something about it fast. She scatters those she doesn't kill and God only knows how many we have lost. You are the only man who can get her, Tim. We want you to go after her. It won't take you so long with your experience. Now wait till you hear our proposition,' he hastened to add as Tim moved to speak. 'We know you have retired from the game, so to speak, but . . .'

They all paid tribute to his skill as a dogger. Everybody said he was the only man who would bring in her scalp. They were all agreed on this. They would stake him, buy his grub, supply him with horses and packs, pay him a hundred pounds for her scalp. He was still remarkably fit. You only had to look at him. They recalled him coming down from the top in snow storms, they remembered the time he had ridden ninety-four miles between sunrise and sunset.

'You couldn't kill him with an axe,' one remarked to another.

They continued to praise him, but Tim wasn't listening. He was looking at the walls of his hut. Many things hung there, all with a tongue — an old bridle, a rusty broken trap, the skin of a dingo, faded photographs in frames of painted cork, frames of seashells, pictures of horses cut from the pages of magazines . . . How many times had he sat and looked at them! It was his life he looked at and it was a protection. He only had to turn his head and there through the window were the mountains with a thin track winding up into the cold and the loneliness, the loneliness that had often sat with him in this room.

'You couldn't kill him with an axe,' he thought.

Their words were sweet to him. The pains, the aches, the digestive troubles his mind had fashioned from boredom and which seemed to lurk within him awaiting the trigger of purposelessness to release them, suddenly vanished and a deep breath filled his lungs with a new strength. He'd show them, these men who could discard a friendship like an old shirt. They needed him now. All the others had failed. He wouldn't fail.

'I'll bring you back her hide,' he said.

They took him down to the pub and shouted for him. They gave him advice. They all knew how the bitch could be caught.

'You'd probably bring her into the traps using piss as a lure,' said one of the men, a grazier whose wife, tired of life in the bush, was living in a Melbourne flat. 'They'll follow the trail for miles.'

Tim didn't reply. He knew all the lurks. Tie a bitch on heat so that she has to stand on a sheet of galvanised iron, catch her urine in a tin and bottle it — it would lure a male dingo into the traps or within reach of a rifle, but didn't this bloke realise he was dealing with a slut? It had no appeal to her.

His mind even now was planning the methods he would use. He was remembering past triumphs when with unresented patience he followed a dog for months until he knew its every habit, its peculiarities, its weaknesses . . . He would do the same again.

Four days later he was following Barlees Track across Reads Flat. The Geehi flowed nearby, fed by the melting snow that still lay in drifts on the Snowy Mountains. He was making for a cattleman's hut not far from Wild Cow Flats where the tracks of the Three-legged Bitch had been seen by several sheepmen preparing to take their flocks up above the tree-line to graze during the Summer months.

She had not yet killed, they said, though one of the men who had seen her several times trotting down from the Grey Mare Range said she was in good condition after the Winter.

'She knows when you haven't got a gun,' he said. 'She stood and watched me one day — only about forty yards away. You could tell what she was thinking.'

For two months Tim camped in the hut. He used it as a base from where he ranged the surrounding country. He had found her tracks, listened to her howl as he sat over his log fire.

He thought a lot about her while sitting before his fire. He developed a strange affection for her. *Was* she as merciless and cruel as they said? *Was* she evil? He had earned his living by killing. And he had got joy from it. He had looked down on the trapped dog with excitement. Then he had killed. Now he didn't like thinking about this. He didn't like thinking how he loved the admiration of other men, an admiration earned by killing.

'There's nothing you don't know about dingoes.'

'I'll hand it to you — you're the best dogger in Australia.'

Then he had seen her. He had been riding back with a load

of stores he had bought at Jindabyne when he came to an outcrop of rock just off the track. Huge boulders leaning one against the other formed cavities that made a perfect shelter. He dismounted, left his reins hanging and began searching around the rocks for tracks. The indentation of each claw was always absent from her tracks. They had been worn down by age and travel and she left only the impression of her pads. The claw tracks of young dogs were always deeply impressed into the ground.

She had been there all right. He looked at her tracks. She was older than he thought. He noticed the mark of her injured paw. He turned and looked up the mountain side as if expecting to see her slinking among the boulders. Suddenly she shot from a cavity to the left of him. She bounded on to a flat rock and then stood looking at him for a few swift heartbeats. His gun was back with the horses. Then she was gone. She seemed to flow over the rock upon which she had been standing. She glided through the trees and rocks making of each one a cover that stood between them.

Tim saw her many times over the next few months. He got to know her well. She had a deep curiosity. She often studied him from the shelter of some rock on the mountain side before slipping quietly away. He had seen other dogs, too, mongrels with her blood in them. But he was not involved with them. He had set out to destroy one animal — the dingo bitch. She was famous, so was he.

He studied her for months. He knew she always came in fairly fast. She trotted along a track, her head low, her tongue dripping. She never paused but kept up her tireless trot for miles. She always went out by a different track. When making back to the higher country she went slowly, pausing to roll on the grass or sniff at a tree-trunk she knew would attract other dingoes. She had killed and her hunger was satisfied.

When coming in on wild moonlight nights, she sometimes stopped and raised her head and her throat would vibrate in a quavering howl, a sound that always gave Tim a disturbing feeling of fear. His reaction to the howl of a dingo had never been removed by familiarity with the sound. The uncomforted voice of the bitch drew him into an experience of utter loneliness. It was the cry of a living thing in isolation and it united his yearnings with her own.

He discovered an old sheep track coming down from the craggy top of the range where it ended on a treeless flat. Here sheep were often grazing. He set two traps on this track. He set them with skill and left them. Some day she would use that track. Months of rain and sun would remove all evidence of their existence. They would wait.

He sought the sheep tracks she had used recently. On one that followed the crest of a spur he found her tracks, clear and distinct, unweathered by rain and wind. She always trotted along ridges rather than through valleys. She liked open country for travel and avoided those tracks that demanded she cross a creek. She was always reluctant to leave a cattle or sheep pad on which she found herself. She followed them for miles lifting her front legs high in a style that had been cultivated on the tussocky uplands above the tree-line. On this track Tim set his traps in the form of a letter 'H'. He selected a spot where the track was flanked by bleached tussocks that formed a dense cover she would naturally avoid.

The dog-traps Tim was carrying were like oversized rabbit-traps, each with two springs. The teeth of the wide jaws did not meet. This prevented the dog's leg from being severed instead of held.

Tim wore old gloves which were caked with the dried blood of a brumby. He spread a bag on the track, placed a trap beside it, then cut an outline round the trap with an old shearblade, pushing the blade deep into the soil. He removed the outlined sod by prising it free with the blade until it could be lifted intact and placed carefully on the bag. He placed the topsoil on one corner, the bottom soil on another so that he could return them to their original position in the set. The set trap fitted exactly into the excavation.

He enjoyed doing this. All his past experiences were directing him and they grew in value as he pondered on his skill and knowledge. He suddenly felt linked with all men who knew their craft and worked well, a great army of men with whom he walked shoulder to shoulder.

He never touched the soil. He transferred each root-bound lump with the blade. Beneath the raised plate he thrust dry

The Three-Legged Bitch

grass, pushing it carefully into position to prevent soil collecting there. He did not place paper above the plate as in rabbit trapping. It would be likely to rustle when a dog stepped close to it.

He buried the chains attached to the traps with the same care. At the end of each chain a strand of wire increased its length and ended by being fastened to a 'drag', a log of wood Tim had selected because of its shape. They were not too heavy and would enable the dingo to drag them some distance without subjecting her leg to a strain that would sever it.

When the traps and chains were covered he carried the bag on which surplus soil was lying and shook it some distance away. He then used the bag to 'blow' the set. He waved the bag above the set blowing away loose crumbs of earth. Using the shearblade he scattered dry leaves and broken cow manure above the area on which he had been working until all evidence of his work had vanished.

He stood up and looked down at his work with satisfaction. The longer the traps stayed in the ground the better his chance of catching her.

He passed near the set two days later but it hadn't been disturbed, then on the fourth day after a gusty night of wind he reined his horse beside the track and looked down on the scarified earth over which he had worked so carefully. Two of the traps had been sprung. Dirt and stones had been scratched over them in what seemed to be a gesture of contempt. She had come trotting down the track, following it with her head down. She had continued between the arms of the 'H' then stopped dead at the bar. Here she had stood a moment deadly still — the last four pawmarks were deeply indented — sniffing at the polluted air. She had then backed carefully out, stepping into the tracks she had already made, until she was free of the enclosure. It was here she had turned and ripped up the stones and earth in an attempt to render the hidden steel harmless. Tim sat on his horse and looked at her answer. There was a faint smile on his face.

In the months that followed he tried every trick he knew. Wearing gloves stained with blood he had dropped poisonous crystals into slashes made in the flanks of freshly-killed brumbies. He had shot only thin horses. He believed a dingo, knowing it had swallowed poison, could throw up the flesh of a fat horse. She had eaten round the slashes. He tried poisoning the carcasses of sheep she had slain. She ignored them.

But still she killed, leaving a trail of dead animals on the Swampy Plain, out by Bogong, on the slopes of the Blue Cow. She was killing with more than usual ferocity as if danger had made her desperate.

He dragged putrid legs of sheep by a rope tied to his saddle, leading her for miles to baits of fresh liver with deadly mouths slashed into them. She often followed these trails, scratching dirt over each bait as she reached it. On one occasion she had carried two of the baits and dropped them on top of a third that lay on an open pad beneath the sun. Beside this pile of poisoned meat she had left her dung.

A further symbol of her contempt? Tim kicked it to one side and smiled. She had no mind for such gestures. It was the heavy odour of putrid flesh that inspired her to leave the smell of her presence for the benefit of other dogs.

On a small flat open to the sky Tim found a pool of clear water. The banks were undermined, and matted dry grass clung to these banks and hung over the water immersing their pale, brittle stems beneath the surface. On one side there was a gap in the encircling grass and here on a tiny beach of grey mud she had left the imprint of her battered paws.

Tim studied them, then looked around him. The flat was treeless except for a bushy snow gum growing some twenty yards away. He knew that after a dingo drank she would trot to the nearest tree where she would stand or lie down for a while in the shade. There were no tracks to the tree — the grass was too thick — but there was an impress on the grass beneath it that suggested she had lain there.

He set four traps around the tree. When he had finished, the grass, the earth, the littered bark were as if no hand had touched them. He was pleased and stood for a moment anticipating victory.

Two days later he stood there again. She had sprung the tracks with scratched dirt. She had drunk at the spring, trotted to the tree and stood there a moment with senses alert while her sensitive nose detected the evidence of his work. Then the fear and the destruction of what she feared. Tim understood her.

The Three-Legged Bitch

He loaded the traps on to his horse and rode away and there was no anger nor resentment in him.

He followed her with rifle and fired at her from distances that demanded keener eyes than he possessed to hit her. He watched the spurt of dust rise near her feet then trailed her until her tracks petered out among rocks that littered the uplands.

She became increasingly wary of him — she feared guns and rifles — and he began finding it difficult to get within sight of her. He moved from hut to hut on the high country, following reports of her killing, and camping for weeks in some remote shelter built by cattlemen and only visited for a week or two each year.

He wintered at the Geehi Hut on the track to Khancoban. He packed in his stores and was never short of tucker. He was used to solitude. When Spring came to the mountains he followed the retreating snow to the top. For a week he searched for her tracks then found them criss-crossing the pitted earth behind a flock of climbing sheep. She had killed one of the stragglers.

There were moments when he felt she was indestructible, that all his skill was useless against her instinct to survive. He sometimes felt there wasn't a trail from the top in which he hadn't buried his traps; no clearing he hadn't baited.

He had made it a habit to make a regular visit to the old trail in which he had set his traps when first he came to the mountains. Almost a year had passed since he had hidden them beneath the track she once had made. Snow had covered them since then; bleak winds had flattened the soil above them, sun and rain and frost had removed all trace of man and the track wound upwards in an unbroken line that smelt of wild grass and the presence of Spring.

His mare knew the way. She moved at a brisk walk through the tussocks while he sat relaxed in the saddle, the reins drooping from her neck. He had no feeling of anticipation. This visit had become a habit.

When he first saw her crouched upon the track, draggled, panting, surrounded by the torn earth of her struggling, he experienced a leap of excitement that was almost a pain, so intense it was. The air had no motion and he sat in a still silence savouring his triumph. He could hear distant shouts of acclaim from beyond the accusing mountains, cheering . . .

The moment passed and his shoulders sagged to the burden of the accusation. He alighted from the mare and walked to her. Two traps held her helpless, their naked jaws clamped on a front and hind leg. They had lain in darkness beneath the track for more than a year and the smell of the earth had become their smell. The chains were taut from the drags which had prevented her from struggling into the concealing grass.

As he approached she wriggled backwards taking up what slack was available to her, then she faced him, crouching low, her muzzle resting on the earth, her fangs bared in a soundless snarl.

They confronted each other, the old man and the greying dingo, both killers who had reached a final reckoning. And Tim knew it in a clouded way. Hundreds of slain dingoes marked the trail of his lonely passage. Her pathway was a line of torn sheep lying motionless across the mountain uplands where she was born. He was surprised that she didn't reveal in her appearance the murderer of her reputation. Sheepmen saw her as inspired by an evil joy in slaughter. The mind that directed her was to them the cold and calculating instrument of a criminal. Now Tim saw her as a lonely old dingo scarred by pellets of shot, by traps and the teeth of hunters' dogs. He was a bit like that himself, he thought, but his scars didn't show. They lay beneath the confident smile, the pride in killing; hers denied him his pride.

'I'll bring you back her hide,' he had told them.

But when I kill her, he reflected, I kill myself. I'll go back to being an old-age pensioner. No more slaps on the back, shouting in pubs. No more invitations to stay at the homesteads of wealthy graziers. I'll return to my hut and die in my hut and that will be the end of it all.

He stood watching her, torn by indecision. He wanted to go on living with himself, he wanted to be able to walk with his head up, with dignity. When he did act it was with sudden desperation. Reason had bowed its head.

He seized a heavy stick and advanced upon her, his face twisted with an anguish his powerful arms denied. She waited for him, shrinking closer to the earth, her glaring eyes

The Three-Legged Bitch

desperate. The snarl she had held in silence now found voice in a vibrating growl of defiance and she sprang as he raised the stick aloft. She took up the slack of both chains in her spring and the blow he brought to the side of her head jerked her sideways as the tightened chains arrested her leap. She fell on her side to the ground, her head thrown back, her four legs taught and quivering.

He hit her again, not with frenzy but with a kind of despair, then turned and walked back to his mare. He suddenly felt old and tired and he walked stiffly. With his head resting against the saddle he drew deep breaths of replenishment until the cold sense of betrayal passed and he could stand erect.

He walked back to her body lying prone on the ground and released her paws from the grip of the traps. He dragged her to one side, her head bouncing loosely over the stones. Her worn teeth were bared in one last horrible grimace from which Tim turned his eyes.

He'd made up his mind. He buried her there beneath the tussocky grass and he did it with the same care he used in setting a trap. When he straightened up, the grass was waving in the mountain wind above her grave and the sheep track was the same as it was before he'd strewn it with death. Cloud shadows rippled up the mountain side like the quick and silent passing of her feet, and an eagle soared down the wind.

It was a good place to rest.

Christ, the Devil and the Lunatic

John Morrison

I was an atheist for several years before I met Hester, and never at any time during my courtship did I make a secret of it. She herself was a devout Anglican, and we married under an agreement that we would pursue separately our spiritual paths, and that our children would be taught to follow her. My paganism wasn't as clearly reasoned then as it is now. I couldn't, therefore, see how cruelly wrong it was to deliberately put into a child's mind beliefs which I myself had long ago rejected. Perhaps it was the influence of Hester herself. She was the serenest creature I have ever known, and I fell into the very forgivable error of ascribing her serenity to Faith. I wanted my children to grow up just like her.

Anyway, our arrangement worked very well, so well, indeed, that only once in all our married life have we had occasion to review it. That was when, in the bad year of 1931, I took a job as personal attendant to an imbecile.

It is of this that I wish to tell, because I believe it embodies an interesting, even if grim, study in the contentious subject of Faith.

We were living in Richmond at the time, with two children, and having a desperately thin time of it. I had been a musician in a picture theatre, but the arrival of the 'talkies' had put me out of a job, and for more than twelve months Hester and I had barely scratched an existence. My profession placed me at a tremendous disadvantage in competing for other kinds of work, and all that came my way was an occasional day's gardening and Saturday mornings helping a friend who owned a woodyard. I

Christ, the Devil and the Lunatic

had a few pounds saved, but they soon went, and before long we had to move out of our little cottage into a flat. Our clothes wore out; we became shabby. We lived on porridge, bread and jam, mincemeat, and cabbages and potatoes, considering ourselves fortunate indeed when we could afford a little butter or a few chops. Hester and I didn't mind much for ourselves, but it was hard seeing the children go short. They were both boys, six and eight years old, ages when there is no bottom to the appetite.

Through it all Hester was splendid. That congested flat, with the boys sleeping in the living room, and the constant worry of seeing that they didn't annoy other tenants, must have been heartbreaking for her after the little four-roomed cottage with its garden full of flowers and vegetables. All through two stifling summers she cooked at an open fireplace, for although we had a gas stove we found wood to be cheapest. Of a winter's night we used to go to bed very early, that being the only place where we could keep warm for nothing. Yet never once did I hear a word of complaint or criticism. Hester was the real true-blue Christian, consoling herself in adversity by reminding herself of those still worse off. Some knowledge of the real causes of social suffering made me bitter, but there were times when I envied my wife her faith. 'If ignorance is bliss, 'tis folly to be otherwise'. To me, the monster so euphemistically known as the Depression was something wholly horrible and unjust; to Hester it was but the working of a Divine Scheme. Now and again she would appeal to me to try to cultivate Faith, but that's impossible. Reason insisted that I was right and she was wrong. Yet, I repeat, I envied her, because Faith gave her peace and courage, however spurious, and thereby she suffered less than I the pagan.

All of which is not to suggest that she did not suffer at all. Perhaps deep in her indomitable heart she felt everything, but I was rarely allowed to see it. On returning home after a futile search for work—that was the time. A woman has a way of looking at a man then. Question and answer are so unnecessary. Hester would hear me coming, and always I would find her in some attitude of arresting action, facing the door, her expression a study of mingled hope and fear. One glance at me was always enough. We simply smiled at each other and didn't talk about it. What was the use?

One morning I saw in the paper an advertisement requiring the services of 'a respectable young man as attendant to a mental patient, afternoons only.' The position was, of course, far out of my line, but in the past year or so I had chased stranger jobs. I therefore wrote a letter begging the favour of an interview. That, as is well known, is the correct procedure. One 'begs'. Three hundred years ago, Rousseau lamented that 'Man, who was born free, is everywhere in chains.' He should see us now, begging for the chains.

However, the favour was granted me, and I kept an appointment at an address in Cotham Road, Kew. On enquiring for 'Mr Storey', according to instructions, I was shown by a housemaid into an apartment, half office and half sitting-room, where a little bald-headed man was writing at a desk. He attended to me immediately, laying down his pen and asking me abruptly, though quite civilly, if I had brought the originals of my references. I had. His keen eyes examined me frankly as I held them out. I liked him immediately. Experience had taught me that men who look straight at you and don't fumble for words are to be respected.

After the papers came the usual questions. How old was I? What occupations had I followed besides those mentioned in my testimonials? Was I an Australian? How long had I been out of work? Was I married?

To all except the last I returned a truthful answer, believing that as a single man I would stand a better chance of getting the job. When he asked me what I proposed to do with the rest of my time should he engage me, I knew he had already made up his mind. Here again, however, I deemed it wisest to prevaricate, saying that most of my mornings were already taken up. He gave me a searching look.

'The wage,' he said, 'is only one pound a week.'

I nodded, and he proceeded, without taking his eyes off mine: 'It's necessary that you should not be wholly dependent on this position. There are opportunities for — ah — ' He hesitated, then went on with a dry smile, 'It is, in a very modest way, a position of trust, Lewis. No considerable sum is involved, admittedly, but it is essential that I have an honest man. Your charge — his name is Peter Lawson — comes of very wealthy people, and an allowance of ten shillings per day is made solely

Christ, the Devil and the Lunatic

for his amusement. It will be one of your duties to handle that money.'

Mr Storey paused, as if to allow this to sink in. I remained silent, returning his gaze as frankly as I could.

He resumed: 'That ten shillings I will give to you each day, and you will lay it out as far as possible in accordance with Peter's fancies. Your job, in short, will be to take Peter out every afternoon and help him to spend his pocket money. Spend all of it, and manage it so that it lasts until it is time to come home.'

'What does he usually buy?' I naturally enquired.

Storey smiled and shrugged his shoulders. 'He spends it just as a child would, in Coles's emporium and in sundae shops. The job has its amusing side, I assure you. You'll come back every day full of chocolates and ice cream and loaded with toys and rubbishy knick-knacks. I'm taking it for granted that you have your own mind made up — you want the job?'

'I certainly do, Mr Storey.'

'Excellent. You'll find Peter erratic, difficult at times, but quite harmless. Take him round the shops with his few shillings and he won't give you much trouble. If he takes a fancy to something which is too dear, just tell him it costs two pounds. He'll believe you.' Here Storey leaned forward, solemnly wagging his forefinger at me for emphasis. 'Now listen carefully, for this is something you must thoroughly understand. Peter has a currency all his own. It has four values, and it would be useless to talk to him of any other. To him everything costs either six and elevenpence or two pounds, every coin is either a "penny" or a "silver penny", and every note is one pound. Anything which he can buy costs six and elevenpence; anything which he can't buy costs two pounds. Therefore — mark this particularly — it is not a ten shilling note which I give you each day, but a pound note. Be careful always to refer to it as a pound, because mention of anything else would only confuse and upset him. Get to know him as quickly as possible; he has many little peculiarities you must find out for yourself. The all-important thing in the treatment of the mentally afflicted is to avoid the unusual, keep to routine, amuse them without exciting them. Peter, like all of them, is inclined to be suspicious, but once you've gained his confidence you'll be able to do as you please with him.'

There was quite a lot more in the same strain. Storey was a

man with his whole heart in his work, and I had to sit listening to him with an appearance of absorbed interest while really I was itching to get away to break the glad news to Hester. For it was glad news. One pound a week was a tragically inadequate income, but at least it would secure rent and insurances. Besides, I still had every morning in which to look for a real job.

That night we had a modest celebration, squandering two precious shillings on pork chops, butter, and bananas.

'Perhaps this is the turning of the tide,' suggested Hester.

'Perhaps!' I assented dryly. 'To him that hath shall be given!'

'Cynic! The only time I ever hear you quoting the scriptures is when you wish to be sardonic.'

I was musing on the ten shillings a day squandered by a lunatic.

'Tomorrow,' I said thoughtfully, 'I'll help the idiot to eat ten shillings' worth of lollies; afterwards I'll come home and watch my children eat bread and treacle because I can't afford to give them butter.'

I was speaking more to myself than to Hester, but must have sounded particularly bitter, for she came round the table and laid her hands on my shoulders. 'Tom, you don't really look at it that way, do you?'

'It's a grand world! I know a little family — so do you! — not far from here, who have an imbecile child, and they love every hair of his head. The wouldn't part with him, although they've only got to say the word and he'd go into a Home tomorrow. They go short themselves to feed him the best. Peter's people have everything, but they won't suffer the indignity and inconvenience of having him attached to them. And I, because I have nothing, must shoulder their responsibility.'

'Last night,' said Hester quietly, 'we were in the dumps. There was no job at all, and we were talking of selling the bedroom suite and your mother's wedding present. Now we don't have to do that, and — you grumble.'

'But you must admit it's terribly unjust, dear,' I protested.

'To you, yes, because you see no object in it. Tom, we mustn't question. Let us be thankful, or even this little may be taken from us.'

'By Him who ordained in the first place that I receive it!'

Nevertheless, I was in good humour when, punctually at one

Christ, the Devil and the Lunatic

o'clock the next day, I presented myself at 'The Glen', as Mr. Storey's private mental hospital was called. Peter, all wriggles and smiles, was formally introduced to me and we set off immediately, the 'pound' note reposing hypocritically in my trousers pocket.

I'd had some novel jobs since leaving the theatre, but before we'd gone a hundred yards Peter had made it painfully clear that I had yet to learn how some poor devils make a living. Dignity, I decided sadly, must go by the board. Considerably bigger than myself, grotesquely ugly, and without a scrap of physical discipline, Peter Lawson was a living hell-broth of all the monsters I had ever read of. All through the first hour I was constantly expecting him to dilate his horse-like nostrils and wag his piggish ears; both feats would have been horribly becoming. His brutal and disorderly energy frightened me. He was like a villainous marionette out of control. He didn't walk; he lurched and staggered and shambled, rolling his head, swinging his arms, and flapping down his slovenly boots as if there were no feet in them.

Never as long as I live will I forget that first outing with Peter. The whole enterprise was so odd, so fraught with petty anxieties, and so utterly lacking in decorum, that the wonder is I didn't push the crazy fool under a tramcar. He was as stubborn as a cow, as clumsy as a baby, and as helpless as a dead dog. At Victoria Bridge, where we changed from an electric into a cable tram, he immediately made for a front seat so that he could pretend to be driving, with me hanging on to the seat of his trousers. At the Town Hall, where we alighted, I had to wait a full half hour before he got tired of watching the policeman on point duty. From there we turned north, pursuing a devious and troublesome course along the crowded pavements as far as the Royal Mail Hotel. Here, from the familiar display under the green tiled walls, Peter selected his first purchase — *Truth, Smith's Weekly,* and *Sporting Globe.* In a tone of peevish authority that made me sizzle with rage I was instructed to give the newsvendor six and elevenpence — and carry the papers!

A few minutes later at the Bourke Street Post Office he said he was tired, sat down, and began to scan one of the papers upside down. When, thinking to calm myself, I began to roll a cigarette he instantly demanded one.

'Sure. Have this one, Peter,' I said, holding it out.

But he insisted on making one himself, and I had to watch anxiously while he spilled my precious tobacco and mutilated several papers. Then, without the slightest warning, he got up and started off across the road. Faithfully I followed, up Bourke Street to Swanston Street, then southwards as far as the Capitol Theatre, where I was doomed to pass one of the most wretched hours of my life. Peter wanted to go in, and Storey's definite instruction was to keep him out of theatres.

'We'll go in here,' announced Peter with disarming confidence. I had been assured that he understood perfectly well this was forbidden ground, but would probably try to take advantage of a new custodian.

'They won't let us in there, Peter,' I replied. 'It costs two pounds.'

I kept walking, but the bluff didn't work, for when I looked back he was standing stiffly at the booking window glaring at me with an expression of sullen defiance. I returned.

'It's time we had something to eat, Peter,' I suggested hopefully. 'We can come back this way later.'

He indicated the painted beauty in the box, who, with the commissionaire, was watching us delightedly. 'Give her six and eleven. I'm going in.'

Argument, I now knew, was useless, so I settled down to try and wear him out. The commissionaire, who seemed to see nothing but humour in the situation, persuaded the accursed fool to stand away from the booking window, while I took up a position on the opposite wall. And there we remained for a whole agonizing hour. Now and then I took a turn up and down the pavement, or passed a word with the commissionaire, but Peter never once moved. Idiots must have the physical hardihood of religious fanatics, for Peter's posture was one I couldn't have sustained for ten seconds. Every time I caught his eyes he scowled.

'He's harmless, I suppose?' said the commissionaire.

'That depends on what you mean by harmless!' I fumed. 'I'm the dangerous one at the moment. If it doesn't move soon you can take it home and whack it up with the wife and kids!'

Heaven alone knows how long the stalemate would have lasted had not a group of lascar seamen come along. Their

Christ, the Devil and the Lunatic

outlandish costumes and excited yabberings and gesticulations completely bewitched Peter, drawing him as the Pied Piper drew the rats. And without as much as a glance at me he fell in behind and tailed them along the street. My luck seemed to have turned, for the seamen actually entered Coles, where Peter soon lost them in the crowd.

Any hopes I had, however, of an easy run home were soon dissipated, for it was in Coles that the real adventures of that day really began. Storey had warned me, but Peter far surpassed my most gloomy anticipations. He handled everything, wanted to buy everything, barged all over the place like a vulgar woman, giving voice every now and again to a crazy high-pitched cackle that made everybody stop to stare at us. He bought balloons and wanted them blown up on the spot. He bought a large kewpie, threw away the bag, and gave the damned thing to me to carry. He paid sixpence for a mouthorgan and created a traffic block trying to play it. He bought a box of tacks, went to count them, and spilled the lot. He bought a mousetrap and got his fingers caught trying to set it. Every purchase he immediately and ruthlessly divested of its wrapper. He bought a feather duster and began to sulk when I objected to being tickled with it. In an effort to restore his good humour I bought him a packet of petunia seeds. The pretty little envelope delighted him.

'That's cheap for six and eleven, eh?' he beamed, and promptly ripped off one end, scattering the tiny seeds on the floor.

We must have made a sensational picture when, about five o'clock, we came out onto Swanston Street again. Peter had the handle of the feather duster rammed down the front of his trousers, with the bunch of scarlet feathers ornamenting his chest. In one hand he held aloft a vivid and fully extended toy sunshade, in the other the mouthorgan on which he gaven an occasional hideous blast. From one jacket pocket protruded a packet of lunchwraps, from the other a smelly bundle of firelighters. My share was the kewpie, a wooden Mickey Mouse on a swing, a bottle of turpentine, and the newspapers. I was utterly exhausted, and trying hard to decide what to say to Mr. Storey when I got back.

I had yet to learn that Peter could keep it up until the final gong. While waiting for a tram at the intersection he discovered that something was pricking his leg. I had to run him over to the public lavatory near the Town Hall and take down his trousers. He must have rescued some of the tacks off Coles's floor, for I found several in his underpants. Coming back he insisted on buying a bunch of flowers, which he graciously gave me to carry. In Victoria Street his sunshade was blown away, and he made such a hullabaloo that the gripman stopped the tram while I raced back along the track. Then he took to playing with the Mickey Mouse, finishing up by stamping the thing to smithereens because it wouldn't work to his satisfaction. At Victoria Bridge I had to blow up the balloons and tie them with his bootlace, while all the way up Cotham Road he tickled me with the feather duster. Several people — more lunatics, I assumed — were in the grounds of 'The Glen' when we arrived, and I regarded it as an ominous sign that they took little notice of us. Mr Storey wasn't about, so I handed Peter over to an attendant and fled.

That night I told Hester everything. Dear girl! Her calm voice was celestial music to me after the crazy cackles of Peter.

'Tell me what you bought,' she said.

I named everything from the newspapers to the bunch of flowers. Every now and then she shook her head, murmuring sadly: 'God help him! God help him!'

'God undoubtedly is helping him!' I once replied shortly. In the sane atmosphere of my home I was quickly losing my ill humour, could even see something to chuckle at in Peter's antics. Nonetheless there was a rankling sense of injustice and ignominy that became stronger as I thought of it all. I said: 'A few hours ago, in Bourke Street, an ice-cream nearly choked me; you and the boys haven't tasted ice-cream for months.'

Hester looked at me reproachfully. 'Tom, you're brooding on this.'

'My dear, that only half describes it. I'm rebelling at a—a tyranny that's so terribly subtle one can hardly name it. I suppose a beetle feels like this when it's being poked around a box with a bit of stick. This afternoon Peter and I were Waste and Want parading hand in hand. Imagine it! That Frankenstein with a sunshade! Newspapers he can't read! A mousetrap he can't set! Fire-lighters, and no fire to light! Dolls, turpentine, flower seeds!'

I really was angry, but thank Heaven for the grace of

Christ, the Devil and the Lunatic

humour. Even as I spoke I saw again the ludicrous figure of Peter, trousers down over his boots, with his scarlet feathers and sunshade, patiently and smilingly waiting while I picked tacks out of his underpants. I burst out laughing, Hester joined in, and for the rest of the evening we talked of Peter only with pity and amusement. Hester appealed to me to be patient with him.

'It's only for a little while, dear,' she said. 'By and by we'll get over our troubles, but poor Peter will always be like that.'

I spent the following morning in the usual way, looking for work, and with the usual result. At one o'clock I returned to 'The Glen', feeling, no doubt, just as Daniel must have felt entering the lion's den.

That was the day Peter made love to me. At the Victoria Bridge tram terminus we had ice-creams, and for five minutes my precious lunatic studied me with a brooding and silent intensity that made me wonder what devil's scheme he was hatching now. He began the performance by sidling coquettishly along to the far end of the seat.

'I like you!' he announced with a mirthless smile.

'That's nice of you, Peter,' I replied cautiously.

'Do you like me?'

'Sometimes, when you're a good fellow and do as I tell you.'

He frowned. 'I like you all the time.'

'How much, Peter?'

The next instant I could have bitten my tongue off. Laying his Caliban's head on the back of the seat he half closed his eyes.

'I love you!' he whispered.

Two tram conductors standing within earshot tittered. I didn't mind that much, for they probably knew Peter. What did worry me was the question of where the little comedy was going to end. Evidently Peter had been overhearing things and was giving me the benefit of it. I tried to wriggle out of the trap by winking at him and nodding significantly in the direction of the conductors.

'You shouldn't tell me that now, Peter. Wait till we get on the tram.'

He scowled again. 'I'm not going on the tram.'

I exhibited the 'pound' note. 'What about this? Don't you want to see the shops?'

'I want to stay here with you. I love you.'

I went to get up, but he caught me by the arm, stretching his great bull neck and protruding his thick and slobbering lips. 'Kiss me!' he grunted.

I kissed him.

That same day he stopped outside a big delicatessen in Swanston Street and pointed to some saveloys. 'How much are they?'

'Two pounds each!' I gasped. 'Come on!'

His last tamer, however, must have indulged him, for he began to sulk. 'I want some.'

I defied him for a little while, but had to yield in the end. I bought three, which he promptly dragged out of the bag with a savageness that made me shudder. Fair in the middle of the crowded pavement he giggled and shook them at me, three wretched saveloys.

'How much were they?' he screamed.

'Six and eleven. Put them in your pocket. The dogs will snap at them.'

He cast a wild and predatory look at the shop window. 'I want some more.'

It was frightful. Five times he drove me into the shop, finishing up the proud owner of two dozen saveloys. In the midst of hilarious spectators I baulked at giving him the last lot.

'I'll carry these, Peter,' I said affably. 'The dogs—'

'I want them!' he bawled, snatching, and in an instant saveloys were strewn everywhere.

It takes the responsibilities of married life to develop self-control in a man. Thinking of Hester and the boys I cleared a ring while my poor idiot gathered up his precious bags of mystery. And off we set again, Peter with saveloys sticking out of every pocket and as many as he could clutch in his ape-like paws. Thus laden he made me steer him into Sargent's Cafe, where he dumped all the infernal things on a table and called for crumpets and tea. The wonder is that we were allowed in. Perhaps they took pity on me, for I must have looked pretty haggard. Staying there, however, was another matter. Peter followed his afternoon tea with a passionfruit ice and one of the seeds got under his top dental plate. I saw immediately what he was going to do, and reached out a restraining hand, but he shook me off.

'Leave me alone!' he screeched. 'I know what I'm doing.'

Everybody had stopped eating. From the far side of the cafe a manageress was watching me resentfully, but I was helpless. There was a barbaric violence about everything the idiot did that frightened me. So I just sat and simmered while he painstakingly cleaned the dental plate with his handkerchief. Then, just as he was about to return the thing to his mouth, he got one of those fantastic ideas which can come only to the utterly demented. His hysterical gaze fixed itself on the nearest saveloy, he gave a shrill crazed laugh, and before I could move a finger to stop him he jammed the teeth fair into it. And as if that weren't enough he had to whip out his lower plate, turn the saveloy over, and complete the bite on the other side, driving the teeth in with a thump of his fist that shook the table.

We were ordered to leave, of course. The manageress wanted to ring for the police, and only after some persuasion accepted my assurance that the situation was not quite out of control. I had to bribe Peter with chocolate eclairs before he consented to follow me out into Swanston Street. That used up the last of his money, yet at Victoria Bridge he refused to board the tram until I had bought him a cauliflower. That came out of my own money, as did the fares. Moreover I had to carry the caulifower, and between it and the saveloys our homecoming was little less spectacular than that of the previous day. We finished up with a magnificent dog-fight right outside 'The Glen', a pack of mongrels losing all interest in a little bitch to follow the trail of Peter's saveloys. It made my blood boil when Peter began to feed them, for in spite of all ill-treatment they were still good saveloys. I rescued four by pretenting to have a couple of poor starving dogs of my own at home.

Storey showed nice understanding when I told him of having spent some of my own money. He advised me to deduct it from the ten shillings next day.

'You find him a bit difficult?' he enquired.

'Mr Storey, the job's worth a pound a minute!' I replied vehemently. 'Couldn't you get his people to raise my pay a little?'

'My boy, I've already tried. Your predecessor asked for an increase, but I had to let him go, although he understood Peter as no one else has ever done.'

'And his people are wealthy!' I exclaimed bitterly. 'It's a hard world, Mr Storey.'

Quite kindly he laid a hand on my shoulder. 'Young man, never generalize about morality. The world's a very beautiful place, only it has some very mean things in it. It's a bad thing to get bitter at your age. Don't wait until too late, as so many of us do, to discover that the ideal philosophy is to make the best of things as you find them. Don't run your head against the inevitable. Understand?'

I understood I was being lectured, but didn't mind that very much, even though I found the argument rubbish. Storey had a way with him. His steady friendly gaze had a soothing effect on me after the crazy antics of Peter.

I nodded resignedly. 'I took the job at a pound a week, and if I'm not satisfied I don't need to stay, eh?'

My tone was still bitter, but he replied patiently: 'It comes to that, although I'd be sorry to lose you. The situation is that Peter's people allow three pounds a week for his pocket and one pound for special attendance, and I've been unable to get them to improve on it. You see I admit the position is worth more.'

'It ought to be one pound for his pocket and three pounds for special attendance,' I said. Storey's candour, however, had got the better of me, and I smiled. 'Thanks for the admission, anyway!'

He gave me a friendly pat. 'Go home and refresh yourself, my boy. Troubles are always a little smaller when you've rested and eaten. Ask for me tomorrow if there's anything you want to tell me.'

Not until I laid the four rescued saveloys on the table at home did I observe that one of them bore the clear imprint of Peter's teeth. Thank Heaven again for the gift of humour. My first impulse was to throw out all four, but when I got to telling Hester about the scene in the cafe, I had to laugh, and the three unblemished specimens went into the pan. Hester laughed also, but afterwards I knew by her subdued air and the thoughtful glances she kept giving me exactly how she felt about it all. She gave the boys one each and made to lay the other on my plate.

'No thanks,' I said. 'I've had all sorts this afternoon. You have it.'

She demurred at first, but gave in when I insisted, and began to eat. Watching her covertly I saw a pathetic study in the martyrdom of pride. She really did carry her scruples to

Christ, the Devil and the Lunatic

ridiculous lengths. Those saveloys had been begged for; I had used cunning and falsehood in order to wheedle them off a helpless idiot. For her, therefore, they held no relish. On the other hand she knew also at what cost to my own dignity they had been acquired, and wanted to eat to please me.

'They're not very tasty without sauce,' I remarked drily.

She smiled weakly. 'It's quite nice. I just don't seem to be very hungry tonight.'

I knew better, though, and without speaking picked the saveloy off her plate and threw it into the bucket under the sink. She uttered no protest, and as I sat down again her hand stole across the table and settled gratefully upon mine.

'I was thinking of you, Tom,' she said quietly.

Nevertheless, I didn't regret bringing the infernal things home, for the boys enjoyed their portions. Later, when we were alone, Hester and I fell into discussing the problem of living. We rarely talked of anything else those days, for nothing else mattered. All the talking in the world won't increase one's income or bring down the cost of commodities, yet in the anxieties of poverty it is impossible to leave the subject alone. One returns to it again and again in the wretched unreasoning hope that, perhaps, on investigation things will prove to be not quite as bad as appeared.

Therein, incidentally, lies the explanation of the comparative lack of fine taste in the working class. For, in the name of Creation, how can a man give his mind to exalted things when his boots are worn through and his belly empty? Anxiety is the great sickness of the lowly, for no organic disease causes more universal suffering than the prolonged and dreadful scheming to make ends meet, and the abiding fear of what tomorrow may fail to bring forth.

That night Hester suggested quite seriously that I give up the job. She contended that it was doing us no good, that even in two days I had become horribly cynical and irritable.

'Confess,' she said, 'that it hurts you to help Peter spend that money. You're brooding over it. You think it outrageous that the poor fellow should waste it so when we and so many others are in serious want.'

'Yes, in want!' I echoed emphatically. 'Our boys are at an age when they should be building constitutions to see them right through life. And they aren't doing it. They hardly know the taste of eggs, while that pop-eyed barbarian—'

'At least they're sane, Tom. It's God's will—'

I made an impatient gesture. 'That's all very well, my dear, but I can't see God's purpose. Less than ten shillings a day would raise two useful citizens, yet what have we? Good meat thrown to the dogs! Mousetraps! Sunshades! Flowers! I can't grasp it at all.'

Hester eyed me sadly. 'If only you believed!'

I kept silent, because she'd have been hurt by the only thing I could honestly have said.

'Don't go back, Tom. It isn't worth it,' she said a moment later.

'The rent,' I reminded her.

'We'll manage somehow. We'll sell the suite. Something must come along soon.'

'No.' I was beginning to feel ashamed, and made an effort to throw off the black reflections which oppressed me. 'I'm not grumbling at the job itself, sweetheart, as much as at the—the wicked—oh, ethics of it all. It's so preposterous. But never mind. The point just now is that you're broke?'

She smiled ruefully. 'I have fivepence, and there's hardly anything in the house. I thought Mrs. Baker would have paid me today, but she said she didn't have it. Fivepence to get lunch and tea with tomorrow. You'll have to try to bring something in yourself if Peter pays you.'

Mrs. Baker was a neighbour for whom she sometimes did a little sewing.

'I'll pay myself,' I said grimly.

It was Wednesday night. Counting what I had loaned Peter, we had exactly thirty pence on which to live until Friday.

On the following morning Mr. Storey's greeting was particularly affable. Obviously he was out to placate me, and I wasn't surprised when, in the course of the short conversation, he admitted that the position was one which he had experienced some difficulty in keeping filled. After I'd listened patiently to another of his invigorating 'tonic talks', he cautioned me not to mention my little debt to Peter.

'Just take what is due to you and put it in a separate pocket. He wouldn't understand if you attempted to explain, and it isn't in the least necessary.' He gave me one of those warm frank stares that I found so attractive. 'It should do you no harm to learn that I liked the way you told me about that last night.'

'I had to recover it, Mr. Storey. I'm broke.'

'That isn't what I meant. Some fellows wouldn't have mentioned it at all. They'd just have taken it, probably a bit more than their due. And the temptation to repeat the practice would have been irresistible. I know now that I'm dealing with a very straightforward man. That's why I don't want to lose you.'

He wouldn't have said that had he known what was in my mind. I thanked him, passed some inept remark about thieves never prospering, and felt a miserable hypocrite. Between thoughts of Hester and Storey, and the usual antics of Peter, I passed a mentally strenuous day. Paganism doesn't imply immorality. In all my life I'd never been guilty of stealing, and the certain knowledge that two very good people had unbounded faith in my integrity made my first transgression infinitely difficult. The fact is, however, that I did transgress. Perhaps if Peter had been at all merciful that day I would have remained honest, but he made me carry a bowl of goldfish and a bundle of rhubarb all the way from Victoria Market to the Town Hall, and — the Devil won.

That evening Hester and I had our first really serious difference when, on returning home, I laid five packages on the table. Suspecting nothing at first, she gave me the customary kiss, told me to sit down and rest for a few minutes before washing, and turned to inspect my purchases.

'You seem to have got good value,' she remarked smiling.

The boys were climbing all over me, but I hardly noticed them. Hester's smile didn't last long. There was half a pound of butter, a pound of lamb chops, six eggs, two pounds of apples, a pound of tomatoes, and a wholemeal loaf. She looked at them for quite a minute, turning them over again and again, no doubt totalling up their cost, before turning her puzzled face to mine.

'Wherever did you get them, Tom?'

'I earned them.'

'But how?'

'Taking care of a raving maniac for four benighted hours!'

The boys transferred their attentions to the packages. I got up, and with affected unconcern began to take off my collar and tie. But Hester took hold of me by the arms, turning me around so that I was forced to look down into her face.

'Tom, you used Peter's money?'

I understand better now just what it meant to her, but at the time the implied reproach seemed outrageous. I'd anticipated something of the sort, but had hoped that she would, at least, let us all enjoy a good meal and postpone discussion until the boys were in bed.

'Look here, Hester,' I said, 'there's less than four shillings' worth of tucker there, and I've earned it a thousand times over in the last few days. We haven't had a decent meal for weeks. There's one there, and nobody else a hoot the worse off—'

'It's stealing, Tom, no matter how you like to look at it.'

'Hush, the boys are listening!' Annoyance came quickly, for I'd been reasoning the thing out all the afternoon and was thoroughly convinced of the justice of what I had done. I believed that only a coward or a religious fanatic would have acted otherwise. Nevertheless I controlled myself, and fell to appealing. My immediate concern was to get the frying pan onto the fire and see Hester and the boys digging into the chops. Even now Dick and Bob were clamouring for apples. I told them to help themselves, and tilted my wife's chin so that her worried face was raised to mine.

'Couldn't we eat now and talk afterwards? Maybe I'll promise not to do it again.'

'You meant to do this when you went out this morning.'

'I did. Are we going to eat, or shall I throw them out? I can't return them either to the shops or to Peter.'

'Please don't be angry with me, Tom. I can't help it. I never thought—I didn't want to come down to this. We—' She broke off, biting her lip, on the point of tears.

Torn between pity and exasperation I clasped her to me, and for some moments we stood thus in silence. Dick, the eldest boy, asked me with a mouth full of apple what was wrong with Mummy, and I told him to shut up. It's a wicked thing to snub a child, and his timid and curious gaze as he backed away cut me to the heart. My eyes fell on the contentious packages. Beyond them there seemed to hover, ugly and menacing, the distorted image of Peter. I felt his vile presence, I heard his insane laugh. I tasted again his graveyard kiss, and reflected that since then I

Christ, the Devil and the Lunatic

had kissed Hester. Strange fears gripped me. I sensed contamination and calamity. Peter had followed me home! Something nameless and unclean was in the air, and with a smothered curse I tore loose from my wife's arms.

'Tom, what are you going to do?'

'I'm going to do what you want me to do. Willingly! Hand me that bucket, Dick!'

'No, you musn't! Please —' Hester, with tears streaming down her face, fastened her arms around me again. 'Tom! Wait . . . I'll cook them! Don't throw them out . . . please . . . this once . . . we can talk it over. Dear . . . listen to me! . . . I was selfish . . . I wasn't thinking of the boys . . . I know you did it for them . . .'

I had one hand free and had already swept some of the things into the bucket before self-control returned. Hester and the boys were clinging to me, coaxing and whimpering. The whole scene was horrible, so foreign to our home. The simple fact is that we had momentarily broken down. Two years of ceaseless anxiety, that was it. People can't live under such conditions without changing. We had, without knowing it, got to that stage where any sudden emotional strain was liable to precipitate collapse. In Hester collapse took the form of fear and despair; in me it awakened a fiend of hate and destruction. I wanted, more than anything else, to get my hands on something I hated . . . to rend, to smash, to destroy. If, by any extraordinary trick, Peter had walked into that room just then I would have killed him.

But Peter didn't walk in, and firmly disengaging myself from Hester I sat down. She, poor girl, turned the chops into the frying pan and the butter into a dish with a haste that shamed me. I watched her in silence, feeling inexpressibly weary and nauseated. Everything oppressed me all at once — the cramped room with the wretched remains of our furniture, Hester's shabby frock and down-at-heel shoes, the threadbare tablecloth, the frayed sleeves of Dick's jersey, the patches in Bobby's pants, and more than anything else, the long vista of Tomorrows . . . poverty, anxiety, little hopes, big disappointments. We seemed to have travelled so far from the little cottage in Powlett Street.

Meanwhile Hester was busy. The table was laid, bread was cut, the chops sizzled. I caught her anxious sidelong look, and not knowing what to say I got up, rolled up my sleeves and went out to wash.

Neither of us referred to the matter as we sat down and began to eat. We talked, of course, but it was the boys who got things going and brought us back to normal. Children are great peacemakers, and in the irresponsible chatter of Dick and Bob, Hester and I found ourselves again. At the same time the meal was hardly a success. It was the case of the saveloys all over again. Hester smiled whenever I looked at her, but I knew her too well to be deceived. I still believed that I had done right, but her scrupulous loyalty to her Faith compelled respect. This, I knew, was an issue on which she would never yield.

Later, when the boys were asleep, there came the reckoning. For half an hour I read a newspaper and my wife knitted without either of us saying a word. Each of us was waiting for the other to begin, and I was relieved when she asked quietly, without looking up:

'Were you very angry with me tonight, Tom?'

'I wasn't angry with you at all,' I replied. 'I was simply exasperated at the predicament we found ourselves in.'

She knitted for a minute or two. Then, in the same quiet tone: 'What are you going to do about it?'

Welcoming this straightforward approach, I laid aside my paper. 'If you mean am I going to rob Peter again, the answer is no. Not without your full approval, anyway. I don't want any more scenes like that one. They're right out of our line.'

Hester gave me a caressing glance. 'It was horrible, Tom.' She came and sat beside me, laying her hand on mine. 'You must give in to me in this, dear. You must promise not to do it again.'

'Of course I promise, but under protest!'

'But this is so unlike you. You used to be so . . . so fussy. It's stealing, no matter how you try to justify it. You'd keep on doing it, and there'd be so little difference between stealing from somebody else. You'd take away the only precious things we have left, our pride and honesty. Don't you value them?'

'Hester,' I replied confidently, 'I haven't stopped thinking of this for twenty-four mortal hours. And for the life of me I can't see how I'm offending God or hurting anyone on earth. Peter went home today as happy as a schoolboy. Mind you, I am giving in; I won't touch his money again. But I still maintain that all this fuss is uncalled for. Our first duty is to those two children.'

'That's just what I'm concerned about, only we see it in

different ways. I wish you'd never taken this job.'

'So did I a couple of hours ago. I had an uneasy feeling that Peter had somehow got between you and me. But I've been turning it all over again. We're still soft, kid, that's what's wrong with us. We're too sensitive, too conscientious. We'll have to toughen up or we'll go under. Christianity wasn't made for this social order. The great captains of industry they talk about . . . Professors of Exploitation I call them . . . are they Christians?'

'Christianity was made for all time,' murmured Hester sadly. The simple sentence was spoken with a depth of sincerity and conviction that almost awed me.

'If Christ came back to earth tomorrow,' I exclaimed bitterly, 'there'd be a bigger clean up than ever there was in the Temple.'

'Christ is always with us.'

'I can't believe it, my dear. If He sees all this, and is indeed omnipotent, then what is His object? All this inequity, and useless suffering. Why, why, why?'

Hester's hand came up reprovingly. 'Tom, you promised . . .'

'I promised never to attack religion. True, but . . .'

'Wait! We can leave religion out of it. There's something else. Do you want me to think of you as a thief?'

'A man isn't a thief when, in order to feed his family, he takes what no one else needs.'

'His family doesn't want it. Yes, I'm speaking for the boys too.' Hester spoke confidently and quickly, as if afraid of losing the thread of her argument. 'I want them to grow up respecting you. They needn't know the truth, I admit, but I couldn't bear hiding something from them that I was ashamed for them to know. And if I'm to teach them, then I must respect you myself. I want to keep on admiring you, as I've always done. I don't mind going hungry, you must know that by now. And it hurts me as much as it does you to see the boys going short. But, Tom, it can't last forever. Work must come sooner or later, and then we must have nothing to regret. We've lost so much; let us, at least, keep our self-respect. There's Mr. Storey too. Don't you value his confidence? He also trusts you. You told me Storey gives an impression of honesty. Those were your very words. That doesn't spring from nothing, you know. Storey *is* honest. Don't you want to impress people in the same way? Storey trusts you. How could you look him in the face if you were secretly betraying that trust? If the temptation is too much for you then give up the job.'

'Not on your life!'

'You intend to go on with it?'

'I do.'

'And you'll play fair?'

'I'll play fair . . . according to the lights of society!'

Hester smiled ruefully. 'I know you're not a bit impressed by what I've said. Still, you've made a promise, even if it was . . .'

'Extorted!' I smiled. I was weary of the whole business, and wanted to put Peter right out of mind until tomorrow.

'Some day you'll be glad I . . . kept you in order. We've had some bad luck, and God will reward us.'

I laughed. 'They say the Devil also looks after his own!' And before she could reply I had caught her in my arms and closed her lips with a kiss.

'You're a frightful heathen, Tom,' she gasped a moment later.

'And you're a darling to bear with me!'

Hester's relief at what she regarded as a victory over sin must have infected me, for there was a happier atmosphere in the home than there had been for many a long day. Later in the evening she asked me for some music, and I wiped the dust from my long-neglected violin and played to her. Afterwards we fell to talking over old times, of the cottage in Powlett Street, of the flowers we used to pick from the tiny garden, of Sunday mornings when we used to loaf in our pyjamas on the sunlit back verandah, of Saturday nights, when Hester always used to come to the theatre and walk home with me. Great days. Talking of them didn't make us at all sad, and we went to bed with the firm, though quite unreasonable, conviction that better times really must come soon.

Better times did come, but not until three months later. In those three months three forces combined to torment me: Christ, the Devil, and the Lunatic. Christ in the faith of Hester, the Devil in the temptation provided daily by Peter's money, and Peter himself. I knew no peace, but that one pound a week was indispensable, and I carried on. Never again did I appropriate a penny of Peter's money. Every weekday for three months I took him out and deliberately squandered ten beautiful shillings. It was grotesquely infamous. Often I came home sick from eating

Christ, the Devil and the Lunatic

ice-creams and chocolates to sit down with Hester and the boys to a meal of tea and bread and jam. For I reasoned that the more Peter and I ate the less conspicuous would we be. Better a shilling's worth of candy in my stomach than a balloon or a bundle of rhubarb in my hands. Each day I could have taken two shillings out of Peter's allowance without him being a whit less content, for I acquired quite an art of interesting him in cheap trifles.

'Spend it all every day,' Storey had said, and faithfully I did spend it all. It was criminal. I got to a stage when meals at home were an ordeal, when I would sit gloomily reflecting: 'And we could be eating meat and vegetables, perhaps even a pudding. And eggs for breakfast!'

There was the indignity of the job, too. Most nights I came home looking like an idiot myself — grimy, perspiring, and dishevelled. No wonder Hester told me I was losing pride in myself. She said I was getting vulgar and careless. A score of times she begged me to give up, but there was nothing else and I would tell her gruffly to let the matter rest. We talked little of an evening. As often as not I fell asleep on the sofa. We took each day as it came, a makeshift hand-to-mouth existence. Storey's one pound a week paid rent, firewood, and insurance. For the rest we depended on what Hester could pick up with her needle and I at odd jobs.

The end came with a completeness that sent us both almost hysterical with joy. A friend got me a position in a warehouse in Flinders Lane at four pounds a week. Constant work at four pounds a week! Hester handed me a letter with the glorious news when I came in one day, and we did a jig round the table with the boys watching us in bewilderment. Four pounds a week! It was explained, moreover, that I was to begin as soon as possible. It was then Tuesday night and, quite naturally, I decided to drop Mr. Storey and Peter there and then, and begin the new job next morning. By so doing I would collect two pounds on Friday night instead of Storey's one. When Hester began preaching to me about fair play in regard to Mr. Storey I exploded:

'Hang Mr. Storey! Would he consider himself obliged to give me warning if he had no further use for me?'

'You needn't take your morals from other people, Tom,' she replied quietly. 'In your own heart you know what's right, and you must do it.'

'My first duty is to provide for this home. Mr. Storey comes second.'

'Your duty is to do as your conscience tells you. Mr. Storey has treated you fairly. He trusts you. Tomorrow he will be waiting for you . . .'

'He'll just have a job to fill. That'll be easy, with a thousand other unfortunates choosing between looking after Peter, or starving.'

'It isn't worth it, dear. Give him notice tomorrow and finish on Friday night. God has sent you work; let us be grateful. We've come through without being unkind to anyone. Don't betray a trust for a paltry twenty shillings.'

'A paltry twenty shillings!' I ejaculated.

Still, she prevailed, as she always had. My ultimate capitulation was, I suppose, only a just reward for her fortitude. Her example throughout had been so consistently brave that it would have been unkind to ignore this final appeal.

At nine-thirty on Wednesday morning, therefore, I presented myself at Mr. Storey's establishment. The throwing up of a thoroughly detested job is, I declare, one of the few pleasures of life exclusive to the working man, and that summer morning I gave myself over to it with epicurean enthusiasm. This was my moment, and I lived it. I had a job, a real job, dignified and remunerative, and I approached 'The Glen' warm with the wine of independence.

A housemaid, immaculate in black and white even at that hour, answered my ring and I asked if I might see Mr. Storey. She thought Mr. Storey was busy just then with one of the patients, but if I would step inside for a moment she would take him a message. She knew me, of course, but I didn't tell her my business.

'Just ask if I could have a few words with him, please,' I said. 'It's important, but I won't keep him long.'

She departed, returning in less than a minute to say that Mr. Storey could not come immediately but if I would wait in his office he would be glad to see me as soon as he was at liberty.

Grandly assuring her that time was of no value to me that morning, I allowed myself to be shown into the same cosy little room where, twelve weeks ago, I had had that momentous initial

Christ, the Devil and the Lunatic

interview. Here, after seeing me settled in an easy chair, and indicating with a friendly smile the morning paper lying on the desk, the housemaid left me.

I didn't touch the paper. In a mood of luxurious indolence, I just lay backwards, heaved a sigh of contentment, and fell to musing on Mr. Storey's charming office. It was comfortable, simple, and above all orderly, like the man himself. Nothing ornate, nothing superfluous, nothing out of harmony with the whole. A settee in the window recess, three easy chairs and a plain chair, a plain green carpet, a big cedar bookcase. On the mantelpiece two white plaster casts of classical figures, a pair of Chinese vases, and a marble clock. Lastly the desk, with its daily calendar, its stationery rack, inkstand and blotter, and morning's mail . . . the latter opened and sorted into two or three neat piles ready to begin work on.

I felt a pang of envy. Everything breathed rest and security, the workroom of a man at peace with himself and all the world. Outside birds were singing in the garden, and faintly I could hear the clatter of dishes in the diningroom. It was odd to reflect that this was a mental hospital. By turning sideways I could read the titles of some of Storey's books: Lord Avebury's *Pleasures of Life*, *The Meditations of Marcus Aurelius*, Wordsworth's *Poems*, and an apparently complete set of the works of Henri Fabre the great French naturalist. Here again was something characteristic of the man — simple philosophy, simple poetry, simple science, elementary textbooks on exalted subjects. It was easy to picture Storey taking down the *Meditations* and conning it, leisurely and reverently, by the fireside of a winter's night. What a contrast to the life I had been living during the past three months! It came to me suddenly with terrific force that this room had been just like this all the time. That afternoon, for instance, at the very moment when Peter had sunk his mouthless teeth into the saveloy, this room had been just like this. A little pool of peace and knowledge, with the muffled songs of birds, and the sunlight, filtering through the trees in the garden, making a pattern on the half-drawn curtains. Just like this.

I think it was at this stage in my reflections that my eyes fell on the name 'Peter' occurring on the top sheet of one of the little piles of correspondence. Had it been any other name I probably wouldn't even have noticed it. As it was, though still quite idly, I

Australian Short Stories

read the few words immediately following. They interested me. I looked at the address at the top. Then at the signature at the end. Finally, with a peculiar tingling sensation at the roots of my hair, I slowly read the letter right through. It was as follows:

'Dear Mr. Storey, — I thank you for your letter dated January 14th. It came as a surprise to me to learn that it has been necessary to engage a new attendant. Peter is, I well know, a big handful, but in these hard times I would have thought the remuneration sufficient to retain the services of any man seriously mindful of his welfare. It is unfortunate you did not inform me immediately of Arthur's impending departure, as I have lately been involved in some financial loss and find it necessary to curtail Peter's expenditure. As you are aware I have always allowed more than I was legally obliged to, but circumstances now compel me to come down to the exact terms of Father's will. It would have been convenient if the new attendant had been engaged on those terms; nevertheless an adjustment must be made. Will you, therefore, inform him that his wage is forthwith reduced from forty to thirty shillings per week? Peter, on his part, must content himself with ten shillings per day instead of the fifteen he has been accustomed to. This latter is, of course, a matter for yourself alone.

I am sorry to have to impose on you what will doubtless be an unpleasant duty, but I have no alternative. Will you please inform me of the working of the new arrangement as early as possible? I will be in Melbourne on business some time in April and will make a point of seeing you.

Yours faithfully,
Herbert Lawson.'

Comment on the letter is unnecessary. Before leaving that room I compelled Storey, under threat of exposure, to hand over to me a cheque for all the money he had wrongly appropriated while I was in the job, a total of thirty pounds. Hester still thinks I won it on a racehorse, for I never had the heart to tell her the truth. I've never been a racing man, and she hasn't even yet got over her amazement at the one little flutter I was unable to resist.

The Incense Burner

John Morrison

It was a one-way trip, and I paid off in London in the middle of winter with twenty pounds in cash, a wristwatch worth fifteen pounds, and a good kit of clothes, half on my back and half in a suitcase. And a fair bit of experience for my nineteen years.

I put up at somebody's 'Temperance Hotel' near King's Cross Station because I was sick of the drunken orgies that had marked every port of call coming over from Australia, and was knocked up at eleven o'clock the first night by a housemaid innocently armed with dust-pan and empty bucket who asked me if there was anything I wanted. There wasn't. That also was something I'd got sick of on the way over.

At the end of a fortnight I had added something to my experience and was down to thirty shillings, a pawn-ticket in place of the watch, and the suitcase, still with contents. So I left the hotel, took a room in a seamen's lodging-house down near the East India Docks, and started to look for a ship home.

I wasn't long in finding out that I'd left my gallop a bit late. In 1929 a seaman looking for a ship out of London needed something better than thirty shillings and a brand-new discharge book. I had only one entry in my book, and Second Engineers and shipping officials weren't impressed. Thousands of good men were haunting the docks every day. Real seamen, with lifetimes of experience behind them, and rubbed old books to prove it. I came to the conclusion after a few days that my book was more of a handicap than a help. I'd had enough of London, and I wanted a ship bound for Australia and nowhere else. And my book made it all too clear. Second Engineers and Second

Mates used to flick it open, drop the corners of their lips, and pass it back to me with a dry smile. I had it written all over me — Adelaide to London. They wanted men for a round voyage, not homesick Australians who would skin out at the first port touched.

I lasted two weeks; ten shillings a week for my room and ten shillings the fortnight for food. I did it by getting in sweet with a ship's cook, a Melbourne man, on one of the *Bay* ships laid up for repairs. I got breakfast out of the black pan every blessed day of the fortnight. Sometimes tea, too, until he told me not to make it too hot.

There were some good feeds, but not nearly enough, and it was all very irregular, and I was only nineteen, and as fit as they come, and walking up to fifteen miles every day, and I got hungrier and hungrier. There were days when I could have eaten my landlady. She was a skinny, sad-looking woman with bulging fish's eyes and a rat-trap mouth. I thought she was the toughest thing I'd ever met in my life. I was out all day every day, and on the rare occasions when I saw her she didn't seem to care whether she spoke to me or not. I used to turn in fairly early and lie reading, and until a late hour every night I could hear the thumping of a smoothing-iron in the kitchen at the far end of the passage. She was a widow; with only one other lodger, a pensioner, she had to support herself by taking in washing. It was a dark, silent, dismal hole of a place, smelling perpetually of wet clothes and yellow soap.

I saw the other lodger only once, an old man in a beard and long overcoat, vanishing into his room as I came in one night. I heard him often enough though. Too often. He had one of those deep, rumbling coughs that seem to come all the way up from the region of the stomach. He would go for minutes on end without stopping. He used to wake me up every night. Sometimes I thought he was going to suffocate.

His name was Burroughs — 'old Burroughs' to Mrs. Hall. I knew nothing about him — or about Mrs. Hall either, if it came to it — until my last day in the house. I had sevenpence-ha'penny left, and the rent of my room was due that night. It was a cold, raw day with skies you could reach up and touch, and a threat of snow. In the morning I did the usual round of the docks, missed out on a last feed on the *Bay* ship, and went back to

The Incense Burner

Finch Street to tell Mrs. Hall I was leaving. I'd had to recognize the fact that I was well and truly on the beach; that there was nothing for it now but the Salvation Army 'Elevator', an institution about which I'd heard plenty in the past two weeks.

I was to learn that day that my landlady's forbidding manner was nothing more than a front deliberately built up over years of contact with tough London seamen. She had a heart of gold, but like a lot of good people had become afraid to let the world see it.

She talked to me at the kitchen door, and as I told her what I was going to do she stared past me down the length of the short passage with her grim little mouth tightly shut and an expression of sullen bitterness on her dour face. I felt I was telling her an old and familiar and hated story. She must have seen a lot of defeated men in her time. Behind her was a table piled with washing; two or three ramshackle chairs, a linoleum with great holes rubbed in it, and a stove with several old-fashioned irons standing at one side.

'It's a damned shame, that's what it is,' she burst out with a vehemence that startled me. 'Good, clean, respectable, young men walking the streets.' She sniffed and tossed her head. For a moment I thought she was going to cry. Instead she asked me in for a cup of coffee. 'I was just going to make one. It'll warm you up.'

It was the worst coffee I'd ever tasted, half a teaspoonful of some cheap essence out of a bottle, mixed with boiling water. And a slice of bread to eat with it. Stale bread spread thinly with greasy margarine. But I was cold and hungry, and friendly words went with it. God help her! It was all the hospitality she could offer me. One glance around that wretched room convinced me that I had been living better than her.

I told her I didn't want to take any good clothes into the hostel with me, and asked could I leave my suitcase with her until my luck turned.

'You can leave anything you like. Only no responsibility, mind you.' She went on to tell me that she never knew from one day to another who she was going to have under her roof, and in the middle of it there came a muffled sound of coughing from along the passage. She stopped to listen, holding her breath and pulling a face, as if she were actually experiencing some of the old man's distress. 'I'm not saying anything about *him*. He's all right. I can go out and leave anything lying around. Poor old soul! There's many a time I give him a cup of coffee, and I'll swear to God it's the only thing that passes his lips from morn till night. Where he gets to when he goes out . . .'

'He's pretty old, isn't he, Mrs. Hall?'

'Not that old. He was in the war. He's a sick man, that's what's wrong with him. One of these days I'll wake up and find I've got a corpse on my hands. You just ought to be here when he gets one of his foreign parcels.'

'Foreign parcels?'

Mrs. Hall finished her coffee, got up, and began sorting the things on the table. 'Don't ask me where it comes from. He never tells me anything, and I never stick my nose into another body's business. But he's got somebody somewhere that hasn't forgotten him. Every few months he gets this parcel. Not much — a pair of underpants or socks, or a muffler — just bits of things. And a little bundle of dry leaves, herbs for his cough I suppose. My God, you just ought to smell them! He burns them in a bit of a tin pan he's got. They stink the house out. And there he sits and just sucks it in. It's beyond me how he can stand it. I've got to get out till he's finished.'

Mrs. Hall sniffed and blew, as if the smell of the herbs from the foreign parcel were in her nostrils even then. °'He's been here three months, and if it wasn't for that I wouldn't care if he stopped for three years. He never bothers nobody, and he keeps his room like a new pin. I've never yet seen him with drink in, and that's a change from some of them I get here, you mark my words. I know *you're* not the drinking kind, otherwise I wouldn't have asked you in here.'

Poor Mrs. Hall!

She wished me good luck and promised to keep my suitcase in her own room until I came back for it.

Travelling light, I walked all the way to the Salvation Army headquarters in Middlesex Street, stated my case to a 'soldier' just inside the door, and was sent over to an elderly grey-haired 'officer' seated at a desk piled with papers. All this happened a long time ago, and many of the details are hazy, but I'm left with an impression of newness, of spacious floors, of pleasant faces, of friendly efficiency.

The Incense Burner

The officer asked me what it was I wanted them to do for me. I told him.

'I'm an Australian. I worked my way over as a ship's trimmer. I wanted to see London: you know how it is. Now I'm broke, and I'm looking for a passage back home. I've got to find somewhere to live while I look for a ship.'

'Where have you been living?' Nothing inquisitorial about the question. He was taking quiet stock of me all the time. I had no reason to deceive him, but I felt it would be a waste of time anyway, that I was dealing with a man full of experience.

'In lodgings down in Custom House near the East India Docks. I've got to get out tonight, though; I haven't a shilling left.'

'You didn't jump your ship, did you?'

Only a man who knew sailors would have asked me that. 'No, I've got a clean book.' My hand went to my pocket, but he stopped me with a gesture.

'It isn't necessary for me to pry into your affairs, my boy. You understand that if you go into the Elevator you won't have much time to look for a ship?'

'I know I'll have to work, but that's all right. I could get some time off now and then, couldn't I?'

'Yes, as long as you did your task. But that's the responsibility of the commandant down there.' He reached out and picked a form off a little pile at his side. 'I'll give you a note to take down. I can't promise he'll have room for you, but it's worth while trying. What's your name?'

'Thomas Blair.'

'Do you know where Old Street is?'

They took me in, and for a little over three weeks I earned food and lodging by sorting waste string at the establishment known as the Elevator, down in Spitalfields.

It was the strangest three weeks I have ever experienced, and the most generally hopeless company of men I was ever mixed up with. There were about forty of us, of whom perhaps twenty were professional tramps wintering in. Of the others, fellows in circumstances more or less similar to my own, I got an impression that only a few were still trying to get their heads above water again. Conversation was not primarily around the prospect of finding employment, as I expected it to be, but around the petty incidents of the day, that evening's bill of fare, a certain current murder trial, and every triviality of hostel administration they could think up. At the time, I was thoroughly contemptuous of it all, but I understand better now. Those men had had a lot more of London than I had; I was still fresh to the struggle . . .

We worked nine hours a day; seven-thirty in the morning until five-thirty in the evening, with an hour off for dinner.

I was never able to find out why they called the place the Elevator, unless because it was intended as an elevator of fallen men. That's likely enough, but I'm not sure that it worked out in practice. I'm not questioning the good faith of the Salvation Army officers charged with its administration, but the prevailing atmosphere was far from elevating. On the first morning a short conversation with my immediate bench-mate served to reveal in a flash the spirit permeating the entire establishment.

'Been in before?' he asked me.

'No.'

'Stopping long?'

'No longer than I can help.'

'That might be longer than you think, chum. Y'ought to try and get on the staff. It's a sitter if they don't know you.'

'What staff?'

'Here, and up at the hostel. Sweeping out, making beds, cooking and serving. They're all chaps that come in off the streets, like you. Not much money in it, but everything's turned on free. All you got to do is get saved.'

'Saved?'

'Go out to the penitent form at one of the prayer meetings. Give your heart to Jesus . . .'

And that was it. It was a home for the destitute, largely run by some of the destitute. And if you weren't particularly anxious to move on, and were sufficiently unscrupulous, you could be one of the running brigade. And the way to muscle into the running brigade was simply to get 'saved'. I discovered that some of the old hands got saved every year as soon as the winter winds began to blow and the roads frosted up.

All the charge-hands at the Elevator were such brands clutched from the burning, and a more foxy-looking crowd I never set eyes on. They were on a sweet thing, and in their

The Incense Burner

anxiety to stick to it they took good care that precious little of the spirit of Army benevolence got beyond the corner of the building where the commandant had his little office. Beggars-on-horseback, they ran the place with much of the efficiency, and even less of the humanity, of an ordinary factory.

The Elevator was simply a depot for the collecting and sorting and re-packing of waste paper, rags, and string. All day long motor-trucks, horse-drawn lorries and handcarts kept coming in heaped with salvage which was unloaded and dragged to various parts of the great concrete floor for sorting out.

I was put onto the string bench, and each morning was given a one-hundredweight bag of odds and ends of string which I had to disentangle and distribute into a row of boxes marked 'cotton', 'sisal' — I forget the other names.

That was my task for the day, the price I paid for three meals and a bed to sleep in at night. Anything I did over and above that was paid for, if I remember correctly, at the rate of half-a-crown a hundredweight. In the three weeks I was there I earned just enough cash to keep me in cigarettes, carefully rationed, and nothing more. And there was no getting out of it if you wanted those three feeds and the bed. I tried, on the very first day — seizing a moment when I thought nobody was looking, and ramming a double handful of unsorted string into the sisal box. But one of the foxes saw me from a distant part of the floor and made me drag it out again under the threat of instant expulsion.

We didn't live at the Elevator. An old shop next door had been converted into a dining-room, and every day at 12 o'clock we trooped in and received dinners served from hot-boxes brought down from some Army cookhouse. And at the end of the day's work each man was given three tickets on the hostel in Old Street a mile or so away, one for tea, one for bed, and one for breakfast next morning.

The Old Street hostel was one of the biggest in London, and was run on much the same lines, and much the same spirit, as the Elevator. There was a washhouse with neither soap nor towels, dormitories — barrack-like but quite clean — and a spacious dining-room where the men could sit for the rest of the evening after eating. I understood that most of the food — 'leftovers' of some kind or other — was donated or bought cheaply from hotels, cafes, shops, and bakehouses. But it was priced so low that a man could usually eat plenty; it was dished up with every appearance of cleanliness, and I can't say I ever found it anything but appetising. Meal tickets were valued at 1/3, and we could choose what we liked from the bill of fare stuck up at the end of the serving counter: slice of bread and margarine 1d., pot of tea or coffee 1d., soup 2d., roast beef or mutton 3d., stew 3d., kippers 1d. each, vegetables 2d., apple tart 3d.

All a bit primitive, if you like, but I had a two weeks' hunger to work off, and they were the most enjoyable meals I ever had in my life. Food was, indeed, the only thing that made life at all worth living just then. I would open my eyes every morning thinking of breakfast, and when it was over I'd grit my teeth and stagger through the next four hours sustained only by thoughts of dinner. And when that was over there came thoughts of tea.

One red-letter day I cashed two tea tickets. My neighbour on the string-bench got on to something better for that evening, and gave me his. When I lined up at the counter the second time the fox in the white apron gave me a cold stare.

'What's this? I've served you once.'

'Don't be funny,' I replied. 'How many tickets d'you think we get?'

Still staring, he became positive, threw the ticket into the tray, and turned to the next man in line, dismissing me with a curt: 'Move on, chum, you've had it.'

He should have known better, because there are two things for which a man is always prepared to fight, and food is one of them. I reached out and seized his wrist.

'Come up with it, Mister! I'm in the Elevator. I worked for that ticket — '

He shook himself free, but I must have looked as savage as I felt because he served me without further argument.

I was like that all the time, hostile on the whole infernal world and ready to take it out on anybody. Each week I got leave off for half a day and went the familiar round of the docks, but a ship seemed to be as far off as ever. I hated London as I'd never hated any place before, began to lose hope, and fell into a mood of gloomy self-pity that made me impatient and contemptuous of everybody around me. Those men didn't talk much about their private affairs, and with the egotism and intolerance of youth I assumed that none of their troubles was as great as mine. A man

The Incense Burner

with youth and good health, and no responsibilities, should find any tussle an exhilarating adventure, but some of us don't realize that until youth is past. I used to try to cheer myself up by comparing my circumstances to those of old Burroughs coughing his life away down in the hovel in Finch Street, but that only made matters worse. Visions of the old man creeping along the dark passage, or crouched over his periodical burning of the herbs, positively frightened me. For he also had had a youth, and somewhere in the past there had been a beginning to the road that led to Finch Street, and that assuredly would go on from there nowhere but to the grave.

The hostel was full of them, shivering watery-eyed old men, who wandered the streets all day, and stumbled in at nightfall to stand for a long time studying the bill of fare with a few miserable coppers clutched in their stiff fingers. Nobody took any notice of them. No doubt they would have envied old Burroughs, for nobody ever sent *them* parcels with mufflers and 'bits of things' in them. All the same, they moved me to horror and fear more than to pity, for were they not life-members of a fraternity of which I had become a novitiate?

And if during the day all my dreams were of food, then at night-time all my dreams were of home. The coughing of old Burroughs had nothing on the wheezings and mutterings of that refuge of lost men. Sleep came to me slowly, and was often broken, and in the wakeful moments I would lie with wide eyes and tight lips, deliberately torturing myself with nostalgic longings.

Some building close by had a clock that chimed the hours, and whenever I heard it I would think carefully and call up a scene in Australia that I knew was true and exact of that very moment.

At midnight I would say to myself: it's ten o'clock in the morning, and the hotels down Flinders Street are just opening, and the wharfies coming away from the first pick-up are crossing from the Extension and dropping into the Hotham and the Clyde for a quick one before going home to lunch. And there's a white sky and a smell of dust, and trembling pavements which by noon will be hot enough to fry eggs on. And down at St Kilda beach lazy little waves are lapping in, and some of the Fortunate Ones are crossing the Promenade from the big apartment houses and spreading their towels on the sand for a brown-off. And even though it's a week-day, the Point Nepean Highway down the Peninsula is already lively with cars heading for the bush and more distant beaches. And there's a place down there in the heath country where my mates and I used to go rabbiting on Sunday afternoons. And the big loose-limbed manna gum where we found the parrot's nest is still there, its thin foliage hard and sharp against the sky in that way that always reminded me of the figures on a Japanese willow-pattern plate. And somewhere on the scrubby slope that runs up to the road a wallaby sits with drooping paws and pricked ears. And the air is full of the scent of the paperbarks down in the swamp, and of the whistlings and twitterings of grey thrushes and honeyeaters and blue wrens. And every now and then, on the breathlike puff of a breeze that comes out of the north, there is another smell that I know well, and over in a saddle of the distant Dandenongs a column of smoke marks where the bushfire is burning . . .

For three weeks.

Then — suddenly, like most bad things — it was all over.

One morning at breakfast time I got talking with a stranger who turned out to be a sailor. And within a few minutes he knew what I was looking for.

'Why don't you give the *Tairoa* a go?' he asked me. 'Ever done a trip as a steward?'

'No. What about the *Tairoa*?'

'She's leaving for Australia today, and they were signing on single-trippers yesterday. A lot of the New Zealand Company's packets do it. They go out stuffed with emigrants in the 'tween-decks. At the other end they dismantle the accommodation and fill up with cargo for home. They only want most of the stewards one way.'

'How is it I've never heard about this? I've walked those docks —'

'Well, you wouldn't be looking for Chief Stewards with that book, would you? Anyway, the Shore Superintendent's the chap you want to see. He's got an office down at the East India somewhere. You'll have to look lively if you want to try the *Tairoa* — she's up for noon . . .'

She's up for noon — oh, the friendly, intimate jargon of the sea! There was promise in the familiar phrase that raised my excitement to fever-heat. I never met that seaman again, but I'll love him till the day I die.

It took me two hours to find the Shore Superintendent, and less than five minutes to get the ship. He was a busy man all right. I was at his office by half-past eight, but they told me he had just left for a certain ship, and it was half-past ten before I caught up with him. I can't at this distance of time, trace my wanderings in those two hours, but I must have visited at least six vessels at widely separated berths, always just a few minutes behind him. However, I was after something that drew me like the very Holy Grail, and I nailed him at last just as he was about to get into his car. I knew I was on the right track as soon as he stopped to listen to me.

'We don't want trimmers,' he said after a glance at my book. 'We want stewards.'

'That's all right with me,' I replied. 'I want the passage. I'll sign as a steward. I've worked in hotels.'

He passed the book back, taking me in from head to feet.

'Where's your gear?'

I cold hardly speak for excitement. 'Up in my room in Custom House—'

'You'd have to be aboard by twelve o'clock.'

'I can do that. Where's she lying?'

He told me. 'Give us your name.' He pulled out a pocketbok. 'Report to the Second Steward and give him this note.'

She's up for noon . . .

Finch Street was two miles away, but I'll swear I made it in twenty minutes. There was plenty of time, but I had it in mind there was a suitcase to lug over the return trip, and I wasn't taking any chances. It was a cold foggy morning, but I was sweating from the long chase and the fever of success. And the grey buildings, and the shrouded figures that passed me on the pavement, were like things seen through the enchanted mists of fairyland. All the world had become beautiful, and I strode along puffed with triumph and springing on my toes with physical well-being. I told myself that youth and strength and pertinacity had to tell in the long run. You couldn't keep a good man down. Not when he had something big to struggle for. Those old men of the hostel had lacked the spur, inspiration, a vision . . .

No more Elevator. No doubt I wore a silly smile, because

more than once I caught a curious glance directed at me as I hurred on. Perhaps my lips were moving too, because the magical phrase 'she's up for noon' rang in my head until it took the tune of a well-known military march. I could have danced to it, shouted it aloud.

She's up for noon . . .

I remember afterwards holding back to let an ambulance pass me as I was about to cross into Finch Street, but the fact that it was an ambulance didn't register at the time — only a car of some kind, and in a hurry.

But I did observe instantly the women out at their doors all along both sides, and the little knot of gossipers in front of my old lodgings.

I thought first of Mrs. Hall, then of old Burroughs. But the humour of pitiless superiority was still on me, and I hardly quickened my pace. I'd come back for a suitcase, that was all, and in a few minutes these people . . .

They turned their heads and watched me as I came up. I saw Mrs. Hall in the doorway, her popping eyes red with weeping.

'It's the old man, Sailor. They've just took him off. The poor old soul.'

Some of the arrogance and detachment left me. I wasn't interested in old Burroughs, but this woman had given me a cup of coffee and a few words of sympathy when I needed them most. The other women stood aside, and I moved into the passage, taking the landlady by her elbow and drawing her after me. Something tickled my nostrils, but all my attention was on something else.

'He's an old man, you know, Mrs. Hall. What happened?'

'They think it's a stroke.' She began to weep again, dabbing her nose with the lifted end of her tattered apron. 'God help him! He tried to talk to me. He got one of them parcels this morning, them herbs. He's been sitting there — you got a ship, Sailor?'

She could think of me too.

'Yes, I'm going aboard in an hour. Where've they taken him?'

But I didn't hear her reply.

Because that something which had been tickling my nostrils got right inside, and I lifted my head like a parched bullock scenting water, and stared along the passage, and sniffed, and licked my lips — and drew in a mighty inhalation that filled my

The Incense Burner

lungs and sent me dizzy with the sickness that had been eating into me for five mortal weeks. I seized Mrs. Hall with a violence that made her stare at me in sudden fright.

'Mrs. Hall! — that smell — those herbs — where did they come from?'

As if I didn't know!

'Sailor —'

Burning gum-leaves! O, shades of the bush and smell of my home!

Pushing her from me, I was down the passage in two frenzied leaps and throwing open the door.

But nothing was left save the belongings of a lonely old man, a wisp of blue smoke rising from a tin set on an upturned box, and a digger's hat hanging on a nail driven into the mantelpiece.

The Man Who Liked Music

E.O. Schlunke

Alex Denholm was a pleasant enough man who could have been popular with his neighbours if it had not been for his queer streak. Alex had no sense of proportion. Until the neighbours got to know him they would hurry across to his farm to help him fix his tractor or his combine, only to find that there was nothing wrong with them; Alex had actually stopped work in the middle of the wheat-sowing season to go inside to listen to the Music Lover's Hour on the radio. And he would come out with his red hair standing up from the way he rumpled it in his excitement, his reddish-brown eyes glowing like fire, and his face, which was rugged and ruddy, shining in an absurdly delighted and boyish manner, to tell them he had just heard the Vienna Philharmonic Orchestra playing Mozart's E Flat Symphony.

Opinion about Alex's wife was divided. Some said she was a heroine for putting up with him; others that she was a fool for not leaving him.

The neighbours were very amused when they heard that Alex was getting an Italian prisoner-of-war to work for him.

'That'll be two of a kind,' said some.

'Don't be too hard on the Ities,' said the others.

The Control Centre men were a bit apologetic about the Italian they brought to Denholm's place. He was a small, obsequious fellow, who looked exactly like a waiter in a second-rate Italian restaurant.

'I don't think he knows anything about farm work,' said the sergeant-major, 'but you'll have no trouble keeping him in order.'

All the C.C. staff chuckled at this and Mario looked at them

The Man Who Liked Music

nervously, with his big soft brown eyes sliding from one to the other. Alex gave his prisoner a cheerful smile, as if he were sure he would discover some good in him. It did not take him very long. The very first night when he took him in to tea and they were both feeling awkward and embarrassed because they could understand only a few words of each other's language, Alex switched on his radio to his usual programme of classical music. An orchestra was playing selections from Italian operas. Mario looked and listened with intense interest.

'Rossini,' he said.

'Rossini good,' said Alex.

'Good! Good!' said Mario enthusiastically, and they smiled delightedly at each other. The orchestra played the first three notes of the next air and Alex shouted, 'Mascagni!'

Mario looked at him admiringly. 'Mascagni good!' he said.

They went on 'Verdi good', 'Leoncavallo good', 'Bellini good'.

After that Mario could do no wrong. Alex taught him to milk the cows and do the odd jobs about the place. For a prisoner-of-war Mario had a very happy existence. He liked milking the cows, and gave them new Italian names — the names of girls he had loved in Bari. The beautiful, friendly red one with fat round hips he called after Domenica, his latest and best love, even though she had not written to him for three years. He always sang while he milked, and while he milked Domenica it was always *'Che gelida manina'* from *La Bohème*. He sang it very feelingly and very sadly, just like the ill-fated lover in the opera, and Alex wasted a great deal of time listening outside the cowshed. Mario was really good. Alex boasted about it to everybody he met. He had a sister who was a music-teacher in the nearby provincial city of Waghurst. He lost no time in telling her about his sensational discovery, and bringing her out to hear him.

Theresa Denholm was a Dip. Mus., an S.T.S. and an A.T.M. She was also a master of the art of attracting large numbers of pupils and keeping them paying tuition fees long after they should have realized that they had neither the physical nor the intellectual gifts required in an interpreter of music. She was a bright, attractive, and lively young woman, though not so young that she wasn't somewhat troubled by the problem of keeping her hips and bust within the limits of elegance. On the way to Denholm's place she listened with every appearance of rapt attention, though with the inner boredom of the professional musician, to Alex's praise of his Italian singer.

But when she saw Mario come in to sit at the 'low' end of the old twelve-foot family table, looking so foreign and exotic, and really rather fetching with his big eloquent eyes and sensitive face, she was greatly interested.

'Is that the man who sings so well?' she said, letting her big and somewhat babyish blue eyes roll admiringly at him.

Mario had been a prisoner and had lived a harshly masculine life for four years, and here was a *bella donna* with curves like the most alluring Italian girl *and* blonde hair. Mario could not take his eyes off her, and though he was only a poor, wretched prisoner-of-war Theresa blossomed under his admiration. She was gay and bubbled with laughter; she joked with Alex; she teased his wife; she caressed and played with the children. Mario couldn't swallow a single mouthful.

Ina, the girl carrying plates in and out, full of resentful bewilderment because Mrs. Denholm had impressed on her most emphatically not to play up to the Italian because it was a condition of his parole that he was to have no contact whatever with women, pointed meaningly at his plate each time she passed him. But Mario heeded her not at all, though usually his glances followed her hungrily enough.

When Mrs. Denholm rose from the table it was the signal, among other things, for the Italian to retire to his hut. But tonight Theresa stopped him with an entreating cry. She wanted to have Mario in the lounge-room so that she could hear him sing at the piano. Mrs. Denholm objected. The prisoners should be kept in their places, she said, and she told them the nasty things the neighbours were saying about Alex for being too friendly with a P.O.W. There were some brisk exchanges between Mrs. Denholm and Theresa, Mario not understanding a word, but looking on with an expression of embarrassed self-pity. Theresa finally won through sheer egotistic inconsideration.

But Mario appeared very reluctant to go into the lounge. He eyed the carpet as if he dared not step on it; he would not take a chair but remained standing, tense and nervous.

'No *possible* me siddown,' he said, 'me *prigioniero*.'

Theresa gave him a melting smile, and a roll of the eyes that

The Man Who Liked Music

made him momentarily sag at the knees. She went to the piano and played softly and sentimentally. She began to sing, flashing glances at Mario until she saw that he was so full of music that his throat muscles had relaxed. She invited him to sing, tactfully helping him along when he had difficulty with the rather elaborate piano accompaniment. Theresa certainly knew the job of music-teaching. She soon had him going with great enthusiasm, leading him into exaggerated expressions of passion and sorrow until the tears ran down his cheeks. She stopped abruptly.

'Very good,' she said, giving him an up-and-down look as if it were decidedly incredible.

But Mario shook his head with a sort of pessimistic modesty. 'Me no good. Plenty *prigionieri* sing similar me.' Then he caught the look in Mrs. Denholm's eye, and hastily departed with many 'Scusami's', taking long steps to avoid treading too much on the carpet. Alex turned triumphantly to his sister.

'Isn't he as good as I said? Did you notice his marvellous *forte*?'

'It's the best natural singing voice I've ever heard,' said Theresa enthusiastically, 'do you know what I've been thinking? I'll have to have him in my pupils' concert.'

Mrs. Denholm said with deceitful sympathy, 'It's a pity you can't, but he's under strict military discipline. Otherwise it wouldn't really matter that he isn't a pupil of yours, would it?'

Theresa gave her sister-in-law a blank unreceptive look.

'I must have him,' she said. 'That man Foll has a fine young tenor. His voice is so good that even Foll's ridiculous old Marcesa methods can't ruin it. His opera singing is supposed to be particularly good, but Mario would make him look silly.'

Alex's eyes began to shine. 'Wouldn't he make them sit up? A beautiful, fresh young voice like that.'

Mrs. Denholm said, 'For goodness' sake Alex, don't let Theresa make a fool of you again.'

Alex tried to remember what she was referring to, but soon gave it up as unimportant.

'He really *must* be heard, he's so good,' he said.

Theresa turned her eyes up in her thoughtful pose.

'Isn't that Captain Adkins in charge of the prisoners?' she asked, then she broke into contented smiles. 'I know him. He's an awfully nice man.'

Captain Adkins was an amiable gentleman who ran the Waghurst P.O.W. Control Centre as if it were a welfare centre for Italian immigrants. The large room where the staff worked was always cluttered with prisoners whose employers had brought them into town for a hair-cut, to see the doctor, or just for an afternoon off. They always made a great deal of noise, seizing each other by the hands, exclaiming like long-lost brothers and even embracing and kissing each other. Theresa soon became quite well known at the Centre. She cultivated Captain Adkins, learnt the names of all the sergeants, corporals and other ranks, and dropped *buon' giorno's* to the prisoners, who soon got the notion that she was the *prima donna* at the local opera house. When she felt that she had established so much goodwill in Captain Adkins' heart that he could deny her nothing, she asked him if Mario could sing at her pupils' concert. The Captain looked somewhat taken aback.

'Now,' he said, looking at the ceiling, 'if it were just a private entertainment of invited guests, held at your brother's place, at which the prisoner would make a brief appearance dressed in his maroon uniform, and all the guests were informed beforehand of his position and had no objections, then it would be quite all right.'

Despite her carefully cultivated woman-of-the-world control, and her rather lavish make-up, some disappointment was discernible in Theresa's face. Her pupils' concerts were always held in one of the biggest halls in the city, the public was bidden to attend by cunningly and rather deceitfully worded advertisements, and a charge was made for admission. She smiled very warmly on Captain Adkins and put a hand on his sleeve in an innocently beseeching manner.

'So many people want to come to my concerts —' she began.

But the captain held up a warning hand.

'Those are the regulations,' he said, and then he smiled, 'but then, I don't know any more about your concert than you choose to tell me.'

Theresa nearly blushed as she realized how close she had gone to being guilelessly confidential. She rose and said, 'I'm having a little cocktail party at my studio tomorrow afternoon, I do hope you can come.'

On her way out she didn't remember as many of the ser-

The Man Who Liked Music

geants' names as usual. She was too preoccupied in thinking of ways and means. The advertisement, for instance, might be worded as an invitation — and a charge could still be made to defray expenses. She went and bought the most expensive tie in the town, and sent it to her brother, omitting to remove the price tag. She had an idea she would need a lot of co-operation from him.

The story went the rounds of the musical circles in Waghurst that a mysterious Greek tenor was going to sing at Theresa Denholm's concert. It transpired that he was a famous partisan patriot deep in the confidence of the Allied War Council. Every blossoming young soprano was dying to meet him, but the Nazis still maintained a fabulous price on his head, and all his comings and goings were made in the utmost secrecy.

On the night of the concert Alex smuggled Mario into the hall dressed in a suit of his own clothes, with a very bright blue shirt and crimson tie to give him a bit of dash and to make him look less like an Italian waiter. He faced the audience rather nervously, but he sang very well, with Theresa at the piano giving him great moral support. The audience loved him; they thought his modesty becoming in a foreigner of his reputation. Captain Adkins was there and seemed to enjoy his performance as much as anyone. The crowd clapped for an encore, but Theresa was pushing him out of the back door, where Alex seized him and rushed him away, the well-disciplined prisoner carrying out the orders of his *padrone* without question. Only when they were safely at home did a glimmer of pride light Mario's eyes.

'Me sing good?' he asked.

Mr. Foll, the eminent music-teacher, went about with one of his handsome iron-grey eyebrows sardonically elevated, telling people there was something phoney about the whole business, that the story of the tenor's romantic origin was only a poor publicity stunt, and that any Mediterranean would have a much more convincing Italian enunciation. He personally recognized the voice as belonging to a yodelling milkman employed by a dairy-farmer just outside the town. It was a freakish, unnatural voice, and nobody would be fooled by it for long.

But the *Waghurst Daily Diverter* said, 'Here is the voice which Waghurst can match with pride against the cream of Sydney and

Melbourne at our forthcoming eisteddfod.'

Queues of new pupils blocked the way to Theresa's studio door, where she received them with a most winning and gracious condescension. Next week-end she was at Alex's place again, still seething with excited triumph.

'Now I'll just have to enter him in the eisteddfod! I could win one of the major sections with him, against all comers. Then I'd be able to double my fees.'

Mrs. Denholm said darkly, 'That would be very nice for you, but do you know what we've found out? The penalty for supplying a prisoner-of-war with a suit of civilian clothes is five to ten years' jail.'

'There isn't much risk,' Theresa said brightly.

'What about Mr. Foll and all the other jealous music-teachers? They'll be nosing round,' said Mrs. Denholm.

But Alex sat with a bemused smile on his face.

'I believe Mario could win the operatic aria,' he said, as if everything else were unimportant.

Theresa said with brisk, easy confidence, 'I'll go and have a confidential talk to Captain Adkins. He'll fix everything for me.'

She started training Mario immediately. Mrs. Denholm interrupted rather frequently to send Mario to do some job, and stayed to criticize.

'Is it necessary,' she asked, 'to hold his hands and tell him how good he is all the time?'

'That's building up his confidence,' said Theresa professionally. 'Voice without personality will get him nowhere in an eisteddfod. He's got to learn to put it over. I have to make a study of his psychology, and find out how to put a bit of backbone into him.'

Back in Waghurst Theresa took the first opportunity to call at the P.O.W.C.C. As soon as she entered she was aware of a difference in the atmosphere. There was no noise except the sounds of men at work. There were no surplus personnel in either khaki or maroon loitering about. The few N.C.O.s were so busy at their desks that they barely had time to glance up at her. She felt quite relieved when a prisoner-of-war came in, bowing with extravagant politeness and smiling at her in the friendliest manner. She was greeting him warmly when she suddenly saw his face go blank and pale. She turned round in

The Man Who Liked Music

surprise to see a huge man towering over her with the pips of a captain on his massive shoulders. A pair of cold, opaque, hardened blue eyes were fastened mercilessly on the cringing prisoner. He said in a well-controlled, but definitely menacing voice, 'Take that fellow out of here.'

Two sergeants and a corporal sprang from their seats and advanced so swiftly and threateningly on the Italian that he fled like a rabbit to the cells at the back of the Centre, hitherto used for storing blankets. After he had heard the clang of the door Captain Pillory turned his eyes on Theresa. She searched his face for something that might suggest a line of approach. It was the face of one in authority — one who knew what he knew, and knew it so well that it was futile to tell him anything else. He said to her with all the arrogant assurance of a man securely entrenched in a man's world, and bolstered by an infallible set of man-made rules, 'Now, madam, just what is your business in here?'

Theresa looked round at all her friends at the desks, but none of them offered to introduce her. She looked back at Captain Pillory and knew that it was neither the time nor the place to make an impression on him.

'Oh, I must have made a mistake,' she said with an airy smile, 'I wanted the place next door.'

The next Thursday was 'canteena' day at Denholm's place. Captain Adkins had always left the tours of inspection and supply to his staff, but Captain Pillory came personally to see that his new order was established. Mario's smile of welcome dribbled off his face when he saw the new 'uffishaal'. Pillory reproved him sharply for the way he was dressed, for not polishing his boots, for the way he kept his room. Captain Pillory scorned to make use of the interpreter. Experience had taught him that if he glared hard enough, shouted loudly enough, and towered high enough, the b_____s understood him very well. Mario certainly understood that he was very unpopular with Captain Pillory; he stood at a rather lop-sided attention, his face pale yellow with fright, trying hard to be correct and respectful. The N.C.O.s treated him severely, too. They handed out only half the usual tobacco ration without making any explanation. They refused to issue new clothing unless the old were worn to disgraceful shreds, and they didn't allow Mario more than five minutes of his favourite futile sport of trying to get into a pair of boots two sizes too small for him.

When they had finished Pillory had Mario paraded before him again. He said to Alex, sternly, 'How has he been behaving?'

'Splendidly,' said Alex. Pillory looked quite disappointed.

'Isn't this the fellow who sings?' he asked, with something very like a sneer.

Alex's face lit up.

'Oh, marvellously!' he said, with his usual enthusiasm. 'A true lyric tenor with only a little development required in the upper register to make him one of the great *bel canto* singers of our day.'

Pillory looked hard at Alex, as if he were having some trouble in militarily classifying him.

'Is that so?' he said, feeling his way, but letting his face relax a bit so that his staff could think he was pulling Alex's leg.

'Yes,' said Alex, 'it is. His voice has something of Gigli's quality, with Schipa's lightness of inflection.'

The captain cleared his throat and set out to do some intelligence work.

'Tell me, who are these fellows, Gigli and Schipa? Sounds to me as if they're just a couple of dagos.'

Alex's ruddy face flamed with indignation.

'Gigli and Schipa are the greatest operatic tenors in the world. Thousands of people flock to hear them whenever and wherever they sing.' He ran his eye over the captain's various insignia of rank with a none too respectful glance, and burst out again. 'Why, Gigli would be paid as much for a tour of a few weeks as ten generals would get in a year.'

Captain Pillory maintained his undaunted and unimpressed expression, but he repeated, 'As much as ten generals,' as if that had got through to the responsive core of his being. An incredulous and vastly curious look crept slowly over his face.

'But surely this—' he glanced towards Mario as if he couldn't think of the word to describe him — 'this Italian isn't good enough to get among the money like that.'

'Would you like to hear him?' Alex said eagerly, 'and compare his voice with gramophone records of the world's best tenors?'

But Pillory was not going to be led in beyond his depth. He

The Man Who Liked Music

glanced at his watch, and said, 'Not today, thanks, we haven't time.'

One glance round and the N.C.O.s sprang onto the truck. They roared away to terrify some more prisoners.

When Theresa came out next week-end Alex had a copy of the eisteddfod agenda, and was shouting with excitement.

'Look here,' he said, 'the very thing for Mario, "Selection from Italian Opera in Costume". He can sing some of Canio's part from *Pagliacci*. No one would know who or what he is in a clown's make-up.'

Theresa gave him a shrewdly calculating look to make sure he was determined, then said, 'Oh, you wonderful man, to think of that, and to be willing to take such a risk for me!'

'There's no need to worry,' Alex said. 'That new captain might be strict, but he's not very bright. Would you believe it, he'd never heard of Gigli or Schipa! I've got it all worked out. Mario can wear his red uniform and pull the clown's overall over the top of it. That will give us a chance to talk our way out if Pillory does stumble on us. See? No civilian clothes, no disguise that would help him escape, and wearing his red uniform.'

Mrs. Denholm, who had come in with her face full of suspicion of Alex's excited talk, said ominously, 'Did you hear about the man who took his prisoner into a hotel for a drink? The mob threw both of them out and Captain Pillory sent the prisoner back to the camp for punishment.'

Theresa looked at her with a dead, bored expression, then rushed out and called Mario to come and have a practice. He was just about to go and milk the cows, but he dropped the buckets and came. Alex went out and picked up the buckets.

A week before the eisteddfod Theresa invited Alex and Mrs. Denholm to give Mario an 'audience test'. She asked them particularly to notice his growing confidence. It was apparent as soon as they entered the lounge. Mario was relaxing comfortably in an armchair, but he sprang out of it quickly enough when Mrs. Denholm gave him one of her looks.

Theresa stood Mario where he could watch her while he sang. They noticed his eyes turning to her continually, and the way he responded to her every look and gesture. He sang extremely well, Alex complimented both Theresa and Mario profusely.

But Mrs. Denholm said, 'He'll be all right, provided you can keep him hypnotized until after the eisteddfod's over.'

When Mario had gone Theresa confided, 'He's not going to fail, because I've taught him to be more afraid of letting me down than he can possibly be of the audience or adjudicators.'

Mario went about the farm with an earnest expression, practising conscientiously at all hours of the day and night. While he milked the cows, instead of his old light-hearted singing, he ran through his scales and arpeggios or roared dramatically his *'Ridi pagliaccio.'* Even the cows seemed to know there was something portentous about it all, and gave (on the average) a pint less of milk per day per cow. Alex took elaborate precautions against Mario getting too hot or too cold, and running the risk of a chill. His wife went about wearing an expression of apprehensive resignation.

There was tremendous public interest in the Waghurst eisteddfod that year. Mario was greatly impressed with the throngs of people about the town hall.

'Me similar Caruso,' he said, thinking they had all come to hear him.

They kept him discreetly in a closed car until it was nearly time for him to sing, then they brought him into the wings 'to get the feel of the theatre'. At the back of the stage there was a concourse of people in every degree of excitement. Young girls nearly palsied with fright, proudly holding sheets of music in their hands to show they were competitors, but getting sudden pitiful expressions on their faces as if they would have sold their souls to be back at home washing the dishes; teachers hovering; neurotic women combining the solicitous protectiveness and fierce aggressiveness of mothering hens; temperamental men teachers, and young men performers affecting calm self-possession but forgetting themselves to fall into fits of passionate nail-biting.

Most of them forgot their troubles to stare at Theresa Denholm's Greek tenor, who could easily have been a Dutchman or a Negro under the heavy clown's make-up that Theresa had plastered on him for safety. Mr. Foll came drifting to Theresa's side, despite her uninviting look, and, glancing at Mario's costume said loudly enough for him to hear, 'Singing *'Vesti la giubba'* I see. Unfortunate, that. Another man sang it a while

The Man Who Liked Music

ago. A strange thing happened. The note the accompanist gave him was half a tone flat. The poor fellow sang flat all the way through.'

Theresa thanked Mr. Foll and smiled more warmly than he expected, because she was thinking how ineffective his nerve war was on uncomprehending Mario. She encouraged him to retire and mind his own business.

The mysterious Greek tenor got a great reception. It seemed as if most of the audience really had come to hear him. And they were not disappointed. Theresa and Alex hugged each other in the wings as he went on from one thrilling phrase to the next. Even before the adjudicator announced his decision, everybody recognized it as a great triumph for him and for Theresa Denholm. Captain Pillory was there, to everyone's surprise, looking as if he were determined to get this singing business by the throat.

He was still thinking about it when he next visited Denholm's place. He didn't have much time to spare, but he insisted on Mario singing for him, unaccompanied and in the open air, while the N.C.O.s were getting the issue forms ready for him to sign.

He listened with a very judicial expression, but soon stopped Mario with a curt gesture.

'Quite a voice,' he said commendingly, 'but nothing like that Greek tenor at the eisteddfod. That was the man who has the chance of getting among the big money.'

For once Alex let an obviously wrong opinion about music go unchallenged. He did not encourage the captain to speak any more about the matter, being quite relieved to see him departing. But the interpreter, a mild, soft-spoken, dark little man, who had been ignored by the captain ever since he came, paused by Alex's side for a brief moment, and murmured to him, 'You've got away with it twice, but for goodness' sake don't try it again, because I'll have to do my duty and report you.'

The Last Night

Gavin Casey

We started off that holiday on the wrong foot. We couldn't afford it, for one thing; but I was on the verge of walking in my sleep, so we decided we'd have to have it, afford it or not. That sort of decision leaves you gloomy and savagely aware that you've worked hard for a long time and ought to be able to afford a spell. It's my way to spend pretty freely, too; and when I can't do it I'm not exactly good to live with. I'm generally careful and irritable for a while, and then I burst out, letting the cash fly and damning the consequences. I've lived with myself long enough now to know my habits, and that's one of them that I dislike pretty thoroughly. I wish I disliked it enough to mend it.

Anyway, we didn't start off well. Sadie and I had got used to taking no notice of each other around the house, but it was a sure thing, I thought, that our bad habits would show up more among other people. I wished I could go off on my own, but she needed a rest as much as I did. Maybe more, after about three years of looking after me and the kid, and putting up with my temper, and lacking the change I got at work. It was all or nothing; so we checked over the money we had, and made plans about how to make the best use of it. Plans of that kind disgust me, and then I disgust Sadie. But they had to be made, and that was all there was to it.

We didn't have much to say to each other on the bus, except when Sadie quarrelled with the driver about paying for the kid. That sort of thing always irritates me, though I should know it's only our common purse she's trying to look after. I do know, but not at the time. At the time all I know is that it's not my way to

The Last Night

squabble about that sort of thing, and it ought not to be my wife's. I feel ashamed and angry.

'You needn't try to look as if we didn't belong to you,' Sadie snapped when the bus-driver had gone back to his seat with a red face but no fare for the kid. 'You should have put that beast of a man in his place.'

'Hell!' I said. 'You don't get anywhere by "putting people in their places". If you hadn't gone for him like a mad dog I might have had a word with him.'

'A word with him!' said Sadie bitterly. 'You'd have had a word with him all right! By the time you'd finished talking to him you'd have been paying double fare for the lot of us, and we'd have had to walk home.'

The bus rolled through good country—little farms and gardens, and trees that were the rich, heavy green that you find only where there's plenty of rainfall—but the squabble spoiled it for me. Instead of enjoying it, I felt cheated and angry. I could feel Sadie's dislike and exasperation like a current flowing into my mind, and the kid seemed to feel the tension, too. He sat pretty quiet, but he couldn't keep it up for ever.

'What's that?' he yelled suddenly, pointing. 'What's that?'

I hopped in to answer the question and collar the kid before his mother got him. 'It's a calf,' I said. 'A little calf, Bill.'

'It looks like a cow,' he said, a bit distrustfully.

'It's a calf,' I said. 'A calf's a baby cow.'

The nipper sat quiet for a quarter of a mile, thinking it over. Then he said, pretty seriously: 'I'm a baby man, then, dad. I'm a baby man, aren't I?'

I laughed, but Sadie's face never crinkled. She sat grim and disapproving, staring ahead. I began to hate her pretty thoroughly. If we couldn't have the kid in common there was nothing we could have, I thought. I took the youngster on my knee and ignored her as thoroughly as I could. He was too worked up about all he saw, too keen on getting his questions answered quickly, to worry about who answered them, and he took no notice of her at all. I felt pleased, and hoped it hurt.

When we arrived I was disappointed in the place, too. It was one of those sprawling seaside towns that are not on any railway line. It was covered with flimsy, shoddy, impermanent holiday homes, and the place we'd hired was as bare and jerry-built as the rest of them. From the front veranda I could look out over the big bay, but the bay, all except the blue water in it, seemed frowsy too, and the sand was grey, instead of the dazzling white I'd always associated with beaches. The town was all hotel and change-rooms and ice-cream signs, and the very look of it made my heart start to ache in the way it had been aching lately in the city. But the bay was preferable to the dirty holiday house, with Sadie grim and righteously indignant. After we'd eaten a scratch meal that was mostly bread and jam she started to put young Bill to bed, and I got a fishing-line and stamped out. It would do her good, I thought, to spend the first evening of her holiday alone in the ugly box with no company but the sleeping kid.

The darkness covered up the ugliness of the town, and the papers blowing around were just shadows in the night. The lights were prettier than ice-cream signs, and the whole show was a lot better. The breeze off the sea was fresh and cool, and as I tramped towards the jetty I felt better. I passed others, coming and going, and there were lanterns glowing in boats on the bay. There were purposeful men with rods and lines, talking a jargon I couldn't understand; but my mood had improved, and they were men, anyway. I rambled out over the water and stood alongside a chap who was squatting patiently over a line.

'How're they biting?' I asked.

'Not so good,' he said. 'Should 'a' got a boat. They're gettin' 'em all out there.' He started pulling in his line, and swore when he found the hook bare of bait. I stood behind him, feeling curious as to why the fish should prefer the boats to the jetty, which jutted out further than the places where most of the dinghies lay.

'I don't know much about this game,' I said. 'Why's a boat better, anyway?'

I got no answer for a while, as the chap started rolling up his gear. Then he started to laugh. 'Damned if I know,' he said. 'I don't even know if it is. The talk was just swank, and if you know less than me you're pretty ignorant. I'm a wheat-cocky, an' even the banks have stopped biting up my way.'

'I'm from the goldfields,' I said. 'I've been in the city the last few years, but I've spent most of my life up there, where the fish come in breadcrumbs.'

The Last Night

I felt warm and friendly. I liked his style, and when he said he'd spent twelve months on the fields a few years earlier when things had been tough we started comparing notes, and found the names of a few men we both knew. We squatted on the jetty, smoking and letting the fish bite the piles away from underneath us if they wanted to. After a while it reached what it was working up to, and we tramped up through the sand towards the pub, feeling thirsty and friendly and good. I'd forgotten Sadie altogether, and, of course, I'd forgotten all the money I didn't have to play around with.

It didn't turn out to be an expensive evening after all. There was more talk than beer, and what did trickle down our throats did us a lot of good. He was pretty good company. He was old enough to have been in the 1914 war, and he'd had some of the fields and a stretch among the cane in Queensland, as well as plenty of the wheatbelt. By the time I was ready to get off home my mind seemed to be full of new ideas and friendship.

We hadn't drunk so much, but it couldn't have been so little either, because when I got out into the cool air I started to feel it. All the miserable humpies lining the road seemed the same, and I wasn't sure of ours, but I fluked it first go, and felt pleased with myself. I felt pleased because of that, but I'd have been pleased if I'd had to blunder around for an hour looking for it. My new cobber, Len Martin, was the sort I liked, and in the fortnight we both had at the beach I was looking forward to seeing a lot of him. I blundered into the house, feeling well above myself, and not thinking about the reception I might get.

I switched on the light in the only room worth calling one, and, of course, Sadie and the kid were in bed. The youngster was sprawled out, fast asleep, but Sadie was sitting up, with the blankets gathered around her throat, looking at me in that extra-venomous way she keeps for special occasions. She had a case for complaint, and a good one, and I was feeling so pleased with myself that I might have felt pretty repentant if she'd given me a chance. But she didn't. She never does see when the time is ripe to let a man's own good spirits work around until they make him feel like a worm. She always hops in, bitter and accusing, and drives the pleasure out of me with hate.

'I could smell your breath from the door,' she said. 'There is no need to tell me where you've been. Why did you worry to take the fishing line with you?'

'Well, I haven't brought it back,' I said, suddenly discovering that I must have left it down at the pub. 'Just as well, or I might have strangled you with it.'

That was how things were when I tumbled into bed, lying so far over on my side of it that I practically hung out like a veranda. I lay in the dark, awake, for what seemed like a long time, though it probably wasn't, seething with indignation, and justifying myself for all that had happened, and feeling determined to see plenty of Len Martin, whether Sadie liked it or not.

Next day I did see Len, and he produced a wife, three kids and an old car, so we combined forces. The wife was fat and comfortable, the nippers were likely sorts, two boys and a girl, and we learned a thing or two from the Martins about the best way to handle our one and only. The car used to bulge a bit at the sides, but there was always room for rugs, and if any of the kids got tired before we came home from anywhere they could roll up and go to sleep. It made things better for Sadie, being able to take young Bill when we rambled off to some distant bay or beach, and she seemed to appreciate it at first. But then she froze up on me, and got tight-lipped and silent and disapproving whenever Len and I put in an evening yarning at the pub. Mrs. Martin talked on and on as a rule, and occasionally got sympathetic and understanding, but I wanted to kick Sadie in the face when I thought of her at all.

In the city I suppose you meet as many of your sort as you do anywhere else, and now and again you get a glimpse of their troubles or the things they're enthusiastic about that makes you feel warm towards them. But mostly they disappear into the crowd again, and afterwards you get only glimpses of them at long intervals. If you come from the fields you miss the leisurely yarns in the change-rooms and the pubs and the interesting things that bubble out of pretty unexpected places at times. Len got me back into that atmosphere, with the added advantages of the cool salt sea to swim in and stretches of sand on which we could lie and smoke, talking or not talking just as we felt inclined. It wasn't long before I could look out over the bay and

The Last Night

see the islands and the curling coastline without even noticing the crude buildings that had offended me at first, and, of course, when I reached that stage the holiday was doing me good.

The days of fishing and sun-bathing and running around in Len's car passed too quickly, and when the last one came I was concerned about losing touch with him altogether. We left the women ashore and went out in a rowboat. From where we dropped the anchor we could see the women lying with their hats over their faces and the kiddies running and yelling like young blackfellows. I wished it could go on for ever. I was feeling well and strong, but I wasn't looking forward to the city. We sat in the boat with our lines trailing, feeling the sun on the backs of our necks and each thinking his own thoughts. I hoped that Len would be regretting the end of our couple of weeks of knocking around together, too.

'Well,' I said, 'It'll soon be over, worse luck! D' you reckon on coming down to the coast next year?'

'Not unless I win something,' Len drawled.'Cockies only have holidays once every five years, an' then they can't afford 'em.'

'If you cared to stay with us in town it might make it easier on your pocket,' I suggested.

'I've been thinking a different way.' Len said. 'If you could put up with the wheatbelt we'd like to see you and the wife and kid up in our part of the world.'

It was casual enough, but I knew he meant it, and in one jump I started thinking a year ahead. I felt pretty pleased, because it's always good to know that someone you like likes you, too. We sprawled about the boat, watching the shadow of the jetty grow longer and not needing to say anything until long after the women and kids had gone scrambling over the sandhills. When we pulled ashore it was dusk, and I went towards our place, still feeling good. I was full of the news for Sadie, not because I thought it would please her as much as it had me, but because it was one of those things you've got to talk about to someone, whether you think they'll understand or not. But the opportunity to tell her didn't come for a while. She was busy with the tea, and then the kid was asleep on his feet and had to be put to bed. We tucked him away, and when we went out to sit on the veranda steps I suddenly wanted to sell the idea to my wife, to convince her that next year's holiday would be good, and that

Australian Short Stories

Len was a man who was out of the ordinary. It made it harder to start, having to be careful. Before I got going young Bill, inside, woke up with a yell, and we dashed inside and switched the light on.

He was all right, of course. It must have been just one of those vague dreams that sometimes startle kids out of sleep. His eyes weren't open for more than fifteen seconds, but while they were he mumbled, 'Can't we stay here, dad? I don't want to go home. I want to stop with Tom and Joe and Marjorie.' I saw Sadie's lips tighten, and I guessed that, for some reason I couldn't plumb, she thought it would be a good thing when we were home again. I resented that, and my resentment got queerly mixed up with the things I had been thinking. When we were back on the veranda, sitting on the steps watching the hurricane-lamps twinkling on the bay, I started to talk.

'Len wants us to go up to his farm next year,' I said bluntly. 'It won't cost much, and it'll be healthy for the kid.'

Sadie said nothing, but I knew she disapproved. In the dim light I couldn't see her expression, and I couldn't have understood it if I had.

'It'll only cost the train fare,' I said. 'Three extra mouths to feed aren't anything on a farm.'

'You're very careful about money all of a sudden,' Sadie answered ready to quarrel.

'All right,' I said, 'if that's how you feel. I'll go if it costs all I have, and I don't give a damn if you come or not. I like Len Martin, and I'm glad of a chance to see him again. I thought you liked Mrs. Martin, too, like anyone else would.'

'She's all right,' said Sadie, suddenly pretty passionate and speaking out the venom that was in her. 'It's your damned Len Martin I hate. If you expect me to love him because he keeps you away every minute of the day except when you want to eat or sleep, you're a fool. I hate him, and I wish we were never going to see him again.'

Sadie started to cry, and it softened her and startled me. She wailed miserably, with her head in her arms against the rough boards of the veranda floor, and it was a lonely, discouraged sound, pretty different from her usual cold superiority. Suddenly I tumbled that she was jealous of Len Martin, as jealous as she would have been of another woman, and I felt kinder and a bit

The Last Night

ashamed of myself. I felt good, too, and for the first time for a long time I was aware that Sadie and I were a long way from the end of our interest in each other, even if we did snarl and hate a good deal of the time. I looked at her, curled up on the steps sobbing, and felt for a while as I used to feel about her ten years earlier. I slithered along the step and put my arm around her shoulders.

'Hell, Sadie!' I said. 'There's nothing for you to feel like that about. It's just that a man's got to have man's company sometimes, and if I got more of it, as a rule, I daresay I wouldn't have hogged it so much with Len. I'm sorry if I've overdone it.'

She sat up, and I tried to think of the proper words to use, telling her what was in my mind, but there weren't any words. I remembered how the kid had been so wrapped up in Len's youngsters, too, and I though I could realise for a moment how much my wife had come to feel like the cook and housekeeper around the place. Her holiday had been as bad as mine had been good, I could see, and I pulled her closer to me.

We sat till late, staring out over the bay and at the haze of light where the big port lay a score of miles along the coast. We didn't say much, because there wasn't much that could be said. At the start there was a lump in my throat over the hard deal Sadie and myself, and everyone else for that matter, got, but that dissolved, and I felt warm and comfortable and less alone than I did even with Len. For the evening, anyway, neither of us held any spite or resentment or stored up hatred for wrongs we thought we'd suffered at each other's hands.

My holiday was a good one, and the last night of it was good for Sadie, even if that was all. The last night of it was good for me, too. I've thought about it a lot since, and sometimes it brings me up with a jerk, though often when things go wrong and she's wearing her cold, tight-lipped smile I haven't got enough sense to remember her crying that night on the steps.

Say To Me Ronald!

Hal Porter

Good God! thought Perrot, my nose *twitched*. The golf-bag was the biggest he had ever seen. The biggest in the world? Or perhaps it seemed so because it was three o'clock on a Sunday afternoon in 1942, and there was a war on.

In his Adelaide housemaster's study, more oakishly panelled than Sir Jasper's stage library, the golf-bag totemically stood, its effect admonitory. It had, too, the quality of a menhir, albeit composed of a circus-red species of leather, and *fleur-de-lis*-ed, gusseted, gored and belted with whitest white. Buckles and nodules of nickel ratified its Maya-like power. From its well protruded uncountable . . . weapons? . . . virile insignia? . . . surely not golf-clubs? . . . of some surely Venusian alloy.

It seemed less to have been lugged upstairs by Wee Soon Wat than to have, like an Aztec archpriest bent on sacrificial mayhem, lugged upstairs Wee Soon Wat. Nevertheless, lugee or lugger, Wee Soon Wat was lotus-immaculate and smooth as sesame oil.

'My dear Wee!' said Perrot, who felt that he, all over, as well as the nose he felt he had felt twitch, had changed colour. Pinker or paler he could not tell.

'Say to me Ronald, sah,' mildly although rebukingly said Wee Soon Wat, seventeen, Sixth Form, Chinese, dressed to kill, and odorous of *Soir de Paris*.

'My dear *Wee*,' said Perrot, affecting firmness, feeling older and smaller and unwashed, and — oh, God — changing colour again. 'I can't possibly accept this . . . ah . . .' He squinted at the bag as though it were the sort of woman American G.I.'s took

Say to me Ronald!

out, and he his own Seventh Day Adventist Aunt Edith. The bag merely got bigger than Elsa Maxwell. 'Wee, I can't *possibly*. It's . . . it's too much.'

Wee Soon Wat's face, usually as unmarked as if it were simply portable heredity rather than a private growth capable of illustrating character and emotion, thereupon revealed some sort of character and emotion. It began, moreover, to emit high-pitched sound, courtesan-like, an arpeggio of it. Oriental merriment? It certainly required a fan before it. It ran its course. It petered out. At peace again, its executant seemed purged, and became charming enough to charm a porcupine: 'Too *much*, sah! Whai, mai old man are a millionaire, sah!' Upon this Wee Soon Wat's face got rounder than the moon above the autumn bamboos.

'*Is*,' schoolmasterishly said Perrot, schoolmaster, Senior English, Middle School French, *divorcé*, and in love with someone he had no right to be in love with.

'Sah?' said Wee Soon Wat from above the bamboos, most delicately inquiring of the low-born.

'*Is*, Wee. Singular. Is. *Is* a millionaire, Wee.'

'Oh, sah, s-u-r-r-r-e thing *is*. Yiss, *sah*! Singapore millionaire, as you are knowing to date.'

Wee glimmered with gladness that Perrot understood. His smile was mother-of-pearl itself. Then, less glimmeringly, for life was really serious, and he insisted on being permitted to live on his own kindness to himself, 'Pliss, say to me *Ronald*, sah.'

Say?

Say!

Perrot recognised 'speechless' as his adjective but, 'Ah — Ronald — ah — *Wee*,' he said in a voice nearly resembling his own. 'I am — ah — I am grateful for your kind thought. But *not* necessary. Those few extra lessons in English were . . . I thought you — ah — *quite* understood that I was happy to give them. There was no thought of . . .' Payment? Reward? *Pourboire?* Rake-off? No word fitted the overwhelming receptacle and its protrusions. 'No thought at all, Wee . . . *Ron-ald* . . . ab-so-lute-ly none.'

Slitting his eyes like an adolescent Fu Manchu at the golf-bag, and also in the manner of one who examines another's point of

Australian Short Stories

view to disregard it, 'To date you are thinking, sah,' said Wee Soon Wat, 'she are definitely beauteous?'

'*It* and *is*, Wee. I think *it is*,' said Perrot, governess-like. Then stopped dead. What the governess was saying was indubitably not what Perrot wanted said.

'Theah are Scotch within her and Great British cigarettes,' said Wee Soon Wat stroking the nickel-barnacled white-and-crimson pockets, his manicured nails and delicate fingers aquiver on their pregnancies, an inward smile suggesting one about to feast on human frailty. 'To date theah are this whiskeh and Playah's Please Cigarettes, sah. Oh, gratitude, sah!'

'There *is* . . .' began Perrot.

'No!' cried Perrot. 'The plural, Wee. There *are*. Yes, yes.'

He resisted tearing hairs or beating breasts. He forbore to wail. Using every effort he manipulated the wires of his nature to simulate forcefulness.

'Wee, I can*not* accept it. You must take it back to wherever — to whoever — to *whom*ever — to the shop — to the man — to . . .'

He ceased, apparently made mad and dumb.

The Oriental moon rose fuller and *blander* above . . . well, the bamboo, the ricefields, the Forbidden City.

'It is impossible, im*poss*ible,' suddenly squeaked and gibbered Perrot, dragonfly bamboozled in bamboo, peasant yak-like in ricefields, witless leper at the city gates. 'It is *utterly* impossible, Wee.'

'Say to me Ronald, mai *deah* sah,' said Wee Soon Wat in his angel-white sharkskin coat, one of his Singapore twenty. It was still only a little after three o'clock, Sunday, 1942, and a war decidedly on.

Perrot knew about the war because the School Matron and the Housekeeper had got crisper and leaner than *grissini*, and wore ration-card-snipping scissors on chains in the manner of 1912 shopgirls. The gymnasium was sandbagged. Lavatory paper was thinner; underwear got more raggedy. Charcoal-burners appeared on cars, and tan shoes on boys. All jam had become raspberry. In short, eccentricity was the mode: in becoming more unreal life had become more lifelike.

Of course, vestiges of peace-time past recurred or persisted as no more eccentric than usual: summer, winter, morning hymns,

Say to me Ronald!

examinations. The Headmaster, ever Zeus-like behind rimless spectacles blinding with reflected light, remained correct-weight Olympian without wane. The leather-aproned school-carpenter, the tuckshop Scotswoman, the nag that pulled the groundsman's roller, the cook floury as a cook, all remained, except for time's imperceivably stealthy subtractions and additions, the same.

Elsewhere in the school, the needs and lures of war also effected subtractions and additions, but outrageously, quite without stealth, and in the comic tradition. Maids who had moused about mutchless, yet with the air of wearing mutches, were now elsewhere, pert and jimp as soubrettes, in one or other war-time uniform. They were constantly being replaced and replaced by a rout of mock maids with bigger or springier busts, fingernails like dowager Manchu empresses', more make-up, more crystal necklaces, tinier eyes, hairier legs and voices like tawny frogmouths'.

On the same conveyer-belt, stop-gap schoolmasters incredible as creatures from Dostoiëvski also moved into and out of view, the probability of their having habits or hobbies that could shock trailing them like a reek of burnt stew. The School got noisier than a zoo. Above all this, that and the other, searchlights slid about at night finding clouds, no Japanese warplanes and not even a Zeppelin. However, there were compensating fascinations.

War had side-channelled a number of foreign schoolboys into the School. Not only were they foreign in tint, profile and accent: glamour flickered about them like St. Elmo's Fire from the fact that they had been considered sacred enough or costly enough to be packed up like *objets d'art,* and whisked away from danger. They were less, it seemed, to be educated than put in storage until the war whimpered out.

Most fascinating of the many was a selection of princelings: Batavian, Malayan, Siamese, Balinese — it was impossible to work out which was which. They gazed with deerlike animal intensity, as though fevered with sad love, from the bodies of classes. These gazers were young, yet seemed as ancient as highly-finished statuary of a remote era in which delicacy was the keynote: their wrists, too fine for the coarse activities of schoolboys, suggested poetry and immorality of a jaded kind.

Of the exotics Wee was the most eye-catching. More than his wealth his own nature made him conspicuous, unless it was that wealth had made him flashier, kinder, more imaginative, fantastically overflowing with an excess of *noblesse oblige*, and unsittable-on. Perrot was victim of this florid misconception of the shape of gratitude. Perrot led usually a nicely edited life; his mind usually had all its lights blazing. Wee Soon Wat and the golf-bag, however, had caused a dimming and flickering: a fuse could soon be blown.

Perrot cleared his throat as does a character in a short story.

'Wee,' he implored brutally, 'take the . . . take the bag away, *please*.'

For the first time an expression approaching human stirred the Chinese moon, and yet it was no more than a look of butterfly distress, misty and unattached.

'Oh, sir!' cried Wee, fervently cracking the finger-joints of each hand with the other. 'You have falsed me! To date you are telling me she are definitely beauteous. And now, 'Take away, pliss!' Oh, horror! Oh, badly! What shall poor Ronald Wee believing?'

There was a quarter-second of tragic gloom. Then, victim of a thought of more splendour, Wee Soon Wat became incandescent in worldly and enlightened fashion. After all, his father was rich enough to buy the school, and convert it into a coolie-ridden College-Tudor godown packed with cloud-ear fungus and tinned water-chestnuts.

'Ah *ha*, sah!' he continued. 'You are thinking to date she are definitely beauteous. You have said. But you are thinking she are bad form. Horror and alas! How Ai see! The Awstralian fellohs will be jealousy. Mai sisters have said bad form. How raight Ai see! Su-r-r-re thing: bad form! Ai must thinking. Ai think. To date Ai am thinking raptly.'

A Buddha, he put on thought. He cracked anew his finger-joints.

'A golden wrist-watch!' he cried.

'No, Wee — *no*. Nothing.'

Perrot might not have spoken.

'A watch *not* for the wrist? A chain-watch of Swissland. But *golden*.'

'No, Wee — no.'

Say to me Ronald!

'A desk for wraiting? A desk of fashion.'

'No, Wee.'

'Armchairs with lamps?'

'No.'

'Silken shirts!'

Perrot considered screaming. Perrot did not even sigh. He gazed at his pupil as into a crystal turbulent with some lamentable destiny.

A year-long hour later, he heard himself promise to allow himself (in lieu of accepting wireless-sets, crocodile-skin suitcases, concertinas, an aquarium of goldfish, and a variety of pets) to be entertained by his adamantly grateful pupil, in a fortnight's time, at the flat of the Misses Wee.

At the School Swimming Carnival, Perrot had already glimpsed Wee's two sisters. They had been revealingly enclosed in gowns of un-Australian materials and colours. These shape-gripping *cheong sams* had slendered them to elegance. The skirts, ankle-length, but slit to above the knee on each side, had tempered the old-ivory bandiness of their naked high-heeled legs. Their coiffures had been liquorice moulded into convolutions no hand or wind would dare or could playfully budge. On each black miracle a fragile artificial flower had quivered like something recording a delicious feminine undercurrent.

Distinguished and apart as angel-fish, they had each luminously occupied like enchanted growths the luminous and scented area under their sunshades. The Indian-ink-black of their brush-stroke eyebrows, and the lacquer-red of their lipstick, had caused mothers and aunts, even Boticellian schoolgirls, to feel barbaric and pimpled, to pant like dogs, and wish they had pumiced their legs. Sophisticated agelessness varnished the Misses Wee.

Their apparent fragility had been exported from Singapore to employ safety from war in acquiring a domestic and social extra at an Edwardianly ladylike finishing school. They lived in a flat in one of St. Peter's kurrajong-lined streets towards which, a fortnight later, a taxi-cab — no, no, not a taxi-cab, a vice-regal hire-car without a charcoal-burner — conveyed Perrot and his host.

It was, in the saner world, 106 in the shade, even at four in the afternoon. Wee had not a pore, follicle or gesture betraying consciousness of heat: he was so buffed, so blindingly coated and crisply trousered that Perrot, praying to sweat inconspicuously, felt cumbered and furry as an Eskimo. As the hire-car stopped, Wee leapt from it with the grace and elasticity of Lifar, then, in the manner of one tending a lunatic invalid, his curved hand an inch from Perrot's elbow, almost assisted him from the car. Next, he paid off and over-tipped the driver with a note conceivably minted that noon.

Perrot, stroking hopefully over his hair which felt like Struwwelpeter's with a hand that felt like Struwwelpeter's, was encouraged with dove-like murmurs and infinite tenderness through the gate and along the smooth path as over the skulls and rocks of the Valley of the Shadow of Death.

At the door the brother rang, masculinely, as one expressing unequivocally: Sisters, I am without! *Women*, open!

Soundlessness ensued.

There was no brazen gong, no struck zither, no scuttle, slither, squeak, murmur or breath.

No pin was dropped to be heard.

Silence and time continued.

Then, suddenly, swiftly, silently, the door retreated and 'Good af-ter-noon, Mis-ter Pel-lot,' melodiously and pentatonically in duet chanted the Misses Wee, gorgeous as concubines and, in duet, extended lily hands cold as golfish although the hallway was hotter than outside, infernal, marbled with almost visible blastings of incense, of the Misses Wee's disparate scents, of garlic, gas, and some more disturbing smell like charred mice.

The living-room was small, but the Wees and money had taken every advantage of the spaces left between the landlord's unpleasant furniture. All overhead lights blazed, and four standard-lamps and two large table-lamps suckling current through perilous lianas of flex. Each lamp was of a different design, boudoir jostling military club; each lamp endlessly repeated its image in a mound of many-coloured witch-balls on a fumed-oak refectory table. Vases, containing jammed-in bundles of artificial and tinselled flowers, prevented every flat surface from practical misuse. Fuming incense-burners abounded.

Say to me Ronald!

A cocktail-cabinet, so new that a price-ticket string still hung from a knob, displayed its cut-glass vessels and Saturnalian burden of bottles in a white-hot dazzle. Competently, as though he had often rehearsed this important move, Wee approached the shrine, took up station, shot his cuffs, and the formalities began.

'Would you caring, sah, for whisky-sodah, sah?' said Wee, prepared for no nonsense, and stripping the foil from a bottle-top with the decision of a head-surgeon. The Misses Wee flanked him in attitudes of willowy effacement, as though in a cool iris-garden, but with the air of inwardly abiding a moment, every wire tuned, to be played like musical instruments.

'Thank you, Wee,' said Perrot thinly as a beggar, blinded with blaze, dizzy with heat and odours and the obligations of ritual.

With the social aplomb of an undertaker, and in blood-curdling quantity, Wee poured two whisky-sodas. The moment the second crystal goblet was abrim the Misses Wee abandoned the iris-pool, and flexuously undulated to their appointed duties. Beneath their brother's unwatchingly watchful eye, one placed the drink on a silver tray, one indicated a great hairy armchair, and piped sweetly, 'Pliss to sit with-in arm-chair, Mis-ter Pel-lot.'

As Perrot sank sleep-walkerishly into this hot enclosure she disposed several hotter chenille cushions about and behind him, packing him in like a T'ang statuette, while the other sister presented the drink.

Perrot observed that Wee now held *his* whisky in a position that could only be pre-salutation. First, however: 'Sit!' said Wee Soon Wat with some sternness.

Perrot started as much as he was able. The order was not at him. Sinuously the handmaidens sat, one on each arm of another shaggy chair. They were like things dreamed. Their postures were divine. The stage was set. All eyes slid Wee-wards. Wee elevated his goblet a gentlemanly fraction.

'Cheer-*ho*!' he said, 'Cheer-*ho*, mai deah sah!'

'Cheers, Wee,' said Perrot meekly, commending his sanity and sobriety to any gods.

'Say to me Ronald, kaindly, sah, in mai own abode,' said Wee Soon Wat, tossing off his giant whisky as though he were a dipsomaniac collier. This done, he shot an invisible message to his sisters. Their eyes became still. They smiled like leading ladies. They spoke.

'Hah-oo kaind you have said to Lon-ald,' said the Miss Wee in gold and red, perhaps the elder. She had more and larger teeth.

'Lon-ald is glate-ful,' recited the Miss Wee in silver and green who had the less bowed legs, and smaller but brighter eyes.

'Lon-ald is sad and tlag-ic because goffing-bags are bad form.'

'We have said Lon-ald that goffing-bags are bad form.'

'Lon-ald admires Mis-ter Pel-lot and not admires bad form.'

'Goffing-bags are bad form,' intoned the Misses Wee together.

Then, 'Bad form,' they again said together as though delicately saying 'Incest.'

Upon that, abruptly, the record ran down.

'Pliss, sah,' took up Wee Soon Wat, moderately sternly, hand on bottle. 'Pliss, sah, to drink. To date theah are plenty more wheah that are coming from.'

As under hypnosis Perrot drank to the ruinous dregs with a sense of Gorki-ing through *Lower Depths*. The goblet empty, the Misses Wee unfolded like exquisite serpents. Gold-and-red, agitating a fan, disarranged the heated air uselessly through Perrot's mop while packing the cushions tighter; Silver-and-green brought on her silver tray Perrot's refilled goblet.

The Misses Wee then replaced themselves as before, each holding this time in fingers curved like chrysanthemum petals a claret glass enriched to the brim with liqueur. Miss Gold-and-red held *Cherry Heering*, Miss Silver-and-green *Crème de Menthe*.

'Cheer-*ho*, mai deah sah,' said Wee Soon Wat heartily. 'And sisters,' he added with some distaste.

'Cheer-*ho*, Mis-ter Pel-lot and Lon-ald,' said the Misses Wee in duet.

'Cheers — cheer-*ho*!' said Perrot.

Perrot was never sure at which moment, at which drink, the ship, as it were, left the firm shores of formality, but certainly some solid safety was sometime wantonly abandoned: there was a feeling of mural dipping and ducking, of undulations and fireworks, the floor became perverse, noise took on extra intonations and ran about like bediamonded cats.

It was at this stage, early in the storm, that Wee cried out, quite loudly and un-Orientally, 'Food! Melting Moments! Fastly!'

Say to me Ronald!

The Misses Wee, also crying out but in flutelike voices, 'Melt-ing Mom-ents, Melt-ing Mom-ents!' arose like flames, and disappared apparently into the banks of tinselled flowers.

'Mai sisters have cooking Melting Moments,' said Wee.

Melting moments? Ah, Melting Moments! Perrot remembered these delicacies of his boyhood Sunday suppers: half-spheres of crunchy, pale, sweet biscuit clamped together with icing. They scarcely went with Scotch, but the notion of any sort of food now had its interest. He proposed devouring many of these saccharine spheres which the Misses Wee, chirruping like many birds of paradise behind the lamps or flowers or cocktail-cabinet, were doubtless arranging — for he heard plate-like clinkings — on Ming.

Wee poured another drink. Perrot made a pointless gesture of refusal. Wee, who was turning *eau-de-nil*, scorned the gesture. Perrot accepted the drink just as the Misses Wee re-formed, elated with accomplishment and liqueurs, in the spinning and coruscating prison. 'Melting Moments,' they cried. 'We learn to cooking Melting Moments.'

'I,' gushed Perrot before he could stop himself, before he saw what they tendered on non-Ming plates, 'I love Melting Moments!' Then, sustaining a smile for each Miss Wee, and removing an object from each Miss Wee's plate — how could he dare favour one above the other? — Perrot ate each object in a simulation of relish.

The Misses Wee's Melting Moments were flat, greyish circles gummed together by a pale ooze, and flaccid as Dali watches. That smell of charred mice! The sugar (or was it ground glass?) infesting their plasticine-like texture tasted of garlic — oh, a mere connoisseur's whiff!

The Misses Wee closely watched him eat six. Then, once again arranged on their armchair, holding their gown-matching liqueurs in the petal fingers that had constructed and conveyed to him the Satanic sweetmeats, they continued to watch him as though he were an accident.

Where, meantime, was Wee?

'Where,' said Perrot, 'is Wee Soon Wat?' It suddenly seemed important to know.

The Misses Wee instantly removed their gaze from Perrot as from obscenity, and began to giggle, and continued giggling.

Their manner suggested that an impenetrable wall of humour separated ladies from fact. They began to talk with melodious speech at each other in a language Perrot presumed to be Chinese. Miss Silver-and-green downed her *Crème de Menthe* like an amateur actress playing Anna Christie, and lit a cigarette in an involved way.

The Misses Wee's legs were now being carelessly revealed. As they wildly chattered, vouchsafing nothing, they shot many hyphenated glances at Perrot. He had the impression of such a number of these jet glances *dit-dit-dit-dit* from each that, between the two of them and their four assessing eyes, one solid scrutiny was composed. This and the Chinese hullabaloo were becoming disconcerting, and he blushed. He took vulgar steps: he removed two of the cushions and dropped them callously on the floor; he flicked ash on the science-fiction Melting Moments; he smiled like a fox, and spoke again, more loudly than he intended.

'Where is Wee? Where?'

The schoolmasterliness momentarily terrified the Misses Wee to silence and paralysis. Their eyes raced about like crickets but could not resist, finally, all four of them, moving in one direction towards a door which Perrot now perceived for the first time.

It was a door terribly closed.

It was a bathroom door.

From behind it came the rooster-like sounds of Wee making efforts to avoid being heard being sick. Having faltered in their sisterly camouflage of chatter and false joy the Misses Wee returned their eyes to nowhere, and began more vivaciously and noisily their exchange of . . . of what?

Perrot, in an embarrassment, lowered his lips to his drink. Meeting people unlike oneself does not widen one's vision; it confirms one's notion that one is unique.

He understood now the clamorous smoke-screen of the sisters, but could not fully applaud it for he was certain that they were not discussing the weather or hair-ornaments. No, Perrot thought, they are discussing me, Perrot. Is my hair too mad? Have I Melting Moments surrounding my mouth like a screamingly funny leprosy? Is my fly undone? He could do nothing but drink again. The bathroom door shot open.

'Bad form! Bad form!' cried Wee Soon Wat, paler than the

Say to me Ronald!

heart of a lettuce but immaculate and unchastened. His sisters stopped as though their throats had been cut. 'Bad form to talking Chainese for mai deah sah. Pliss, sah, to drink. To date theah are plenty more wheah that are coming from.'

And once more, like a record one hoped would not be played again, the formalities began. Wee poured. Miss Silver-and-green circumspectly took up her tray. Miss Gold-and-red plugged cushions about her victim.

Their duties done, the Misses Wee replaced themselves like mobile waxworks.

'Cheer-*ho*, mai deah sah,' said Wee restraining a shudder to drink without a shudder.

'Hah-oo kaind you have said to Lon-ald,' intoned a Miss Wee, her eyes still as bullet-holes through which blew a glacial wind.

'Lon-ald admires Mis-ter Pel-lot and not admires bad form,' said the other, without conviction, and smiling by numbers.

'Lon-ald is sad and tlag-ic because goffing-bags are bad form.'

God!

Perrot made an effort. He called up his most dazzling party manners in an attempt to halt the cultured-pearl remarks.

'Too kind, too kind,' he said like the dying Florence Nightingale. 'You are all *very* kind. I cannot tell you how heart-warming to meet and to . . .'

What *am* I saying? he thought. And what the hell shall I say next? His audience impassively confronted him.

'Wee, do ask your charming sisters what they were saying before in Chinese. It really sounded fascinating,' he said.

God is listening to you, you bloody liar, he thought.

'Tell! Tell Mr Perrot!' said Wee, whose face was becoming dewy, in the voice of one about to enter a tunnel.

The Misses Wee imperceptibly stiffened. Their faces stopped at ivory; one could tell that, although their eyes were discreetly directed away from each other's and on some dot in outer space, they were really staring at each other in dismay. Their souls blinked; their spirits winced; their hearts said, 'Barbarians!'

Wee, too, stiffened; the dew on his forehead increased and shone in gems above his pistachio-green face. He was visibly wrestling with some inner demon.

'Tell, pliss,' he said in a voice attempting severity but in the tones of one already somewhere else.

'Not to worry, oh, not to worry, Wee,' said Perrot. The Misses Wee had, however, dutifully begun to translate themselves.

'We say,' said Miss Silver-and-green, 'that we not under-stand-ing Mis-ter Pel-lot, pliss.'

'We say,' continued Miss Gold-and-red, 'we say are Mis-ter Pel-lot laike all Aws-tlalian boy? Are Mis-ter Pel-lot?'

They both stared fixedly and callously at Perrot.

'Yiss, yiss,' said Miss Silver-and-green, suddenly very animated, but in a deadly way. 'Are Mis-ter Pel-lot laike all Aws-tlalian boy? *Are* Mis-ter Pel-lot?'

There seemed nothing to do but try answering.

'Well,' said Perrot, 'well, Miss Wee and . . . and Miss Wee, I think I may say I'm typical. That is typical enough. Well, *fairly* typical.'

The Misses Wee looked at him as if he were a flower arrangement they would like to tinker with. They uttered not a word.

'Tell, tell, tell!' cried Wee, quite strongly. He was less pallid, the will having successfully wrestled the flesh. 'Tell! You cannot clap with one hand.'

'We say we thinking Aws-tlalian boy . . .' and here Miss Silver-and-green made an insulting shrug of great beauty, and an exquisite denigratory hand movement.

Miss Gold-and-red imitated these sending-up movements to perfection.

Then both averted their eyes from Perrot in a commenting way and, in the next instant, began to giggle. Their giggles multiplied. They clutched each other. They writhed divinely in each other's slender arms.

'Bad form! To date most bad form!' shouted Wee, restored to full voice. 'Tell and tell! Fastly tell!'

Entwined and sinuous as salamanders, the Misses Wee gave broken and hysterically bubbling speech:

'Aws-tlalian boy . . .'
'Aws-tlalian boy not . . .'
'Not . . .'
'Mis-ter Pel-lot not . . .'
'Mis-ter Pel-lot . . .'
'Not . . .'
'Not hot stuff!'

'Singapore boy,' sang the Misses Wee, 'oh, Singapore boy hot stuff, hot stuff!'

They screeched, supporting each other on memory's ecstatic behalf.

From whatever plane of banishment he occupied Perrot heard the voice of his host, as suave as though the party were just about to begin and there were no shame in the world.

'Would you caring, sah,' said the voice of one expecting no denial, 'for whiskeh-sodah, sah?'

'Oh, no, Wee,' said Perrot, attempting to stir, to rise. 'Oh, please, *no*.'

Wee Soon Wat was already pouring.

'Not to worrying to date, sah,' he said. 'Theah are plenty more wheah that are coming from.'

As Miss Silver-and-green unwound herself from her sister to carry the silver tray, and Miss Gold-and-red prodded the cushions to embed Perrot more hotly and firmly, 'No, Wee, no. No, Wee, no,' he said.

'Say to me Ronald, mai deah sah,' said Wee Soon Wat, and went on pouring.

Brett

Hal Porter

When Benito Mussolini was Il Duce the Milan railway station was built.

Architecture without much conscience, it is edificial, colossal, and not unfittingly dictatorial. It is also very dreary: an intention to grandeur of the sublime kind doesn't at all come off. A façade of would-be triumphal arches leads into a succession of vast, austere lobbies, seemingly limitless, and far too lofty. Here, misshapen echoes vault cumbrously and forlornly about like headaches with nowhere to settle.

Once through the first dolorous arcade the traveller is confronted and affronted by a cyclopean alp of stairs which suggests by its mathematical cruelty the incline of an Aztec ziggurat. This scarp of livid stone depresses rather than overawes: it must be toiled up to attain the platforms from one of which *l'accelerato* starts south to run through Lombardy towards Parma, Bologna, Florence, and the ever-flowing, ever-cold fountains of Rome.

On a bleak afternoon in late November, a day of drizzle from a steel-grey sky onto a seal-grey city, Jean D. and I were being farewelled at the station by the Australian Consul-General's wife with whom we had lunched. Afterwards she had come with us to a refrigerated Santa Maria della Grazie while, as our planned last sight-seeing in Milan, we looked again at Leonardo da Vinci's *The Last Supper*.

We were both wary again-lookers drifting through the Old World in the direction of the equator, and back to Australia. Middle-aged, unpassionate but firm friends, hard-bitten tourists, we were revisiting together what we had, when younger, separately visited before. To sum up our itinerary — a Harry's Bar or a Trader Vic's was as much part of it as any Gothic polyptych, Byzantine mosaic or Bernini triton.

Somewhat chastened by *The Last Supper*, we were to catch the two-fifty for Florence.

The three of us stood flinching in the maelstrom of draughts at the foot of the grim cliff of stairs while Mario the consular chauffeur unloaded our baggage from the consular Fiat.

It was I perhaps who first noticed the young woman: her face. It was the Consul-General's wife who first spoke of her.

'Now *that*,' she said, 'is what I should be wearing.' She added, 'With my impossible legs.'

Jean D. and I, prudent cowards, looked neither at each other nor the legs we'd already noted as misproportionately strapping beneath the Consul-General's wife's svelte upper, and her delicately hollow face. We gave instead the keenest attention to what the young woman wore, the back-view as she ascended with much grace the Teotihuacán-like steep.

It was the year when the pitiless fashion of the mini-skirt was just giving way to a more humane one; freakish legs were returning to the seductive obscurity of longer skirts. In England, Germany, and France we had already seen numbers of women wearing the new style. The one before our eyes was the first we'd seen in Italy. A maxi-coat recalling a Ukrainian Cossack's, and worn with Russian boots, it was not only fitting wear for the untender wintriness of the day but strikingly set off its wearer's tallness and litheness. The flared skirt and its border of fur lilted romantically as she mounted the steps with all the stylish bravado of a *jeune premier* in a Graustarkian operetta. The two women with me went into analytical raptures which I did not interrupt with:

'But did you see her face?'

Useless to interrupt: had they seen it they would by then have forgotten: the Cossackian coat had become headless to them.

It was clear that what had caught my eye had not caught theirs: a face so like Eleanor da Toledo's in the Angelo Bronzino portrait that I felt myself go actually open-mouthed with amazement. It was, in effect, double amazement. There I was, about to board *l'accelerato* for Florence where one of the reasons for a proposed trek through the endless little salons of the Uffizi Gallery was to moon yet again, for the fifth or sixth time, in front of that very portrait with its sealed, cool countenance, its eyes depthless with indifference. Extraordinarily alike, portrait and passer-by: for an absurd moment it seemed reasonable to accept that Eleanor da Toledo could be a sixteenth-century ancestress of the supple stranger whose face was not only also impassive and impenetrable, a courtly mask, but whose hatless black hair was arranged much as the woman in the painting had arranged hers — was that looking-glass still alive? — more than three centuries ago.

Reason alone, I knew, is too fallible. That glimpse of her, fleeting yet charged, was no more than one from which a poem might be made, taut with regret because both the world and the Milan railway station were boundless enough for me and Eleanor da Toledo's reincarnation never to be breathing again at the same time the same freezing air with its odour of damp metal.

Jean D. and I said good-bye to the Consul-General's wife at the bottom of the steps, and climbed — how much less buoyantly than the tall girl with the still face and swashbuckling coat! — up and up into the skirmish of echoes, and the arctic cross-currents of inexplicable little indoor winds.

It would have matched my mood of Baudelairian spleen to find every seat in the train taken, and the corridor jammed with a rain-soaked herd of pilgrims on their way to Rome. The train was far from crowded. In the eight-seater *seconda classe* compartment where we settled five minutes before departure there were only three passengers.

In one window-seat was a very fat Italian woman, fiftyish, high-bosomed, with an adolescent moustache.

Opposite her sat a stocky young man brutally handsome as a brigand.

Their attire announced that they were possibly of the lower middle class, in any country the most conventional, and therefore the most easily identified. They wore the sort of clothes seen behind the plate-glass of smaller department stores, the uniform of the hide-bound and frugal, unemphatic wear, factory-made of artificial materials. The one thing about them not ersatz was their behaviour; but even that, taking into consideration the melodramatic country we were in, was orthodox enough.

They were patently mother and son: a family profile jutted out of her blubber and his sullenness, and they were so engrossed in a generation tiff that they neither spared us a sideglance nor lost an impassioned syllable when we came in. They were both holding forth at the one time; her soprano railing went volubly on above his fierce baritone declaiming over and over again:

'*Non è stata colpa mia!*' — whatever it was it wasn't his fault — '*Non è stata colpa mia, mamma! Non . . . è . . . stata . . . colpa . . . mia!*'

On the badgered son's side of the compartment, plumb in the middle, the half-clock-face of the airconditioning switch directly above his hair which was like goffered iron, sat another Italian, perhaps seventy, perhaps only sixty: it was hard to tell. Not once in the two-and-a-half hours he was with us did we hear him speak, or catch his eye.

He sat monolithically upright as a stone Rameses, contentedly withdrawn, his scoured, sun-darkened hands inactively set on his hams. The contours and rich rustic colouring of his face reminded me of an Arcimboldi one, a composition of corn-cobs, pomegranates, chestnuts, and onions. He seemed so much of the earth that we'd have to be, one felt, famished oxen or ailing vines, before his attention would turn to us, and his unreflective eyes come to life. He could, of course, have been a rugged solitary who despised the vile world, and played Ravel exquisitely.

I sat on the so-to-speak masculine side of the compartment, in the corner next to the corridor. Jean arranged herself opposite and, as we usually did on train journeys, we began the process of retracting somewhat from each other. She opened her guidebook at, I had no doubt, the chapter on Florence. A loud-speaker voice gabbling truculently against its own several echoes announced that our train was about to leave. I experienced that sensation of feline well-being mingled with here-we-go-again boredom the experienced traveller is apt to experience at such times.

Then, at the last moment, mere seconds before the wheels

turned, the young woman in the Cossack coat flashed radiantly into sight at the doorway, scanned the compartment with lustrous heartless eyes, and appeared to find it worthy of her. From where she stood, and deftly as a basketball player throwing a goal, she tossed her valise onto the rack.

This *coup de théâtre* accomplished, she moved in, and sat with decisive aplomb between Jean D. and the fat mother who, at a climax of son-baiting, her wattles aquiver, spat out a scalding babble of insult. The victim had had enough. Harshly crying, *'Non l'ho fatto apposta!'* — I didn't do it on purpose! — he folded his arms as though barricading himself behind them, set his jaws, and closed his eyes. A door had been slammed in a face.

Furtively, as if sidling from an unhallowed cathedral, the train slipped between the soaring nave piers, through a rood-screen of grimy girders, over the no-altar, and out into the Milanese rain so like all other rains, the dejected industrial outskirts that could have been anywhere.

All this, and a funereal burden of smoke lowering above a palisade of chimney-stacks, I took in from the corner of my senses. For the rest I was covertly but wholly taking in the unbelievable late arrival.

She was, I saw, years younger than Bronzino's Eleanor, but twentieth-century experiences had given her an additional gloss of age in a dimension beyond years. Self-possession's self, she lit a cigarette, and opened a Penguin. The nails of the ringless, long long Renaissance fingers were bitten. That was a touch jarringly too human and modern, and stopped me in my tracks on the poetic by-path I'd taken. The Penguin was Elizabeth Bowen's *To The North*.

So, as well as being a nail-biter, she wasn't a Latin after all! This reversed sign-post was more than intriguing: I contemplated a remark about Elizabeth Bowen. Jean D. was ahead of me.

The proximity of the fur-trimmed Cossack sleeve to her Scotch tweed one generated some electricity of intuition. My friend closed the guidebook in a final way and, with the certainty that the animal in the cage she was entering was of a familiar species, spoke to the young woman. The species certainly was familiar; the animal ready to play, and without reserve. She was also Australian. She had been working for three months, *au pair* but with a small salary, as nursemaid to the baby twins of a Signor and Signora Russo, at Parma. Oh, she was absolutely without reserve. She abhorred Parma, she said, loathed the Signor who was, like all Dago men, sly and a sex maniac; scorned the Signora; and couldn't stand babies. And the meals! *Pasta*, no matter what shape or colour, she hated. Veal too, and sausages containing God knows what. As for the continental breakfast, that was hardly food at all, or at most:

'*Slum* food, actually. Bread-and-jam and cocoa — and I *detest* crusts!'

She was twenty going on twenty-one. Her name was Brett Something-or-Other. Had her mother been reading Hemingway when she was pregnant? I didn't ask although dying to. Maybe, as people do to lighten the hard work of travel, she would come to telling.

Travellers, imprisoned with strangers in foreign trains, ships' bars, air-terminal waiting-rooms, chartered tourist buses lunging through Turkey or Afghanistan, are inclined to foil *ennui* by being as unreticent about themselves as characters in a Chekhov play.

About themselves: how else keep their identity in places they do not belong to?

About themselves: even though the impression they more often than not create is of eccentricity, recklessness, animal cunning, of an incredible toughness shot through with peculiar snobberies and almost-idiot simplicities. Perhaps Brett would later clear up why she had been named Brett. As I listened to her talking to Jean D. in an educated, extravert voice, it was manifest she had no thought of hiding anything.

I am, her manner said, what I am: lump it or leave it.

While exchanging *dragées* and peppermints and cigarettes, the women exchanged more and more of themselves, admitting me to their confidences but offhandedly, as though I were scarcely human, a dummy on the side-line. For all her poise (the panache, for example, with which she'd entered the compartment) she seemed to live in perpetual suspense. Her version of herself was hounded and harassed, a chronic Victim of Fate. It was done humorously, yet, as I laughed, I felt alarm at what catastrophe might be just ahead: some of the past catastrophes, however hilariously she presented them, seemed to me hair-raising, rape or murder an inch off.

She was always losing things, her passport, traveller's cheques, a camera, or leaving her purse with the last of her money in it at some place so disreputable that there was no hope of its being returned. She missed trains or buses to find herself stranded among near-cutthroats at unhealthy hours, drifted solo into the back-alley haunts of criminals and prostitutes; found herself fighting off inflamed lechers in places so out-of-the-way that no Good Samaritan would have heard her scream. Once she and an Australian girlfriend, speeding through Germany in a rented car, had run down a deer on the outskirts of East Berlin at three o'clock in the morning, and had spend three days and nights in a lock-up.

'The food,' she said, 'was miraculous — *Kaffee mit Sahne*, yet!'

She was, she said, in trouble at the moment, with not a brass razoo to her name, down to her last unbroached packet of cigarettes, and nearly three days late in getting back from the week-end she had nagged Signora Russo into letting her spend in Milan.

'Everything, but everything, happens to poor Brett,' she said complacently.

Meantime, outside, a landscape like a rain-botched *grisaille*, sodden Lombardy slid murkily by between the profiles of mother and son. He had been permitted a length of sanctuary behind the barrier of his folded arms and shuttered eyes while she dipped at mechanic intervals into a black plastic carry-all for titbits she chewed with the engrossed mien of a plot-hatcher. A moment arrived when she was sated, and had ruminated her next move into shape. She attacked again, sharply: 'Carlo!'

No response so, more sharply, louder: 'Car-lo, Car-lo!'

Once more, no response.

The jelly of her face stiffened: she knew he heard within the fort. From among the chattels banked up around her she groped out a chubby umbrella, and tapped his knee with the blunt ferrule. He still keep to his asylum; one felt he had his back to the door, hard. A muscle flickered on his cheek.

'Car-*lo*!'

This time she tapped viciously enough to hurt. He didn't wince but his eyes, as inexpressive as all brown eyes are, shot wide open, then immediately became slits. Politely enough, yet gratingly, threateningly, he asked what she wanted, *'Che cosa desidera?'*

She beat on the seat beside her with a fat little hand, and trilled:

'É troppo duro; é troppo duro.'

It wasn't hard at all; on this tourist-ridden line even the second class catered for spoiled foreigners. Anyway, had it been brown sienna marble instead of brown leatherette padded with foam rubber, Carlo's mother was her own luxurious cushions. Marble, fakir's spikes, fire-walker's coals, what could her child have done? Nurse her? Advise her to stand, or swing like a larger marmoset from the luggage-rack? He didn't even bother to answer, shut his eyes, and contemptuously, as though to exclude someone crazy.

Unbearable! Unfilial! Humiliating! — the ferrule prodding maliciously at his entwined fore-arms expressed these for her. He came to angry life, and grabbed the ferrule, far from playfully.

'Carlo, ma no!'

She squealed as if we other four were not there, tug-of-warring frantically as with a real snatch-thief, both hands in use. A new line, femininity, was jolted into being.

'Fa freddo,' she wailed, piping, frail and helpless.

'Fa freddo, Car-lo mi-o!' and pounded her patent-leather trotters girlishly on the floor to indicate their being violet with cold. Suddenly he let go and, as she bounced back with a squeak, stretched out for the air-conditioner switch above the hair of the Rameses man who didn't even slope his head automatically to one side but remained static and sequestered as a private image. Carlo pushed the pointer to its heat limit, *Caldo*, and, as one saying, 'There, boil to death, dear mother, and leave me in peace', again immured himself behind his arms and eyelids.

Brett said very clearly, 'The perverse old bitch! What that overweight madam needs is a back-hander across the chops!'

It was fascinating. Edged with indictment as her voice was, her face remained serene. She might have been praising or blessing the brawlers. They had, however, aroused a sleeping dog. She began again to denigrate Signora Russo and all living

209

Italians. Because of the crystal pitch of her voice, she was as embarrassing as a cruel child. It disordered me. How could she know that the Italians didn't understand English, that she wasn't committing a social atrocity? I suppose, in fact, that she didn't care if every word were intelligible, and that she looked on them as being as culpable as the next Italian.

She hadn't come to Italy to dislike it; its inhabitants had taught her to. She felt blameless: she'd earned her fare over; was paying her way, working her way, conning her way when all else failed, through an Old World she'd been lured into visiting by gilded legends, propaganda ablaze with seductive adjectives. She'd been taken in by a mirage of civilizations accounted superior to her own country's, of breathtaking landscapes strewn with gorgeous cities and enchanting villages alive with diverting and decorative people.

She had been too ingenuous to believe, had not lived long enough to learn, that the Utopias of the pamphlet are what one does one's best to avoid. Now, behind her happy-go-lucky cynicism and audacious front, disillusion stirred like Polonius behind the arras. She spared nothing: Italy was a fifth-rate vaudeville show, the Italians cheap and nasty buffoons. She was revolted by the showy clothes hiding the dismal secrets of uncleanliness; sick of the untrustworthiness, the emotionalism, and jealous pride; infuriated by the sensual, over-confident faces of those who accosted her.

'Brett's *virgo intacta*, and proud of it,' she said almost ringingly. 'But a wise virgin, and not a timid one.'

The terrors of the flesh she held at bay: she had, it seemed, learnt well the perilous lessons of modesty and love but didn't think them shield enough.

'See here!'

She took from her hand-bag a pair of wickedly pointed little scissors.

'They're silver. My great-grandmother used them for embroidery. She'd die again if she knew, poor lamb, what I use them for.'

In queues, crowded trains and trams, cinemas, and public gardens, she carried them in her hand ready to stab into men who touched her. Her intolerance was flawless. Cheek by jowl with Italians in the compartment of *l'accelerato* she was separated from them by an abyss of the spirit. The Italian woman and her son shocked her: she *hated* them, she said, her face as expressionless as a camellia — yet it might have been a serpent speaking.

Curiously, despite a force and stringency in her conversation, one became also aware of odd slacknesses, bewildering non sequiturs. The link between thought and thought seemed especially to dissolve at a direct question. At first I thought she was letting down a safety-curtain on some of Jean D.'s feelers, but her whole-hearted candour made that unlikely. It was just that, with one foot in sophistication, the other in naïveté, dislocations occurred. She was, for example, denouncing Signora Russo for always being underfoot, always hanging over her own babies:

'I don't know why she bothers with a nanny. I might just as well be in Saudi-Arabia. Sometimes I'd like to hit her.'

Jean D., who thinks kindly of most Italians and all babies, said, 'Oh, you can't mean that, Brett. She treats you very well. You have plenty of time off. After all, why shouldn't she dote on her own babies?'

'Because she'll ruin them. Besotted woman — tying and untying their ribbons all the time as if they were dolls.'

'But she's their *mother*.' Jean D., childless, was becoming fervent and stubborn.

'Yes, I suppose the creature is.' To my surprise she spoke mildly, as if she had of a sudden seen the Signora in a new light, a kind of Crivelli Madonna dandling two Holy Children in front of an oriel window-sill crowded with porcelain-like fruit, enamelled-looking flowers, and highly glazed cucumbers.

'Then, surely,' asked Jean D. more in the manner of a sentimental deaconess than I'd have believed possible, 'she can be forgiven, or at least understood?'

'I . . . don't . . . think . . . so.' Brett answered lingeringly, apparently in thought. It couldn't have been thought, for she added, 'No, I *don't* think so. She's far too pretty, and has varicose veins.' She paused. 'Anyway, she's a bank-manager's wife.'

Jean D. was flummoxed enough to say, 'What difference does that make?'

'My father's one, too.'

On the subject of returning to Parma three days late after racketing about Milan with wanderer Australian friends on their way to Venice her thoughts were equally random and unmarried to each other.

'What on earth,' Jean D. had asked, 'will your Signora say?'

'I don't care a damn what she says. Or does. She can rave on like that obese dolly in the window-seat if it gives her a kick. I'll make up some taradiddle or other — tell her I ran out of lire.'

While I was still trying to spot what was askew about this, Jean D. said, 'Heavens, girl, *that's* hardly a convincing lie. If you'd no money how could you afford three extra days?'

'It's not a lie.' How calm she was. From the handbag containing scissors but no money she languidly took her last packet of cigarettes. 'I told you I hadn't a brass razoo.' Finically as a good little girl, she began opening the packet. 'But this morning I had lashings of lucre.'

'You haven't lost your purse again?' Jean D. was getting motherly.

'No. I can't imagine why — but no, the money's not lost this time. I lent it to two blokes who were skint.'

'You *lent* it!' Jean D. was maternally severe. 'So now you're skint. Who were they?' She doubtless pictured a brace of confidence men from Naples pretending to be Veronese counts who'd left their wallets in other suits.

'One was an Australian.'

'I see.' Jean D. was now absolute mother. 'And the other?'

Brett languidly lit a cigarette, languidly exhaled. 'Oh, he was an Australian.'

A silence had to fall. There was nothing to say. Jean D. looked at me, I at her, our eyes as it were shrugging. There was nothing else to do.

At that moment the mother in her discreet production-belt hat animated herself, and intoned with tragic intensity, *'Carlo mio, fa troppo caldo.'*

The son, perhaps truly, like a disciple at Gethsemane, slept on.

'Io sudo,' she whined, dabbing a pink handkerchief on her moustache which was indeed beaded with sweat. *'Io sudo, Carlo. Non posso sopportare il calda.'*

'She can't bear the bloody heat!'

Brett rose up, breathing authentic cigarette smoke, and metaphorical flame. 'Neither can I. Excuse me, talkative,' she said down in the coiffure of the living idol whose self-absorption remained unruffled as she abruptly turned the air-conditioning pointer right back to *Freddo*. 'And I sincerely hope, Mother Macree, that you freeze to death.'

Whatever the words conveyed to us Australians, the tone cannot have conveyed anything to the Italians, particularly as she uttered without a side-glance at them, and had moved to perform her ostensibly gracious act like a well-bred and mobile caryatid on whose carven tresses an invisible burden of marble acanthus leaves and a ton of architrave were being perfectly balanced. Reseating herself, her visage politely neutral, 'God, I *hate* them,' she said.

Beyond the windows a drenched Lombardy was running out; before many minutes *l'accelerato* would be in drenched Emilia.

Sky-scraper crags, bottomless primeval lakes, cascades frothing soapily down gorges, leagues of blue-and-white snow-dunes, unemployed nature in any guise is not to my taste. It would have pleased me, however, had the plains docile from centuries of cultivation not been veiled in vertical water, to look out at them, at the tamed rivers, the food-bearing trees and drink-bearing vines, the wounded towers and castles far-off on their hill-top aeries, the farther-off mountains like penitentiary walls still keeping in something mediaeval and feudal, the fumes of vendetta and foray and, in the veins of the last of the vine-leaves, the blood of battle-axed mercenaries, of war-horses and lords, which had long ago extravagantly irrigated the soil. Since I was unable to see what lay outside, the beauty that is feud's aftermath, I had to make do with the feud in the compartment, and await its aftermath.

It wasn't a situation about which to be flinty. Brett's naïveté was too engaging for that, and her fearlessness rather moving because what was callous in it was not inborn but a culture: necessity its spore. Her fury was, I felt, only that of the displaced and disappointed, transient enough for air to have wafted it into her mind. The faintest movement of the weathervane, and a breath would puff it out.

Perhaps, now, she could never cry, 'Open, sesame!' with the

old wide-eyed expectation — she had learnt too much to want to, but she could still cry, 'Open, wheat!', 'Open, barley!' and not be let down. The consequences of her impercipience meant nothing to her, nothing: it proved nothing except the immeasurable distance between two national minds. She had arrived at the point where civilisation (as she recognised it) was seen, by its absence, to have existed where she came from, not where she had come to. Homesickness can calcify the heart and buckle the vision as quickly and easily as vice.

The train advanced into Emilia and the melancholy borderland of twilight. Perhaps because abhorred Parma, amorous Signor Russo, the doting Signora and her beribboned twins, tomorrow and tomorrow, all swam nearer and nearer through the darkening rain, she fell silent, closed her eyes, and did not sleep.

Her face! — behind its composure an engagement with emotion could be guessed at, but the ivory surface, the Goddess of Mercy blankness admitted nothing: her hands with their bitten nails now and then shifted restlessly on her fashionable lap.

Jean D. opened her guidebook. Would it inform her that for nearly five centuries Florence had been, like Rome and Vienna, Madrid and Paris, a centre of fake antiquities and forged masterpieces?

Night's tide was in when Brett opened her eyes.

'Forgive me, Jean. I was out on business. Really! I've been desperately trying to think of something heart-breaking. Hopeless!'

She gave no explanation, but went on, 'I must have some money. Must. *Must*.'

She was talking to Jean D. rather than to both of us but her wantonly clear voice could no doubt be heard in the next compartment if not farther off.

'Oh, dear, it's maddening. In three weeks' time I want to be out of Parma. You see, there's a promise I've got to keep. Two girl-friends are coming down from Norway. We'll join up at Milan, go down to Rome and Naples, then to Brindisi where we'll get a ship across the Adriatic to Greece. I've been there before, and *loathed* it, but a promise is a promise. Even if I have to sleep in the Parthenon, and get my Vitamin C from those sour oranges that grow on the street-trees in Athens, I'll need *real* money to get there. I was certain I'd have it by now, but everything's gone wrong. Me all over, of course. Time's running out. Poor little Brett's on the horns of a whatsis. No matter how much I try and try, I can't get my suit-case stolen. What would you do?'

'To . . . to get my suit-case stolen?' Jean D. spoke out of a fog. Suddenly it cleared: 'Oh, I see. For the insurance, you mean?'

'Yes. It's money for jam. Or so I thought.'

She had heavily insured everything she'd brought with her from Australia, and losing her expensive camera at a time when she was on the rocks had found the insurance money a god-send. The camera's loss had been an accident; the loss she was now set on was to be deliberate. The case she hoped to collect on was, she said, a costly monster so large that it had to be wheeled on an also-costly fold-up trolley. For the sort of bread-line travelling she and her young friends now did, invaders' skimpily-accoutred Blitzkriegs, the monster, with its attendant contraption, was a hindrance. It was also potential capital.

Her account of attempts to abandon it was very funny, illegal though her intentions. She'd done everything possible to contrive situations in which her head was morally above water, even if only just. Usually she left it on railway platforms next to the most criminal-looking people in sight while she walked conspicuously away, not looking back, to dally in station bars or waiting-rooms or buffets. Time after time she returned to find it, despised loot, exactly as she'd left it. Twice she had deserted it on buses. Once a group of men who resembled the denizens of a thieves' kitchen had yelled and whistled her back; once a wizened old man with a squint had scorched after her on a new-fangled bicycle.

'I suppose,' she said, 'the costly bloody monster *and* its costly trolley are too conspicuous to steal. And — ' She smiled faintly. — 'I'm too conspicuous to be stolen from. It bugs me. Either they're all daft, or I'm fated, or both.'

In a Europe she regarded as an elaborate piece of machinery set up to bilk and pillage the tourist, an honesty she regarded as perverse dogged her.

'I'd contemplated defying the fates, and trying again in Milan, but decided no-no-*no*: better to enjoy myself than have the worry of not losing it again. I've got a better plan. When I get off at Parma . . . *hell*, where are we?'

The train was decelerating, running over points. She recognized, through the streaming panes, some reassuring combination of lights and outlines.

'Ah, thank God this isn't for me.'

It was for Signor Rameses-Arcimboldi who unfolded into an unexpectedly squat man, took an old-fashioned kit-bag from the rack, slid open the door, and wordlessly, on his too-short legs, went out to wait in the corridor.

'Carlo! Che ora è? Quanto ci fermiano qui? Ho sete, Carlo. Ho appetito!' keened the mother.

Carlo, eyes balefully open, said cruelly that he wasn't thirsty or hungry: *'Non ho sete. Non ho appetito.'* Outraged, detonated, she released a torrent of melodious abuse. Like a lip-reader, or someone at a *film muto*, he watched, one felt, rather than heard.

The train stopped. The full-dress tirade didn't. The little platform was bare except for the silent man and his kit-bag jogging through the rain. A dog committing a dire aria could be heard. The train started.

'Oh, do shut up, you neurotic old sow,' said Brett looking at the palm of one hand. 'You know, it's a wonder he doesn't knife the whingeing hag. I'd like to see Signora Giovanni Russo try to bully me like that.'

Right then, it came to me that for all the mother's malicious caterwauling and the son's churlishness, all the domestic discord, the two Italians with their passion-afflicted faces had quieter nerves than Brett with her unmarked brow and tender mouth. Theirs might well have been a happy partnership of hate, for hate has as many allegiances as love, and far less fallible ones. If their faces were, so to speak, chewed, their finger-nails weren't.

'You were saying,' said Jean D., the orchestra-conductor tapping with the baton, 'that when you get off at Parma . . .'

'I'll show them.'

Brett flicked her compact open, reviewed her lips and eyes in the glass, did nothing to them.

'I used to have lovely nails until I took to feasting on them.'

She put away the compact, and gazed tranquilly at her fingers.

'They really are repulsive. It makes me shudder to look at them.'

'Show whom what?' Jean D. was pedantic but persistent. Curiosity gnawed at her like the Spartan youth's fox: she had no intention of letting Brett's riven mind remain unwelded.

'The insurance people, of course. When I get to Parma my new plan goes straight into action.' She inhaled a sighing breath. 'I'm going to report to the Dago station-master that I've lost the monster.'

We said nothing.

'Have I shocked you? Everyone does it. *Have* I?'

Neither of us answered. I saw Jean D.'s face — and felt mine — congeal at non-committal. I said, 'Will they believe you?'

'Oh, don't say that! They'll *have* to believe me. I'll make them. I used to be quite an actress at school; Portia, you know — "it droppeth as the gentle rain", and so on.'

She went into a kind of trance, enacting what she'd devised, running over her pathetic script.

'I'll tell them that the case was so enormous it couldn't fit on the mingy little second-class rack, so I left it in the corridor. What else could I do? Why didn't I book it through in the luggage-van? Because, poor maiden, I didn't get to the station in time.' She dropped the mediumistic manner, and absurdly pleaded, 'You saw that, didn't you, Jean, my leaping on just as the train was moving out?' Then she returned to her other fiction. 'I was desperate. I'd been lost for *hours* in Milan, all all alone, and was worried frantic about getting back to the dear, sweet, lovely *bambini*. In the train I was so exhausted from trailing around Milan in the downpour that I fell asleep, and didn't wake up until we arrived at Parma. When I went out into the corridor to get my case — *mamma mia! il mio bello, bello bagaglio* — gone! I'll burst into tears. *"Mamma mia, mamma mia,"* I'll sob, *"Oh, mamma mia, il mio bagaglio!"*

The snatches of Italian interrupted the bickering in the window-seats; mother and son turned their simmering, feral eyes on the elegant foreigner. She sensed their attention. Without deigning to look at them, she said, 'Stare, stare, monkey bear! Mind your own bloody business, slobs!'

I think Jean D. and I thought that, surely this time, some Mediterranean extra-sensory gift might have been at last brought into play, and the rudeness understood, for we both quickly spoke.

'Will it work?' was hers; 'It won't work,' was mine.

'It has to. I promised the girls I'd meet them outside the Milan cathedral at midday on the fifteenth of next month, traveller's cheques and all. I couldn't let them down. I've got to be a get-rich-quick maiden this time. All this mess wouldn't have happened if one of the nit-wits had had the nous to pinch the case instead of trying to pinch my you-know-what. Imagine poor Brett weeping and wailing in front of a lecherous gang of porters! *"Ah, poverina, poverina",* they'll croon, and pat me, and I won't be able to use my scissors. And then there'll be the police, and I'll have to repeat the entire *mamma mia* performance.'

She inhaled another, deeper, sighing breath.

'One must martyr oneself for oneself,' she said blandly.

Jean D. was near tears. It wouldn't have surprised me if she'd drawn the regal head down to her bosom.

'But aren't you worried, Brett?'

Did she really mean morally worried? Did she mean, on a lower plane, worried about attempting blatant perjury without any of the technique of the Duse it would require to make it work? Did she, on the lowest plane, mean worried at the possibility of being not believed? Which sort of worried did she mean?

'Worried! Of course. I spent my last lire in that clinical buffet on the Milan station to mop up a few fortifying vinos. I'm worried *stiff*.'

She — which sort of worried did she mean? She consulted the compact again, this time using a lipstick, wiping powder on, fussing with her scarf, touching up the leading lady or preparing the victim. Worried? The touched-up face was as pacific as a tarn nothing is reflected in.

She put a cigarette between her lips, and struck a match. The quivering of the tiny flame made it clear that her hand was unsteady.

'Oh dear,' she said, 'poor Brett.'

She blew out the match without lighting the cigarette, and admonished herself: 'Stop that instantly, you silly maiden.

Stop, right now.'

The aristocratic hands with their gnawed nails, held out before her, became still.

'Anyway,' she said, putting the cigarette back in the packet, 'there's no time.'

She stood, reached for her valise, put it on the seat, and sat again, tilting her head back, closing her eyes. She kept them closed for five minutes, ten minutes, until the train, jerking over points, passing through a lighted suburb, came to Parma, and stopped.

She opened her eyes. 'Yes, Jean,' she said, rising, and taking up her valise. 'I'm *very* worried. I've been trying to think of something sad so that I can cry for those galoots out there. Good-bye.'

At the door she spoke once again, and then went. The train started. We passed her, pliant and untouchable in the Cossack coat, moving over the brilliant reflections on the wet platform. The rain had gone. Her last words had not: we kept on hearing them.

'I'm terrified. What's going to happen now? All I need is tears, and I can't think of a single unhappy incident in my whole life.'

Warrigal

Dal Stivens

'You'll have to get rid of that dingo before long,' my neighbour Swinburne said to me across the fence. 'Why, he's an Asiatic wolf —'

'No one of any authority says that the dingo is an Asiatic wolf,' I said. 'The Curator of Mammals at the Australian Museum classifies the dingo as *Canis familiaris* variety *dingo* — that is, a variety of the common dog. Another eminent authority says it's most unlikely that the dingo is descended from the northern wolf —'

'I know a wolf when I see it,' this classic pyknic said. 'I don't care what some long-haired professors say. I was brought up in the bush.'

As my wife Martha says, I can be insufferable at times — particularly when I'm provoked. I said: 'So much for your fears of this animal attacking you — it's most unlikely as long as he continues to look on you as the *gamma* animal. Of course, you need to act like a *gamma* animal at all times.'

I thought for a moment he was going to climb over the paling fence that divided our properties and throw a punch at me.

'You be careful who you call an animal!' he said. His big red face and neck were swelling like a frog's. It was pure Lorenz and Hediger I was throwing at him. This was during my animal behaviour period.

'I'm not calling you an animal,' I said. 'I'm just explaining how the dingo sees you. He sees me as the *alpha* animal — *alpha* is Greek for A. I'm the pack leader in his eyes. He sees my wife, Martha, as the *beta* animal. *Beta* is B and *gamma* is C. He probably sees you and your wife and kids as *gamma* or *delta* animals. *Delta* is D. While you behave like *gamma* or *delta* animals, you'll be O.K. He'll defer to you.'

He seemed a little assured — or confused, anyway.

'This *gamma* stuff,' he began uncertainly. 'You're sure of it, now?'

'I'll lend you a book,' I said.

'All the same, he's got pretty powerful jaws,' he said, pointing to Red, who was crouching at my feet, his eyes not leaving me. The jaws were, as he said, powerful, and the white shining canine teeth rather large. The head was a little too large, the prick ears a bit too thick at the roots for Red to be a really handsome dog, but there was a compact power in his strong tawny chest and limbs.

'No more than a German shepherd's,' I said. There were two of them in Mansion Road — that wasn't the name but it will do.

'I suppose so,' he said doubtfully.

'If I hadn't told you Red was a dingo you wouldn't be worrying,' I said. 'I could have told you Red was a mongrel.'

'Are you trying to tell me I wouldn't know a dingo?' he started in belligerently.

Before I could answer, his own dog, a Dobermann Pinscher and a real North Shore status job, came out and began challenging Red. Both dogs raced up and down on their sides of the fence, the Pinscher growling and barking and Red just growling. (Dingoes don't bark in the wilds. When domesticated some learn to do so but Red hadn't.)

Red ran on his toes, his reddish-brown coat gleaming and white-tipped bushy tail waving erect. His gait was exciting to watch: it was smooth, effortless and one he could maintain for hours.

'This is what I mean,' he said. 'Your Asiatic wolf could savage my dog to death.'

'Yours is making the most noise,' I said. The Pinscher was as aggressive as his master.

'Noise isn't everything,' he said. 'Look at that wolf-like crouching.'

'Innate behaviour,' I said. 'Dingoes have acquired that over thousands of years of attacking emus and kangaroos. They crouch to avoid the kicks.'

'So your wolf is getting ready to attack, is he?'

'Not necessarily,' I said. 'No more than yours is. Of course, if one dog were to invade the other's territory, then there would be a fight. But they won't invade.'

'Yours could jump the fence,' he said. 'I've seen him. He could kill my dog and clean up my fowls.'

'Not into your place,' I said. I was beginning to lose my temper. 'He wouldn't. He knows it isn't his.'

'So he's moral, is he?' he shouted. 'This wild dog —'

'They're all moral although the term is anthropomorphic. Wild dogs or domestic dogs usually won't invade another's territory.'

'So you say,' he said. His face was purpling. 'I warn you now yours had better not. If he does I'll shoot him. The law's on my side.'

I was so angry I went inside and got a hammer. I started knocking palings out of the fence.

'Hey!' he shouted. 'That's my fence. And I meant what I said about shooting that Asiatic mongrel.'

'Pure-bred dingo,' I grunted. I was out of condition and the nails were tough. 'Our fence.'

I got four palings out and, as I knew would happen, the dogs kept racing past the gap and ignoring the chance to enter and attack. I was dishing out pure Lorenz.

'It's just bluff,' I said. 'You can see it for yourself. They talk big. After they've said their bit, they'll knock off.'

'Perhaps,' he said, doubtfully.

'Call your dog out into the street,' I said. 'I'll call mine. They'll meet in the middle and sniff each other's anal quarters but they won't fight. There's nothing to fight about — none lays claim to the centre of the road. Of course, the footpath is different.'

'I won't risk it,' he said and he called the Pinscher and started off. 'You may be right and your dingo ought to be at home in your garden.'

It might have sounded conciliatory to you. But there was a crack in it. This was during my Australian native flora period. When I bought this block I had the house built well down the hillside and left all the trees and shrubs. I wanted a native bushland garden and I had left what the other people in Mansion Road called 'that rubbish' in its near-natural state. I had planted some more natives — waratahs like great red Roman torches, delicately starred wax flowers and native roses, piquantly scented boronias, flannel flowers, and subtly curving spider flowers. This was in keeping with my newly acquired feeling for *furyu*, which is often used to described things Japanese. It can be translated as 'tasteful', but the Japanese characters convey a fuller meaning of 'flowing with the wind' — the acceptance of nature, of the material itself, and of the patterns it imposes. Transferring the concept to Australia, I was accepting nature and learning to appreciate the muted beauty of Australian shrubs and flowers.

The neighbours didn't approve. They all had lots of lawns and terraces and beds of perennials and annuals. They'd chopped down most of the native trees and planted exotics. They thought my garden lowered the tone of the street. And they thought the same about our unobtrusive low-line house, blending with the slim eucalypts and the sandstone outcrops. They preferred double-fronted mod. bungs.

We'd have got on a lot better if we had lived in Mansion Road during my azalea and camellia period. At our last house Martha and I had gone in for landscaping — vistas, focus points and the rest. And we'd used azaleas and camellias for much of the mass planting. I'd got myself wised up on azaleas, particularly, and I knew as much as most about Wilson's fifty Kurumes; I once engaged in some learned discussion in a specialist journal as to whether or not some experts were correct in thinking Pink Pearl (*Azuma Kagami*) was, indeed, the progenitor of all the pink-flowered forms.

That was some time ago, and although I still like azaleas, the love affair was then over. Not everyone appreciates Australian natives. We went away for a week once and when we came back someone had dumped two tons of rubbish into our place. We had no fence at the street level and someone had thought it was a virgin block. The house is well down the slope and hard to see from the street. Of course, he should have noticed the rather heavy concentration of native flora. He had tipped the rusting tins, galvanized iron, mattresses, and so on, onto a stand of native roses, too.

We didn't really fit into Mansion Road for a number of reasons. First, there was my profession as a journalist and writer. And moreover, Martha and I were in our Chagall period; our earlier Rembrandt love affair might have been accepted.

And there was the car business. They all had one or two cars but we didn't see the need when there was a good taxi and hire car service. When they finally got the idea that we could afford a car but wouldn't have one, it struck them as un-Australian or something.

The dingo business was merely another straw, though Swinburne seemed to be trying to push it a bit further.

'Why get yourself angry?' Martha reproached me when I went inside.

'A conformist ass!' I said.

'You can't educate him,' she said.

'I know,' I said. 'I was having a bit of fun.'

'Whatever you call it, we'll probably have to get rid of Red,' she said.

'Where?' I said.

That was the question. I wasn't giving him to the Zoo, as some in Mansion Road had hinted I should. Dingoes are far-ranging, lively, intelligent creatures and it would be cruelty to confine him. And I couldn't release him in the bush now that he was a year old and had had no training in hunting for himself. Normally, he would have acquired this from his mother, but I'd got Red as a pup. A zoologist friend had brought him to Sydney and then found his wife wouldn't let him keep a dingo.

I didn't see Swinburne again until the next week-end. He called me over the fence.

'What you say about that dingo might be true at present but he'll revert to type,' he said. 'The hunting instinct is too strong. It will be someone's chicken run eventually even if it's not mine.'

'He hasn't been taught to hunt fowls — or anything else,' I said. 'So why should he? He's well fed.'

'Primitive instincts are strong,' said Swinburne.

'We don't know what his primeval instincts are,' I said.

'He's a wild dog.'

I said, insufferably: 'Professor Konrad Lorenz, who is one of the world's greatest authorities on dogs, says that the dingo is a descendant of a domesticated dog brought here by the Aborigines. He points out that a pure-blooded dingo often has white stockings or stars and nearly always a white tip to its tail.

He adds that these points are quite irregularly distributed. This, as everyone knows, is a feature never seen in wild animals but it occurs frequently in all domestic animals.'

'Has this foreign professor ever seen a dingo in the wilds?' he asked.

I couldn't see what his question had to do with the paraphrase I had given him, but I told him that while Lorenz had not been to Australia so far as I knew, he had bred and studied dingoes.

He changed the subject abruptly.

'You seem to know all about animals and birds,' he said. 'Perhaps you have a cure for a crowing rooster? Mine is upsetting some of the neighbours by crowing during the night. He answers other roosters across the valley.' (There were farms there.) 'In a street like Mansion Road, you have to fit in.'

He was getting at me but I ignored it.

'I think so,' I said.

'I'd like to hear it,' he said, too sweetly.

'You have to get on with people, as you say,' I said, also too sweetly. 'But roosters can be stopped from crowing in a very simple fashion. A rooster, as you know, has to stretch its neck to crow. I'd suggest tacking a piece of hessian over the perch, a couple of inches above his head. When he goes to stretch his neck, he'll bump the hessian and won't be able to crow.'

He took it in after a few questions and said he'd try it. It took him and his fifteen-year-old son most of the afternoon. I must say they were thorough. It took them ten minutes to catch that White Leghorn and then they held him with his feet on the ground and measured the distance to a couple of inches over his head. They measured the hessian meticulously and then they had a conference during which they kept looking towards me. I was sowing some flannel flower seeds. I'd gone to the near-by bushland reserve several times to observe the soil and aspect of flannel flowers so that I could plant the seeds in the right place in my garden.

Swinburne came over to the fence finally. 'I'm sorry to trouble you,' he said. This was a change. 'But there are several perches in the hen house.'

'The top one,' I said. 'He's the *alpha* animal.'

They fixed it there and Swinburne asked me to come and

have a beer at his place. But he hadn't changed his mind much about the dingo because he and his wife started telling me about the merits of budgerigars as pets.

'Now, budgerigars make marvellous pets,' he said. 'Our Joey is a wonderful talker.'

The bird, a male pied blue, was perched on his hand, and while Mrs. Swinburne smiled dotingly, it displayed and then, with wings down-dragging, it tried to copulate with Swinburne's big red hand.

'Isn't he quaint?' asked Mrs. Swinburne. 'He does that by the hour.'

Poor bloody bird, I thought.

'No wonder,' I said aloud.

'What do you mean?'

'Nothing,' I said. 'I mean it's wonderful.'

'And they tell me budgerigars don't talk in the wilds,' said Mrs. Swinburne.

'No,' I said. 'Only when they're caged.' I refrained from saying anything about mimicry being due to starved sexuality, to banked-up energy.

I couldn't see Mansion Road letting up on Red – Swinburne was just the official spokesman as it were, one of the *alpha* members in the street, the managing director of a shoe factory. I knew the others were saying the same things among themselves.

They said them to me a few nights later. Mrs. Fitter called. If Swinburne was an *alpha* male, she was *the alpha* female. Her father had been a drapery knight and had built the big house in which the Fitters lived with a feature window and two cars.

'I've come on behalf of the mothers of Mansion Road,' she started in. She was a large dark woman with a hint of a moustache. 'They're very frightened that ravening wild dingo will attack their children. They have to pass it on their way to school and it crouches in the gutter.'

She was laying it on. Most of the children were driven to school.

'It won't attack them,' I said. 'He lies in the gutter because that's his territorial boundary. Like ourselves animals are land owners.'

'And what's more he barks at them,' she said, going too far.

'Dingoes don't bark,' I said, gently, but I was getting angry.

Matha was making signs.

'And at cars, too,' she said. 'I had to swerve to miss him. And he slavers at the lips.'

'He has well-developed salivary glands,' I said. 'I assure you he won't attack anyone, but in any case the solution is simple. Your Schnauzer owns your footpath, Mrs. Fitter — or thinks he does. I respect his property right and don't walk on his footpath and we get on very well.'

It wasn't tactful but I didn't want to be.

After Mrs. Fitter had left, Martha said, 'Red has been going out after cars the last couple of days.'

'But not barking?' I asked.

'No,' she said.

Three nights later a young policeman called. Mrs. Fitter had complained that Red had killed one of her fowls.

'Did she see him?' I asked.

'No, but she is convinced it could only have been the dingo,' he said.

'Well, constable, you know the legal position as well as I do,' I said. I didn't like it but I had to tack a bit. 'Every dog is allowed one bite — but not two. I don't admit that Red did kill the fowl. It could have been any one of the dogs in the street. And, further, Red is not necessarily a dingo. He could be a mongrel. I don't know his parentage. He was found in the outback by a friend and brought to Sydney.'

He went away but was back the next night.

'Mrs. Fitter says that you have admitted that the animal is a dingo,' he said.

'I admit nothing,' I said tacking again. 'I have called the dog a dingo without any accurate knowledge and purely out of a spirit of fantasy. I wanted to indulge in a little fancy. It has been fun to think of Red as a dingo.'

He was a bit shaken and I went on, 'I'm no expert on dingoes, nor is anyone else in this street. Have you ever seen a pure-bred dingo?'

'I think so — at the Zoo —' he said, uncertainly.

'Exactly,' I said. 'And how do you know it was a pure one and even if it was, would you be able to point to any dog with certainty and say that is a dingo or that another was a Dobermann Pinscher —'

'A Dobermann what, sir?'

'Mr. Swinburne's dog is a Dobermann Pinscher. Mrs. Fitter, on the other hand, has a Schnauzer. Of course, the two have points in common, according to the experts. I am of the opinion that a Manchester Terrier is even closer in appearance to a Dobermann Pinscher and that only the well informed can pick one from the other. Now when you come to mongrels, the question of identification is much more complicated —'

There was a bit more of it. He fled in some confusion and Martha and I rolled around the floor, helpless with laughter, and went to bed earlier. But it was getting serious. If I didn't cure Red of going out on the road, Mrs. Fitter, or someone else, wasn't going to swerve next time.

What I did was undiluted Lorenz.

If you want to stop a dog chasing cars you have to fire a small stone at him from behind from a catapult when he is in the middle of chasing. When you do it this way the dog is taken by surprise. He doesn't see you do it and it seems to him like the hand of God. That is anthropomorphic, but you know what I'm getting at; it's a memorable experience for the dog and usually cures him completely.

I stayed home the next day. It took me an hour to make a catapult that worked properly and I had to practise for twenty minutes. Then I was ready. I cured Red that morning with two hits, which were, I hope, not too painful. The gutter and the street were abandoned by him. Encouraged, I decided to cure him of establishing himself on the footpath. I achieved that, too.

I knew it only won a respite for the dingo. I had to return him to the wilds. The alternatives of giving him to the Zoo, or having him put away, I'd already rejected. Swinburne came home early that day.

'I see you're still insisting on keeping that Asiatic wolf,' he said.

'*Canis familiaris* variety *dingo*,' I corrected. 'But you're wrong about keeping him. I'm returning him to the wilds.'

'But they're sheep killers.'

'Not where there are no sheep.'

'There are sheep everywhere,' he said stubbornly.

'Australia's a big place,' I said. 'There ought to be a place somewhere where he can live his own life. But he'll have to be taught to hunt before I can release him.'

'You mean on wild animals?'

'What else?' I said.

'You'll soon have the fauna protection people after you,' he said.

'Rabbits aren't protected,' I said.

'They're vermin — and so are dingoes!' he said.

They didn't give me time to put my plan into operation. I had thought it just possible that they might give Red a bait. But I couldn't believe they hated him so much. Besides it's an offence to lay baits and they were most law-abiding in Mansion Road. They didn't poison Red. What happened was that Red went wandering off one day through the bushland reserve and a poultry farmer on the other side of the valley shot the dingo, as he was legally entitled to do.

'Sorry to hear about that dog of yours,' said Swinburne later.

'But why should he go off?' I asked.

'I know a bit about dingoes,' he said and his eyes were gleaming. 'Most likely he followed a bitch on heat. It's a question of studying animal behaviour.'

I knew then that he'd done it with a farmer in on the job. They were legal in Mansion Road. But I wouldn't be able to prove anything.

'It's better to keep budgerigars as pets,' I said, blazing inside. 'You keep them sex-starved and they'll try to mate with your hand.' Only I used a blunter word. 'It's all nice and jolly and they'll talk, too.'

I was sorry afterwards for losing my temper. Swinburne wrung the budgerigar's neck the next time it displayed on his wife's hand.

We sold out soon afterwards. I was coming to the end of my Australian native flora period, anyway.

Down at the Dump

Patrick White

'Hi!'

He called from out of the house, and she went on chopping in the yard. Her right arm swung, firm still, muscular, though parts of her were beginning to sag. She swung with her right, and her left arm hung free. She chipped at the log, left right. She was expert with the axe.

Because you had to be. You couldn't expect all that much from a man.

'Hi!' It was Wal Whalley calling again from out of the home.

He came to the door then, in that dirty old baseball cap he had shook off the Yankee disposals. Still a fairly appetizing male, though his belly had begun to push against the belt.

'Puttin' on yer act?' he asked, easing the singlet under his armpits; easy was policy at Whalleys' place.

''Ere!' she protested. 'Waddaya make me out ter be? A lump of wood?'

Her eyes were of that blazing blue, her skin that of a brown peach. But whenever she smiled, something would happen, her mouth opening on watery sockets and the jags of brown, rotting stumps.

'A woman likes to be addressed,' she said.

No one had ever heard Wal address his wife by her first name. Nobody had ever heard her name, though it was printed in the electoral roll. It was, in fact, Isba.

'Don't know about a dress,' said Wal. 'I got a idea, though.'

His wife stood tossing her hair. It was natural at least; the sun had done it. All the kids had inherited their mother's colour, and

Down at the Dump

when they stood together, golden-skinned, tossing back their unmanageable hair, you would have said a mob of taffy brumbies.

'What is the bloody idea?' she asked, because she couldn't go on standing there.

'Pick up a coupla cold bottles, and spend the mornun at the dump.'

'But that's the same old idea,' she grumbled.

'No, it ain't. Not our own dump. We ain't done Sarsaparilla since Christmas.'

She began to grumble her way across the yard and into the house. A smell of sink strayed out of grey, unpainted weatherboard, to oppose the stench of crushed boggabri and cotton pear. Perhaps because Whalleys were in the bits-and-pieces trade their home was threatening to give in to them.

Wal Whalley did the dumps. Of course there were the other lurks besides. But no one had an eye like Wal for the things a person needs: dead batteries and musical bedsteads, a carpet you wouldn't notice was stained, wire, and again wire, clocks only waiting to jump back into the race of time. Objects of commerce and mystery littered Whalleys' back yard. Best of all, a rusty boiler into which the twins would climb to play at cubby.

'Eh? Waddaboutut?' Wal shouted, and pushed against his wife with his side.

She almost put her foot through the hole that had come in the kitchen boards.

'Waddabout what?'

Half-suspecting, she half-sniggered. Because Wal knew how to play on her weakness.

'The fuckun *idea*!'

So that she began again to grumble. As she slopped through the house her clothes irritated her skin. The sunlight fell yellow on the grey masses of the unmade beds, turned the fluff in the corners of the rooms to gold. Something was nagging at her, something heavy continued to weigh her down.

Of course. It was the funeral.

'Why, Wal,' she said, the way she would suddenly come round, 'you could certainly of thought of a worse idea. It'll keep the kids out of mischief. Wonder if that bloody Lummy's gunna decide to honour us?'

231

Australian Short Stories

'One day I'll knock 'is block off,' said Wal.

'He's only at the awkward age.'

She stood at the window, looking as though she might know the hell of a lot. It was the funeral made her feel solemn. Brought the goose-flesh out on her.

'Good job you thought about the dump,' she said, out-staring a red-brick propriety the other side of the road. 'If there's anythun gets me down, it's havin' ter watch a funeral pass.'

'Won't be from 'ere,' he consoled. 'They took 'er away same evenun. It's gunna start from Jackson's Personal Service.'

'Good job she popped off at the beginnun of the week. They're not so personal at the week-end.'

She began to prepare for the journey to the dump. Pulled her frock down a bit. Slipped on a pair of shoes.

'Bet *She*'ll be relieved. Wouldn't show it, though. Not about 'er sister. I bet Daise stuck in 'er fuckun guts.'

Then Mrs. Whalley was compelled to return to the window. As if her instinct. And sure enough there She was. Looking inside the letter-box, as if she hadn't collected already. Bent above the brick pillar in which the letter-box had been cemented, Mrs. Hogben's face wore all that people expect of the bereaved.

'Daise was all right,' said Wal.

'Daise was all right,' agreed his wife.

Suddenly she wondered: What if Wal, if Wal had ever . . .?

Mrs. Whalley settled her hair. If she hadn't been all that satisfied at home — and she was satisfied, her recollective eyes would admit — she too might have done a line like Daise Morrow.

Over the road Mrs. Hogben was calling.

'Meg?' she called. 'Margret?'

Though from pure habit, without direction. Her voice sounded thinner today.

Then Mrs. Hogben went away.

'Once I got took to a funeral,' Mrs. Whalley said. 'They made me look in the coffun. It was the bloke's wife. He was that cut up.'

'Did yer have a squint?'

'Pretended to.'

Wal Whalley was breathing hard in the airless room.

'How soon do yer reckon they begin ter smell?'

'Smell? They wouldn't let 'em!' his wife said very definite.

Down at the Dump

'You're the one that smells, Wal. I wonder you don't think of takin' a bath.'

But she liked his smell, for all that. It followed her out of the shadow into the strong shaft of light. Looking at each other their two bodies asserted themselves. Their faces were lit by the certainty of life.

Wal tweaked her left nipple.

'We'll slip inter the Bull on the way, and pick up those cold bottles.'

He spoke soft for him.

Mrs. Hogben called another once or twice. Inside the brick entrance the cool of the house struck at her. She liked it cool, but not cold, and this was if not exactly cold, anyway, too sudden. So now she whimpered, very faintly, for everything you have to suffer, and death on top of all. Although it was her sister Daise who had died, Mrs. Hogben was crying for the death which was waiting to carry her off in turn. She called: 'Me-ehg?' But no one ever came to your rescue. She stopped to loosen the soil round the roots of the aluminium plant. She always had to be doing something. It made her feel better.

Meg did not hear, of course. She was standing amongst the fuchsia bushes, looking out from their greenish shade. She was thin and freckly. She looked awful, because Mum had made her wear her uniform, because it was sort of a formal occasion, to Auntie Daise's funeral. In the circumstances she not only looked, but was thin. That Mrs. Ireland who was all for sports had told her she must turn her toes out, and watch out — she might grow up knock-kneed besides.

So Meg Hogben was, and felt, altogether awful. Her skin was green, except when the war between light and shade worried her face into scraps, and the fuchsia tassels trembling against her unknowing cheek, infused something of their own blood, brindled her with shifting crimson. Only her eyes resisted. They were not exactly an ordinary grey. Lorrae Jensen, who was blue, said they were the eyes of a mopey cat.

A bunch of six or seven kids from Second-Grade, Lorrae, Edna, Val, Sherry, Sue Smith and Sue Goldstein, stuck together in the holidays, though Meg sometimes wondered why. The others had come around to Hogbens' Tuesday evening.

Lorrae said: 'We're going down to Barranugli pool Thursday. There's some boys Sherry knows with a couple of Gs. They've promised to take us for a run after we come out.'

Meg did not know whether she was glad or ashamed.

'I can't,' she said. 'My auntie's died.'

'Arrr!' their voices trailed.

They couldn't get away too quick, as if it had been something contagious.

But murmuring.

Meg sensed she had become temporarily important.

So now she was alone with her dead importance, in the fuchsia bushes, on the day of Auntie Daise's funeral. She had turned fourteen. She remembered the ring in plaited gold Auntie Daise had promised her. When I am gone, her aunt had said. And now it had really happened. Without rancour Meg suspected there hadn't been time to think about the ring, and Mum would grab it, to add to all the other things she had.

Then that Lummy Whalley showed up, amongst the camphor laurels opposite, tossing his head of bleached hair. She hated boys with white hair. For that matter she hated boys, or any intrusion on her privacy. She hated Lum most of all. The day he threw the dog poo at her. It made the gristle come in her neck. Ugh! Although the old poo had only skittered over her skin, too dry to really matter, she had gone in and cried because well, there were times when she cultivated dignity.

Now Meg Hogben and Lummy Whalley did not notice each other even when they looked.

> 'Who wants Meg Skinny-leg?
> I'd rather take the clothes-peg . . .'

Lum Whalley vibrated like a comb-and-paper over amongst the camphor laurels they lopped back every so many years for firewood. He slashed with his knife into bark. Once in a hot dusk he had carved I LOVE MEG, because that was something you did, like on lavatory walls, and in the trains, but it didn't mean anything of course. Afterwards he slashed the darkness as if it had been a train seat.

Lum Whalley pretended not to watch Meg Hogben skulking in the fuchsia bushes. Wearing her brown uniform.

Down at the Dump

Stiffer, browner than for school, because it was her auntie's funeral.

'Me-ehg?' called Mrs. Hogben. 'Meg!'

'Lummy! Where the devil are yer?' called his mum.

She called all around, in the woodshed, behind the dunny. Let her!

'Lum? Lummy, for Chris*sake*!' she called.

He hated that. Like some bloody kid. At school he had got them to call him Bill, halfway between, not so shameful as Lum, nor yet as awful as William.

Mrs. Whalley came round the corner.

'Shoutin' me bloody lungs up!' she said. 'When your dad's got a nice idea. We're going down to Sarsaparilla dump.'

'Arr!' he said.

But didn't spit.

'What gets inter you?' she asked.

Even at their most inaccessible Mrs. Whalley liked to finger her children. Touch often assisted thought. But she liked the feel of them as well. She was glad she hadn't had girls. Boys turned into men, and you couldn't do without men, even when they took you for a mug, or got shickered, or bashed you up.

So she put her hand on Lummy, tried to get through to him. He was dressed, but might not have been. Lummy's kind was never ever born for clothes. At fourteen he looked more.

'Well,' she said, sourer than she felt, 'I'm not gunna cry over any sulky boy. Suit yourself.'

She moved off.

As Dad had got out the old rattle-bones by now, Lum began to clamber up. The back of the ute was at least private, though it wasn't no Customline.

The fact that Whalleys ran a Customline as well puzzled more unreasonable minds. Drawn up amongst the paspalum in front of Whalleys' shack, it looked stolen, and almost was — the third payment overdue. But would slither with ease a little longer to Barranugli, and snooze outside the Northern Hotel. Lum could have stood all day to admire their own two-tone car. Or would stretch out inside, his fingers at work on plastic flesh.

Now it was the ute for business. The bones of his buttocks bit into the boards. His father's meaty arm stuck out at the window, disgusting him. And soon the twins were squeezing from the rusty boiler. The taffy Gary — or was it Barry? had fallen down and barked his knee.

'For Chrissake!' Mrs. Whalley shrieked, and tossed her identical taffy hair.

Mrs. Hogben watched those Whalleys leave.

'In a brick area, I wouldn't of thought,' she remarked to her husband once again.

'All in good time, Myrtle,' Councillor Hogben replied as before.

'Of course,' she said, 'if there are *reasons*.'

Because councillors, she knew, did have reasons.

'But that home! And a Customline!'

The saliva of bitterness came in her mouth.

It was Daise who had said: I'm going to enjoy the good things of life — and died in that pokey little hutch, with only a cotton frock to her back. While Myrtle had the liver-coloured brick home — not a single dampmark on the ceilings — she had the washing machine, the septic, the TV, and the cream Holden Special, not to forget her husband. Les Hogben, the councillor. A builder into the bargain.

Now Myrtle stood amongst her things, and would have continued to regret the Ford the Whalleys hadn't paid for, if she hadn't been regretting Daise. It was not so much her sister's death as her life Mrs. Hogben deplored. Still, everybody knew, and there was nothing you could do about it.

'Do you think anybody will come?' Mrs. Hogben asked.

'What do you take me for?' her husband replied. 'One of these cleervoyants?'

Mrs. Hogben did not hear.

After giving the matter consideration she had advertised the death in the *Herald*:

> MORROW, Daisy (Mrs.), suddenly, at her residence,
> Showground Road, Sarsaparilla.

There was nothing more you could put. It wasn't fair on Les, a public servant, to rake up relationships. And the *Mrs.* — well, everyone had got into the habit when Daise started going with Cunningham. It seemed sort of natural as things dragged on and on. Don't work yourself up, Myrt, Daise used to say; Jack will

Down at the Dump

when his wife dies. But it was Jack Cunningham who died first. Daise said: It's the way it happened, that's all.

'Do you think Ossie will come?' Councillor Hogben asked his wife slower than she liked.

'I hadn't thought about it,' she said.

Which meant she had. She had, in fact, woken in the night, and lain there cold and stiff, as her mind's eye focused on Ossie's runny nose.

Mrs. Hogben rushed at a drawer which somebody — never herself — had left hanging out. She was a thin woman, but wiry.

'Meg?' she called. 'Did you polish your shoes?'

Les Hogben laughed behind his closed mouth. He always did when he thought of Daise's parting folly: to take up with that old scabby deadbeat Ossie from down at the showground. But who cared?

No one, unless her family.

Mrs. Hogben dreaded the possibility of Ossie, a Roman Catholic for extra value, standing beside Daise's grave, even if nobody, even if only Mr. Brickle saw.

Whenever the thought of Ossie Coogan crossed Councillor Hogben's mind he would twist the knife in his sister-in-law.

Perhaps, now, he was glad she had died. A small woman, smaller than his wife, Daise Morrow was large by nature. Whenever she dropped in she was all around the place. Yarn her head off if she got the chance. It got so as Les Hogben could not stand hearing her laugh. Pressed against her in the hall once. He had forgotten that, or almost. How Daise laughed then. I'm not so short of men I'd pick me own brother-in-law. Had he pressed? Not all that much, not intentional, anyway. So the incident had been allowed to fade, dim as the brown-linoleum hall, in Councillor Hogben's mind.

'There's the phone, Leslie.'

It was his wife.

'I'm too upset,' she said, 'to answer.'

And began to cry.

Easing his crutch Councillor Hogben went into the hall.

It was good old Horrie Last.

'Yairs . . . yairs . . .' said Mr. Hogben, speaking into the telephone which his wife kept swabbed with Breath-o'-Pine.

Australian Short Stories

'Yairs . . . Eleven, Horrie . . . from Barranugli . . . from Jackson's Personal . . . Yairs, that's decent of you, Horrie.'

'Horrie Last,' Council Hogben reported to his wife, 'is gunna put in an appearance.'

If no one else, a second councillor for Daise, Myrtle Hogben was consoled.

What could you do? Horrie Last put down the phone. He and Les had stuck together. Teamed up to catch the more progressive vote. Hogben and Last had developed the shire. Les had built Horrie's home. Lasts had sold Hogbens theirs. If certain people were spreading the rumour that Last and Hogben had caused a contraction of the Green Belt, the certain people had to realize the term itself implied flexibility.

'What did you tell them?' asked Mrs. Last.

'Said I'd go,' her husband said, doing things to the change in his pocket.

He was a short man, given to standing with his legs apart.

Georgina Last withheld her reply. Formally of interest, her shape suggested she had been made out of several scones joined together in the baking.

'Daise Morrow,' said Horrie Last, 'wasn't such a bad sort.'

Mrs. Last did not answer.

So he stirred the money in his pocket harder, hoping perhaps it would emulsify. He wasn't irritated, mind you, by his wife — who had brought him a parcel of property, as well as a flair for real estate — but had often felt he might have done a dash with Daise Morrow on the side. Wouldn't have minded betting old Les Hogben had tinkered a bit with his wife's sister. Helped her buy her home, they said. Always lights on at Daise's place after dark. Postman left her mail on the veranda instead of in the box. In summer, when the men went round to read the meters, she'd ask them in for a glass of beer. Daise knew how to get service.

Georgina Last cleared her throat.

'Funerals are not for women,' she declared, and took up a cardigan she was knitting for a cousin.

'You didn't do your shoes!' Mrs. Hogben protested.

'I did,' said Meg. 'It's the dust. Don't know why we bother to clean shoes at all. They always get dirty again.'

Down at the Dump

She stood there looking awful in the school uniform. Her cheeks were hollow from what she read could only be despair.

'A person must keep to her principles,' Mrs. Hogben said, and added: 'Dadda is bringing round the car. Where's your hat, dear? We'll be ready to leave in two minutes.'

'Arr, Mum! The hat?'

That old school hat. It had shrunk already a year ago, but had to see her through.

'You wear it to church, don't you?'

'But this isn't church!'

'It's as good as. Besides, you owe it to your aunt,' Mrs. Hogben said, to win.

Meg went and got her hat. They were going out through the fuchsia bushes, past the plaster pixies, which Mrs. Hogben had trained her child to cover with plastic at the first drops of rain. Meg Hogben hated the sight of those corny old pixies, even after the plastic cones had snuffed them out.

It was sad in the car, dreamier. As she sat looking out through the window, the tight panama perched on her head lost its power to humiliate. Her always persistent, grey eyes, under the line of dark fringe, had taken up the search again: she had never yet looked enough. Along the road they passed the house in which her aunt, they told her, had died. The small, pink, tilted house, standing amongst the carnation plants, had certainly lost some of its life. Or the glare had drained the colour from it. How the mornings used to sparkle in which Aunt Daise went up and down between the rows, her gown dragging heavy with dew, binding with bast the fuzzy flowers by handfuls and handfuls. Auntie's voice clear as morning. No one, she called, could argue they look stiff when they're bunched tight eh Meg what would you say they remind you of? But you never knew the answers to the sort of things people asked. Frozen fireworks, Daise suggested. Meg loved the idea of it, she loved Daise. Not so frozen either, she dared. The sun getting at the wet flowers broke them up and made them spin.

And the clovey scent rose up in the stale-smelling car, and smote Meg Hogben, out of the reeling heads of flowers, their cold stalks dusted with blue. Then she knew she would write a poem about Aunt Daise and the carnations. She wondered she hadn't thought of it before:

Australian Short Stories

At that point the passengers were used most brutally as the car entered on a chain of potholes. For once Mrs. Hogben failed to invoke the Main Roads Board. She was asking herself whether Ossie could be hiding in there behind the blinds. Or whether, whether. She fished for her second handkerchief. Prudence had induced her to bring two — the good one with the lace insertion for use beside the grave.

'The weeds will grow like one thing,' her voice blared, 'now that they'll have their way.'

Then she began to unfold the less important of her handkerchiefs.

Myrtle Morrow had always been the sensitive one. Myrtle had understood the Bible. Her needlework, her crochet doilys had taken prizes at country shows. No one had fiddled such pathos out of the pianola. It was Daise who loved flowers, though. It's a moss-rose, Daise had said, sort of rolling it round on her tongue, while she was still a little thing.

When she had had her cry, Mrs. Hogben remarked: 'Girls don't know they're happy until it's too late.'

Thus addressed, the other occupants of the car did not answer. They knew they were not expected to.

Councillor Hogben drove in the direction of Barranugli. He had arranged his hat before leaving. He removed a smile the mirror reminded him was there. Although he no longer took any risks in a re-election photograph by venturing out of the past, he often succeeded in the fleshy present. But now, in difficult circumstances, he was exercising his sense of duty. He drove, he drove, past the retinosperas, heavy with their own gold, past the lagerstroemias, their pink sugar running into mildew.

Down at the dump Whalleys were having an argument about whether the beer was to be drunk on arrival or after they had developed a thirst.

'Keep it, then!' Mum Whalley turned her back. 'What was the point of buyin' it cold if you gotta wait till it hots up? Anyways,' she said, 'I thought the beer was an excuse for comin'.'

'Arr, stuff it!' says Wal. 'A dump's business, ain't it? With or without beer. Ain't it? Any day of the week.'

240

Down at the Dump

He saw she had begun to sulk. He saw her rather long breasts floating around inside her dress. Silly cow! He laughed. But cracked a bottle.

Barry said he wanted a drink.

You could hear the sound of angry suction as his mum's lips called off a swig.

'I'm not gunna stand by and watch any kid of mine,' said the wet lips, 'turn 'isself into a bloody dipso!'

Her eyes were at their blazing bluest. Perhaps it was because Wal Whalley admired his wife that he continued to desire her.

But Lummy pushed off on his own. When his mum went crook, and swore, he was too aware of the stumps of teeth, the rotting brown of nastiness. It was different, of course, if you swore yourself. Sometimes it was unavoidable.

Now he avoided by slipping away, between the old mattresses, and boots the sun had buckled up. Pitfalls abounded: the rusty traps of open tins lay in wait for guiltless ankles, the necks of broken bottles might have been prepared to gash a face. So he went thoughtfully, his feet scuffing the leaves of stained asbestos, crunching the torso of a celluloid doll. Here and there it appeared as though trash might win. The onslaught of metal was pushing the scrub into the gully. But in many secret, steamy pockets, a rout was in progress: seeds had been sown in the lumps of grey, disintegrating kapok and the laps of burst chairs, the coils of springs, locked in the spirals of wirier vines, had surrendered to superior resilience. Somewhere on the edge of the whole shambles a human ally, before retiring, had lit a fire, which by now the green had almost choked, leaving a stench of smoke to compete with the sicklier one of slow corruption.

Lum Whalley walked with a grace of which he himself had never been aware. He had had about enough of this rubbish jazz. He would have liked to know how to live neat. Like Darkie Black. Everything in its place in the cabin of Darkie's trailer. Suddenly his throat yearned for Darkie's company. Darkie's hands, twisting the wheel, appeared to control the whole world.

A couple of strands of barbed wire separated Sarsaparilla dump from Sarsaparilla cemetery. The denominations were separated too, but there you had to tell by the names, or by the angels and things the RCs went in for. Over in what must have been the Church of England Alf Herbert was finishing Mrs.

Morrow's grave. He had reached the clay, and the going was heavy. The clods fell resentfully.

If what they said about Mrs. Morrow was true, then she had lived it up all right. Lum Whalley wondered what, supposing he had met her walking towards him down a bush track, smiling. His skin tingled. Lummy had never done a girl, although he pretended he had, so as to hold his own with the kids. He wondered if a girl, if that sourpuss Meg Hogben. Would of bitten as likely as not. Lummy felt a bit afraid, and returned to thinking of Darkie Black, who never talked about things like that.

Presently he moved away. Alf Herbert, leaning on his shovel, could have been in need of a yarn. Lummy was not prepared to yarn. He turned back into the speckled bush, into the pretences of a shade. He lay down under a banksia, and opened his fly to look at himself. But pretty soon got sick of it.

The procession from Barranugli back to Sarsaparilla was hardly what you would have called a procession: the Reverend Brickle, the Hogbens' Holden, Horrie's Holden, following the smaller of Jackson's hearses. In the circumstances they were doing things cheap — there was no reason for splashing it around. At Sarsaparilla Mr. Gill joined in, sitting high in that old Chev. It would have been practical, Councillor Hogben sighed, to join the hearse at Sarsaparilla. Old Gill was only there on account of Daise being his customer for years. A grocer lacking in enterprise. Daise had stuck to him, she said, because she liked him. Well, if that was what you put first, but where did it get you?

At the last dip before the cemetery a disembowelled mattress from the dump had begun to writhe across the road. It looked like a kind of monster from out of the depths of somebody's mind, the part a decent person ignored.

'Ah, dear! At the cemetery too!' Mrs. Hogben protested. 'I wonder the Council,' she added, in spite of her husband.

'All right, Myrtle,' he said between his teeth. 'I made a mental note.'

Councillor Hogben was good at that.

'And the Whalleys on your own doorstep,' Mrs. Hogben moaned.

Down at the Dump

The things she had seen on hot days, in front of their kiddies too.

The hearse had entered the cemetery gate. They had reached the bumpy stage toppling over the paspalum clumps, before the thinner, bush grass. All around, the leaves of the trees presented so many grey blades. Not even a magpie to put heart into a Christian. But Alf Herbert came forward, his hand dusted with yellow clay, to guide the hearse between the Methoes and the Presbyterian, onto Church of England ground.

Jolting had shaken Mrs. Hogben's grief up to the surface again. Mr. Brickle was impressed. He spoke for a moment of the near and dear. His hands were kind and professional in helping her out.

But Meg jumped. And landed. It was a shock to hear a stick crack so loud. Perhaps it was what Mum would have called irreverent. At the same time her banana-coloured panama fell off her head into the tussocks.

It was really a bit confusing at the grave. Some of the men helped with the coffin, and Councillor Last was far too short.

Then Mrs. Hogben saw, she saw, from out of the lace handkerchief, it was that Ossie Coogan she saw, standing the other side of the grave. Had old Gill given him a lift? Ossie, only indifferently buttoned, stood snivelling behind the mound of yellow clay.

Nothing would have stopped his nose. Daise used to say: You don't want to be frightened, Ossie, not when I'm here, see? But she wasn't any longer. So now he was afraid. Excepting Daise, Protestants had always frightened him. Well, I'm nothing, she used to say, nothing that you could pigeonhole, but love what we are given to love.

Myrtle Hogben was ropeable, if only because of what Councillor Last must think. She would have liked to express her feelings in words, if she could have done so without giving offence to God. Then the ants ran up her legs, for she was standing on a nest, and her body cringed before the teeming injustices.

Daise, she had protested the day it all began, whatever has come over you? The sight of her sister had made her run out leaving the white sauce to burn. Wherever will you take him? He's sick, said Daise. *But you can't*, Myrtle Hogben cried. For

243

there was her sister Daise pushing some old deadbeat in a barrow. All along Showground Road people had come out of homes to look. Daise appeared smaller pushing the wheelbarrow down the hollow and up the hill. Her hair was half uncoiled. *You can't! You can't!* Myrtle called. But Daise could, and did.

When all the few people were assembled at the graveside in their good clothes, Mr. Brickle opened the book, though his voice soon suggested he needn't have.

'*I am the resurrection and the life*,' he said.

And Ossie cried. Because he didn't believe it, not when it came to the real thing.

He looked down at the coffin, which was what remained of what he knew. He remembered eating a baked apple, very slowly, the toffee on it. And again the dark of the horse-stall swallowed him up, where he lay hopeless amongst the shit, and her coming at him with the barrow. What do you want? he asked straight out. I came down to the showground, she said, for a bit of honest-to-God manure, I've had those fertilizers, she said, and what are you, are you sick? I live 'ere, he said. And began to cry, and rub the snot from his snivelly nose. After a bit Daise said: We're going back to my place, What's-yer-Name — Ossie. The way she spoke he knew it was true. All the way up the hill in the barrow the wind was giving his eyes gyp, and blowing his thin hair apart. Over the years he had come across one or two lice in his hair, but thought, or hoped he had got rid of them by the time Daise took him up. As she pushed and struggled with the barrow, sometimes she would lean forward, and he felt her warmth, her firm diddies pressed against his back.

'*Lord, let me know mine end, and the number of my days: that I may be certified how long I have to live*,' Mr. Brickle read.

Certified was the word, decided Councillor Hogben looking at that old Ossie.

Who stood there mumbling a few Aspirations, very quiet, on the strength of what they had taught him as a boy.

When all this was under way, all these words of which, she knew, her Auntie Daise would not have approved, Meg Hogben went and got beneath the strands of wire separating the cemetery from the dump. She had never been to the dump before, and her heart was lively in her side. She walked shyly through the bush. She came across an old suspender-belt. She stumbled over a

Down at the Dump

blackened primus.

She saw Lummy Whalley then. He was standing under a banksia, twisting at one of its dead heads.

Suddenly they knew there was something neither of them could continue to avoid.

'I came here to the funeral,' she said.

She sounded, well, almost relieved.

'Do you come here often?' she asked.

'Nah,' he answered, hoarse. 'Not here. To dumps, yes.'

But her intrusion had destroyed the predetermined ceremony of his life, and caused a trembling in his hand.

'Is there anything to see?' she asked.

'Junk,' he said. 'Same old junk.'

'Have you ever looked at a dead person?'

Because she noticed the trembling of his hand.

'No,' he said. 'Have you?'

She hadn't. Nor did it seem probable that she would have to now. Not as they began breathing evenly again.

'What do you do with yourself?' he asked.

Then, even though she would have liked to stop herself, she could not. She said: 'I write poems. I'm going to write one about my Aunt Daise, like she was, gathering carnations early in the dew.'

'What'll you get out of that?'

'Nothing,' she said, 'I suppose.'

But it did not matter.

'What other sorts of pomes do you write?' he asked, twisting at last the dead head of the banksia off.

'I wrote one,' she said, 'about the things in a cupboard. I wrote about a dream I had. And the smell of rain. That was a bit too short.'

He began to look at her then. He had never looked into the eyes of a girl. They were grey and cool, unlike the hot, or burnt-out eyes of a woman.

'What are you going to be?' she asked.

'I dunno.'

'You're not a white-collar type.'

'Eh?'

'I mean you're not for figures, and books, and banks and offices,' she said.

He was too disgusted to agree.

'I'm gunna have me own truck. Like Mr. Black. Darkie's got a trailer.'

'What?'

'Well,' he said, 'a semi-trailer.'

'Oh,' she said, more diffident.

'Darkie took me on a trip to Maryborough. It was pretty tough goin'. Sometimes we drove right through the night. Sometimes we slept on the road. Or in places where you get rooms. Gee, it was good though, shootin' through the country towns at night.'

She saw it. She saw the people standing at their doors, frozen in the blocks of yellow light. The rushing of the night made the figures for ever still. All around she could feel the furry darkness, as the semi-trailer roared and bucked, its skeleton of coloured lights. While in the cabin, in which they sat, all was stability and order. If she glanced sideways she could see how his taffy hair shone when raked by the bursts of electric light. They had brought cases with tooth-brushes, combs, one or two things — the pad on which she would write the poem somewhere when they stopped in the smell of sunlight dust ants. But his hands had acquired such mastery over the wheel, it appeared this might never happen. Nor did she care.

'This Mr. Black,' she said, her mouth getting thinner, 'does he take you with him often?'

'Only once interstate,' said Lummy, pitching the banksia head away. 'Once in a while short trips.'

As they drove they rocked together. He had never been closer to anyone than when bumping against Darkie's ribs. He waited to experience again the little spasm of gratitude and pleasure. He would have liked to wear, and would in time, a striped sweat-shirt like Darkie wore.

'I'd like to go in with Darkie,' he said, 'when I get a trailer of me own. Darkie's the best friend I got.'

With a drawnout shiver of distrust she saw the darker hands, the little black hairs on the backs of the fingers.

'Oh well,' she said, withdrawn, 'praps you will in the end,' she said.

On the surrounding graves the brown flowers stood in their jars of browner water. The more top-heavy, plastic bunches had

Down at the Dump

been slapped down by a westerly, but had not come to worse grief than to lie strewn in pale disorder on the uncharitable granite chips.

The heat made Councillor Last yawn. He began to read the carved names, those within sight at least, some of which he had just about forgot. He almost laughed once. If the dead could have sat up in their graves there would have been an argument or two.

'In the midst of life we are in death,' said the parson bloke.

JACK CUNNINGHAM
BELOVED HUSBAND OF FLORENCE MARY,

read Horrie Last.

Who would have thought Cunningham, straight as a silky-oak, would fall going up the path to Daise Morrow's place. Horrie used to watch them together, sitting a while on the veranda before going in to their tea. They made no bones about it, because everybody knew. Good teeth Cunningham had. Always a white, well-ironed shirt. Wonder which of the ladies did the laundry. Florence Mary was an invalid, they said. Daise Morrow liked to laugh with men, but for Jack Cunningham she had a silence, promising intimacies at which Horrie Last could only guess, whose own private life had been lived in almost total darkness.

Good Christ, and then there was Ossie. The woman could only have been at heart a perv of a kind you hadn't heard about.

'Forasmuch as it hath pleased Almighty God of his great mercy to take unto himself the soul . . .' read Mr. Brickle.

As it was doubtful who should cast the earth, Mr. Gill the grocer did. They heard the handful rattle on the coffin.

Then the tears truly ran out of Ossie's scaly eyes. Out of darkness. Out of darkness Daise had called: What's up Ossie, you don't wanta cry. I got the cramps, he answered. They were twisting him. The cramps? she said drowsily. Or do you imagine? If it isn't the cramps it's something else. Could have been. He'd take Daise's word for it. He was never all that bright since he had the meningitis. Tell you what, Daise said, you come in here, into my bed, I'll warm you, Os, in a jiffy. He listened in the dark to his own snivelling. Arr, Daise, I couldn't, he said, I couldn't get a stand, not if you was to give me the jackpot, he said. She sounded very still then. He lay and counted the

247

Australian Short Stories

throbbing of the darkness. Not like that, she said — she didn't laugh at him as he had half expected — besides, she said, it only ever really comes to you once. That way. And at once he was parting the darkness, bumping and shambling to get to her. He had never known it so gentle. Because Daise wasn't afraid. She ran her hands through his hair, on and on like water flowing. She soothed the cramps out of his legs. Until in the end they were breathing in time. Dozing. Then the lad Ossie Coogan rode again down from the mountain, the sound of the snaffle in the blue air, the smell of sweat from under the saddle-cloth, towards the great, flowing river. He rocked and flowed with the motion of the strong, never-ending river, burying his mouth in brown cool water, to drown would have been worth it.

Once during the night Ossie had woken, afraid the distance might have come between them. But Daise was still holding him against her breast. If he had been different, say. Ossie's throat had begun to wobble. Only then, Daise might have turned different. So he nuzzled against the warm darkness, and was again received.

'If you want to enough, you can do what you want,' Meg Hogben insisted.

She had read it in a book, and wasn't altogether convinced, but theories sometimes come to the rescue.

'If you want,' she said, kicking a hole in the stony ground.

'Not everything you can't.'

'You can!' she said. 'But you can!'

She who had never looked at a boy, not right into one, was looking at him as never before.

'That's a lot of crap,' he said.

'Well,' she admitted, 'there are limits.'

It made him frown. He was again suspicious. She was acting clever. All those pomes.

But to reach understanding she would have surrendered her cleverness. She was no longer proud of it.

'And what'll happen if you get married? Riding around the country in a truck. How'll your wife like it? Stuck at home with a lot of kids.'

'Some of 'em take the wife along. Darkie takes his missus and kids. Not always, like. But now and again. On short runs.'

Down at the Dump

'You didn't tell me Mr. Black was married.'

'Can't tell you everything, can I? Not at once.'

The women who sat in the drivers' cabins of the semi-trailers he saw as predominantly thin and dark. They seldom returned glances, but wiped their hands on Kleenex, and peered into little mirrors, waiting for their men to show up again. Which in time they had to. So he walked across from the service station, to take possession of his property. Sauntering, frowning slightly, touching the yellow stubble on his chin, he did not bother to look. Glanced sideways perhaps. She was the thinnest, the darkest he knew, the coolest of all the women who sat looking out from the cabin windows of the semi-trailers.

In the meantime they strolled a bit, amongst the rusty tins at Sarsaparilla dump. He broke a few sticks and threw away the pieces. She tore off a narrow leaf and smelled it. She would have liked to smell Lummy's hair.

'Gee, you're fair,' she had to say.

'Some are born fair,' he admitted.

He began pelting a rock with stones. He was strong, she saw. So many discoveries in a short while were making her tremble at the knees.

And as they rushed through the brilliant light, roaring and lurching, the cabin filled with fair-skinned, taffy children, the youngest of whom she protected by holding the palm of her hand behind his neck, as she had noticed women do. Occupied in this way, she almost forgot Lum at times, who would pull up, and she would climb down, to rinse the nappies in tepid water, and hang them on a bush to dry.

'All these pomes and things,' he said, 'I never knew a clever person before.'

'But clever isn't any different,' she begged, afraid he might not accept her peculiarity and power.

She would go with a desperate wariness from now. She sensed that, if not in years, she was older than Lum, but this was the secret he must never guess: that for all his strength, all his beauty, she was, and must remain the stronger.

'What's that?' he asked, and touched.

But drew back his hand in self-protection.

'A scar,' she said. 'I cut my wrist opening a tin of condensed milk.'

For once she was glad of the paler seam in her freckled skin, hoping that it might heal a breach.

And he looked at her out of his hard blue Whalley eyes. He liked her. Although she was ugly, and clever, and a girl.

'Condensed milk on bread,' he said, 'that's something I could eat till I bust.'

'Oh, yes!' she agreed.

She did honestly believe, although she had never thought of it before.

Flies clustered in irregular jet embroideries on the backs of best suits. Nobody bothered any longer to shrug them off. As Alf Herbert grunted against the shovelfuls, dust clogged increasingly, promises settled thicker. Although they had been told they might expect Christ to redeem, it would have been no less incongruous if He had appeared out of the scrub to perform on altars of burning sandstone, a sacrifice for which nobody had prepared them. In any case, the mourners waited — they had been taught to accept whatever might be imposed — while the heat stupefied the remnants of their minds, and inflated their Australian fingers into foreign-looking sausages.

Myrtle Hogben was the first to protest. She broke down — into the wrong hankerchief. *Who shall change our vile body?* The words were more than her decency could bear.

'Easy on it,' her husband whispered, putting a finger under her elbow.

She submitted to his sympathy, just as in their life together she had submitted to his darker wishes. Never wanting more than peace, and one or two perquisites.

A thin woman, Mrs. Hogben continued to cry for all the wrongs that had been done her. For Daise had only made things viler. While understanding, yes, at moments. It was girls who really understood, not even women — sisters, sisters. Before events whirled them apart. So Myrtle Morrow was again walking through the orchard, and Daise Morrow twined her arm around her sister; confession filled the air, together with a scent of crushed fermenting apples. Myrtle said: Daise, there's something I'd like to do, I'd like to chuck a lemon into a Salvation Army tuba. Daise giggled. You're a nut, Myrt, she said. But never *vile*. So Myrtle Hogben cried. Once, only once she thought how she'd like to push someone off a cliff, and watch

Down at the Dump

their expression as it happened. But Myrtle had not confessed that.

So Mrs. Hogben cried, for those things she was unable to confess, for anything she might not be able to control.

As the blander words had begun falling, *Our Father,* that she knew by heart, *our daily bread,* she should have felt comforted. She should of. Should of.

Where was Meg, though?

Mrs. Hogben separated herself from the others. Walking stiffly. If any of the men noticed, they took it for granted she had been overcome, or wanted to relieve herself.

She would have liked to relieve herself by calling: 'Margaret Meg wherever don't you hear me Me-ehg?' drawing it out thin in anger. But could not cut across a clergyman's words. So she stalked. She was not unlike a guinea-hen, its spotted silk catching on a strand of barbed-wire.

When they had walked a little farther, round and about, anywhere, they overheard voices.

'What's that?' asked Meg.

'Me mum and dad,' Lummy said. 'Rousin' about somethun or other.'

Mum Whalley had just found two bottles of unopened beer. Down at the dump. Waddayaknow. Must be something screwy somewhere.

'Could of put poison in it,' her husband warned.

'Poison? My arse!' she shouted. 'That's because *I* found it!'

'Whoever found it,' he said, 'who's gunna drink a coupla bottlesa hot beer?'

'I am!' she said.

'When what we brought was good an' cold?'

He too was shouting a bit. She behaved unreasonable at times.

'Who wanted ter keep what we brought? Til it got good an' hot!' she shrieked.

Sweat was running down both the Whalleys.

Suddenly Lum felt he wanted to lead this girl out of earshot. He had just about had the drunken sods. He would have liked to find himself walking with his girl over mown lawn, like at the Botanical Gardens, a green turf giving beneath their leisured feet. Statues pointed a way through the glare, to where they finally sat, under enormous shiny leaves, looking out at boats on water. They unpacked their cut lunch from its layers of fresh tissue-paper.

'They're rough as bags,' Lummy explained.

'I don't care,' Meg Hogben assured.

Nothing on earth could make her care — was it more, or was it less?

She walked giddily behind him, past a rusted fuel-stove, over a field of deathly feltex. Or ran, or slid, to keep up. Flowers would have wilted in her hands, if she hadn't crushed them brutally, to keep her balance. Somewhere in their private labyrinth Meg Hogben had lost her hat.

When they were farther from the scene of anger, and a silence of heat had descended again, he took her little finger, because it seemed natural to do so, after all they had experienced: they swung hands for a while, according to some special law of motion.

Till Lum Whalley frowned, and threw the girl's hand away.

If she accepted his behaviour it was because she no longer believed in what he did, only in what she knew he felt. That might have been the trouble. She was so horribly sure, he would have to resist to the last moment of all. As a bird, singing in the prickly tree under which they found themselves standing, seemed to cling to the air. Then his fingers took control. She was amazed at the hardness of his boy's body. The tremors of her flinty skin, the membrane of the white sky appalled him. Before fright and expectation melted their mouths. And they took little grateful sips of each other. Holding up their throats in between. Like birds drinking.

Ossie could no longer see Alf Herbert's shovel working at the earth.

'Never knew a man cry at a funeral,' Councillor Hogben complained, very low, although he was ripe enough to burst.

If you could count Ossie as a man, Councillor Last suggested in a couple of noises.

But Ossie could not see or hear, only Daise, still lying on that upheaval of a bed. Seemed she must have burst a button, for her breasts stood out from her. He would never forget how they laboured against the heavy yellow morning light. In the early light, the flesh turned yellow, sluggish. What's gunna happen to

Down at the Dump

me, Daisy? It'll be decided, Os, she said, like it is for any of us. I ought to know, she said, to tell you, but give me time to rest a bit, to get me breath. Then he got down on his painful knees. He put his mouth to Daise's neck. Her skin tasted terrible bitter. The great glistening river, to which the lad Ossie Coogan had ridden jingling down from the mountain, was slowing into thick, yellow mud. Himself an old, scabby man attempting to refresh his forehead in the last pothole.

Mr. Brickle said: *'We give thee hearty thanks for that it hath pleased thee to deliver this our sister out of the miseries of this sinful world.'*

'No! No!' Ossie protested, so choked nobody heard, though it was vehement enough in its intention.

As far as he could understand, nobody wanted to be delivered. Not him, not Daise, anyways. When you could sit together by the fire on winter nights baking potatoes under the ashes.

It took Mrs. Hogben some little while to free her *crêpe de Chine* from the wire. It was her nerves, not to mention Meg on her mind. In the circumstances she tore herself worse, and looked up to see her child, just over there, without shame, in a rubbish tip, kissing the Whalley boy. What if Meg was another of Daise? It was in the blood, you couldn't deny.

Mrs. Hogben did not exactly call, but released some kind of noise from her extended throat. Her mouth was too full of tongue to find room for words as well.

Then Meg looked. She was smiling.

She said: 'Yes, Mother.'

She came and got through the wire, tearing herself also a little.

Mrs. Hogben said, and her teeth clicked: 'You chose the likeliest time. Your aunt hardly in her grave. Though, of course, it is only your aunt, if anyone, to blame.'

The accusations were falling fast. Meg could not answer. Since joy had laid her open, she had forgotten how to defend herself.

'If you were a little bit younger' — Mrs. Hogben lowered her voice because they had begun to approach the parson — 'I'd break a stick on you, my girl.'

Meg tried to close her face, so that nobody would see inside.

'What will they say?' Mrs. Hogben moaned. 'What ever will happen to us?'

'What, Mother?' Meg asked.

'You're the only one can answer that. And someone else.'

Then Meg looked over her shoulder and recognized the hate which, for a while, she had forgotten existed. And at once her face closed up tight, like a fist. She was ready to protect whatever justly needed her protection.

Even if their rage, grief, contempt, boredom, apathy, and sense of injustice had not occupied the mourners, it is doubtful whether they would have realised the dead woman was standing amongst them. The risen dead — that was something which happened, or didn't happen, in the Bible. Fanfares of light did not blare for a loose woman in floral cotton. Those who had known her remembered her by now only fitfully in some of the wooden attitudes of life. How could they have heard, let alone believed in, her affirmation? Yet Daise Morrow continued to proclaim.

Listen, all of you, I'm not leaving, except those who want to be left, and even those aren't so sure — they might be parting with a bit of themselves. Listen to me, all you successful no-hopers, all you who wake in the night, jittery because something may be escaping you, or terrified to think there may never have been anything to find. Come to me, you sour women, public servants, anxious children, and old scabby, desperate men . . .

Physically small, words had seemed too big for her. She would push back her hair in exasperation. And take refuge in acts. Because her feet had been planted in the earth, she would have been the last to resent its pressure now, while her always rather hoarse voice continued to exhort in borrowed syllables of dust.

Truly, we needn't experience tortures, unless we build chambers in our minds to house instruments of hatred in. Don't you know, my darling creatures, that death isn't death, unless it's the death of love? Love should be the greatest explosion it is reasonable to expect. Which sends us whirling, spinning, creating millions of other worlds. Never destroying.

From the fresh mound which they had formed unimaginatively in the shape of her earthly body, she persisted in appealing to them.

I will comfort you. If you will let me. Do you understand?

But nobody did, as they were only human.

For ever and ever. And ever.

Leaves quivered lifted in the first suggestion of a breeze.

So the aspirations of Daise Morrow were laid alongside her small-boned wrists, smooth thighs and pretty ankles. She surrendered at last to the formal crumbling which, it was hoped, would make an honest woman of her.

But had not altogether died.

Meg Hogben had never exactly succeeded in interpreting her aunt's messages, nor could she have witnessed the last moments of the burial, because the sun was dazzling her. She did experience, however, along with a shiver of recollected joy, the down laid against her cheek, a little breeze trickling through the moist roots of her hair, as she got inside the car, and waited for whatever next.

Well, they had dumped Daise.

Somewhere the other side of the wire there was the sound of smashed glass and discussion.

Councillor Hogben went across to the parson and said the right kind of things. Half-turning his back he took a note or two from his wallet, and immediately felt disengaged. If Horrie Last had been there Les Hogben would have gone back at this point and put an arm around his mate's shoulder, to feel whether he was forgiven for unorthodox behaviour in a certain individual — no relation, mind you, but. In any case Horrie had driven away.

Horrie drove, or flew, across the dip in which the dump joined the cemetery. For a second Ossie Coogan's back flickered inside a spiral of dust.

Ought to give the coot a lift, Councillor Last suspected, and wondered, as he drove on, whether a man's better intentions were worth, say, half a mark in the event of their remaining unfulfilled. For by now it was far too late to stop, and there was that Ossie, in the mirror, turning off the road towards the dump, where, after all, the bugger belonged.

All along the road, stones, dust, and leaves, were settling back into normally unemotional focus. Seated in his high Chev, Gill the grocer, a slow man, who carried his change in a little, soiled canvas bag, looked ahead through thick lenses. He was relieved to realise he would reach home almost on the dot of three-thirty, and his wife pour him his cup of tea. Whatever he understood was punctual, decent, docketed.

As he drove, prudently, he avoided the mattress the dump had spewed, from under the wire, half across the road. Strange things had happened at the dump on and off, the grocer recollected. Screaming girls, their long tight pants ripped to tatters. An arm in a sugar-bag, and not a sign of the body that went with it. Yet some found peace amongst the refuse: elderly derelict men, whose pale, dead, fish eyes never divulged anything of what they had lived, and women with blue, metho skins, hanging around the doors of shacks put together from sheets of bark and rusty iron. Once an old downandout had crawled amongst the rubbish apparently to rot, and did, before they sent for the constable, to examine what seemed at first a bundle of stinking rags.

Mr. Gill accelerated judiciously.

They were driving. They were driving.

Alone in the back of the ute, Lum Whalley sat forward on the empty crate, locking his hands between his knees, as he forgot having seen Darkie do. He was completely independent now. His face had been reshaped by the wind. He liked that. It felt good. He no longer resented the junk they were dragging home, the rust flaking off at his feet, the roll of mouldy feltex trying to fur his nostrils up. Nor his family — discussing, or quarrelling, you could never tell — behind him in the cabin.

The Whalleys were in fact singing. One of their own versions. They always sang their own versions, the two little boys joining in.

Show me the way to go home,
I'm not too tired for bed.
I had a little drink about an hour ago,
And it put ideas in me head . . .

Suddenly Mum Whalley began belting into young Gary – or was it Barry?

'Wadda *you* know, eh? Wadda *you*?'

'What's bitten yer?' her husband shouted. 'Can't touch a drop without yer turn nasty!'

She didn't answer. He could tell a grouse was coming, though. The little boy had started to cry, but only as a formality.

Down at the Dump

'It's that bloody Lummy,' Mrs Whalley complained.

'Why pick on Lum?'

'Give a kid all the love and affection, and waddayaget?'

Wal grunted. Abstractions always embarrassed him.

Mum Whalley spat out of the window, and the spit came back at her.

'Arrr!' she protested.

And fell silenter. It was not strictly Lum, not if you was honest. It was nothing. Or everything. The grog. You was never ever gunna touch it no more. Until you did. And that bloody Lummy, what with the caesar and all, you was never ever going again with a man.

'That's somethink a man don't understand.'

'What?' asked Wal.

'A caesar.'

'Eh?'

You just couldn't discuss with a man. So you had to get into bed with him. Grogged up half the time. That was how she copped the twins, after she had said never ever.

'Stop cryun, for Chrissake!' Mum Whalley coaxed, touching the little boy's blowing hair.

Everything was sad.

'Wonder how often they bury someone alive,' she said.

Taking a corner in his cream Holden Councillor Hogben felt quite rakish, but would restrain himself at the critical moment from skidding the wrong side of the law.

They were driving and driving, in long, lovely bursts, and at the corners, in semi-circular swirls.

On those occasions in her life when she tried to pray, begging for an experience, Meg Hogben would fail, but return to the attempt with clenched teeth. Now she did so want to think of her dead aunt with love, and the image blurred repeatedly. She was superficial, that was it. Yet, each time she failed, the landscape leaped lovingly. They were driving under the telephone wires. She could have translated any message into the language of peace. The wind burning, whenever it did not cut cold, left the stable things alone: the wooden houses stuck beside the road, the trunks of willows standing round the brown saucer of a dam. Her too candid, grey eyes seemed to have deepened, as though to accommodate all she still had to see, feel.

It was lovely curled on the back seat, even with Mum and Dad in front.

'I haven't forgotten, Margaret,' Mum called over her shoulder.

Fortunately Dadda wasn't interested enough to inquire.

'Did Daise owe anything on the home?' Mrs. Hogben asked. 'She was never at all practical.'

Councillor Hogben cleared his throat.

'Give us time to find out,' he said.

Mrs. Hogben respected her husband for the things which she, secretly, did not understand: Time the mysterious, for instance, Business, and worst of all, the Valuer General.

'I wonder Jack Cunningham,' she said, 'took up with Daise. He was a fine man. Though Daise had a way with her.'

They were driving. They were driving.

When Mrs. Hogben remembered the little ring in plaited gold.

'Do you think those undertakers are honest?'

'Honest?' her husband repeated.

A dubious word.

'Yes,' she said. 'That ring that Daise.'

You couldn't very well accuse. When she had plucked up the courage she would go down to the closed house. The thought of it made her chest tighten. She would go inside, and feel her way into the back corners of drawers, where perhaps a twist of tissue-paper. But the closed houses of the dead frightened Mrs. Hogben, she had to admit. The stuffiness, the light strained through brown holland. It was as if you were stealing, though you weren't.

And then those Whalleys creeping up.

They were driving and driving, the ute and the sedan almost rubbing on each other.

'No one who hasn't had a migraine,' cried Mrs. Hogben, averting her face, 'can guess what it feels like.'

Her husband had heard that before.

'It's a wonder it don't leave you,' he said. 'They say it does when you've passed a certain age.'

Though they weren't passing the Whalleys he would make every effort to throw the situation off. Wal Whalley leaning forward, though not so far you couldn't see the hair bursting out of the front of his shirt. His wife thumping his shoulder. They were singing one of their own versions. Her gums all watery.

So they drove and drove.

'I could sick up, Leslie,' Mrs. Hogben gulped, and fished for her lesser handkerchief.

The Whalley twins were laughing through their taffy forelocks.

At the back of the ute that sulky Lum turned towards the opposite direction. Meg Hogben was looking her farthest off. Any sign of acknowledgement had been so faint the wind had immediately blown it off their faces. As Meg and Lummy sat, they held their sharp, but comforting knees. They sank their chins as low as they would go. They lowered their eyes, as if they had seen enough for the present, and wished to cherish what they knew.

The warm core of certainty settled stiller as driving faster the wind paid out the telephone wires the fences the flattened heads of grey grass always raising themselves again again again.

The Voice

Peter Cowan

The staff-room was warm. He closed the door on the wind that seemed concentrated along the corridor as if it had blown nowhere else. He crossed to the fire in the glass-fronted fireplace, one pane of glass missing so that beyond the small cube the flames held a sudden reality, before he saw that she was sitting in the easy chair by the long window.

He had thought he might have, briefly, the room to himself, like some respite from the endless impact of personalities, from the words that must be found, the demand of faces.

He said, 'Cold enough. Still.'

'Yes. This room is warm, though.'

He looked up quickly from the fire. He saw her every day, without particular note. Quite a time ago she had deepened her hair in colour to black. Before that he seemed to remember indeterminate shades, neutral, in keeping with her rather broad, quiet face, that her glasses with their emphasized rims seemed to guard. It was a face that revealed little, he thought, except a rather determined pleasantness, and he was aware suddenly how slight had been his curiosity or his interest. And nothing that he saw as he looked at her now would have changed his feeling. But her voice was so altered that for a moment it seemed grotesque, as if some joke had been played on him.

She smiled faintly, as if she read his thought.

'Laryngitis. Isn't it stupid? I'm helpless in class.'

'Yes,' he said. Her voice had ordinarily been different, a little high-pitched, with something of a childish quality. Now, it seemed to hold authority, and something that eluded him. He

The Voice

could have laughed at a certain wariness in himself, afraid still this might be some trick.

'I'm going home last period. I've no class then.'

'It's the only thing to do,' he said. 'I remember a headmaster once, more noted for his voice than any minor qualities such as intelligence, saying to me when I'd had the flu, "You're pretty helpless without a voice." It was the nearest I ever saw him come to self-revelation. And to smiling.'

He realized as he spoke that his joke was not communicable and he was irritated with himself for having placed the pointless words between them. But she smiled and said, 'That wouldn't have been Pete?'

'Yes. Did you know him?'

'He terrified me. When I was just out of training college. I can still hear his voice booming down corridors.'

'Always.' He laughed. 'It's a few years since I knew him. He retired quite a while back.'

She nodded. He thought probably she did not want to talk, but he would have liked to hear her voice. The change intrigued him, its tone somehow provocative, what one might have called, he thought suddenly, suggestive. He almost smiled. It was exaggerated, a bit stagey, as if she were acting in some not very competent theatrical. He looked at her quiet, rather serious face that he had always felt to be too plainly reserved, prim, and he thought how incongruous the voice was. But her eyes met his and she might somehow have shared his amusement, so that he was suddenly uncertain.

'I've nothing to read,' she said. 'You haven't a good thriller, something light?'

'I don't know — I don't think so. Not here. What would you like?'

'As long as it's not serious I don't care. I've finished all the exam marking and I just want to relax. And with this throat on top of it all I'm a bit fed up.'

'As are we all,' he said. 'I'll see what I can find in the library.'

'I've looked.'

'Oh. Nothing?'

'Not that I haven't read. It doesn't matter. It was only for tonight.'

She stretched herself, her arms lifting, and then let her hands

261

fall suddenly, her fingers spread, her palms upturned towards him. He looked down at the fire.

'I'm getting lazy here.'

'Why not?' he said.

'In this hive? It must be the fire.'

'I could get you a couple of books,' he said. 'I think I've some would do.'

'It doesn't matter.'

'It's no trouble. I could run them round to you.'

Once or twice, after late staff meetings, he had taken her home, with two other teachers who lived in the direction of his own suburb.

'Do you think you could?'

'Yes. I've a games practice after school, I may be a bit late—'

'After tea,' she said. 'There's no hurry. It's good of you—'

The bell broke the classrooms to sound and deliberate disorder. He looked up towards the window and the rain was moving greyly across the buildings and the black quadrangle.

The flat was on the ground floor of a small block of four. As the door opened and she stood beneath the light of the small entrance hall he felt a surprise that he realized she perhaps perceived. He had expected some evidence of the invalid. Heavy clothes. A thick sweater, perhaps. Even a scarf about her throat. Now that he thought of it, a bandage would have been possible. It would not have been out of keeping with the practicality he had always associated with her nature. Just as in winter she wore a shapeless grey raincoat like a man's. And heavy flat shoes.

'Come in,' she said. Her voice was deep, faintly strained. He had wanted to hear it again. But as he followed her into the room he had not been prepared for the white blouse, short-sleeved, the thin brown skirt that suggested so plainly her hips and thighs. He could no longer remember the anonymity of the clothes she wore to the school. She looked quickly at him, perhaps aware of his comparison.

'My voice is strained,' she said. 'It's not the flu or anything like that. I'm not really an invalid.' She smiled. 'It was good of you to bother with these.'

He handed her the books.

'You said something light —'

The Voice

'Thank you. These look just what I wanted. Sit down, Max.'

There was a heater near the fireplace. She went across to the corner of the room and turned on the television. He looked at the meaningless images that steadied to a pattern he did not bother to encompass.

'Mother is out,' she said. 'She plays bridge on Tuesdays.'

He looked about the room that seemed crowded with small pieces of furniture that achieved no particular balance, and he wondered if the personalities of herself and her mother had somehow reached a stalemate in the furnishings of this main room of the flat. It might have been that the furnishings of two different periods found an uneasy common ground, the old, ornately carved china cabinet and the clear, rather sharp lines of the low coffee table, the wide, high-backed settee and the chrome television chairs, contrasts so obvious as to seem deliberate. He had never met her mother.

She asked him about one of the books he had brought, and they discussed the writer, neither of them, he realized, interested, the words giving them excuse. About her wrist she wore two thin silver bracelets that slipped along her arm, they drew his gaze, for he could not remember her affecting any such adornment at the school.

He said suddenly, 'We've both been round at the school quite a time.'

She laughed, seeming not to find his remark unexpected.

'I suppose so. I was going to get a transfer about a year ago, but nothing came of it.'

'I'm used to the place,' he said. 'Probably I'll stay until I'm moved perforce.'

'That doesn't sound very cheerful.'

'Well — you know yourself, there are enough times it seems an insane asylum, and the warders the least sane.'

'Oh yes.'

He shrugged. 'Somehow one stays.'

'Perhaps we're afraid to go outside,' she said.

He looked at her quickly, but she was watching the television. Her fingers moved the thin bracelets back along her arm. For a time they allowed the shadows that moved in the diminutive world to hold them. Once or twice he noticed her lift her hand to her throat, and he wondered if her voice was painful to use, despite her denial. But it seemed to him that the evening had somehow broken, deriding them, as if it had offered some promise now withdrawn. Or perhaps, he thought, promise that had existed only in his own mind, unformed and now unlikely to find form. There was the beginning of uneasiness between them. He could find no words that might confirm their own reality, that after all this time they should be here, in the room of her flat, and she met his few obvious commonplaces too quickly. As the inanity of advertising filled the small screen before them, she stood up, smoothing briefly her thin skirt.

'I'll make some coffee. I won't be a moment.'

While she was out of the room he went across to the bookshelf and looked at the neat, even lines of the books. There was one strong section of travel, perhaps her mother's, he thought, but the rest held a queer neutrality almost like some disguise of a personality, the books perhaps expected of a teacher, of one who had been educated. As she came in he turned away.

She said, 'Nothing very much there.'

He stood close to her, taking the cup from the small tray. Her features were attractive, he thought in faint surprise, no longer marked with the air of rather conscientious worry she had always seemed to affect, and which he had found irritating. She smiled at him suddenly, and he had again the sense that his feeling must have been obvious, but the restraint between them seemed to have passed, and they talked without awkwardness, content to allow pauses to lengthen between them while they looked idly at the film, which reflected some of the tinsel of another age.

When again advertising without subtlety broke upon the screen as if to cancel all that had existed before it, he said,

'I must go. I've kept you late, and with your throat like that — you must be tired — '

'Oh no.' She rose with him. 'Those old films are curious — to think we felt like that — accepted all that as valid —'

He laughed. 'And the same will happen to today's.'

'Yes.'

He said, 'Your voice — I'd like you to go on talking —'

'My voice — ' She laughed.

He was standing close to her, and seemingly without volition he reached towards her, touching her arms, and she looked up at him. He thought she seemed without coquetry or evasion as she

The Voice

was without the forced jollity, the careful good-fellowship he had associated with her.

'It's not yours, really, I suppose.'

'Isn't it? How do you know?'

The television screen was suddenly blank, and she smiled, moving to turn it off.

He said, 'I didn't know it was as late as that.'

'It's not really.'

He said, 'If someone — suddenly isn't that person — '

She began to laugh and he said, 'It's very confusing.'

'It must be. How could it happen, Max?'

'I'm not sure.'

They heard the front door of the flat open, and he thought that for a moment she looked startled, and her mother came quietly into the room.

'Hullo,' she said. She looked at them as they stood near the television set. 'I wondered how you were. We finished early, so I came straight home to make sure you were all right. And meet Mr Webster. Evelyn said you would lend her some books. It was good of you.'

As they spoke, and he made his excuses for leaving, he looked at the small woman, whose quiet manner held something of authority. There was a certain fussiness about her, as though she did not like things disturbed, or to be unexpected, a suggestion of the fixity of routine that was perhaps also in the younger woman who came to the door with him, thanking him again for the books.

She did not come to school the next day. He had thought of ringing to ask how she was, but in the haste of activity that seemed so often meaningless he did not get to the phone. The following day, just before morning break, he came into the staff-room and she was standing by the window, talking to the history teacher. He went towards them and she looked up. As soon as she spoke he knew that the kind of strain, the depth, the faint suggestiveness her voice had seemed to hold was gone.

He said, 'You're better.'

Her smile had a briskness. 'Oh yes. A day home worked wonders.'

'Something we could all do with more often.' The history

teacher laughed at his own commonplace.

As he looked at them she seemed so much as he had always known her that he thought perhaps his feeling had been imagination, that he had somehow, on the verge of making a humiliating revelation, been reprieved. Or, as he listened to her laugh which echoed only an impersonal gesture, he thought it might have been that a mask had been replaced, the revelation not his alone, and he would suddenly have spoken to her. But she was offering some triteness to match that of the history teacher, the mask would perhaps not slip again. He turned away as the bell rang for the morning break.

On Our Safari

Thelma Forshaw

We saw them arrive from our kitchen-window. Four of them, picking their way clumsily through the rough grass paddock up to their house. They all paused a decent distance from the cow roped to a stump in the yard, and I'll guarantee the diagram of a cow's carcass in Nell's cookbook isn't so neatly calculated as that animal was then. 'All present and correct?' and 'Moo-moo, sir!' That's how it was.

You just got the feeling. Or is it because you've heard that sort of thing about them so often, you expect it?

The old lady was of globular construction, and she rolled along like a sailor, from one foot to the other. She led the party. The husband was built square, from head to boots — short and square — and, like a square, you knew nothing could get into him and nothing could get out either, as with all frightened people. The girl was tall, and with that blackish look their girls have — all hair, and a little face tucked into it to break the monotony. The young bloke, only about eighteen, was good-looking in the swashbuckling way of boys who've seen someone like themselves in the films and live up to it.

They carried coats on their arms, and you knew if they put them on, the hems would clear the ground only by about three inches, making their feet seem bigger than they were. They talked very loud — like a good row — and you could catch bursts of the lingo all mixed together, as they moved up to the house where the fowlsheds were ranged side and back, a-squawk with their busily strutting inmates.

Australian Short Stories

The talk resembled a composition for full orchestra, all the instruments coming in together and saying their bit, then weaving in and out of each other, tailing off, only to come in again in twos and threes. The conductor and first violin was the old lady.

Wherever she moved, wherever she stopped, the other three did likewise. It was the longest umbilical cord I'd ever seen, and put me in mind of a crew of mountaineers roped to each other on some Alp.

Nell shouldered in next to me at the window and said, 'Wonder what they are.'

'Reffos.'

'Yes, but where from?'

'Any place that's giving them the boot at the moment — could be Germany, Czechoslovakia, Austria, Poland . . . any of those. Don't you follow the Hitler serial?' There isn't any other she misses between 9 a.m. and 8 p.m. Eastern Standard Time.

'Oh, you!' She pushed me with her elbow. 'Suit you better to see if you can give them a hand, instead of staring the daylights out of them.'

'The proper study of mankind is man, ducks,' I said, by way of ennobling my peasant curiosity.

She's a good girl — any woman who'd give up her gay town life to satisfy my middle-aged whim for a little poultry-farm just out of the city must be. I'd been a white-collar boy — the glossy, well-starched variety that sometimes calls for a bow-tie — for twenty years, and that did me. Nell had exchanged her cocktail apron for the utility sort to oblige, so it's to be expected her tongue would get a fine cutting-edge to it.

I left the refs in peace, and went back to my paper. Nell gave me a look. 'There's plenty of work to be done, you know, Fred.'

'Sure, sure,' I agreed enthusiastically. 'Love the stuff. Can't stay away from it. But a little self-denial'll do me good.'

She ought to know by now that I enjoy poultry-farming without working at it. I watched her go out to feed the chooks, herself, with her thin-lip back. I could tell her moods for a whole week without seeing her face. She has a very eloquent back, Nell has.

The poultry country we're in is almost urban the way there's very little distance between the various runs. Each wouldn't pan out to more than twelve acres, if that. Only the sparse bush, which always puts me in mind of a man losing his hair, and the dusty road corrugating along from the railway keeps up the illusion that we're far from the madding throng of Sydney. We are, in fact, a bare thirty miles, but it'll do.

One has moments when the refinements of civilization have their appeal, and then one gives way to an orgy of cityism. This starts off with shopping, ranging from the utility type down to the fine nuances, a decent sort of pub-crawl, dinner among the plush, and, if the fever's still running high, a leery play or a front stall at the Tiv. After which, one comes home feeling debauched, hailing the good clean country life hysterically, and works it all off in a few days' hard yakka. Purified again, you might say.

It's a crave, like the grog, the city life, once you've abandoned it, but most of the time you're a passive addict, only bursting out in periodic sprees.

The general run of our colleagues in the neighbourhood are the real McCoy, though. They've grown right out of the place — not 'slips', like Nell and me. We rub along fine, because we all love poultry-farming, but not what you would call working at it . . . And straight from scratch, our newchums, the reffos, stood out like sore toes, because, right way or wrong way, brother, they *worked* at poultry-farming!

Next day, Nell tucked some scones under her wing, and we started over to their place with the idea of giving them a leg-in to the community.

It had rained overnight, summer-hard, but the heat had recharged itself long before the first cock shot off its big beak. Poppa Ref and Baby Ref were ready for it. There they were, attired like a couple of pukka sahibs, toeing it gingerly through the sheds, flicking grains of feed at the hens like pinches of salt. Both wore tropical sun-helmets of the aggressively African type, soap-ad shirts, and long white shorts that touched the tops of kneeboots. Outsize sunglasses balanced like little black scales across their noses. Mouths and chins were left recklessly exposed to the fury of the outer-Sydney tropics.

Nell got behind a tree. 'God forgive me!' she choked and, having summoned divine sanction, gave way to her uncharitable mirth. I stood thoughtfully watching the little safari as it trudged

Australian Short Stories

manfully through the fowlsheds, appeasing the savage hunter of wild and woolly poultry.

'Come on, pull yourself together,' I snapped, 'or I'll haul out those spike-heels you brought up with *you*, and line 'em up outside the gate.'

That adjusted her perspective, and we went on, giving them a hail as we climbed through their fence.

Round they whirled — there's no other word for it — and stood waiting with a tension so strong it could have been rented out to playwrights for thirty per cent of the gate.

'You can forget about the S.S. out here, mates,' I muttered, a bit unnerved by the huge apprehension of their expectancy, as we bore down on them.

Nell nervously held out the scones. 'These will save your lady work at morning-tea,' she shouted.

The big sunglasses flashed like headlamps towards the house and focused there.

'Mumma!' barked the boy.

'Halloo! Halloo!' Poppa brayed with desperate breeziness. I thought of a couple of poddy-calves threatened by dingoes.

Mumma lumbered out, wiping her hands on an apron as big as a car-tarp. 'Vot is? Vot is?' she bellowed, and finally came to a ponderous halt, head and shoulders below all of us.

Nell seemed near tears. She's very sensitive to atmosphere, of which we keep very little round our place. She held out the scones again, and talked in her 'deaf voice', which is keyed for hailing a party of lost bush-walkers in the Blue Mountains.

'Scones!' she shouted. 'For your morning-tea!'

'Shkon?' The old lady frowned. 'Ve not much English. Only *drei* month coming from Wien. Vot is shkon?'

'*Kuchen*,' I swaggered, and her face lit up. She caught my hand. 'You must come! Come!' She pulled, gesturing at the house with her head, free hand, and the part where her apron tied at the back. 'I making coffee mit *schlag*.' She smiled, and her shrewd old porous face beamed with it. She turned her back on the menfolk, and pushed us both before her into the house like a hospitable bulldozer.

'Ah, coffee with cream,' I said for Nell's benefit. 'Not too hot for our weather? Er — *nicht zu heiss, Frau* — ?'

'Jones,' she said, pronouncing it 'Chones'. 'Frau Jones.'

270

On Our Safari

Oh, yes, I thought. Well, it's a wee improvement on Frankenwurtzenheimer.

She brought out some very nifty china, and I took a good dekko at the stuff they had already managed to shove into the positions prescribed for turning a house into home. You could see into one of the bedrooms from where I sat, and the beds were the twin sort, which seem to be a fetish with foreigners, very low and decoratively covered, too. There was a Persian carpet, and very nice brocaded curtains — altogether rather rich icing for such a plain cake as a farmhouse.

As we sat drinking the coffee with cream, the sweat popped out of our pores like beads of syrup. Out of sheer pity I introduced the topic of tea.

'Ah, tea,' she sighed. 'So very dear, no? In Wien is not to buy.'

I threw out my arms expansively. 'Any amount, Frau Jones. You know — *sehr viele* — everywhere in Australia, tea.'

'So?' She nodded, impressed. 'Is very hot here. Tea is being *besser?*'

The suspicious faces of her menfolk peered round the doorway, and she summoned them in with a rattle of German. They stood, staring at us, and I imagined the girl had fled at the first sound of our voices, and was probably listening behind a closed door.

'In Wien,' Frau Jones confided, 'we leaving very much. I have three shops, all very goot business. Karlchen — *sitz du!*' she commanded the boy, who was eyeing my rough garb — or semi-nakedness — up and down, a red flush of comprehension staining his neck. His threatened manhood overrode his mother's inducement to sociability, and he disappeared for a few minutes, sidling back stripped of half his safari clobber.

Assimilation begins, I thought with a grin. But bet your life Herr holds out to the bitter end.

'Yes, in Wien,' chanted Frau Jones lingeringly, 'I am having housemaids for my work. This — I never doing!' She indicated her apron, and I felt Nell's sympathetic tremor. 'But Hitler — he taking all. And so we have only enough to buy chicken-farm.'

I shook my head, in a combination of astonishment and sympathy.

'We see only hen on *table*, in Wien,' she explained, 'never before on feet, walking. In Wien, is not necessary for me, *verstehen sie?'*

Nell gave a hysterical giggle, which I covered with a fusillade of vehement 'Yah's'. I caught an ironical dart from her eye. She gets jealous of my adaptability in all sorts of company, and I was enjoying my role of cosmopolite.

I told Frau Jones reassuring things about her neighbours, all good sorts, and of the major, a real gentleman, who could also speak a little German with her, being an Old Digger.

'Ah, Dicker,' she sighed. 'This is something for a war, no? The man' — she jerked her head, and I could see old Mac, the handyman who'd passed over to them with the farm, knocking about outside, in his spuriously busy fashion — 'ven he speak, you think war is something for a *dicker*, no?'

I nodded. Old Mac had never come back from Flanders. He had parley-voo-ed, toot-sweet-ed and French-tabby-ed right up to the Lili Marlene period, which was then with us.

Presently I noticed a certain rhythm about the comings and goings of Herr Jones and Karlchen. They would stand about for a while, listening blankly, then snatch up egg-baskets and duck outside, sidling back in again, murmuring and grunting together feverishly. The next time I observed these shenanigans, they stamped in, hooting exultantly and I saw that the cause of their glee was three eggs. Frau Jones's eye gleamed and she nodded approval. After a decent interval, off they went with the baskets, returning with faces as long as your arm, eggless.

I could see fascinated disbelief on Nell's face, as she followed these sorties. And it dawned on me that they regarded a live hen as a kind of doughnut-machine, and expected her ladyship to give with a one-two-three-egg routine round the clock. I felt tired just thinking of it. And a little stern, in R.S.P.C.A. style. Hens, after all, were not Austrian shopgirls. Not that it actually worried me. I'll stake a hen to call the tune right up to the minute her neck's wrung.

Nell opened her mouth, closed it and looked at me, but I said nothing. My line of thought was too entrancing . . . If it came to the point, they weren't expecting the hens to do more than they'd do themselves. Now, if the Frau Joneses could have laid the eggs themselves, there'd be a mighty pretty profit in no time. Yes, I could quite see the frustration of just sitting there and waiting for those hens to lower away. But they'd soon lose that urgent, let's-press-on-time's-flying attitude and learn to adjust their tempo to La Chook's.

I got up — well entertained, but not the greedy type. 'Work to be done, Frau Jones,' I said heartily, 'so we'll be off. If we can be of any help to you, you will let us know, eh?' We're only next-door. Don't be shy.'

She nodded blankly and vigorously, reading my intentions in face and tone.

We noticed the scones had not been touched, and I could imagine them all, after we'd gone, bending over, their heads together pulling them apart, sniffing and tasting gingerly.

'Well, for Heaven's sake,' Nell began, as we went indoors, 'you might have told them you only collect eggs twice a day — '

'Look, ducks, they wouldn't have believed me.' I eyed the teapot pointedly. 'They'd think I was trying to hold 'em back.'

'Poor silly devils,' she said, putting the kettle on. 'What possessed them to take it up? They'll be broke in six months.'

I smiled. Nell knows the smile. It was often cast in our college plays — with me as a sort of frame for it. She gave it answer. 'Oh, go on! In all that tropical get-up and egg-hunting!' She looked at me doubtfully, but I held it. The Mona Lisa wouldn't have got a look in.

As the Frau Joneses settled, I was over there more often than at our own place, and Nell put up with my absences for the sake of the stories I brought back to her, playing Penelope to my Ulysses.

Then came the heatwave. It always does, of course, but this was the Frau Joneses' first. After laying out my dead, I strolled over to sympathize, flopping down on their back doorstep with a lassitude and resignation I expected to find duplicated by similarly bereaved Joneses.

'How many you lost?' I asked.

'None! None!' shouted Frau Jones. 'Not to sit there, mister, please!'

I came indoors, suddenly feeling a mere fleck of dust in their cosmos. The air was charged with urgency. Just as I'd got out of the way, Herr Jones and Karlchen and the girl came storming across the yard, cradling stonkered hens in their arms. They hurtled into the kitchen and delivered up their burdens to Frau

Jones, who was squatting vastly on the floor, surrounded by stricken fowl.

'Papa! Karlchen! Quick! Bring der coffee! Bring me coffee! Quick!' Karlchen scattered and came running with a big enamel jug. This she snatched from him and, with a spoon, began ladling the cold brew into a sunstruck chook.

'Ice! Ice!' she screamed. They skidded up with it, and she applied an iceblock to the bird's comb. The patient was then borne off and tucked into the sink with the tap running. She turned to the next casualty. First the dose of black coffee, then ice to the fevered brow and to bed in Ward Sink.

The out-patients' deparment on Anzac Day wasn't in it! Sun-smitten chooks staggered round, bumping into the walls and dripping with melted ice. Meanwhile, the St. John Ambulance service kept running between the yard and the kitchen, Herr Jones and the kids reeling in with armfuls of fresh invalids. In the middle of it all, Florence Nightingale kept on ministering with the fury of seven devils.

She paused between patients. 'We lose none,' she said deeply, looking at me with shining fanatical blue eyes, straggles of hair clinging to her steaming face.

I looked bitterly at the hens. 'Best of everything, you b.b.'s,' I thought, 'and me sitting here half-cooked.'

Out of a whirling vortex of questions I chose one: 'Why coffee?'

'Ice, Lottchen! You must me bring more ice!' She dripped coffee into a gasping beak and answered without turning, 'Coffee is good for the heart, no?' Then, 'I tell you, mister, I not lose one. I promise you this.'

Somehow I loped home to Nell, and sat looking deflated for a long time. Partly heat. In a sober voice I related the doings over at Frau Jones's, and while she laughed till she cried, I kept saying reverently, 'But it works! How does it work? But it works!'

When the neighbourhood tallied its losses after the heat-wave, it was found that the Frau Joneses had lost least of all, and an aura of witchcraft hovered over them. They kept on doing everything wrong side up, but somehow coming out sunny side up. And our topics of conversation ranged in this order: (a) the b. war, (b) the Mad Foreigners, and (c) poultry-farming.

On Our Safari

None of us ever bothered about dressing, being content to load our eggs off to the market and be done with it. It was a tidy enough living. But the Frau Joneses launched into dressing, and the farm ran with gore. Anyone could see them, as they passed by along the road — Frau and Herr Jones, Karlchen and Lottchen, standing at big tables outside the kitchen-door.

Herr Jones, out of innate squeamishness, which, I confess, I shared with him, loudly declined butchery, and was assigned to plucking; Karlchen stood and wrung neck after neck with his deft, neat hands moving as cool and unconcerned as if he were tying Boy Scouts' knots. Lottchen also plucked and did the fiddly bits, but where the gore flowed thickest, where entrails abounded, amid the thousand ills that fowl is heir to — there was Frau Jones.

Her fat, short arms worked like little pistons, yanking away intestines by the yard, as though she were on the ribbon-counter at Woolworths, slitting stomach-bags, undismayed by the morbid surprises chook-dressing sometimes presents. Then, off to the fridge with the slaughtered, all lights carefully collected. Yea, and in death they were not divided. Not with Frau Jones on the job.

After that, Herr Jones was seen sullenly pushing a barrow between the farm and the railway, laden with big suitcases. Up and down he went, narked about it, you could see, but the whip had cracked and he had to jump. The stationmaster pulled me aside one day. 'What the buggers up to? Smuggling?'

'Dressed poultry,' I assured him. 'Messiest damn' job under heaven. Haven't you noticed the boy's been running up and down to Sydney? Canvassing for orders.'

We looked at each other, mouths turned down. Of course, we shrugged, if you can take it — if you like it that way — if you want to work yourself into your grave . . .

From time to time, the Frau Joneses paused to have company. Sponsors, I supposed, or cobbers they'd kept in touch with who'd come out here in their turn. One day, after they'd had visitors, I went across and found Herr Jones muttering to himself in his usual rage of the chronically scared.

'What's up, Herr?'

It was the sanitary-pan. We all knew how he felt about it. It was just that bit too far out for the sanitary service and we all performed the unlovely chore ourselves.

'Fisitors!' he grieved, 'I not wanting them. Only the others. *They* want. Always I must empty — ' He cursed down a wave of nausea. 'I tell the others they can go in the paddock, but fisitors! They come — eat, eat, eat all day and then they go to the lavatory. And always I — I must it empty. Let them empty themself. I am not the toilet-putzer.'

He did have his paddy up. I said, 'Ah, come on, now, Herr. That's not very hospitable of you.'

'And the boy. Always there is trupples,' he went on, tipping his begrimed sun-helmet back to mop the sweat. 'Now the Army. We so short, and the handyman so lazy — and *he* want to go in the Army. All day he talk — Army, Army. Nothing else. I am sick of it. He cannot go. Ve poultry-farmer and poultry-farmer is not for Army.'

'That's right, Herr, we're exempt. Still, he's only a boy, and he doesn't see much life round here — you know — no pleasure — '

He blew his top. A very active crater, Herr was.

'Pleasure!' he cried. 'I must working all day. I haf no pleasure. Why must he pleasure?'

I saw his point reluctantly. Frau Jones had a job on her hands, keeping them all free of the young country's corrupting playfulness. Herr, himself, had all the earmarks of the thwarted *bon vivant*, and I knew he balked as hard as the young 'un, and for that reason was all the more determined to block Karlchen's efforts to scat. He didn't mention Lottchen, but we all knew Billy Worthing, one of the neighbouring farmers, had his eye on the solid, dark-visaged fraulein.

Months moved on, and we spent an occasional evening over at the Frau Joneses'. Nell wasn't too keen. She couldn't follow everything that was said, and when she sat knitting, one time, in the Frau Joneses' kitchen, rather resented the old lady grabbing the wool and showing her 'how ve *stricken*' (she called it) in Europe. 'So, with the left hand, and the wool here. Chinesesch also *stricken* in this way. What *you* doing — this is English.'

'Well, I *am* English,' Nell burst out, a little inaccurately, and the old lady flared back: 'And I — *I* am a Wienerin.'

I thought there would be fireworks, but the Frau was a clever — and theatrical — old devil. After her spirited come-back, she smiled beguilingly and, gazing into our eyes with her head on one side, began to sing in a quavering tremolo, '*Wien, Wien, Mein Wien*', playing up the tourist conception of Vienna — wine, women and waltzes — for all she was worth, with the moistening eye and the little rueful smile. The boy squirmed uncomfortably, the girl was silent as usual, but Herr seemed entranced, lapping it up.

'Come! Ve haf a drink,' he said emotionally, and went to the fridge, hauling out a bottle of Sauterne. 'Lottchen, bring glasses.'

Frau Jones quavered thrillingly on, sprinkling nostalgia everywhere, and Herr Jones said gruffly, 'I show you *gespritzen*. Wine mit soda-water. This we drink always in Vienna.' He shattered quarter glasses of Sauterne with full toppings of soda-water, which we sank with surprised pleasure.

'Ahhh, ahhh, ahhh,' sang Frau Jones, with a glass of *gespritzen* in one hand, singing in her obstinate tremolo. Yet the lively blue eyes and the spirit behind the old girl's play-acting did get across something of brave gaiety — *galgenhumor* they call it — to sing while the heart breaks, joke on your way to the gallows.

I think she knew the young 'uns were tugging on the umbilical cord. Lottchen's rustic suitor, many years older than herself, had started paying open court, and the girl was anything but unwilling. Then suddenly I got the feeling Frau Jones was singing to *them*, and saying, 'Remember, remember, remember.'

That was a funny sort of evening, and Nell said after she felt embarrassed with Frau Jones singing like that, the way people do when they're drunk.

'It's the only way she cuts loose,' I said. 'When you've had it, you go to town and blow a week's money. She gives with the *galgenhumor*.'

'The whatta?'

'Forget it. Did you hear Herr calling their big black cockerel a blutty bucker today?'

'Yes, I think it's a shame picking up the worst words like that.'

'That, my girl,' says I, 'is assimilation.'

'Where I come from,' Nell says, 'it's bad language.'

And it was, too, from behind a dozen kitchen-windows the day the Frau Joneses swept down the road in their big, shiny new car. We thought of our bombs, and when we got together the grumbling was general.

'I dunno how they do it —'

'They come out here —'
'Prack'ly taking the bloody bread out of our mouths —'
'Whatya make of it, Fred?'

I smiled. The old Act Two, I-know-who-done-it smile. I would have liked a good homely allusion to top it off. But all I thought of was — a safari.

Poppy Seed and Sesame Rings

Elizabeth Jolley

Tante Bertl collapsed and died without my being able to do anything about it on the steps of the Art Gallery and Museum. It was on the way home from a short afternoon visit to Grossmutti.

We sat, all three together, in the watery green light of her small apartment, the room opened into a conservatory and the winter sun, fading, made a delicate pattern of fern shadows on the coffee coloured lace table cloth. Tante Bertl sighed repeatedly.

'Das schmeckt mir,' she said, taking a third cream filled pastry. 'Wirklich gut!' Tante Bertl's voice was contented.

'Only try and walk,' I implored her, pulling at her plump hand. It was such a public place though, at the time, no one was walking there or sitting on the benches. She had insisted on getting off at the Museum. A light rain was falling.

'Let us make a little rain walk,' she said and, clambering on her short fat legs from the tram, she sank down on to the bottom step of that wide flight which seemed to reach up behind her to the sky.

As if I were the cause of her difficulties I felt ashamed and embarrassed. I glanced round quickly and nervously, anyone could see us there, even the pigeons could notice us in our trouble. I was afraid she was going to be sick there on the pavement.

I tried to pull her from the step but she only sighed and, making no attempt to get up, she simply leaned forward and died. I ran straight home leaving her there with the pigeons and the coming darkness.

'Tante Bertl wanted to walk,' I told them so they did not expect her for a time.

I thought I heard Mother crying in the night, her subdued sighs followed my father creaking on bent legs about the shop. I knew Tante Bertl was dead. All night long I pictured her huddled all alone on the steps of the Museum with its strange and grotesque treasures piled up behind her. Would the pigeons come to her I wondered, or would they avoid a dead old lady smelling of the vague warm sweetness of old age and so stuffed with pastries.

'Go to sleep, it's all right, go to sleep,' in the candle light my father crawled flickering across the ceiling crouching doubled on the cupboard, 'it's nothing, it's all right, everything's all right, go to sleep.' Flickering and prancing he moved up and down the walls big and little and big and I heard Mother crying and crying.

Next day Mother had to go to the mortuary. My father said to me, 'You go with her and comfort her.' I did not want to go but my father could not leave the shop he said, and I knew this was so. Mother felt so strange in the New Country and she tried to make friends with the few customers we had. She was always giving away packets of groceries or bars of chocolate and washing soap.

'Take ziss too, but take ziss,' she said, trying to imitate the tone and the accent of the people who were now her neighbours. She wanted to be accepted by these people and she pushed the presents my father could not afford to give into the spaces in their shopping baskets.

There were not many corpses in the mortuary. Tante Bertl's body looked so small as if it had been cut in half. I wondered if there would be a mess of blood and pastry, a body cut in half would be a terrible sight unless there was some clever method that I didn't know about. While Mother was being led away towards the white enamelled door, I hurriedly lifted the bottom end of the cloth.

Tante Bertl's unexpected feet gave me a shock. I had never seen her bare feet before, they were plump and neat and very clean. They were wide apart. I supposed this was because of her fat thighs.

It seemed then, that a person was very small in death.

Poppy Seed and Sesame Rings

At once Grossmutti came to stay. With her tin trunk and wickerwork baskets, she sat in the back room and disapproved of Mother's marriage to a shopkeeper. When Grossmutti came she usually stayed for several weeks, her disapproval mounting daily until, after a series of small explosions, she entered into a grand packing and a departure, after which things went on as before. Except that this time there would be no Tante Bertl to nudge Mother softly and whisper with her in the back room.

Mother wept aloud and wished for Bertl.

'Recha!' said Grossmutti. 'Stop sniffing and get my bed made up in the spare room and send Louise up with some hot coals, the room's sure to be damp.'

The night was long and I heard my father creaking to and fro over the floorboards.

'Who's that!' Grossmutti's voice crackled in the darkness, she always kept her door open keeping an unasked for vigil over her son-in-law and his house.

'It is only me,' he replied softly. 'I am looking for fly spray. Mosquito.'

'No mosquito this time of year. More likely vermin!' And then she called, 'What for is Recha crying?'

'It is all right,' my father patiently explained. 'She is homesick that is all.' Grossmutti made a sound of scorn and disbelief.

I often heard Mother crying in the night. When I called out my father always explained in a soft voice, 'She is homesick, that is all.' So I always knew what was the matter. Sometimes, after those times, Mother sent me out for fillet of veal cut in thin slices, she hammered the meat on the red tiles of the kitchen floor and sang,

'Mein' Schätzlein ist sauber ist weiss wie die Schnee —'

And after dinner, when the shop was closed, my father got up from the table, slapped his thighs and leapt across the room, and Mother, with a demure expression, danced sedately round and round the dinner table with him.

My poor mother was always homesick. She longed for the scenery and the smells and for the people of her homeland. She blamed her marriage for all that she was suffering.

'Why are you crying so?' my father, perplexed, would ask her. 'We have a nice house and a shop and a good life safe here in the New Country. What you wanted isn't it? You and your sister

Australian Short Stories

and your mother. Really it is as if I have married all three of you to bring you here, all safe, and you are not satisfied,' he scratched his fine sandy hair. 'And,' he said, 'And I bring Louise too because you are used to her even though she will soon be too old to work,' his voice climbed in indignation. 'Really it is as if I marry four women to bring out,' he said. He looked at me, 'But five,' he said and shrugged helplessly.

Mother longed for the bread she had been used to all her life at home. Though we had poppy seed bread and sesame rings, she said they were not the same at all. Often she took a small roll from the glass sided cupboard where the bread was kept and she broke the bread and sniffed it and dipped it in her coffee.

'It is not the same,' she moaned softly.

I too liked to break the fresh bread and sniff it and pile it into my coffee and pick up the succulent fragrant lumps with a spoon. But with Mutti in the back room we had to refrain from these habits only fit for shopkeepers.

At school I learned the alimentary system of the rabbit. I knew the rabbit from the pinna to the tail. I learned all the Latin names of the human skeleton by heart and all the details of internal combustion and gaseous interchange. I sorted out in my mind the mingling and exchanging of the various juices involved in the process of digestion. And when we had examinations I was always top of the class.

Because of old age, Louise had to leave us and then Grossmutti died. No catastrophe, she just fell asleep quietly like a doll in the little bedroom.

And the years went by one after the other.

'Your mother has no one,' my father said to me in his soft concerned voice. He was so busy in the shop, his skin was paler than ever from being indoors all the time. He never went anywhere and the shop did not change. It did not prosper and it did not give up. The same foods were there and the same customers starting at half past seven in the morning wanting small purchases until nine o'clock at night. The shop was only closed on Good Friday and on Christmas Day. Our own holidays and feasts were pushed aside left in a bygone life. I had been too young when we left to remember this other life but Mother continued to weep alone in the dingy room at the back.

'She is alone all the time. You might try and come and see her

Poppy Seed and Sesame Rings

more often,' my father said at the end of one of my rare visits. He was in the closed shop with me, the smell of mixed delicatessen and spices seemed sharper because of the dark. I had to be back at the hospital for the night.

'I'm pretty busy these days,' I made the excuse.

'Yes yes but your mother is always waiting for you to come,' he made a movement of self effacing apology with his hands in which, even his shoulders and neck and head, even his whole body, took part.

'Your father is working all the time,' Mother reproached me during the short visit. 'He has never a holiday, always working and working so that you can study and pass your exam.'

She always spoke as if I had only one examination to pass. My whole life had become a series of tests and examinations and the only friends I had were books and scalpels and test tubes and dry dead bones. My father toiled so that I could study so that is what I did.

I promised my father I would come home more often and I ran like a thief, with nothing stolen except some hours from my studying, through the empty streets all the way to the hospital.

I resolved to find a friend and to take her home with me the very next week to end my loneliness and to please Mother.

Of course it took longer than I expected and I did not go home for a whole month.

'Go in to her!' my father was just closing the shutters. 'Every day she waits and waits hoping you will come.' She was sitting in the back behind the shop, that was all she had to do, just sit. There was scarcely enough work for two people in the shop.

I explained quickly I was coming on Sunday.

'I'm bringing Marion,' I said trying to make it sound like a treat.

'Who is Marion?' Mother asked. 'Who is this Marion?'

'She is my friend from the hospital,' I explained nervously.

'Does she study too for exam?' Mother asked.

'She works in the hospital,' I said.

'How can she work there and not study?' Mother wanted to know.

'There is other work,' I said, 'all kinds of work.'

'Sunday, you close the shop,' Mother said to my father, 'we have a visitor coming.' She seemed pleased. 'Sunday afternoon, we close the shop,' she said.

'So!' my father said. 'Good! good!' he rubbed his pale soft hands together. I hoped Marion would be a success, but at the back of my mind were some grave doubts.

As soon as we arrived Mother made it very clear that she had not rested, that she had worked without stopping for some days. The table was covered with dishes, bean salad, herring salad, potato salad, even cabbage salad, the air was heavy with their various dressings. There was a large flat plate of cold meat, veal coated with sauce, liver sausage and salami slices and hard boiled eggs, enough for a dozen people. There were cakes too, pastries filled with jam and cream and little heart shaped biscuits.

'She has not made these things for years,' my father said happily. But he had not yet noticed Mother's face as I brought in Marion. I hardly knew my new friend. I had chosen her because she looked healthy and very clean and was the nearest one to speak to at the counter in the hospital administration department. She had seemed pleased to be invited to my home on Sunday. She was a big girl, bigger than all of us, I had not noticed this before. Her pink blouse filled our living room. She kept talking too, from the minute we entered, trying to be well behaved and say the right things. Mother's face was dark with disapproval and it became worse especially as Marion couldn't pronounce our name. She kept calling Mother Mrs. Mosh.

'I love the embroidered cushions Mrs. Mosh, did you make them?' and 'That's a dream of a dress you have on Mrs. Mosh.'

'Nothing but personal remark!' Mother snapped at me in the scullery.

'She is only trying to be friends,' I whispered uneasily.

'She is not any friend for you, she is not ours!' she said so vehemently, I knew she could never receive anyone for me from this New Country as she still thought of it. Just then the radio came on. Mother flew into the living room.

'In this house I switch on or off the wireless!' she said grimly. Years of unhappiness had made her like this I knew but I wished she would try to be agreeable.

Marion blushed.

'It's a lovely radio,' she said. 'Pardon me! but I just love music. Do you like classical music Mrs. Mosh?' There was a silence

Poppy Seed and Sesame Rings

after Mother had switched off, Marion hummed quietly.

'Tell your friend she is not Beethoven,' Mother said coldly. And then she helped Marion to a big plateful of meats and salads even though Marion protested,

'Oh no more thank you Mrs. Mosh! If I eat all that I'll be like the side of a house!' She was buried in egg and salami.

In his embarrassment my father stood up and passed plates to Marion all in the wrong order.

'Cake?' he said in his gentle voice. 'Biscuit? All home-made!' I wanted to ask him to wait. I felt it was all my fault this terrible afternoon.

'Oh very nice I'm sure,' Marion thanked him, 'But I'll have to refuse. I'll be putting on pounds. I've got a spare tyre already!'

'Look such waste!' Mother snatched Marion's plate from me angrily in the scullery. 'You see she does not like our food even!' she scraped the plate noisily into the pail under the sink.

I felt I couldn't face the impossible evening which lay ahead but Marion solved this.

'Well,' she said smiling all round the table, after the meal. 'I'll just have to be going now. I have enjoyed myself really I have Mrs. Mosh. Thank you so very much Mrs. Mosh for having me and thank you Mr. Mosh.'

My father, who was already on his feet, gave a little bow which seemed to involve his whole body, and I jumped up gratefully.

'I'll go with you,' I said, and I fetched our rain coats. At the bus stop Marion said there was no need to go all the way with her, she would be all right, she said. She waved to me from inside the bus and, from the wet pavement, I waved to her.

I thought I ought to go back home.

I ran straight back and Mother was quite different. There was a smell of fresh coffee and she had put some stale poppy seed rolls and a sesame ring from the shop into the oven. All her photograph albums were on the table. Not a word was said about Marion. It was as if she had never been there. We spent the evening in another world with Tante Bertl, Grossmutti and Louise and myself when I was a child. At intervals my father exclaimed in his gentle voice,

'Ach so! Look at this one!' and, 'this is a good picture, take a look at your mother in this picture she has not changed has she.'

It was just as if we were looking at the photographs for the first time. Mother talked and laughed and recalled the materials and the colours of our dresses, and the various occasions. One happy time after another, she described them all.

Then she busily packed up some cold meats and pastries and I had to run all the way to catch the last bus to the hospital. The hard boiled eggs were coming through the wet paper, so I left the parcel in a deserted waiting room on the ground floor.

Upstairs I sat at my table and tried to read and write and study but I kept writing Marion's name everywhere.

I thought about her. I kept thinking about her without being able to do anything about it.

Because of her it seemed that the diagram of the systemic circulation was all wrong. Suddenly it was clear to me that blood flowed in all directions at once. The twelve pairs of cranial nerves, I knew them all by heart, were said to govern the special senses but now I knew these special senses had no government. I thought I would write about the lymphatic system, but instead I began to write about quiet lakes and deep pools which have no reflection and no memory; I wrote too about the excitement of the secluded places where land and water meet.

In my thoughts I found I had an unknown store-house of feelings and I wrote them into half remembered sunsets and half known ways leading through secret woods and along hidden river banks. As I wrote during the night of these strange and grotesque treasures it seemed as if the fragrance of fresh grass came from somewhere not far beyond the hospital and the roof tops and the chimneys. Somewhere in the world I knew there were mountains and more mountains. I wanted a whole mountain to myself. In the night I wanted to be on the mountain climbing up to reach the clear air and the magic place on the peak just when the first sunlight would reach it too.

In the morning I wrote Marion's name again and again on every piece of paper on my study table. And in my hand my pen had an innocence I did not quite understand.

The Cost of Things

Elizabeth Harrower

Dan Freeman shut the white-painted garage doors and went across the paved courtyard to the house which was painted a glossy white, too. *A lovely home.* Visitors always used these words to describe it and Dan always looked intent and curious when they did, as if he suspected them of irony. But the house did impress him for all that he wasn't fond of it.

When the Freemans bought the place they said apologetically to their friends that they couldn't afford it *but* . . . People just looked unfriendly and didn't smile back. Then came the grind, the worry, fear, boredom, paring down, the sacrifices large and small of material and, it really did seem, spiritual comforts, the eternal use of the negative, habitual meanness, harassment. And it wasn't paid for yet, not *yet*. They had been careful, he and Mary, though, to see that the children hadn't — to use Mary's phrase — gone without.

Lately Dan had begun to think it mightn't have done any harm if Bill and Laura *had* been a bit deprived. They might now be applying themselves to their books occasionally, and thinking about scholarships. But, oh no! They had no doubt their requirements would all be supplied just for the wanting. Marvellous! The amount of work they did, it would be a miracle if either of them matriculated.

'Hullo. You're late. Dinner's ready,' Mary called as the back door closed.

Leaning round into the kitchen, he looked at her seriously and sniffed the air. 'What is it?'

'Iced soup. Your special steak. Salad with —'

He rolled his eyes. 'There's the paper. Five minutes to get cleaned up and I'm with you.'

Mary was an excellent cook. The Freemans had always eaten well, but since Dan had come home from his six months' interstate transfer, she had outdone herself. 'I experimented while you were away,' she explained, producing dinners nightly that would have earned their house several stars in the *Guide Michelin* had it ever been examined in this light.

'Experimented!' Dan laughed in an unreal, very nearly guilty, way the first time she said this, because he was listening to another voice in his head reply smartly, 'So did I! So did I!'

Feeling the way he felt or, rather, remembering the name Clea, he was shocked at the gleeful fellow in him who could treat that name simply as something secret from Mary. And he thought *I am ashamed* although he did not *feel* ashamed to find himself taking pride in the sombre and splendid addition to his past that the name represented. Clea, he thought, as if it were some expensive collectors' item he had picked up, not without personal risk, for which it was not unnatural to accept credit. At the sound of that guilty laugh or the puffing of vanity, Dan mentally groaned and muttered, 'I'm sorry. I'm sorry.'

For the first weeks after his return to Melbourne, he had blocked all memories of those Sydney months since he could not guarantee the behaviour of his mind, and if to remember in such ways was to dishonour, he had emerged out of a state of careful non-consideration with the impression that to remember truly might not be wise. But lately, lately . . . He realized that lately when he was alone he sat for hours visualizing his own hand reaching to grasp hers. And each time he produced this scene its significance had to be considered afresh, without words, through timeless periods of silence. Or he pictured her walking away from him as he had once seen her do. An occasion of no significance at all. She had merely been a few steps in front of him. And he pictured her arms rising. For hours, weeks, he had watched her walk away. Then for nights, days and weeks he had looked at the movement of her arms.

He could not see her face.

Wrenching his mind back with all his energy and concentration, he set about tracking down her face, methodically collecting her features and firmly assembling them. The results

The Cost of Things

were static portraits of no one in particular, faded and distant as cathedral paintings of angels and martyrs. These faces were curiously, painfully undisturbing, as meaningless as the dots on a radar screen to an untrained observer.

In their elaborate dining-room, he and Mary sat at the long table dipping spoons into chilled soup.

'Where are the kids?'

'Bill's playing squash with Philip, and Laura's over at Rachel's. They're all going on to a birthday party together.'

'At this time of night?'

'They have to go through some records.'

'What about their work? I thought they agreed to put in three hours a night till the end of term?'

'You can't keep them home from a party, Dan. All the others are going.'

'All the others don't want to be physicists! Or they've got wealthy fathers and don't have to win scholarships. These two'll end up in a factory if they're not careful.'

Mary looked at him. 'You *are* in a bad mood. Did something go wrong at the office?'

'They're irresponsible. If they knew what a depression was like, or a war —'

'Now don't spoil your dinner. How do you like the soup? At the last minute I discovered I didn't have any parsley and I had to use mint. What do you think? Is it awful?'

She hadn't altered her hair-style since they were married. She still chose dresses that would have suited her when she was twenty and wore size ten. Her face was bare of make-up except for a rim of lipstick round the edge of her mouth. And there was something in the total of all this indifference that amounted to a crime.

How easily she had divested herself of the girl with the interests and pleasant ways. And what contempt she had felt for him and shown him, for having been so easily deceived, when she was sure of her home, her children. She had transformed herself before his eyes, laughing.

Anyway, he gave in when she wanted this house, which was pretentious and impossible for them, really. But he even thought he might find it a sort of hobby, a bulwark, himself. You have to have something.

'What are you looking at? Dan? Is it the mint? Is it awful?' She was really anxious. He lifted another spoonful from his plate and tasted it. Mary waited. He felt he ought to say something. 'Mary . . .' What had they been discussing? 'It's — extra good,' he said very suddenly.

'*Extra* good.' She gave a little scoffing laugh. 'You sound like Bill.'

Not raising his eyes, he asked, 'What sort of a day have you had?' and Mary began to tell him while the creamy soup slid weirdly down his throat, seeming to freeze him to the marrow. He shivered. It was a warm summer night. Crickets were creaking in the garden outside.

'— and Bill wants to start golf soon. He asked me to sound you out about a set of clubs. And while I'm at it, Laura's hinting she'd like that French course on records. She says it'd be a help with the accent.'

'*Mary*,' he protested bitterly and paused, forgetting. 'For God's sake!' he added on the strength of his remembered feeling, gaining time. Then again, as before, the weight descended — the facts he knew, the emotions. 'What are you trying to do? You encourage them to want — impossible things. Why? To turn me into a villain when I refuse? You know how we stand. Your attitude baffles me.' Mary's expression was rather blank but also rather triumphant. He went on, and stammered slightly, 'I want them to have — everything. I grudge them nothing. But these grown-up toys — it can't be done. If Laura would stay home and work at her French — and Bill already has so many strings to his bow he can't hold a sensible conversation about anything. They'll end up bus conductors if they're not careful.'

Mary looked at him sharply. 'Have you been drinking, Dan?'

'Two beers.'

'I thought so! . . . Really, if I have to hear you complain about the cost of their education for the next six years, I don't think it would be worth it. Not to them either, I'm sure.'

He said nothing.

'*We* aren't going without anything. We've got the house and car. And the garden at week-ends. It isn't as if we were young.' Mary waved an arm. 'But if you feel like this, ask them to re-pay you when they've qualified. They won't want to be indebted to you.'

The Cost of Things

He stared at her heavily, lifted his formal-looking squarish face with its blue eyes and stared at her, saying nothing. Mary breathed through her nose at him, then collected his plate and hers and went away to the kitchen.

'Clea . . .' It was a groan. Tears came to his eyes. It was the night he had thought to go away with her. They could *not* be parted. How could he explain? It was against nature, could not *be*. He would sell everything and leave all but a small essential amount with Mary and the children. Then he and Clea would go — far away. And great liners trailing music and streamers sailed from Sydney daily for all the world's ports. Now that he'd found Clea, he would find the circumstances he had always expected, with their tests that would ask more of him than perseverance, resignation. They would live — somewhere, and be — very happy.

Commonsense had cabled him at this point: this would all be quite charming except for one minor problem that springs to mind.

What would they live on? A glorified clerk, his sole value as a worker lay in his memory of a thousand details relating to television films bought by the corporation. Away from the department he had no special knowledge, no money-raising skills. Could he begin to acquire a profession at forty-five? Living on what, in the meantime?

'There. At least there's nothing wrong with the steak.' Mary looked at him expectantly, and he looked at the platter of food for some seconds. 'It's — done to a turn.'

'*Over*done?'

'No.' He thought of saying to her pleased face, 'I thought of deserting you, Mary.' And he had, oh, he had. 'What? . . . Yes, everything's fine.' The only trouble was that unfortunately, unfortunately, he was beginning to feel sick.

'Dan, I forgot to mention this since you got back. You're never here with all this extra work —'

'Yes?' Here it came: the proof that he had been right to return, that he and Mary *did* have a life in common. How often had he pleaded with Clea in those last days, 'You can't walk out on twenty years of memories.' (Not that she had ever asked or expected him to.)

'It's the roof. The tiles. There was a landslide into the azaleas while you were away. I thought you'd notice the broken bushes.'

'Oh.'

'So do you think I should get someone to look over the whole roof?'

'Yes, I suppose so.'

'Well, it's important to get it fixed before we start springing leaks.'

'Yes. All right. Ring Harvey. Get him to give us an estimate.'

'Dan? Where are you going? You haven't touched your dinner!'

'I'm sorry. I've got to get some air. No, stay there. Eat your dinner.'

'Aren't you well?' She half-rose from her chair, but he warded her off and compelled her to sink back to the table with a large forbidding movement of his arm. Mary shrugged, gave a tiny snort of boredom and disdain, and resumed eating.

Sydney . . . At the end of a week he had begun to look forward to getting back to Mary's cooking. The department wasn't lavish with away-from-home expenses for officers on his grade, and he had the usual accounts flying in from Melbourne by every post, in addition to an exorbitant hotel bill for the very ordinary room he occupied near the office. The hotel served a 'continental' breakfast and no other meals. At lunchtime he and Alan Parker leapt out for beer and a sandwich which cost next to nothing, then by six o'clock he was famished. Somehow surreptitiously, he started to treat himself to substantial and well-cooked dinners in restaurants all over the city. In Melbourne he only patronised places like these once a year for a birthday or anniversary. He felt rather ill-at-ease eating, so to speak, Mary's new dress or the children's holidays, and he was putting on flesh. But — everything was hopeless. You had to have something. But money harassed him. He felt a kind of anguished dullness at the thought of it. It made him dwell on the place where it was cheaper and less worrying to be: home.

As the representative of his department, he was invited one Friday evening to an official cocktail party. A woman entered the building as he did, and together they ran for the row of automatic lifts, entered one, were shot up to some height between the fourth and fifth floors and imprisoned there for over half an hour. Clea.

The Cost of Things

Dan's first thought was that she looked a bit flashy. Everything about her looked a fraction more colourful than was quite seemly: the peacock-blue dress, and blond hair — not natural, the make-up, and, in another sense, the drawling low-pitched voice. (This would certainly have been Mary's view).

Then while the alarm bell rang and caretakers and electricians shouted instructions at one another, they stood exchanging words and Dan looked into her eyes with the usual polite, rather stuffy, slightly patronising expression.

He was surprised. Under gold-painted lids, her blue eyes glanced up and actually saw him, with a look that twenty years, fifteen years, ago he had met daily in his mirror. It was as familiar as that. She wasn't *young*. It wasn't a young look. It was alarmingly straight. It was the look by which he had once identified his friends.

At the party when they were finally released, however, Clea treated him with wonderful reserve, recognising nothing about him. She remained steadfastly with the group least likely to succeed in charming the person Dan imagined her to be, smiling a lazy gallant smile, bestowing gestures and phrases on their sturdy senses. Showing pretty teeth, laughing huskily, she stood near them and *was*. When Dan approached, though, that all appeared to have been illusory. She was merely quiet, watchful, sceptical, an onlooker.

Ah, well! He put her from him. He expected nothing. It had been a momentary interest, and this wasn't the first time, after all, that circumstances had separated him from someone whom he would in some way always know.

But he met her one day in the street accidentally. (Though Sydney is two million strong, people who live there can never lose touch, eager though they might be to do so.) He remembered they said something about the party, and something else about the lift, and then they said good-bye and parted. It wasn't till he had gone some eight or nine steps that Dan realised he had walked backwards away from her.

The following Saturday night they met at another interdepartmental party and after that there were no backward steps till this inevitable, irrevocable return to hearth and home.

Clea had a flat — kitchen, bathroom, bed-sitting room — in a converted habourside mansion, and a minor executive job with a film unit that paid rent and food and clothing bills. Once she had been an art student but at the end of four years she stopped attending classes and took a job.

'You were too critical of yourself,' Dan said. 'Your standards were too high.'

She smiled.

In her spare time she had continued to paint, she told Dan, and he had an impression of fierceness and energy and he felt he knew how she must have looked. So she had painted. And it was why she was sane. And why people who knew nothing whatever about her liked to be near her. But ages ago, and permanently, she had laid it aside. That is, laid aside the doing, but not the looking, not the thinking, not finally herself.

Dan insisted on being shown the few pieces of work that she hadn't destroyed, and he examined them solemnly, and felt this discarded talent of Clea's was a thing to respect. In addition (and less respectably, he knew) he saw it as a decoration to her personality not unflattering to himself. From talk of art, which he invariably started, he would find he had led the way back to that perennially sustaining subject — their first meeting.

'At the party that night, why were you so — cold?'

'For good reasons. Which you know. How many times do you think I can survive this sort of thing?'

They were in Clea's room on an old blue sofa by the fire. Dan turned his head away, saying nothing. She said, 'It's no fun. You get tired. Like a bird on the wing, and no land. It's — no fun. You feel trapped and hunted at the same time. And the weather seems menacing. (No, I don't mean now. But there have been times.) And in the long run, it's so much less effort to stay where your belongings are . . . Wives shouldn't worry too much. And even other women shouldn't. By the time they find themselves listening to remorseful remembrances of things past they're too — killed to care. And they find they can prompt their loved one with considerable detachment when he reels off the well-known items — old clothes and family illnesses, holidays and food and friends . . . Make me stop talking.'

It mattered very little to them where they went, but they walked a lot and saw a few plays. They went to some art galleries. And once they had a picnic.

'It's winter, but the sun never goes in,' he said.

The Cost of Things

'Except now and then at night. Sydney's like that.'

In the evenings Clea sometimes read aloud to Dan at his suggestion. And he would think: *The fire is burning. I am watching her face and listening to her voice.* And he felt he knew something eternal that he had always wanted to know. One night Clea read the passage in which Yury Zhivago, receiving a letter from his wife after their long and tragic separation, falls unconscious.

Because Clea existed and he was in her presence, Dan felt himself resurrected and so, though what she read was beautiful and he thought so, he laughed with a kind of senseless joy as at something irrelevant when she stopped.

'All right, darling, I suppose it is wonderful. That Russian intensity. If *I* could ever totter to a sofa and collapse with sheer strength of feeling, I'd think: "Congratulations, Freeman! You're really living."'

Clea laughed, too, but said, 'Ah, don't laugh. Because if you can laugh, you make it impossible . . . '

One thing Clea could not do was cook. It took Dan some weeks to accept this, because she wasn't indifferent to food. If they ate in a restaurant, she enjoyed a well-chosen meal as much as he did. But when he discovered that she could tackle any sort of diet with much the same enthusiasm, he was depressed.

'What do you live on when I'm not around?' he demanded, a little disgruntled.

She thought. 'Coffee.'

He was proud of her. He even liked her a lot. But he couldn't help saying, 'I get hungry.'

She looked abstracted. 'Dan, I — You're *hungry*. Oh . . . We had steak?'

'Yes, but no — no *trimmings*,' he tried to joke. 'No art.'

'Dan — '

'I take it back about no art.'

'I'll — tomorrow — '

'I take it back about no art.'

'I will do better.' And after this she tried to cook what she thought were complicated meals for him, and he didn't discourage her.

It was the night they came back from their picnic in the mountains that he had the brilliant idea of asking her why she had never married.

295

She laughed.

'You wouldn't have had any trouble,' he insisted, trying to see her face.

Still smiling, she said, 'The candidates came at the wrong time or they were too young for me when I was young.' She looked at him, raising her brows. 'How old were you? When you married.'

'Twenty-one.'

'I wouldn't have liked you then.'

'You'd have been right. But *you* — tell me.'

She moved restlessly on the sofa, and spread her arms along the back. He felt it was cruel to question her, but knew he would never stop. She said, 'Oh . . . I met someone, and bang went five years. Then some time rolled by while I picked myself up. Then I met — someone else who was married. Names don't matter.'

He looked at her.

'All right, they do. But not now . . . So, by the time you look round after that, you're well into your thirties. And a few of the boys have turned into men, but they're married to girls who preferred them — quite young.'

'Are you saying this to blame me? You are, aren't you?' He heard the rhetorical note in his voice. He knew he had asked her.

Clea seemed to examine the stitches of the black hand-knitted sweater he was wearing. She jumped up quickly and out in the kitchen poured whisky into two glasses, carrying one back to him.

'I can only say, Clea — if things were different — things would be different . . . All right, it sounds lame. But I *mean* it. What do you *want* me to do?'

'And what would you *like* me to say? You'll go back to Mary. Do you want me to plead with you?'

He could see that it was neither reasonable nor honourable in him to want that, but in her it would have been more *natural*, he felt. He said so.

Clea was biting the fingernails of her left hand, cagily. He saw again that it was cruel to talk to her like this, but he knew he would never stop.

She glanced at him over her hand. 'You're beginning to think about your old clothes and family holidays just as I said. And why shouldn't you? These intimate little things are what count in the end, aren't they?'

And she disposed of her hand, wrapping it round her glass as she lifted it from the floor to drink. She rolled a sardonic blue eye at Dan and he gave the impression of having blushed without a change in colour, and frowned and drank, too. Because of course his mind *had* turned lately in that direction. He *had* begun to remember the existence of all that infinitely boring, engulfing domesticity, and his vital but unimportant part in it. It was all *there*, and his. What could he do about it?

Clea knew too much, drank too much, was nervy, pushed herself to excess, bit her fingernails. She was the least conditioned human being he had ever encountered. She was like a mirror held up to his soul. She was intelligent, feeling and witty. He loved her.

'Many thanks.' But she wouldn't meet his eyes.

'Marriage,' he said, harking back suddenly. 'When I think of it! And you're so independent. What could it give you? Really? No, don't smile.'

Still, she did smile faintly, saying nothing, then said irritatingly, 'Someone to — set mouse traps and dispose of the bodies.'

He brushed this away. 'You hate the office. Why?'

'Dan.' She was patient.

'Why do you hate the office?' He did feel vaguely that he was torturing her. 'Why?'

'I don't see the sun. I lose the daylight hours. The routine's exacting, but the work doesn't matter. It takes all my time from me and I see nothing beautiful.'

'And just what would you do with this time?' he asked, somehow scientifically. He would prove to her how much better off . . .

With her left hand, distracted, she seemed to consider the length and texture of the hair that fell over her ear. 'Oh. Look about. Exist.'

Dan thought of Mary. 'Some wives are busy all day long.' He was positive that Mary would be in no way flattered if it were ever suggested that *she* had had time to practise as a student of life. 'In fact,' he went on, 'though cultivation is supposed to be the prerogative of the leisured classes, I think women in your position form a sort of non-wealthy aristocracy all to themselves.'

'Do you?' Clea shifted the dinner plate from her lap and went over to the deal table where she had a lot of paraphernalia brought home from the office spread out. At random she picked up a pencil and tested its point against the cushion of her forefinger saying, 'That's an observation!'

'No, don't be angry.' He turned eagerly to explain to her over the back of the sofa. 'What I mean is that however busy you are from nine till five, you have all the remaining hours of the day and night to concentrate on yourself — your care, cultivation, understanding, amusement . . .'

She smiled at him. 'Don't eat that if you can't bear it. I'll make something else.'

He said, 'Forgive me.'

They quarrelled once, one Thursday evening when he passed on Alan and Joyce Parker's invitation to drive out into the country the following Sunday.

Alan Parker was a tall mild man of fifty, who clerked with dedication among the television films of the library. His wife, whom both Clea and Dan had met at official parties, was friendly and chatty. The Parkers knew Dan was married, and they knew that (as they put it) Dan and Clea had a thing about each other. But they liked Dan because he wasn't disagreeably ambitious though he was younger than and senior to Alan, and they implied a fondness for Clea. Dan guessed that they would be the subject of Joyce's conversation for a week after the trip, but he couldn't find it in his heart to dislike anyone to whom he could mention Clea's name.

But she said swiftly, 'Oh no, I couldn't go with them.'

He paused, amazed, in the act of kicking a piece of wood back into the fire. 'What do you mean? Why not?'

'No, I just couldn't go,' she said definitely, beginning to look for her place in the book she was holding.

'But *why*?' Dan fixed the fire, buffed some ash from his hands and turned to sit beside her on the sofa. He took the book from her, thrust it behind his back, and forced her to lift her head.

Her look daunted him. He said in parenthesis, 'I'm addicted to that eye-shadow.' He said reasonably, 'Only last week you talked about getting out of town.'

'I'd be bored, Dan.'

'Bored? I'd be there!' he rallied her, smiling in a teasing way.

The Cost of Things

'And Joyce's going to produce a real French picnic lunch.'

There was a smile in her that he sensed and resented.

She said, 'I'm sorry.'

'And *I'm* sorry if the fact that I like to eat one meal a day is offensive to you.'

'Darling. Please go, if you'd like to. No recriminations. Truly.'

Mondays to Fridays he didn't see her all day. He couldn't have borne to lose hours of her company. Six months, he'd had, just days ago. Now there were ten weeks.

He said unpleasantly, 'You do set yourself up with your nerves and your fine sensibility, Clea. When you begin to feel that a day in the company of nice easy-going people like the Parkers would be unbearably boring, *I* begin to feel you're carrying affectation too far. If you pander to yourself much more you'll find you're unfit to live in the world at all!'

She didn't answer that, or appear to react. Instead she caught his wrist in her right hand and smoothed her thumb against the suede of his watch-strap. 'In their car, Dan, I'd feel imprisoned. I have to be able to get away. I'd be bored, Dan.' She said, 'I don't love them.'

He stared, jerked his arm away, gave a short incredulous laugh and stood up. 'Don't *love* them!'

She added, 'As things are.'

Throwing on his coat he went to the door still uttering sarcastic laughs. 'Don't *love* them! Well — *good* — *night* — *Clea!*'

In ten minutes he returned. And the ten weeks passed.

'Dan? How are you now?' Mary peered down at him, then glanced abruptly right and left, bringing her chin parallel with each of her shoulders in turn. It was dark on the balcony. 'Do you still want your dinner? It'll be ruined, but it's there if you want it . . . Dan!' She leant over him.

'What?'

'Well, for heaven's sake, you can still answer when I speak to you! I thought you'd had a stroke or something, sitting there like an image.' She bridled with relief and exasperation.

'No.'

In a brisk admonitory voice she said, 'Well, I think you'd better get yourself along to Dr. Barnes in the morning. It's all this extra work. And you're not eating. Sometimes I think you don't even know you're home again.'

He said something she couldn't catch.

'What? Where's *what?* . . . Your dinner's in the oven.' Mary waited for him to speak again. 'Smell the garden, Dan . . . We'd better get ready, then. Jack and Freda'll be over soon.'

'What?' He stirred cautiously in the padded bamboo chair. He felt like someone who has had the top of his head blown off, but is still, astonishingly, alive, and must learn to cope with the light, the light, and all it illuminated.

'I told you this morning,' Mary accused him. 'You hadn't forgotten?'

Carefully he hauled himself up by the balcony railing. 'I'll be bored,' he said.

In the soft black night, Mary went to stand in front of him, tilting her face to look at him. 'Bored, Dan?' she sounded nervous. 'You know Jack and Freda,' she appealed to him, touching his shirt-sleeve.

'I don't care for them,' he complained gently, not to her. And added, 'As things are.'

'Oh, Dan!' Mary swallowed. Tears sprang to her eyes. She caught his arm and walked him through the front door, and down the carpeted hall to their bedroom. 'Lie down, Dan. Just lie there.'

He heard her going to the telephone. She rang the doctor. Then she rang Freda and Jack to apologise and ask them not to come. He heard her crying a little with fright as she repeated his uncanny remark in explanation.

And Dan took a deep breath, and looked at the ceiling, and smiled.

Africa Wall

Morris Lurie

Breakfast in Tangier for Isaac Shur was a short loaf of bread, a tin of sardines or tuna, half a small watermelon, sometimes too a bottle of Coke. No coffee. Isaac Shur had no facilities for making coffee, his apartment had neither electricity nor gas, and though he could easily have bought a small primus stove, he preferred to leave his life the way it was. Unencumbered. Uncluttered. Everything he owned in Tangier fitted into two small canvas bags. He could leave in a minute. He had a trunk of books and clothes with a friend in London, and at odd moments he thought it would be nice to have them here, to have all his things together, but then he thought of porters and taxis and the fuss at customs and the worry of thieves — everyone was a thief in Tangier — and he decided, no. He didn't really need all those books and clothes. He didn't need anything. He was happy the way he was. Perfectly happy. Isaac Shur had been in Tangier, now, for five months.

He bought his bread and his melon and his Coke and his sardines or tuna always at the same place, the first shop down the hill from where he lived. He was there every morning at seven o'clock. He ordered by pointing, miming, smiling, shaking his head. Isaac Shur knew a few words of Spanish, Arabic and French — the lingua franca of this once international city — but he rarely used them. Speaking in a foreign language always made him feel that he was at a disadvantage. The first words he said, in a café, or restaurant, or shop, were 'Do you speak English?' and when the answer was no, or a puzzled look, or a shake of the head, as it almost invariably was, then Isaac Shur would smile, *that* fact established, made clear, out of the way, good. Then he would launch into his performance of pointing and mime, happier with this, really, than speaking in English. In the shop at the bottom of the hill he was served each morning by the owner, a short, shuffling, always smiling Moroccan, shapeless in a dun-coloured jellaba, the Moroccan's cheeks, at that hour, frosted with grey bristles. The owner welcomed Isaac Shur each morning like a long-lost friend, throwing out his hands, calling out greetings, smiling hugely. Isaac Shur would smile back, then without further ado begin his business of pointing and mime. There were two black cats in the shop, lying about on sacks or on the floor just inside the door, warming themselves in the morning sun. The shop smelled of fruit and oil and Arabic coffee and bread and dust, and there was another smell too, surrounding all these others. This smell was not just in the shop. It was everywhere in Tangier. Isaac Shur had sniffed it in Spain too, and in Greece, but in Tangier it was sharper, more pervasive, impossible to ignore. Its exact cause or component was to Isaac Shur a mystery, but he had a name for it. He called it, to himself, the smell of poverty. He planned one day to write about it. Isaac Shur was a poet and a playwright. His first play had been bought by the BBC. Three of his poems had been published in magazines, one in the *New Statesman*. He was twenty-six years old, an Australian.

Isaac Shur sliced his watermelon with the Swiss army knife he had bought in Copenhagen. He was sitting at the table where in half an hour he would begin work, his typewriter and papers pushed to one side, the door open, the windows open, the shutters folded back, his view of bushes and trees, his garden. Sun fell onto the tiled floor. A breeze passed through the trees onto his face. Isaac Shur looked at his watch. Ten minutes past seven. Good. He felt alert and alive, as he did every morning. This was the best time of the day. From now till ten. Three hours. After that it would be too hot, too hot to think, too hot to work. Three hours. Two and a half. Well, that was enough. That was plenty. He would work till ten, maybe even till ten-thirty, and then walk into town, have his morning coffee, buy a newspaper, a magazine, sit, stroll. Then lunch. Then . . . well, he would see.

Africa Wall

Isaac Shur wiped the blade of his Swiss army knife on his jeans. He used this same blade for watermelon, bread, forking out sardines, sharpening his pencils. He finished his bread, washed it down with Coke. His apartment was really just one room, but large, and odd-shaped: where he slept was up two steps and around a corner. Sitting at the table, finishing his breakfast, he could see only the foot of his bed. His two canvas bags beside it. A spare shirt. The kitchen was a narrow space behind him, a sink and a tap. The toilet, behind it, had to be flushed with a bucket. There was an oil lamp beside the bed, another one here on the table. Isaac Shur's was the garden apartment in a block of three floors. Isaac Shur brushed the breadcrumbs from his table and from his lap, lit a cigarette, and stepped outside.

It was a walled garden, the wall made of grey concrete blocks, and along the top of it a glittering necklace of broken bottles and shards of sharp glass set in cement: the terrible teeth of all walls in Tangier. Isaac Shur ignored this. He had learnt not to see it. The garden was wild and unkempt, shaded and private, Tangier locked out. Except in one place, where Isaac Shur stood now, where the ground rose, affording a view beyond the wall, as though the wall were not even there. A view that sailed clear of the hill, past the rubbish dump just beyond the wall — a dusty, smelly mound of earth and iron and feathers and bones and newspapers and broken bricks and God only knew what else. Sailing past all this, quickly, barely touching it, away, and then along a green valley, a soft green cleft that ran as far as he could see, into the fuzziness of distance, into the vague shape of hills.

Isaac Shur stood with his cigarette. The valley was why he had taken this apartment. He had looked along it, that first time, and the doubts he had had about living in a place that had no electricity, no gas, that was half an hour's walk from the centre of town, a walk he would have to do at least twice a day, probably four times. But more than that, the place was so isolated, no one he knew lived anywhere nearby, and the rubbish dump just outside... but then he had looked along the valley, that first time, and all his doubts fell away. Yes, he had said to himself at once, the decision made. I will work well here. I will be happy. This is what I want. Yes. The valley was green at all times of the day, no matter how hard the sun blazed down, and always that same green, soft and hazy, an English green, the green of Hampshire and Sussex and the other counties Isaac Shur had travelled through. And though, at that particular time, he had felt no especial rapport with the English countryside — regarding it merely as pleasant scenery, as he had seen the countryside in France or Denmark or Germany — now, seeing it in Tangier, it struck a chord, it awoke something inside him, some memory, some need. He never tired of it, he could stand for hours looking along its greenness, his eyes endlessly travelling its hazy length. Halfway along the valley there was a village, and then a second, and then a third. Three clusters of white buildings patterned onto the green, but the second, Isaac Shur knew, was not a village but a cemetery, the tricks of perspective and light housing the dead as it did the living.

Isaac Shur threw away his cigarette. He turned his back reluctantly on the view. Time to work.

Isaac Shur had begun, a week ago, a poem on his mother's hands. His mother had died when Isaac Shur was twenty-two, and then his father had died, a year later, a year to the day. Isaac Shur's method of work was to write down, in grammatically perfect sentences, everything he could remember. His mother's hands slicing bread. Putting on lipstick. Dialling on the telephone. Flying to her heart when she laughed. Her fingers. Her wedding ring. Her nails. Her palms. His mother's hands covered, so far, twenty-odd pages. Isaac Shur felt he had hardly begun. There would be twice that number of pages again, at least. And when that was done, when he had recalled everything, he would put the pages away, unread, never look at them again, and then he would write his poem. He wrote quickly but carefully, his letters large and well-formed, and when he heard the clamour at the gate, his mouth fell open, as though he had just been woken from a deep sleep. For a moment he didn't know where he was. And then he did, and he knew what was happening. It was the same thing that happened every morning. Isaac Shur rushed out into his garden, waving his hands, shouting.

There they were, as they were every morning, clambering over the gate. Two of them were already inside the garden.

'Go away!' Isaac Shur shouted. 'Beat it! Scram!'

The two in the garden stood there, smiling idiotically. Isaac Shur ran at them. They ducked behind a bush. A third dropped down from the gate.

'Get out of here!' Isaac Shur shouted, wheeling around. 'Leave me alone!' Now the other two were in too, not just smiling but laughing, dancing on thin legs, waving their arms. Isaac Shur ran at them, but they were too fast, they were always too fast, ducking effortlessly out of reach, and then standing still, taunting him with their idiotic smiles. He ran again, his hands grabbing empty air, and then he remembered, instantly panicking, that his door was wide open, the windows, the shutters. Two of them were already inside, the little one, the one he called The Hot Shot Kid, and the tall one, the one with the shaved head. When they saw him, they ducked behind the table, overturning his chair. Isaac Shur saw that The Hot Shot Kid had his Swiss army knife. And what else? What else had they taken? His papers lay in turmoil all over the floor.

Isaac Shur, in true anger now, slammed the door. Right! Rushing for The Hot Shot Kid, he stumbled over the chair. The tall one laughed, and then was gone, fast as water, out of the window. Then he appeared at another window, smiling like a loon. Isaac Shur ignored him. He advanced on The Hot Shot Kid.

'The knife!' he shouted. 'Put down that knife! Put it down!'

The Hot Shot Kid, for the first time, looked afraid. He was a small boy, about five or six years old. He looked over his shoulder, at the slammed door. The game had become serious. Isaac Shur lunged and grabbed him. He grabbed the knife. The Hot Shot Kid broke free and ran for a window. Isaac Shur let him go. He was shaking. He was wet with sweat.

The shutters, the windows. He locked everything. He shot the bolt on the door. They were laughing outside now, calling out. Isaac Shur picked up his papers. The Swiss army knife was in his pocket. What else had they taken? His pencils, his pen? No. Nothing. It was all there. He picked up the fallen chair, sat down. They were throwing dirt now, at the shutters, at the door. In another minute it would be stones. Isaac Shur saw, when he lit a cigarette, that his fingers were trembling.

It was his fault, of course. He had encouraged them. The

Hot Shot Kid lived in the apartment above. Two of the others lived in the block too. The rest were from somewhere around, local kids, playing most of the time on the rubbish dump. Isaac Shur had noticed them there, vaguely, on that first afternoon, when he had moved in. On his first morning in his new apartment, Isaac Shur, walking around his garden, had seen them standing at the gate, looking in. He had waved to them, and smiled, and then, having bought a too-large piece of watermelon that morning, he had offered them each a slice, and some Coke too. He had unlocked the gate. They came into the garden. Isaac Shur had felt sorry for them, for their thin legs, their thin arms, their ragged clothes. He had given them some bread too, bread and sardines. They were polite that first day, standing in the garden, looking in his open door but not going inside, and Isaac Shur had invited them in, showed them his typewriter, his pencils, his papers, his Swiss army knife, explaining to them, pointing and miming and smiling and shaking his head, his work, his reason for being here, his life. That was the first day. On the second morning they had appeared in his garden. The gate had been locked, they had climbed over. They were still polite, still well behaved, but smiling more now, laughing, friends. Isaac Shur shared his watermelon with them again. From there to how it was now had happened in a rush. And getting worse every day. Worse and worse.

Stones banged against his closed door. Isaac Shur sat furious at his table, puffing on his cigarette. Ignore them, he told himself. Don't make a sound. They'll go away. He reached for his papers. With the door closed, with the shutters closed, it was almost too dark to see. Isaac Shur lit the oil lamp on the table. He picked up a pencil. Her hands when she sewed on a button. The way she held the needle. The little finger of her left hand. The needle dipping. Her hand pulling the thread tight. The oil lamp pushed out heat in solid waves. Isaac Shur unbuttoned his shirt, and then took it completely off. He flung it away savagely on the floor. And then his jeans too, his shoes and socks. He was enormously hot. He could hardly breathe. The smell of his crushed-out cigarette was foul in the room. He lit another. Now they were kicking his door, shouting wildly, banging the shutters with sticks.

Africa Wall

Isaac Shur had written his play in London in a large cold room in Maida Vale, the upstairs front room in a cracked grey house of bedsitters, on the slum fringe. His view, when he looked, was of identical cracked houses both ways down the street, as far as he could see. His only heating was a tiny gas fire set in the wall. The windows rattled with wind. A draught blew under the door. The linoleumed floor was ice to his feet. Isaac Shur was cold when he went to bed at night, cold when he awoke each morning. He had written his play in ten days, then ten days more for a second and final draft, typing as fast as he could, cold all the time. His fingers were white with cold. Coming back from his literary agent, he had seen, at Oxford Circus, a large colour photograph, a poster, an advertisement, for South Africa. The photograph showed three girls in skimpy bikinis laughing and jumping into the sea, and Isaac Shur had felt his muscles tighten with pain, looking at those bare bodies. He had shivered violently. He had felt sick with cold. His literary agent phoned him that night, ecstatic with praise, and a week later the play had been bought by the BBC. Beginner's luck? Isaac Shur knew no other writers, he had no experience of rejection or waiting, and though he was, of course, delighted, delighted and thrilled, the full measure of his success was unknown to him. This is the way it happens, he thought. Good. He had been in London, then, for a month and three days. Before that, for a year, he had travelled, never staying anywhere longer than two or three weeks. A week in Vienna. Ten days in Prague. Three weeks in Copenhagen, two in Stockholm and Oslo. This was his first time in Europe. He wanted to see it all.

Two days after his play had been accepted, Isaac Shur was at the flat of a friend, a fellow Australian who had been in London for two years. This friend, Graham Tinsdale, was a film editor. They sat before a small fan heater. Wind rushed unimpeded through the bare branches of the trees in the square outside, the windows of the flat uncurtained, cold black rectangles of night. Isaac Shur told Graham Tinsdale the details of his sale to the BBC. Graham Tinsdale looked amazed. 'That's terrific,' he said. 'Are you going to do another one?' Isaac Shur looked at the black windows. 'I don't know how anyone can live in England,' he said. 'It's so cold.' 'Go to Greece,' Graham Tinsdale said. 'Greece is good in winter.' 'I've been to Greece,' Isaac Shur said. 'I think I'll go to Tangier.' Isaac Shur had no idea why he said this. Tangier. He knew nothing about the place, he had no real desire to see it, it was just something that had come into his head. Tangier. He heard the wind rushing outside. He shivered. 'When?' Graham Tinsdale asked. 'I don't know,' Isaac Shur said. 'Tomorrow. The day after. Listen, is it all right if I leave a few things here? They're all in a small trunk. Won't take up much room.' Two nights later Isaac Shur was in Paris, waiting to board the midnight train to Madrid. He stayed in Madrid for four days, and from there hitchiked down, and the closer he got to Tangier the more he recognized that he was afraid.

Why am I doing this? Isaac Shur asked himself. Because I had said to a friend in London that I would? That was nothing. I could have stayed in Madrid. Madrid was warm. Blue skies every day. The Prado. Good wine. Isaac Shur hitchiked down, through Valencia, and then along the coast, Malaga, Estapona, travelling not very far each day, staying in hotels, rooms, and each night the fear growing. Why? Why?

All new cities are fearful places, but Tangier remained fearful to Isaac Shur longer than anywhere else he had ever been. And not only at night but during the day too. He was frightened of the shopkeepers, the touts, the beggars, the endless boys forever plucking at his sleeves, always with the same litany: 'How are you, my friend?' What frightened him more than anything else was that he knew his fear was visible to all. He radiated, he knew, not only discomfort but vulnerability. It was in his eyes, in the way he sat at a café, in the way he walked down a street, in everything he did. He wondered should he go somewhere else, but he didn't know where. He could think only of London, but that was too cold. No, he told himself, I don't want to travel. Not yet. I've had enough travelling for a while. Hotels, rooms. I want to be in one place. I want to do some work. Then Isaac Shur began to meet people, Americans, mostly, people his age, other writers, painters, college dropouts, kids having a good time. He moved from the hotel where he was staying to a cheaper one, he established habits and routines, he settled into good work. He developed a manner of walking down a street, of sitting at a café, of not seeing those things that he didn't want to see, of ignoring the hands forever plucking at his sleeves, the litany of pestering voices. He erected around himself the necessary shell or disguise that everyone developed, he told himself, to exist in this city. He learnt to keep his right hand always in his pocket, tight over his wallet and passport and traveller's cheques. Very quickly, he did this without thinking; it became second nature to him.

A large stone slammed against Isaac Shur's door. The door shuddered, daylight, for an awful instant, showing all around. Isaac Shur leapt up from his table, a shout in his throat.

What was the use? What was the point? Isaac Shur knew that even if he chased them away, which was probably impossible, even if he sat them out, did nothing, waited, didn't utter a sound, it would make no difference. The best hours of the day were gone. His brain was in turmoil now. The morning was ruined. He looked at the last words he had written. They lay on the page. They meant nothing.

In the kitchen Isaac Shur splashed himself with cold water, combed his hair. He dressed again in his jeans and shirt. Passport, money. There was a wild scramble in the garden when Isaac Shur stepped outside. Isaac Shur didn't look up. He locked his door, unlocked the garden gate and locked it again, then pushed the keys deep in his pocket under his passport and wallet. Still not looking up, paying no attention whatsoever to the children waving and shouting and advancing and dancing back on their thin legs on the edge of his vision, he started down the hill. Just before the shop where he went every morning he saw a woman sitting on the ground, a baby on her lap. The palm of the woman's held-out hand was as crinkled as a dead leaf. Isaac Shur kept his hand tight in his pocket over his wallet and passport and traveller's cheques. The only acknowledgement he allowed himself to make of her presence was a curt shaking of his head. Give to one and you give to them all, he had learnt long ago. They were endless. Anyhow, he told himself, I don't have any small change.

It was not yet ten o'clock, but the day was already hot. Dust swirled in the road. That smell that Isaac Shur called the smell of poverty filled his nose. July. August, Isaac Shur had been told, was the worst month. Everyone went away in August.

August in Tangier was unbearable. Even the nights were hot. Isaac Shur thought for a moment of going to Portugal, a month somewhere on the Atlantic coast, but the idea of travelling again, just now, of finding a place to stay, of having to establish his habits and routines all over again, was annoying, too complicated, and he pushed it away. He would think about that later, another time. Instead, quickly, he thought about where he would go for his morning coffee.

Isaac Shur had no one particular place. He left it, each morning, for his mood to decide. Some mornings he enjoyed the Café de Paris, on the corner of the Avenue Louis Pasteur, diagonally across from the French Consulate. This is where he had sat that morning when the *New Statesman* with his poem in it had arrived, the magazine open nonchalantly at his page — or so he had hoped it looked — sipping his coffee, smoking cigarette after cigarette, his eyes casually moving over the elegant lamps and the mirrors and the burgundy-coloured leather seats and the waiters in their clean aprons and stiff white shirts and black bow ties, and the parade of people moving past in the street, and the French Consulate with its classical facade and the tall palm trees in the garden, the tall iron gates, the black official cars. Isaac Shur's eyes drifting over all this and then back, again and again, to his poem on the marble table. The Café de Paris was expensive, but Isaac Shur didn't mind that. On the mornings that he went there he usually bought *The Times*, and took his time with it, sitting there for an hour at least, reading every word, even the obituaries and Court Circular. At the Café de Paris Isaac Shur was always alone, and he liked that too. He enjoyed the quiet hour, his newspaper, his cigarettes, the coffee.

Or he would go to Claridges, which was further along the street, on the other side, and sit inside, on a stool at the bar, and have a croissant with his coffee, sometimes two, looking up from time to time to see himself reflected in the mirror behind the bar, his face serious and dimly lit amongst the bottles of whisky and brandy and liqueurs and gin. At Claridges Isaac Shur felt international, a seasoned traveller, mature and self-contained, someone who knew the ropes.

No, Isaac Shur wasn't in the mood for the Café de Paris this morning. Nor for Claridges. He continued down the street that led down to the Socco Grande, past the Minzah Hotel, where, Isaac Shur had been told, Ian Fleming had always stayed whenever he had been in Tangier. Isaac Shur had had his morning coffee there several times, in the garden, sitting under a vast umbrella by the blue pool. The doorman, a turbanned and costumed tall black African, stepped out of the way on the narrow pavement as Isaac Shur went past.

In the Socco Grande Isaac Shur saw the usual crowds milling around the usual dilapidated buses, the usual vendors with their portable stalls — the man who sold scissors, the cakes man, the man with the scarves and belts — and the usual beggars, the usual touts, the endless wheeling boys. Hands reached out for his arms, his shirt. Faces appeared, serious, smiling. 'How are you, my friend?' Isaac Shur walked not quickly but not dawdling either, crossing the large dusty square, his right hand firmly in his pocket, his eyes enjoying the scene, but his face fixed straight ahead. The cafés. The shops. The different sudden smells, of charcoal and meat, of noodle soup, of gasoline, of bread, of chickens, of dung.

Halfway across the square Isaac Shur saw, standing together, in their usual place, the fatimas. Isaac Shur had employed a fatima only once. An old Fleet Street journalist, a man who had stepped ashore at Tangier on his way to somewhere else in 1939 and never left, had told Isaac Shur about the fatimas. 'Go down there, Isaac,' he had said, 'and for three dirhams you'll get your clothes washed and your floors scrubbed and your bed made — they'll even cook your lunch. But don't pay them more than three dirhams, understand? Not a penny more.' Isaac Shur had gone down to the Socco Grande at eight o'clock in the morning, pointed to the nearest woman, and then taken her back with him to his apartment on the bus, a thin woman with lined hennaed hands. Isaac Shur had sat in his garden in his shorts while the woman washed his clothes and his sheets and his towel, washed them in cold water, pounding and pounding them, and then spread them out on bushes to dry. After she had scrubbed his floors, she had come out to where Isaac Shur sat in the garden and mimed eating, her thin hands flying to her mouth, and then pointing at Isaac Shur, raising her eyebrows. At first Isaac Shur had thought that she wanted to make him lunch. He shook his head, no, he didn't want lunch, he wasn't hungry, he would eat later. Then he realized that she was telling him that she was hungry, that he had to feed her. 'Oh,' Isaac Shur had said, blushing red, and had run down to the shop where he bought his breakfast every morning and he bought what he always bought, a tin of sardines, bread, a melon. The fatima had eaten these in the kitchen, crouched in the furthest corner, her back turned on the open windows, the trees and bushes, the view. When she had finished Isaac Shur gave her three dirhams and she had fallen to her knees on the floor and blessed him, and at the gate had told Isaac Shur, pointing and miming and smiling, that she wanted to come again, that she would always come, that she would be his fatima. Isaac Shur had wanted to give her another dirham, for the bus, but his hand stayed in his pocket.

Isaac Shur entered the street that led down to the Socco Chico, the arched entrance to the market on one side, with its wet smell of flowers, a tight, steeply downhill street crammed with tourist shops. He walked faster here, both hands in his pockets, the left one touching his Swiss army knife, feeling its smooth, familiar shape. A sudden gust of boys — three? four? Isaac Shur didn't look — appeared around him, touching, laughing, crying out, and then they were gone, and Isaac Shur was in the Socco Chico.

Saint-Saëns had written his *Carnival of Animals* here, in the front first-floor room of the hotel to Isaac Shur's right. Tennessee Williams, Isaac Shur had been told, had sat here too, often, at one of these cafés, and watching the endless parade had conceived *Camino Real*. And William Burroughs had sat here. And Paul Bowles. And a young Truman Capote. The whole world passed through the Socco Chico, if you sat here long enough. This, anyhow, was the constant refrain of the Americans, the painters and writers and college dropouts whom Isaac Shur had met and befriended, in particular, George Matthews, a black-bearded New Yorker who was Isaac Shur's closest Tangier friend. George Matthews was a great sitter. Four or five hours at a stretch was nothing to him. That was his norm. George Matthews would sit, sometimes, the whole day through, and then, after dinner, come back, around ten or eleven, and sit another three or four hours, ordering, from time to time, a cup of coffee or hot chocolate, smoking a cigarette or two, but mostly doing nothing, just sitting. George Matthews always had a book with him, Spinoza's *Ethics*, or something by Hegel or Toynbee or Kant, once it was Marx's *Das Kapital*, but Isaac Shur had never seen him reading. A book was just something that George Matthews always had with him, a justification for sitting, a prop. He had graduated from Columbia University, but not in Philosophy, as Isaac Shur had supposed. His thesis had been on how to win at Monopoly.

Isaac Shur saw George Matthews sitting at his usual table at the Café Central, his left hand resting lightly on a small green book. 'George,' Isaac Shur said.

George Matthews looked up. His black-bearded face, which always looked gruff, broke instantly into a naïve, innocent smile. 'Hi,' he said, seeing Isaac Shur. 'Hey, sit down, whatcha doin'? How's things?'

Isaac Shur pulled out a chair. There were three other people sitting at the table, two painters named Vincent and Berkeley, and a girl everyone called Bunny. Isaac Shur said hello to them, and then turned back to George Matthews.

'Those kids,' Isaac Shur said. 'Those kids are driving me crazy. I couldn't do any work this morning. Again.'

'Naah,' George Matthews said. 'Kids is nothin'. Don't let 'em hassle ya. Kids is kids.'

'Not these kids,' Isaac Shur said. 'These kids are vultures. They won't leave me alone. You know what happened this morning? One of them grabbed my knife. The little one, The Hot Shot Kid. I went crazy.'

'Yeah?' George Matthews said. 'The Hot Shot Kid, eh?' He smiled. 'He's some kid. So clip him one in the ear, he won't hassle you no more.'

Isaac Shur lit a cigarette. 'A clip in the ear,' he said. 'If you can catch him.'

'Listen, don't let 'em hassle ya,' George Matthews said. 'You want hassle, go to New York. Man, that's the capital of hasslin'. Here, you just relax. Take it easy.'

'Yes,' Isaac Shur said.

The usual waiter appeared, the one everyone called Dopey because of his drooping lids and bald head and slow, faraway manner. *'Con leche?'* he said to Isaac Shur, not quite looking at him. Isaac Shur nodded. The waiter poured out the coffee and milk simultaneously from the two silver pots he always carried, hardly looking at the cup, but getting it, as always, exactly right.

'How ya doin' there, Dopey?' George Matthews said. The waiter smiled the faintest smile and shuffled away. 'Isn't he terrific?' George Matthews said. 'The most terrific coffee pourer on the whole damn continent of Africa. In the middle of an earthquake, I bet he still wouldn't spill a single drop.' He laughed, and then turned back to face the square, his eyes darting, taking in everything, vastly alive, endlessly amused, under his black brows. Isaac Shur sipped his coffee and smoked his cigarette.

Ten minutes passed, fifteen. There was some talk at the table, the sort of talk there always was, small talk, light gossip, never about work. Work was never mentioned. Work, if you did it — or didn't — was your own business, a private thing. When Isaac Shur's poem had come out in the *New Statesman*, he had shown it to George Matthews, here, at the Café Central, at this table, and to the other people who had been here too that day, one of whom, a thin, crew-cutted Canadian named Steven, was a writer, working on a novel. Isaac Shur, excited, had not only let everyone read his poem but then launched into an exposition of his method of work, how he filled page after page with sentences in prose, and then put them away, unread, in a drawer, and wrote his poem. When he had finished telling everyone about this — it was the first time he had ever explained his work to anyone in his whole life — Isaac Shur had expected that there would be some talk about it, that Steven, anyway, would talk about how he wrote, but there wasn't. No one said anything. The talk, when it began again, moved where it always did, into small things, light gossip, and Isaac Shur wondered if this was Tangier or whether all creative people everywhere kept themselves buttoned up. Whatever, Isaac Shur had never talked about his work again.

Another ten minutes, another fifteen. Isaac Shur had finished his coffee. He didn't feel like another. He didn't want another cigarette. A Moroccan youth appeared at the table, a regular at the square. Isaac Shur instinctively put his hand over his cigarettes on the table.

Africa Wall

'Hi there, Muhammad,' George Matthews greeted the Moroccan. 'How's it going?' The Moroccan shook George Matthews' hand, and then slapped him on the back. He shook the painters' hands too, and smiled at Bunny, nodding his head seriously. Isaac Shur ignored the outstretched hand when it came his way, countering it with a short smile, a quick nod, then busying himself with a cigarette. George Matthews invited the Moroccan to sit with them. The Moroccan sat, smiling. After three or four minutes he stood up, shook hands with George Matthews again, with the two painters, nodded and smiled at Bunny and Isaac Shur, and left. Isaac Shur stood up too.

'Hey, where ya goin'?' George Matthews said. 'What's the rush?'

'Well, I thought ...' Isaac Shur began, counting out the money for his coffee. 'I've got some things to do.' He nodded at Bunny and the two painters. 'See you,' he said.

'Wait a minute, wait a minute,' George Matthews said. 'Listen. Why doncha come round for dinner tonight? I'll fry up a chicken.'

'OK,' Isaac Shur said. 'What time?'

'I don't know,' George Matthews said. 'Nine?'

'Fine,' Isaac Shur said. 'Nine o'clock.' Isaac Shur signalled to the waiter, pointing to his money on the table.

'Ya feel like Monopoly?' George Matthews said. 'I'm in the mood.'

'You're always in the mood,' Isaac Shur said, moving away from the table. 'See you. Nine o'clock.' And then, remembering, 'I'll bring the wine.'

It was half past eleven. Isaac Shur, both hands in his pockets, ignoring the bustling bodies all around, walked down the street that led from the Socco Chico to the sea. He would walk along the beach, he decided. He would sit somewhere quiet for a while and think. He would have lunch. He passed, on his left, the mosque, and saw, through the open door, the tiled mosaic walls, the fountain at the entrance, barefoot Moroccans ritually washing, and, further inside, others sitting cross-legged, silent in prayer. Isaac Shur decided that tomorrow he would go to Gibraltar.

Isaac Shur went to Gibraltar about once a fortnight, going

315

on the ferry at nine o'clock in the morning, coming back around six, a two-hour trip each way. Once, suddenly impatient, excited, the prospect of that two-hour trip too much for him, too predictable, too slow, he had taken a cab to the airport, and flown over, and then, at five, flown back, the trip, this way, costing him five times what the ferry did, plus the cabs. It had been worth it though, to see Gibraltar from the air, the thrill of landing on that impossible airstrip, that tiny neck of connecting land, the sea on both sides, the plane coming down on almost no space at all; and then, coming back, for the first time he had seen Tangier the way he had been told by old residents it used to be, in the twenties and thirties, before it had been 'discovered', a magical city floating pale blue on its hills above the Strait.

In Gibraltar, Isaac Shur changed his traveller's cheques — the rate was better than what you got in Tangier, though lately it had been falling — bought a pile of the latest English magazines and newspapers, sometimes too a couple of books, then he had lunch in a Chinese restaurant, and then, in the afternoon, sat in his favourite place, the small park and sailors' cemetery at the end of the main street, and quietly read. In Gibraltar he also bought a bottle of duty-free whisky — Johnnie Walker Black Label or Haig and Haig Pinch — two cartons of Camel cigarettes, and a box of Havana cigars. Ramon Allones, usually. Sometimes Punch. Isaac Shur was no great cigar smoker, but he liked the image of himself smoking a fine cigar in the afternoons whilst sitting in his garden looking across at the green valley and its three white villages. Every afternoon, around six o'clock, the day's heat dying, this is what he did. Unless the children came again. But usually in the afternoons they left him alone.

Yes, Isaac Shur said to himself, tomorrow I'll go to Gibraltar.

The street he was walking down suddenly widened, and Isaac Shur, looking up, saw the sea. Palm trees. Sea-gulls. The road was torn up here, pipes were being laid. There was the usual commotion of tractors and trucks. Isaac Shur, turning left, made for the beach.

He walked for about half a kilometre, and then sat down, on a bench under a tree. He lit a cigarette. Between the beach proper and where he sat there was a row of beach clubs, places where, for a small fee, you could use the changing rooms, hire a locker, shower, buy a drink at the bar, but the real business of the beach clubs was sitting. The beach at Tangier is wide, a long trek across the hot sand to the sea, and Isaac Shur had discovered, on the two or three occasions when he had been to one of these beach clubs, that hardly anyone ever actually swam. Swimming was too much trouble. It wasn't worth it. It was too far. It was a sweat. Instead, everyone just sat, sprawled in deck chairs, smoking, talking, sipping Cokes, for half the day, and longer. Isaac Shur, even when with his friends, or with people he knew, had quickly felt restless, awkward, and each time had left after less than an hour.

Isaac Shur walked the length of the road that paralleled the sea as far as it went, and then back, and lunched, alone, at a noisy café on the harbour. Calimari. A glass of white wine. Coffee and a cigarette. A television set on a shelf above the counter was showing an old film starring Montgomery Clift. The film, dubbed into Spanish, was probably being transmitted from Spain. Isaac Shur didn't know what the film was, he couldn't follow the story at all, but he watched it intently as he ate, not at all bothered by not being able to understand what anyone was saying, enjoying the shots of buildings and cars, the interiors, the details — the telephones, cigarette lighters, elevator doors opening and closing, the clothes. He debated having a second cup of coffee and sitting until the film was over, but the café was too noisy, people coming in and going out all the time, money changers, touts, prostitutes, beggars, and though he would have liked to stay, Isaac Shur knew that he would be pestered if he sat here alone too long.

Isaac Shur walked back through Tangier a different way, up through the French quarter, the New Town. In the windows of the shops he saw cameras and watches and tape recorders and handsomely packaged bottles of aftershave, and Isaac Shur felt growing inside him an acquisitive urge, a desire to own — what? He looked at playing cards, battery-operated record players, transistor radios, silk ties, pondering each item, considering. A Dupont cigarette lighter? A pair of French sunglasses? No, this is ridiculous, Isaac Shur told himself, as he did every day, I am not going to pay these prices. I can get all this stuff cheaper in Gibraltar.

No children rushed at him when Isaac Shur unlocked his garden gate. Nor were they on the rubbish dump. The day was hot with silence. Inside his apartment, Isaac Shur opened the windows but left the shutters as they were. He saw the pages lying on the table as he had left them, his typewriter, his pencils, his pen, and for a moment he thought of sitting down, continuing his work, but no, he was too hot, he was too tired, he shouldn't have had that glass of wine at lunch. He sat down on the end of his bed and took off his shoes and socks. It wasn't the wine. Not just the wine. He unbuttoned and took off his shirt. He thought, if I lived in town, if I didn't have to do that walk every day. He put his passport and wallet and traveller's cheques under his pillow. He was almost too tired to take off his jeans. There was no wind outside, not a breeze, not the faintest stir of air, but Isaac Shur smelt, for an unaccountable instant, that smell of poverty. It filled his nose, his head, and then was gone, replaced by nothing.

What woke Isaac Shur at five o'clock was the garden gate rattling. At first he thought it was the children and felt himself stiffen. Then he remembered. Today was the day he paid his rent. 'Coming, coming,' Isaac Shur called, dressing quickly, but not bothering with his shoes and socks.

She stood at the iron gate, haughty and enormous, wearing the spotless dove-coloured jellaba of the finest wool she always wore on these visits, golden slippers peeping out. Isaac Shur unlocked the gate, smiling apologetically. She swept past him, down the three steps that led to the garden, into the apartment. Isaac Shur, relocking the gate, saw at the kerb the battered black Vauxhall in which she always arrived, her son — one of her sons — sitting at the wheel, staring dumbly through the windscreen straight ahead. Isaac Shur hurried inside.

This woman had once owned, Isaac Shur had been told, the most expensive brothel in all Tangier. Certainly she was rich. She owned, beside this apartment, two buildings in the town, one of them a shop, the other offices and apartments; her mouth flashed with gold; on her left wrist sat a large Swiss watch, there were diamond and gold rings on most of her

Africa Wall

fingers, and the Vauxhall was hers. Yet, when Isaac Shur had gone to see her, to negotiate the leasing of this apartment, gone with the English painter who was relinquishing the apartment and returning home, he had found her living in what looked like abject poverty, in three cramped and crowded rooms in the heart of the Medina. In the first room Isaac Shur had seen an old man asleep in a chair, two young girls sitting on a battered sofa, a baby lying on a scrap of blanket on the floor. Flies crawled everywhere. The only hint of affluence was a television set in a corner. The other two rooms were filled with beds. The smell was appalling. Isaac Shur had had to go outside, to conduct his negotiations in the street. The English painter had done all the talking, in Spanish mostly, but with a few words of Arabic and French. Isaac Shur didn't know the woman's name. He called her Fatima.

'Fatima,' Isaac Shur said, coming into the apartment.

She was walking around the apartment, looking at everything, the typewriter, the two canvas bags, the shirt on the bed, her head high, aloof, completely disregarding Isaac Shur. Isaac Shur remembered that his wallet and passport were still under the pillow, took them out quickly, and began to count out the money for the week's rent.

'Fatima,' he said, holding it out in his hand.

Still she ignored him, looking around the apartment. Isaac Shur placed the money where he always put it, on a corner of the table. He watched the woman's eyes taking in his newspapers and magazines, his bottle of Johnnie Walker Black Label whisky, the Ramon Allones cigars, his cartons of Camel cigarettes. Finally, she sat down in Isaac Shur's chair.

'Whisky,' she said.

Isaac Shur fetched from the kitchen a glass and poured it half full. He handed it to the woman.

'Cigarette,' she said.

He offered his pack of Camels, lit one for her with a match. The woman's face said nothing. She raised the glass to her lips. Then she heard something, they both heard it, a sound outside, a step. The woman dropped the glass of whisky to the floor. The cigarette fell from her other hand. She sat, silent, stone, her eyes on a corner of the ceiling.

Isaac Shur went to the door and looked outside. It was

nothing. There was no one there. The sound must have come from the apartment above.

'Nothing,' he said, holding up his hands, smiling.

The glass was not broken. Isaac Shur poured the woman another drink, lit for her another cigarette. Once more he offered the week's rent. Again she ignored him, sitting straight in his chair, puffing on the forbidden cigarette, but not inhaling, blowing the smoke away. Isaac Shur watched the glass go three times to the woman's lips, but each time it seemed to him the level remained the same. Then there was another sound, and once more she let fall the cigarette and glass.

She stayed for half an hour, never once looking directly at Isaac Shur, but the money disappearing, as it always did, into her jellaba, and when he unlocked and opened the garden gate for her, she swept past him as though she had never seen him before.

Now Isaac Shur stripped again, and standing in the kitchen washed himself all over, shaved with cold water, regretted for an instant not buying one of those handsomely packaged bottles of after-shave, then dressed again, this time putting on his spare shirt, fresh underwear and socks. He rinsed out the glass the woman had used, poured himself a good measure of whisky, selected and trimmed a Ramon Allones, and stepped out into the garden.

Isaac Shur stood with his drink and cigar and gazed along the valley. He felt awake and alert, refreshed by his sleep, his wash and shave, but not as he felt in the mornings. This was a different kind of wakefulness. Or was it wakefulness at all? Isaac Shur thought of the poem he was writing, and at once his brain felt tired, sluggish, annoyed to be forced to think of that. Then of what? Isaac Shur saw, on the rubbish dump, The Hot Shot Kid, the one with the shaved head, another one of them too. He took a step back, quickly, not to be seen. There was a concrete bench under a tree. Isaac Shur sat down.

George Matthews had said that what Isaac Shur needed was a Spanish girl. Spanish girls, he had said, were the best. No complications. No involvement. They knew what was what. He had even picked one out for him, a small frizzy-haired girl with large dark eyes who worked in one of the tourist shops on the Avenue Louis Pasteur. 'Don't be silly,' Isaac Shur had said.

'What are you talking about, "don't be silly"?' George Matthews had said. 'There's nothin' to it. You just go in, give her somethin', I don't know, a bottle of perfume, somethin' like that, then, well, you ask her to come for a walk. Tell her you've got your own apartment, that'll do it.' 'I couldn't do that,' Isaac Shur had said. 'Anyhow, I don't know enough Spanish.' George Matthews had laughed. 'Listen, you don't have to *talk*, for God's sake,' he had said. 'Look, you just rub these fingers together — like this.' George Matthews rubbed his index fingers, two naked bodies, side by side. 'Says the whole thing.'

Isaac Shur wrote once a fortnight to a girl in Australia. They had gone out together for nearly two years, a blonde girl named Ann, an interior decorator, and Isaac Shur knew that all he had to say was 'Come' and she would be in Tangier in a week. He had sent her, from London, a pair of Victorian jet pendant earrings, and she had had herself photographed with them on, three small photographs, pasted on a card, a triptych, two in earnest profile, smiling in the one in the middle. Isaac Shur kept this in his wallet, and each fortnight, before writing to her, he would look at it, at the three faces. Isaar Shur told her, in his letters, what he was doing, what he was seeing, what he was writing, he said how much he missed her, he signed his letters 'love', and as he wrote, what he felt was certainly true, but afterwards, reading his letters over before posting them, he saw how careful they were. They were not his voice; not the voice he employed in his speech or his poems.

Isaac Shur watched his garden filling gently with night. When he stood to refresh his drink, he saw that the valley had almost disappeared. Faint lights in the villages were the only sign of its existence. His apartment, when he went inside, echoed with emptiness, the sound of his shoes enormous on the hard, tiled floor. Isaac Shur poured himself another drink. He threw away his cigar and immediately lit a cigarette. He stood in the centre of the room and looked at the unmade bed, his two small canvas bags, his things on the table, the empty chair. It was still early, not yet seven o'clock. George Matthews didn't expect him till nine. He debated an hour at the Café de Paris with *The Times*, or maybe a stroll down to the Socco Chico, see who was there, a cup of coffee, a cigarette. He remembered he would have to get a bottle of wine. He would get that at the shop down the hill. Gibraltar tomorrow, he remembered. A breeze stirred the trees outside in the garden. Isaac Shur crushed out his cigarette. He felt, suddenly, impatient. He put down his glass of whisky, crossed quickly to the windows and closed them, stepped outside and locked the door. He would buy that bottle of after-shave, he decided, as he unlocked his garden gate, in that shop on the Avenue Louis Pasteur, the shop where the Spanish girl with the frizzy hair and the large dark eyes worked. Yes. He would do that now.

Isaac Shur walked home from his evening with George Matthews. It was after one o'clock, the sky blown full with moon. On the Avenue Louis Pasteur he passed the shop where the Spanish girl worked, where he hadn't gone in, but his thoughts were not on that. Two Moroccans walked hand in hand on the other side of the street. A woman stepped out of a doorway just ahead of him. Isaac Shur, walking past, saw for an instant her eyes above her black veil, the white flash of a naked ankle. Then he was past, walking quickly but not outwardly hurrying, the street empty ahead.

They had played Monopoly, as they always did, five fast games, the board set up and ready when Isaac Shur knocked on the door. They had played during dinner, and then afterwards, game after game, sitting in that curious windowless room in the centre of George Matthews' apartment, a large photograph of Humphrey Bogart hung crookedly on one wall, Beethoven's Fifth booming on George Matthews' record player. He had brought the record player with him from New York. He was never going back there again. He was through, he said, with all that hassling.

George Matthews, as always, had won every game. After the fifth game he had suggested they switch to Scrabble, or chess, but Isaac Shur had said no, he was tired, he wanted to get up early, he had to work in the morning. 'Anyhow, you're tired too,' Isaac Shur had said. 'You're nearly asleep.'

George Matthews had been smoking kif all evening. His eyelids drooped. The smell of his many pipes was sweet in the air. Isaac Shur had never smoked kif, and whenever George Matthews asked him why, as he had again this evening, Isaac Shur laughed, smiled, sipped his wine. 'I haven't got anything against it,' he had said again tonight. 'I just don't need it, that's all. I'm relaxed enough. Come on, it's your go.' There was something childish about George Matthews, Isaac Shur had always felt, something lacking, some essential quality, but exactly what it was Isaac Shur couldn't pin down. But did it matter? Isaac Shur accepted him as he was, accepted the endless games of Monopoly, the endless sitting. He liked him. He was glad that George Matthews was here in Tangier.

A café was still open on the corner where Isaac Shur turned up to ascend the hill to his apartment. Isaac Shur saw Moroccans in drab brown jellabas slumped at the tables, felt them looking at him as he approached, his footsteps ringing loud in the night, and his impulse was to cross the road, but he didn't. Instead, he inspected them coldly as he walked past, his eyes moving from one face to the next, pleased to see each one looking down, looking away, turning from his hard gaze. No one spoke. Isaac Shur began the walk up the hill.

He passed the shop where he bought his breakfast every morning, the shop closed now, but a wan light dimly visible inside, oily and feeble through the dirty window. Isaac Shur felt in his pocket for his keys. He was almost upon her before he saw she was there, the same woman he had seen this morning, sitting exactly as she had sat then, as though she hadn't moved all day, and the baby too, sitting against a wall shadowed by the moon like a pile of dirty clothing thrown there on the broken pavement. Isaac Shur made to step around her, automatically, that reflex action he had done in this city so many times, but she moved, her hand reached out, and when Isaac Shur took another step, quickly, away from her, out onto the road, she came after him, he felt her fingers on the fabric of his jeans. Isaac Shur jumped as though he had been struck. 'Oh, go away,' he said, 'go away!' The sound of his own voice startled him. He hadn't meant to speak, to cry out. He heard his voice as though it had come from someone else, heard the sound of it, the tone. Isaac Shur panicked. He began to run, the key to his iron garden gate already out, gripped hard in his tight hand.

At two in the morning Isaac Shur awoke to hear a sound in his garden, a sound of scraping and chipping, a sound of masonry. He lay dead quiet, too terrified to move, his hands frozen by his sides, his heart thundering high in his throat. He listened, but he didn't have to listen. Isaac Shur knew at once what the sound was, without a second's doubt. Someone was taking away his wall.

Isaac Shur didn't move. He heard the grey concrete blocks being lifted away, one by one. He couldn't move. His fear was enormous. He lay, his heart hammering, naked in the dark. He thought of the oil lamp by the side of the bed, but he knew that to light it was for him, now, impossible. He couldn't move his fingers. He couldn't raise his hands. The room was as black with his eyes open as it was with them closed. Another block, and another. He listened, terrified, to the mortar being chipped away. And then he felt something else, inside him, beside the fear, a first prickle, and then stronger. He began to breathe hard through his mouth, his anger growing, his outrage, growing and growing, pushing aside the fear. He sat up. He stood up. When he opened his door the moon felt inside at his feet like a page of paper.

An old Arab sat cross-legged on the rubbish dump beyond the wall, scraping broken bricks with a knife and putting them into a burlap bag. Curled beside him lay a thin yellow dog, the colour of bad cream in the light of the moon. Isaac Shur stared at the Arab's thin hands, but the Arab's face, bent over his bricks, was to Isaac Shur in shadow, a blackness, a void.

Isaac Shur caught the four o'clock plane to Gibraltar the next afternoon, the connecting flight to London at half past eight.

A Person of Accomplishment

Frank Moorhouse

The invitation to go home with him to his place was absolutely unexpected. There they were writing up test analyses in his office, her mind running a fantasy about going to MIT for a PhD and finding a big buck Negro in a white lab coat, when she'd felt a hand on her knee and heard him say, 'Why don't we stop at this point and go back to my place for a drink?' The pressure of his hand on her knee said drinks and sex.

Her second thoughts were whether she'd stay overnight with him. Whether she'd need a change of clothes for tomorrow and other things. She was also faintly blushing.

She felt like saying 'But we hardly know each other', but that was not a particularly liberated thing to say, and checked it. Nor particularly honest because she'd never made this a real requirement with other men. Unexpected, that was what it was, unexpected. Over the months there hadn't been a sexual breath to stir the clinical atmosphere between them.

'I guess you must have sensed I was going to invite you home one of these fine nights,' he said.

She looked at his smile. 'Well, not exactly . . .'

'You will come, though?'

'Well, yes,' she said. There was the slight obligation of an invitation which comes from an associate professor to a humble research assistant—and then the difference in their ages —twenty-eight and forty, gave him some sort of command. She also felt gently encircled by his clean, serious, American gregariousness. His American geniality.

At his place he took her in his arms in the clean kitchen and with her backside against the stainless steel sink, kissed her very seriously.

'I've been wanting to do that for some days,' he said, with some satisfaction, and having got that out of the way, went about getting her a drink and putting out black bread and cheese — two types — on a cheese board.

He showed her around. Showed her his study with its carved pipe rack, Steel-bilt filing cabinets and Tensor reading lamp.

Besides his doctorate from MIT and his pharmacy degree from the University of Nebraska, Lincoln, framed on the wall, she saw a cup for canoeing and a silver chess piece from some American competition.

'Spacious,' she commented.

'I prefer it to my office at the university,' he said. She mentally corrected it to 'room at the university'.

Back in the living room she ran her fingers along the keyboard of his piano.

'Do you play?' she asked.

'Yes. A little.' Sitting down, he played.

'Schoenberg — discordant? You find it discordant? Twelve-tone system — a rigid intellectual exercise — say, like a sonnet.'

'You seem to have a wide range of interests — chess, canoeing, piano . . .'

'There's a reason,' he said quietly, stopping playing. 'I had a marriage break up on me — years ago — when I was young.' He shrugged, looked at her, and then seemed to decide not to go on.

She felt unable to inquire further.

He swivelled on the piano stool, looking fit and spruce.

She was frightened then for a second that the conversation had lapsed and the situation would become physical. She wasn't ready.

'Do you cook?' she said, looking through at the shadow board and the shelves holding the kitchen utensils — the natural colourings of the handmade wood and pottery and the machined brightness of the duralumin and stainless steel. She could see a cutlet bat, a red casserole dish, brownware dishes, wooden cutting board with inset blades, a crescent-shaped double-handed chopping knife, and a mortar and pestle.

'A playboy cook.' He chuckled. 'Get the woman to do the

vegetables and set the table.' He chuckled some more. 'Yes, I cook, I cook a passable *coq au vin* — provincial style — actually I'm a peasant cook — love the primitive. You must let me cook dinner for you one night.'

Whatever sort of cook you are, she thought, you're not a playboy.

'Oh,' she said, 'here I am at twenty-eight and have never cooked *coq au vin* in my life.'

They sat there, he talked about cooking. She heard Bearnaise, Bordelaise, and vaguely listened while thinking about him, trying to get a feel for him. She was brought back to the conversation by him showing her a hand-written recipe book which she riffled through but could not concentrate on. A book, he told her, begun by his pioneer grandmother, which he had continued. It was in his handwriting, with great clarity — like one of his experiment reports. She saw the headings, Corn Fritter, Rye Bread, Wheat Cake.

'Another drink?'

'Oh yes,' she said, looking at her glass, wanting another drink all right, 'yes please.'

Coming back from the kitchen, smiling, the host, 'Would you like to hear a record or tape?'

He opened a large cabinet containing records and tapes.

'I'm a hi-fi fanatic,' he said. 'Constructed this set-up myself.' And burbled on about sound reproduction as though switched on by the opening of the cabinet.

She went over and knelt beside him in front of the cabinet. 'About five hundred records and as many tapes.' He handed her a catalogue.

'Done by your last research assistant?' she said playfully — it was indexed under title, composer, and musician.

'Oh no,' he said, 'myself — all my own work.'

'How impressive.'

'Not really — clerical, simply clerical.'

She couldn't think of a record — the choice was too great. 'I can't think,' she said. 'You select something.'

'A tape?' he said. 'Let's see — aboriginal music — actual field recording, how's that?'

'Field recording?'

'I was cook on a dig once.'

'Dig? Cook?'

Her queries seemed imbecilic.

'Cook—sound recordist—pharmacist.' He smiled at her. 'I went with some of the Anthrop people—up North—fascinating—actually managed to get a superb collection.'

He put on a tape.

They settled back in their chairs. She didn't know whether one talked during the field recordings. 'May I talk?' she whispered, childlike, above the scrape and clack of the music.

Although there seemed plenty to talk about she had nothing to say.

'When's your book coming out?' she said after a longish pause.

'Which one?' he asked.

'I thought there was only one—*Drugs and Body Chemistry*.'

'Oh, August,' he said, 'but I have another book—poems—a slim volume.'

'You write poems?' she said, almost disbelieving.

'Yes, I'm no Holub, but I have two slim volumes.'

He went to the bookcase and pulled out a couple of books. He handed them to her, *Neutrons and Neurones—Poetic Explorations I-XII*, and *In Praise of the Epigamic—Collected Poems*. She opened them but her mind was still preoccupied with him and his atmosphere and she found she couldn't read. 'I can't concentrate now,' she said. 'May I borrow them?'

'By all means,' he said. 'Better still,' he jumped up, 'let me present you with a copy of *Praise of Epigamic*.'

'I love the title,' she said, as he left the room.

He came back with a copy, autographed. He must have a stock of autographed copies for his lady visitors.

'But this one is different,' she said, comparing it with the other, 'it's a thicker and richer kind of paper.'

'Yes, if you look closely you'll see the binding's different too.'

She examined it.

'I hand-printed it, hand-cut the paper, and hand-bound it.'

'You did it yourself?'

'Yes,' he said without boast, 'I have a friend who has a printery—he taught me the rudiments.'

'But it's beautifully done,' she said.

'Thank you,' he said.

A Person of Accomplishment

'Fancy writing your own poems and then setting about printing and binding the book!'

He laughed. 'This will amuse you too,' he said. 'I mix my own inks.'

'No!' she said, marvelling. She looked again at the ink and saw that it was a delicate strange brown. 'Well,' she said, 'too much,' and then felt that not enough and added, 'I'm impressed once again.'

'You shouldn't be,' he said. 'It's simply a matter of following a recipe — as it happens a fifteenth-century recipe.'

'Fifteenth century!'

'Little more than lampblack, iron, manganese oxides, linseed oil — the early inks are fairly stable — although modern inks probably have greater longevity — we don't know of course,' he grinned, 'superior compounding. I had most of the copies done with modern inks.'

'Oh.'

'Want another little suprise?' he said, boyishly.

'I don't know whether I can stand it.'

'The paper — I made it — even pulped my own wood — sulphite — although it's mainly macerated old rags.'

'I'm flabbergasted.'

They sat there for a few seconds in silence. She could think of a hundred banal questions about how and why but stubbornly resisted asking them, perversely — she didn't want to be an interviewer. To further compliment him would be embarrassing for both of them. For one thing she was running out of natural compliments.

He mended the conversation by saying, 'Have some cheese.' She took a piece.

'I suppose you made the cheese too,' she said, chomping hard as she caught the sound of it — worried that it carried the implication he was a tiresome boaster or that she resented his accomplishments. She willed that it didn't sound that way. He didn't show any offence.

'I didn't,' he said; hesitated and smiled and said, 'I do make cheese — it just so happens that it isn't mine.'

Under her breath she said, oh no. She thought he might be joking and looked again at his face. He wasn't joking. He went to a board in his study containing carefully labelled keys and took down a key. 'Come with me—I have some cheeses ripening.'

He opened a three-quarter door under the stairway, switched on a light and, taking her hand, led her down the stone steps to the cellar.

'I hope I didn't sound offensive just then,' she said, 'about the cheese.'

'About the cheese?' he said, puzzled.

'It doesn't matter,' she said.

She loved the cellar. 'This is a really authentic cellar—just how a cellar should be—stone steps, stone walls, cheeses ripening—oh, and racks of wine.'

She didn't have to ask about the wine because she could see the bottling equipment and the wine press and stainless steel vats in a section at the far end.

'They're not cheeses,' she said hesitantly, pointing at cylindrical moulds hanging from a frame.

'No, they're candles,' he said, 'I turn out my own—God knows why—both paraffin—stearic acid and tallow—I suppose it makes dinner party conversation.'

'Here are my cheeses,' he said, taking her to another part of the cellar, 'still fairly green—that's Brick, sweetish type of cheese—and the rest are dull cheddars.'

She didn't hear his description of the manufacture of cheese—she kept looking around and thinking, my God, he's buried his wife down here.

'I worry about tyrotoxicon—aptomaine—so far I'm still alive.'

'It's rather cool down here,' she said, moving towards the stairs. 'Could we go up?' She didn't want to hear about the candles or the tyrotoxicon—she didn't want to be buried with his wife either. But she wasn't really scared; it was simply a game of nerves.

They went up the steps. He closed the cellar door, locked it, and switched off the light.

He still held her hand. How sweet, he liked it.

'I'd love a drink.'

'Of course.'

'Any other hobbies?' She wondered if 'hobbies' was the correct word.

'Oh, I do a few other things to fill in the time,' he said humorously.

A Person of Accomplishment

Like strangling women. She laughed at herself.

He didn't offer to tell her what they were. But she knew she was obliged to ask although she felt she didn't really want to know. She might even enjoy saying something about herself — but there didn't seem anything to say — he was a hard act to follow. What else could she do?

She asked.

'For instance,' he said, 'I make my own furniture.' She looked around and could see now that it was not factory furniture.

'How unobservant of me. Do you design it?'

'I design it — and also make the glues and the nails — I take the fact you didn't notice it as a compliment.'

She looked at him.

'Did you say "nails"?'

'The nails I make from iron ore — at a small foundry not far from here — a very low grade steel — but my own.'

She must have had a why-for-Godsake look on her face.

He seemed to rush to tell her, 'You see I like to follow a process right the way through — if it's a thing I eat, I want to grow it, harvest it, cure it or whatever. Usually it's not possible,' he said disappointedly. 'I have actually cut the timber for furniture — not this furniture — other pieces I've made . . .' He was scrutinising her and his voice was trailing as though he needed to be reassured that he didn't sound nutty.

'You don't think I'm . . .' he tapped his head.

She shook her head. 'You made the mat then,' she said, looking down at the coarse weave.

'Yes — that's a good case in point.' He gathered new impetus. 'I actually shore the sheep, spun the wool, dyed the wool, made the dyes.'

'What about the machines — the tools — and so on that you use to make things — do you make those too?' It sounded as though she were trying to catch him out.

'Ha! now you've got me — but I have made some simple tools — and I made a spinning wheel — but lathes, no, electric drills, no, saws, no.'

'You didn't build the house,' she said looking around, laughing, almost out of control, almost rudely.

'No, I didn't build the house, but . . .'

331

Australian Short Stories

She interrupted him, 'Let me guess — you could if you wanted to — you know how.'

Modestly, quietly, as though he'd gone too far, he said, 'Back in the States I built a four-room sod cabin using the techniques of the pioneers — up in the Pine Cat Range. It leaked.'

His first joke. She laughed and let herself fall back on the settee. 'Another drink, please,' she said, holding out her glass — noting that she was drinking quickly.

'I didn't make the whisky,' he said, grinning.

'But you did back in the States — in the sod cabin.'

'No,' he chuckled, obviously pleased with his humour, 'it's illegal — all the same I do have a corn mash still under construction — out the back in the workshop.'

She giggled and giggled, shaking her head. 'No — please — excuse me,' she said, choking, 'I can't help laughing — with admiration.'

He knelt in front of her in quick unexpected movement. She stopped laughing instantly. Holding their empty glasses still in his hands he put his head on her lap. She had stiffened. 'You're a very attractive woman,' he said. 'I want very much to impress you.'

'You have,' she said, embarrassed, wanting him to get up, unsettled by his sudden seriousness, 'you have impressed me — and you're a very attractive man,' she said, wondering if in fact he was, and sorry she couldn't do better than directly return his compliment, 'a very attractive man.'

She sensed he felt it time to make advances and to move towards sex.

'Will we take our drinks into the bedroom?' she said softly, trying to make it smooth — and in a way, to get it over with. She was as ready as she'd ever be.

He looked into her eyes, 'I want to make a request.'

She readied herself.

'I hope you have no objections,' he said, perhaps fearfully but certainly determined to ask it, 'and I hope you don't find it insulting.'

'What is it?' she almost shouted.

Still staring into her eyes he said, 'Would you take a bath with me?'

A Person of Accomplishment

The request wasn't as odd as she'd feared. It was his possible motive which perturbed her — he was going to drown her and bury her with his wife.

'I don't mind,' she answered, a little unsteadily. 'Why?'

'I'm glad you will,' he said, relieved, 'I know it sounds a queer deal — but — I like to begin from the beginning.'

'Oh.'

'Are you with me?'

'More or less.' Less than more.

He began to talk very quickly, trying to convince, 'A bath is a symbolic beginning — a rebirth, so as to speak — we remove all connection with the everyday world — our clothes — and we wash away the traces.'

He looked intently at her. 'Odd?'

'I can follow you,' she said, noncommittally.

He coloured. 'I know it sounds odd.'

'Oh no,' she said, lying, but emotionally spellbound by the gregarious pipe-smoking associate professor from MIT on his knees struggling to gain her approval, captured briefly by his mesh of theories and practices. 'It's just different,' she added, for honesty.

'Good,' he said, rising to his feet and guiding her up. 'First, a taste of my wine — light red.'

'Yes, I saw the equipment down in the cellar.'

'I don't grow my own grapes — I buy them.' They went to the kitchen. 'I like to finish the evening with something of my own. Simple vanity.'

In the kitchen he took down two wine glasses and took a bottle of red wine from a rack.

'The glasses!' she exclaimed, 'of course — the glasses — they're home made — you made them.'

'Yes, I blew them,' he said.

He led her then into the bathroom. It was large with a large, almost square, almost Roman, bath — which could hold at least two people. 'Why, this bathroom is fantastic,' she said.

'I didn't make the tiles but I did design it,' he said. 'I very much wanted to build it — but really the only thing of mine is the towels.'

He turned on the taps.

He coughed. 'Could I take your clothes?'

'Oh yes,' she said, swallowing the unnaturalness. She stripped. He stripped along with her.

He took her clothes and his and went out. He was going to burn them and keep her prisoner, she thought—or more likely he was going to fumigate them. Or do something kinky with her underwear.

He came back. 'I use the tallow for both candles and soap,' he said handing her a cake of yellow-brown soap, almost larger than her hand, 'coconut oil—resin—the usual phosphates—and the rest—common household formula. I faintly odourised it with lavender and cassia.'

She smelt it. 'It smells positively caustic,' she said, the cavernous bathroom making her sound like a small girl.

She felt bizarre standing beside the nude forty-year-old American professor, his hand on her arse, holding a cake of handmade soap. It made her think of Nazi prison camps.

'Shall we bathe?' He tried the water. 'It's OK.' They both went into the bath. He began to scrub her with the soap, quite hard. She simply sat there in a half slump. She did as she was told. He washed her as though she were a little girl—between the legs and under the armpits.

'Your hair, too,' he said.

'My hair?'

'Just put it under the water, the soap makes an excellent shampoo.' She wasn't so sure. She wasn't so sure about putting her head under the water with his hand on her neck.

She braced herself for a life or death struggle.

But he was gentle—and practised.

He complimented her on her body.

'Thank you,' she said, aroused in a way by his scrubbing touch and his strong intention—aware that he knew precisely what he wanted to do with her and intended doing it.

After drying her with a coarse handwoven towel he took her upstairs to the bedroom where they lay down on the wide bed which she could see was hewn from logs. He lit a small oil lamp beside the bed. Her damp hair made her slightly uncomfortable.

She was relieved to see her clothes in the room—carefully folded and hung.

'Do you have trouble with orgasm?' he asked, softly.

God. She lay there irritated, without answering, disliking the question.

'I suppose not,' she said, thinking that she'd never had to worry much about it.

'I mean do you take long? Should I wait for you?'

Not only was she embarrassed, she was affronted — did he have a questionnaire? — 'I really don't know,' she said, 'I haven't timed myself.' A little nastily.

'I don't mean to be embarrassing,' he said, apologetically, 'but I always think it's best to get these things out — out of the way.'

He was stroking her legs with his hand and feeling her breast.

'You tell me when you're ready to climax,' he said, 'I'll wait for you.'

She didn't speak. His strong sense of intention had frayed into a desperate effort to please. She was turned off.

'All right?' he asked.

'Yes,' she said, closing her eyes, resigned to enduring it.

'Do you like breast stimulation?'

She didn't answer.

They fucked, she didn't relax and faked climax, telling him by sounds, she hoped, that she'd finished, although he kept saying, 'You right? you right? you finished?', and to stop him she nodded and then he whispered, 'That was great — was it great for you?'

She again nodded, keeping her eyes shut, and reaching blindly for cigarettes she'd put beside the bed.

He chattered for a while about the nature of orgasm; sexual difficulty; being candid about sex; and how few men and women knew women had orgasms. She didn't comment. She wondered how many women had lied to him about himself and about their reaction to him. What could you do?

She stubbed out her cigarette, feeling bad, and feigned sleep.

She was awoken in the morning by him doing his exercises on parallel bars at the far end of the room. He didn't say a word or smile or wink but kept solidly on. She watched him from the bed, dying for a cup of coffee.

When he finished he came over panting and sat on the edge of the bed. 'Started,' he panted, 'on the 5BX — Canadian Air Force — have developed — my own — programme — a hybrid of yoga and Scandinavian gymnastics.'

Australian Short Stories

From a drawer beside the bed he took a book containing hand drawings of various exercise positions and tables—all lettered in his handwriting. 'That's my programme,' he said.

She could think only of coffee. 'I don't even exercise—let alone have my own programme,' she said. 'I'm basically unhealthy,' she said with barely concealed hostility.

He went to the kitchen and returned with herbal tea and meal porridge, hand ground—'See if you like these,' he said.

She left half of both.

And as she smoked her second cigarette he said, 'Well, how do you feel,' anxiously, and she saw that the question was directed at her psyche, health, and mood all at once. As though he was saying, 'How was I?'

'Oh, great,' she said, not wanting to give any sort of analysis of the evening, not wanting to deceive him any more than she had to.

She washed with the home-made soap she now found repugnant, and dressed. They walked through the garden of the house.

'Would you have time to look at my observatory?' He pointed to a dome structure at the back.

'No, must rush, really, some other time,' she said.

'Then there will be another time?' he said.

She'd trapped herself, 'I do have a regular sort of thing with a boy,' she said, as a way out, smiling.

'Then there won't be another time,' he said, logically.

'Let's leave it to chance.'

They walked for a distance without speaking.

'Do you find me a bore?' he asked.

She went on guard. She did. But what could you say? 'But you're a very interesting man,' she said, 'a very accomplished man.'

'My wife—just after we separated—said to me, "The trouble with you, Hugo—you're a damn bore!"'

'That was a fairly destructive thing to say.'

'It gave me a devastating insight—I was a damn bore.'

She went to her bag for a cigarette.

'Her words are forever inscribed on my mind as a warning—and it permitted me to correct the fault—in your words I made myself, "an interesting man".'

336

A Person of Accomplishment

They reached the gate.

The first personal statement made during the whole overnight visit or the months, in fact, that she'd worked with him. She had to get out before she felt she had to be honest with him. She had her own problems.

She kissed him on the cheek and said, 'You are—you are a very interesting man—you must be a very fulfilled man.' It sounded so formal. Too bad.

'But one needs more than that, one needs more, one needs a woman—about the place,' he said, hopelessly, pleadingly, not only to her, perhaps not to her at all, but to all damn womanhood.

She nodded sympathetically. 'I really must rush,' she said, 'I must be off. I must rush.'

Audition for Male Voice

Frank Moorhouse

When we ended up in Bisi's room drunk for a singing party to end the conference, I wondered if there'd be a person who wouldn't have a song to sing as I had once, as a cadet, not had a song to sing, and yes, at this party there was a person who had no song, a young poet from Melbourne. And I'd thought poets always had a song to sing.

'Sing—everyone a song,' said Bisi.

In the old Journalists Club surrounded by older journalists, the older men having taken me, the cadet, to wet my head. 'You'll have to sing a song.' 'Naturally,' I say, not recalling any song, churning at the fear of performance, impersonating an equality with the older men. 'Naturally,' I say, heartily, deep voiced, at seventeen. And to the fifty-year-old journalist who'd just sung, I say, deeply, 'Go on, Fred,' throwing back my beer. 'You'll have to do better than that, Fred.'

The drinking test, to stay on one's feet, the testing session.

'You'll have to sing,' the older journalist says. 'Everyone has sung.'

To have the words, to hold yourself together, to deny shyness, to join with knowingness in age-old drinking rituals, tell a good story, sing a man's song, know the match game. Take the mail to dead man's gulch.

'I will, Fred—I will—don't rush me.' Laughing, inwardly desperate, big-voiced seventeen, the cadet, frying in my self-consciousness. No song coming to my lips.

'Come on, sing a song.'

Audition for Male Voice

To reach seventeen I had climbed higher in a tree, gone into a female lavatory for a bet, sworn at a teacher, had a fist fight with a black, learned to throw a knife and make it stick, shot a rabbit and skinned it, gone into a cemetery at midnight, spat on a church altar, dived off Forty Foot Cliff, touched a girl's breast, touched a girl's cunt, drunk twenty schooners, done the University-to-the-Quay crawl. Asked a barmaid for a fuck.

Come back when you've begun to shave.

'Sing a song.'

I have passed nearly all mine now, and more.

Gone with a whore.

And tests passed more than once.

Fathered a child.

Come back when you've begun to shave.

The tests too of the military.

'I will, Fred — let me finish this beer.'

Cut a body target in two with machine-gun fire, bayoneted a human dummy, endured a route march in full gear, endured a battalion parade without fainting, gone into a gas-filled room.

Bisi was beating the waste-paper bin like a drum, the big Ibo 'high life' music, the music of the market town Onitsha.

'Oh-yes,' he cried, singing, 'oh-yes.'

The moral rearmament man from Samoa was there, not drinking, but smiling, smiling, smiling. Oh-yes. He did an act of pulling in the canoe with his tie, and with great style, squatting on his backside on the college room floor. Pulling in a canoe at UNESCO.

Norman sang Land of Our Fathers, moved by his own voice from the mock-serious to alcoholic dreams of a Coldstream Guard, and back again.

Now the harems of Egypt are fair to behold,

And the ladies the fairest of fair,

But the fairest, a Greek

She was owned by a sheik,

One Abdul-A-Bulbul Emir.

And Ivan Skivinsky Skivar. And The Harlot of Jerusalem. And tools of fools who tried to ride. Hi hi cafoozelum, the harlot of Jerusalem.

Mathers sang Will Ye No Come Back Again, and cried.

I cried. Norman cried. Bisi cried.

'Sing anything.' The old journalist. 'All right Fred, give me a second.' No song to sing, racked. The cadet.

My name is Sammy Hall, Sammy Hall, Sammy Hall. Damn your eyes, blast your soul.

How did they know them, where did they come from?

Why didn't I know?

Painfully — 'All right, quiet everybody, here I go' — painfully my voice leaps. I sing a popular song of the day, eyes closed, stumblingly, in a boy's voice, impersonating a grown man, four lines. Blast my soul. Damn my eyes.

Roll me over, lay me down and do it again.

On Ilkla Moor Baht'at.

Norman sang Land of Our Fathers, became a Coldstream Guard and stayed a Coldstream Guard.

Bisi beat the drums of the market town of Onitsha.

The young poet was asked to sing.

'Go on sing, anything,' I said, my voice the voice of the old journalist. Don't you know —

There was an old man from Cape Horn?

There was a young monk from Siberia?

There was a maiden from Avignon France?

There was a young fellow from Kings?

No.

No?!

'I don't bloody well want to sing.'

'You have to sing,' the voice of the old journalist.

Sing a song. Sing a song.

'I don't want to bloody well sing a song.'

Norman said not to get uptight about it. It was all right.

It was not all right.

'I hate these bloody things,' the young poet cried, temper breaking, reddening. 'I won't be forced into these things.'

'No one is forcing you.'

We are all forcing you.

'I hate this male drinking bonhomie limerick shit.'

There was a young lady from Sydney,

Who took it right up to the kidney.

Bisi, 'You bloody sing a song, young poet, this is a singing party, you sing your song, this is a drinking party, you drink your drink and sing your song.'

Audition for Male Voice

'No daylight, no heel taps,' said Norman, the Coldstream Guard.

The young poet held his temper with the black man.

'I'll go.'

'No, you cannot go. You stay and sing a song.'

Mathers sang Will Ye No Come Back Again, and cried.

Bisi beat the drums.

Norman the Coldstream Guard sang Land of Our Fathers.

The moral rearmament man pulled in the canoe.

I sang Joe Hill.

I dreamed I saw Joe Hill last night, alive as you and me. I?

We sang There is a Green Hill Far Away. The moral rearmament man from Samoa, Bisi from the market town of Onitsha, we all sang:

There is a green hill far away,

Without a city wall,

Where the dear Lord was crucified,

Who died to save us all.

It was on the good ship Venus,

My god you should have see us.

We are gentlemen songsters out on a spree,

Doomed from here to eternity,

Lord have mercy on such as we,

We are poor little lambs

Who have lost our way

Baa, baa, baa.

The poet says, grittingly, 'All right, I'll say the Lord's Prayer. Our father which art in heaven.'

We became quiet. We joined him, all male voices, saying the Lord's Prayer, solemnly, heads bowed. We could have been at an army church parade. Norman was. We joined the poet.

'Our father which art in heaven,

Hallowed be thy name

Thy kingdom come.'

'A,B,C,D,E,F,G,H,I,J, K,L,M,N,O,P,Q,R,S, T,U,V,W,X,Y,Z'

Murray Bail

I select from these letters, pressing my fingers down. The letter (or an image of it) appears on the sheet of paper. It signifies little or nothing, I have to add more. Other letters are placed alongside until a 'word' is formed. And it is not always the word WORD.

The word matches either my memory of its appearance, or a picture of the object the word denotes. TREE: I see the shape of a tree at mid-distance, and green.

I am writing a story.

Here, the trouble begins.

The word 'dog', as William James pointed out, does not bite; and my story begins with a weeping woman. She sat at the kitchen table one afternoon and wept uncontrollably. How can words, particularly 'wept uncontrollably', convey her sadness (her self-pity)? Philosophers other than myself have discussed the inadequacy of words. 'Woman' covers women of every shape and size, whereas the one I have in mind is red-haired, has soft arms, plain face, high-heeled shoes with shining straps.

And she was weeping.

Her name, let us say, is Kathy Pridham.

For the past two years she has worked as a librarian for the British Council in Karachi. She, of all the British community there, was one of the few who took the trouble to learn Urdu, the local language. She could speak it, not read it: those calligraphic loops and dots meant nothing to her, except that 'it was a language'. Speaking it was enough. The local staff at the Council, shopkeepers, and even the cream of Karachi society (who cultivated European manners), felt that she knew them as they themselves did.

At this point, consider the word 'Karachi'. Not having been there myself I see clusters of white-cube buildings with the edge of a port to the left, a general slowness, a shaded verandah-ed suburb for the Burrasahibs. Perhaps, eventually, boredom — or disgust with noises and smells not understood. Kathy, who was at first lonely and disturbed, quickly settled in. She became fully occupied and happy; insofar as that word has any meaning. There was a surplus of men in Karachi: young English bachelors sent out from head office, and pale appraising types who work at the embassies; but the ones who fell over themselves to be near her were Pakistanis. They were young and lazy. With her they were ardent and gay.

Already the words Kathy and Karachi are becoming inextricably linked.

It was not long before she too was rolling her head in slow motion during conversations, and clicking her tongue, as they did, to signify 'no'. Her bungalow in the European quarter with its own lawn, verandah, two archaic servants, became a sort of *salon*, especially at the Sunday lunches where Kathy reigned, supervising, flitting from one group to the next. Those afternoons never seemed to end. No one wanted to leave. Sometimes she had musicians perform. And there was always plenty of liquor (imported), with wide dishes of hot food. Kathy spoke instantly and volubly on the country's problems, its complicated politics, yet in London if she had an opinion she rarely expressed it.

When Kathy thought of London she often saw 'London' — the six letters arranged in recognizable order. Then parts of an endless construction appeared, much of it badly blurred. There was the thick stone. Concentrating, she could recall a familiar bus stop, the interior of a building where she had last worked. Her street invariably appeared, strangely dead. Some men in overcoats. It was all so far away she sometimes thought it existed only when she was there. Her best friends had been two women, one a school teacher, the other married to a taciturn engineer. With them she went to Scotland for holidays, to the concerts at Albert Hall. Karachi was different. The word stands for something else.

Australian Short Stories

The woman weeping at the kitchen table is Kathy Pridham. It is somewhere in London (there are virtually no kitchen tables in Karachi).

After a year or so Kathy noticed at a party a man standing apart from the others, watching her. His face was bony and fierce, and he had a thin moustache. Kathy, of course, turned away, yet at the same time tilted her chin and began acting over-earnest in conversation. For she pictured her appearance: seeing it (she thought) from his eyes.

She noticed him at other parties, and at one where she knew the host well enough, casually asked, 'Tell me. Who is that over there?'

They both looked at the man watching her.

'If you mean him, that's Syed Masood. Not your cup of tea, Kathy. What you would call a wild man.' The host was a successful journalist and drew in on his cigarette. 'Perhaps he is our best painter. I don't know; I have my doubts.'

Kathy lowered her eyes, confused.

When she looked up, the man called Syed Masood had gone.

Over the next few days, she went to the galleries around town and asked to see the paintings of Syed Masood. She was interested in local arts and crafts, and had decided that if she saw something of his she liked she would buy it. These gallery owners threw up their hands. 'He has released nothing for two years now. What has got into him I don't know.'

Somehow this made Kathy smile.

Ten or eleven days pass — in words that take only seconds to put down, even less to absorb (the discrepancy between Time and Language). It is one of her Sunday lunches. Kathy is only half-listening to conversations and when she breaks into laughter it is a fraction too loud. She has invited this man Masood and has one eye on the door. He arrives late. Perhaps he too is nervous.

Their opening conversation (aural) went something like this (visual).

'Do come in. I don't think we've met. My name is Kathy Pridham.'

'Why do you mix with these shits?' he replied, looking around the room.

344

A,B,C,D,E,F,G,H,I,J,K,L,M,N,O,P,Q,R,S,T,U,V,W,X,Y,Z

Just then an alarm wristlet watch on one of the young men began ringing. Everyone laughed, slapping each other, except Masood.

'I'll get you something,' said Kathy quietly. 'You're probably hungry.'

She felt hot and awkward, although now that they were together he seemed to take no notice of her. Several of the European men came over, but Masood didn't say much and they drifted back. She watched him eat and drink: the bones of his face working.

He finally turned to her. 'You come from — where?'

'London.'

'Then why have you come here?'

She told him.

'And these?' he asked, meaning the crowd reclining on cushions.

'My friends. They're people I've met here.'

Suddenly she felt like crying.

But he took her by the shoulders. 'What is this? You speak Urdu? And not at all bad? Say something more, please.'

Before she could think of anything he said in a voice that disturbed her, 'You are something extraordinary.' He was so close she could feel his breath. 'Do you know that? Of course. But do you know how extraordinary? Let me tell you something, although another man might put it differently. It begins here' — for a second one of his many hands touched her breasts; Kathy jumped — 'and it *emanates*. Your volume fills the room. Certainly! So you are quite vast, but beautiful.'

Then he added, watching her, 'If you see what I mean.'

He was standing close to her, but when he spoke again she saw him grinning. 'Now repeat what I have just said in Urdu.'

He made her laugh.

Here — now — an interruption. While considering the change in Kathy's personality I remember an incident from last Thursday, the 12th. This is an intrusion but from 'real life'. The words in the following paragraph reconstruct the event as remembered. As accurately as possible, of course.

A beggar came up to me in a Soho bar and asked (a hoarse whisper) if I wished to see photographs of funerals. I immediately pictured a rectangular hole, sky, men and women in coats. Without waiting for my reply he fished out from an inside pocket the wad of photographs, postcard size, each one of a burial. They were dog-eared and he had dirty fingernails. 'Did you know these dead people?' He shook his head. 'Not even their names?' He shook his head. 'That one,' he said, not taking his eyes off the photographs, 'was dug yesterday. That one, in 1969.' There was little difference. Both showed men and women standing around a dark rectangle, perplexed. I felt a sharp tap on my wrist. The beggar had his hand out. Yes, I gave him a shilling. The barman spoke: 'Odd way to earn a living. He's been doing that for

Kathy soon saw Masood again. He arrived one night with his shirt hanging out while she was entertaining the senior British Council representative, Mr. L., and his wife. They were a cautious experienced pair, years in the service, yet Mrs. L. began talking loudly and hastily, a sign of indignation, when Masood sat away from the table, silently watching them. Mr. L. cleared his throat several times — another sign. It was a hot night with both ceiling fans hardly altering the sedentary air. Masood suddenly spoke to Kathy in his own language. She nodded and poured him another coffee. Mrs. L. caught her husband's eye, and when they left shortly afterwards, Kathy and Masood leaned back and laughed.

'You can spell my name four different ways,' Masood declared in the morning, 'but I am still the one person! Ah,' he said laughing. 'I am in a good mood. This is an auspicious day.'

'I have to go to work,' said Kathy.

'Look up "auspicious" when you get to the library. See what it says in one of your English dictionaries.'

She bent over to fit her brassiere. Her body was marmoreal, the opposite to his: bony and nervy.

'Instead of thinking of me during the day,' he went on, 'think of an exclamation mark! It amounts to the same thing. I would see you, I think, as a colour. Yes, I think more than likely pink, or something soft like yellow.'

'You can talk,' said Kathy laughing.

But she liked hearing him talk. Perhaps there'll be further examples of why she enjoyed hearing him talk.

That night Masood took her to his studio. It was in the inner part of the city where Europeans rarely ventured, and as

A,B,C,D,E,F,G,H,I,J,K,L,M,N,O,P,Q,R,S,T,U,V,W,X,Y,Z

Masood strode ahead Kathy avoided, but not always successfully, the stares of women in doorways, the fingers of beggars, and rows of sleeping bodies. She noticed how some men deliberately dawdled or bumped into her; striding ahead, Masood seemed to enjoy having her there. In an alleyway he unbolted a powder-blue door as a curious crowd gathered. He suddenly clapped his hands to move them. Then Kathy was inside: a fluorescent room, dirty white-washed walls. In the corner was a wooden bed called a 'charpoy', some clothes over a chair. There were brushes in jars, and tins of paint.

'Syed, are these your pictures?'

'Leave them,' he said sharply. 'Come here. I would like to see you.'

Through the door she could feel the crowd in the alleyway. She was perspiring still and now he was undoing her blouse.

'Syed, let's go?'

He stepped back.

'What is the matter? The natives are too dirty tonight. Is that it? Yes, the walls; the disgusting size of the place. All this stench. It must be affecting your nostrils? Rub your nose in it. Lie in my shit and muck. If you wait around you might see a rat. You could dirty your Mem-sahib's hands for a change.' Then he kicked his foot through one of the canvases by the door. 'The pretty paintings you came to see.'

As she began crying she wondered why. (He was only a person who used certain words.)

I will continue with further words.

Kathy made room for Masood in her house, in her bed as well as the spare room which she made his studio. Her friends noticed a change. At work, they heard the pronoun 'we' constantly. She told them of parties they went to, the trips they planned to take, how she supervised his meals; she even confessed (laughing) he snored and possessed a violent temper. At parties, she took to sitting on the floor. She began wearing 'kurtas' instead of 'blouses', 'lungis' rather than 'dresses', even though with her large body she looked clumsy. To the Europeans she somehow became, or seemed, untidy. They no longer understood her, and so they felt sorry for her. It was about then that Kathy's luncheon parties stopped, and she and Masood, who were always together, went out less frequently.

Most people saw Masood behind this — he had never disguised his contempt for her friends — but others connected it with an incident at the office. Kathy arrived one morning wearing a sari and was told by the Chief Librarian it was inappropriate; she couldn't serve at the counter wearing that. Then Mr. L. himself, rapidly consulting his wife, spoke to her. He spelt out the *British* Council's function in Karachi, underlining the word British. 'Kathy, are you happy?' he suddenly asked. Like others, he was concerned. He wanted to say, 'Do you know what you are doing?' 'Oh, yes,' Kathy replied. 'With this chap, I mean,' he said, waving his hand. And Kathy left the room.

People's distrust of Masood seemed to centre around his unconventional appearance and (perhaps more than anything) his rude silences. Nobody could say they knew him, although just about everybody said he drank too much. Stories began circulating. 'A surly bugger,' he was called behind his back. That was common now. There were times when he cursed Kathy in public. Strange, though, the wives and other women were more ready to accept the affair. There was something about Masood, his face and manner. And they recognized the tenacity with which Kathy kept living with him. They understood her quick defence of him, often silent but always there, even when she came late to work, puff-eyed from crying and once, her cheek bruised.

Here, the life of Kathy draws rapidly to a close.

It was now obvious to everyone that Masood was drinking too much. At the few parties they attended he usually made a scene of some sort; and Kathy would take him home. Think of swear words. She was arriving late for work and missed whole days. Then she disappeared for a week. They had argued one night and Kathy screamed at him to leave. He replied by hitting her across the mouth. She moved into a cheap hotel, but within the week he found her. 'Syed spent all day, every day, looking for me,' was how she later put it. 'He needs someone.' When she was reprimanded for her disappearance and general conduct, she burst into tears.

In London, the woman with elbows on the table is Kathy Pridham. She has unwrapped a parcel from Karachi. Imagine: coarse screwed-up paper and string lie on the table. Masood has sent a self-portrait, oil on canvas, quite a striking

A, B, C, D, E, F, G, H, I, J, K, L, M, N, O, P, Q, R, S, T, U, V, W, X, Y, Z

resemblance. His vanity, pride and troubles are enormous. His face, leaning against the tea-pot, stares across at Kathy weeping.

She cannot help thinking of him; of his appearance.

Words. These marks on paper, and so on.

The Man of Slow Feeling

Michael Wilding

After the accident he lay for weeks in the still white ward. They fed him intravenously but scarcely expected him to live. Yet he did live, and when at last they removed the bandages from his eyes, it was found he could see. They controlled what he could see carefully, keeping the room dimmed, the blinds down, at first; but gradually increased his exposure to light, to the world around. Slowly his speech came back. He blocked for some time on words he could not remember, could no longer enunciate; but gradually his vocabulary returned. But he had lost sensation, it seemed. He could not smell the flowers Maria brought into the small private ward. And when she gave him the velvety globed petals to touch, he could not feel them. All foods were the same to him. The grapes she mechanically bought, he could only see. They had neither touch nor taste for him. If he shut his eyes and returned to darkness again, he did not know what he was eating. Yet he was not totally without sensation — it was not as if he were weightless or bodiless. He was conscious of lying in bed day after day, his body lying along the bed — perhaps because the constant pressure reached through to his numbed nerves. But the touch of Maria's fingers on his cheeks, the kiss of her lips against his, he could not feel, nor mouth the taste of her.

And yet as he lay alone in that small white room odd sensations came to him, brushed him with their dying wings. As if, lying there with only his thoughts and imaginings, he could conjure back the taste of grapes, the soft touch of Maria's hand, the searching pressure of her kiss. They surprised him, these sensations; often they would make him wake from a light sleep as

The Man of Slow Feeling

if a delightful dream had achieved an actuality: but when he awoke he was always totally alone, and remembered nothing of any dream. It was often, as he lay there, as if someone had actually touched him, or forced grapes against his palate, and he would want to cry out at the unexpectedness of it. If imagination, it could only have been triggered by the workings of his subconscious. He mentioned it to the nurses, and they said that it could be that he was getting his sensations back. He did not argue with them, pointing out that there were no correlatives to the sensations, no objects provoking them. It was like a man feeling pain in a foot already amputated: a foot he would not be getting back. The sensations were the ghosts of feelings he had once had, nerve memories of a lost past.

Released from hospital, Maria took him back to the house in the country. They made love that first night, but he could not feel her full breasts, her smooth skin, and making love to her was totally without sensation for him. Its only pleasures were voyeuristic and nostalgic: his eyes and ears allowed him to remember past times — like seeing a sexual encounter at the cinema. The thought came to him that the best way to get anything from sex now was to cover the walls and ceilings with mirrors, so that at least he could have a full visual satisfaction to replace his missing senses. But he said nothing to Maria. He said nothing, but he knew she realized that for him it was now quite hopeless.

He was woken in the night by a dream of intercourse, the excitement of fondling a body, the huge relief of orgasm. He lay awake, the vividness of it reminding him bitterly of what was now lost to him.

The early days back in the house he found disorienting. Within the white walls confining the ward experience had been limited for him; he saw little, encountered little; the disturbing nerve memories were few. But released, now they swelled to a riot, as if exposure to the open world had revived dormant, dying memories for their final throes. Released, his body was a continual flux of various sensations, of smell, of taste, of touch; yet still with no sensations from his experiences. He could walk beside the dung heap at the field's corner, ready to manure the land, and though he inhaled deeply hoping its pungency would break through his numbness, he could experience nothing.

When Maria was not looking, he reached his hand into the dung: he felt nothing. A visual repugnance, but no physical sensation, no recoil of nausea.

Yet at tea suddenly the full pungency of the foul dung swept across to him, his hand unfeelingly holding a meringue was swamped in the heavy foul stickiness of the dung. He left the table, walked across to the window that looked out onto the wide lawns. There was nothing outside to provoke his sensations; and if there had been, how could his touch have been affected from outside? His touch and smell had not, as he'd momentarily hoped, returned. Maria asked what was the matter, but he said nothing. He went to the bathroom, but oddly did not feel nausea. He expected to, biting that momentarily dung drenched meringue. But his stomach recorded no sensations. His intellect's interpretation had misled him; his mind was interpreting a nausea he would have felt, in his past life, an existence no longer his.

Yet in bed as he reached out to fondle, hopelessly, Maria who made love with him now more eagerly, more readily, more desperately, uselessly, pointlessly than ever before, his stomach was gripped by a sudden retching nausea, and he had to rush to the bathroom to vomit.

'My poor dear,' said Maria, 'oh my poor dear.'

He wondered whether he should rest again, to recover the placidity he had known in the hospital. But to rest in bed, although he could read or hear music, meant his life was so reduced. At least to walk round the fields or into the village gave him stimulation for those senses that remained.

But activity seemed disturbing. And provoked a riot of these sense memories, these million twitching amputated feet.

Then, one day, he realized his senses were not dead.

It was a compound realization, not a sudden epiphany. In the morning he had driven the car and going too fast over the humpbacked bridge that crossed the canal, had provoked a scream from Maria. He had asked in alarm what was the matter.

'Nothing,' she said, 'it's just that it took the bottom out of my stomach, going over the bridge like that.'

The Man of Slow Feeling

'I'm sorry,' he said, 'I didn't realize I was going that fast. I can't feel that sort of thing now.'

Indeed he had forgotten, till she reminded him, that the sensation existed.

They made love at noon, not because he could experience anything, but because in his dreams and in his waking nerve memories, he so often re-experienced the ecstasy in actuality denied him. He perhaps half hoped to recapture the experience. But never did.

Maria got up to cook lunch, absurdly spending great labour on foods he could not taste, perhaps hoping to lure his taste from its grave. She rushed from the kitchen to his bed when he gave a sudden cry. But he was laughing when she reached the bedroom.

'Sorry,' he said. 'It's just that like you said, your stomach dropped out going over the bridge, and that must have reminded me of it. It just happened this minute, lying here.'

She touched his brow with her cool hand, whose coolness and presence he could not feel. He brushed her away, irritated by her solicitude. As he ate his lunch, he brooded over his cry of alarm. And later, buying cigarettes in the village shop, for the nervous habit he realized that had always caused him to smoke, not the taste, he came on the truth as his body was suffused with the sudden aliveness of intercourse, the convulsive ecstasy of orgasm.

'Are you all right, sir?' the shopkeeper asked.

'I'm fine, fine,' he said. 'It's, it's' (it's nothing he was about to say mechanically, but it was ecstasy); 'it's quite all right,' he said.

Walking back, he was elated at realizing sensation was not denied him, but delayed. He looked at his watch and predicted he would taste his lunch at four o'clock. And sitting on the stile at the field corner, he did. In excitement he ran, his meal finished, to tell Maria, to tell her ecstatically that the accident had not robbed him of sensation, but dulled and slowed its passage along his nerves. When he tripped on a log and grazed his knee without any feeling, he knew, ambivalently, that in three hours the pain would be registered: he waited in excitement for confirmation of his prediction, in anxiety about the pain it would bring.

* * *

But his knowledge was a doubtful advantage. The confusions of senses before had been disturbing, but not worrying. It was the prediction now that tore him with anxiety. Cutting his finger while sharpening a pencil, he waited tense for the delayed pain; and even though cutting his finger was the slightest of hurts, it filled three hours of anxiety. He worked out with Maria that the well-timed cooking of food could appetize his tasteless smelless later meal; but few meals could produce rich smells three hours before serving. He could not do anything the slightest nauseating, like cleaning drains or gutting chickens, for fear of the context in which his senses would later register and produce in their further three hours the possibility of his vomiting. Defecation became nightmarish, could ruin any ill-timed meal, or intercourse. And ill-timed intercourse would ruin any casual urination. He toyed with the idea of keeping a log book, so that by consulting what happened three hours back, he knew what he was about to feel. He experimented one morning, and in a sort of way it worked. For he spent so long noting down each detail in his book, he had little time to experience anything. He realized how full a life is of sensations, as hopelessly he tried to record them all.

He developed a device, instead, consisting primarily of a small tape-recorder which he carried always with him. He spoke a constant commentary into it of his sensate actions and, through earphones, his commentary would be played back to him after a three hours delay, to warn him of what he was about to feel. The initial three hours, as he paced the fields, were comparatively simple, though he worried at the limitations it would impose on his life and experience, having to comment on it in its entirety, each trivial stumble, each slight contact. But after three hours had passed, and his bruised slow nerves were transmitting his sensations, the playback came in. And he found he could not both record his current activities in a constant flow, and hear a constant commentary on his three-hours-back activities, momentarily prior to his sensations of those past ones. He braced himself for the predicted sensation that his recorded voice warned him of, and in doing so forgot to maintain his current commentary for his three hours hence instruction. And maintaining his commentary, he forgot to act on the playback and lost the value of its warnings. And returning again to it,

The Man of Slow Feeling

intent on gaining from its predictions, he began to follow its record as instructions, and when he caught the word 'stumble' from his disembodied voice, he stumbled in obedience, forgetting to hold himself still for the sensation of stumbling. And what, anyway, warned of a stumble, was he to do? Sit passively for the experience to flow through him and pass? What he had recorded as advice seemed peremptory instruction, terse orders that his nerves responded to independent of his volition. The playback possessed an awful authority, as if the voice were no longer his, and the announced experiences (which he had never felt) foreign to him: and at each random whim of the voice, distorted parodically from his own, his sensations would have inevitably to respond. And he the mere frame, the theatre for the puppet strings to be hung and tugged in.

He could never coordinate commentary and playback: the one perpetually blocked the other, as he tried to hear one thing and say another. And he would confuse them and having spoken a sensation into the microphone before him would immediately prepare to experience it, forgetting the delay that had to come. His sensations became as random to him as before in that maze of playback and commentary and memory. And when he did accidentally, reflectively, re-enact the activity his playback warned him to prepare for, then he had to record another warning of that activity for his three hours later sensation: and it was as if he were to be trapped in a perpetual round to the same single repeated stumble.

He abandoned notebooks and tape-recorders. He sat at the window awaiting his sensations. Sex became a nightmare for him, its insensate action and empty voyeurism bringing only the cerebral excitement of a girlie magazine, its consequence a wet dream, the tension of waiting for which (sometimes with an urgent hope, sometimes with the resistant wished-against tension) would agonize him — keep him sleepless or, in the mornings, unable to read or move. And the continual anxiety affected his whole sexual activity, made him ejaculate too soon, or not at all; and he had to wait his three hours for his failures to reach him, knowing his failure, reminded of it cruelly three hours after his cerebral realization.

He could not sleep. Any activity three hours before sleep, would awaken him, bumping into a door, drinking wine, switching off a record player. The sensations would arouse his tense consciousness. He tried to control against this, spending the three hours before sleep in total stillness and peace, but the tension of this created its own anxiety, produced psychosomatic pains: of which he would be unaware until they woke him.

He thought back with a sort of longing to his hospital bed, when without stimulation he had experienced only the slightest of sensations. But in those bare walls of the bare room, he might almost have been in a tomb. If life were only bearable without sensation, what was the life worth that he could bear?

* * *

Maria came back from town one day to find him dead in the white, still bathroom. He had cut his arteries in a bath in the Roman way, the hot water, now rich vermilioned, to reduce the pain of dying. Though, she told herself, he would not have felt anything anyway, he had no sensation.

But three hours afterwards, what might he have felt?

American Dreams

Peter Carey

No-one can, to this day, remember what it was we did to offend him. Dyer the butcher remembers a day when he gave him the wrong meat and another day when he served someone else first by mistake. Often when Dyer gets drunk he recalls this day and curses himself for his foolishness. But no-one seriously believes that it was Dyer who offended him.

But one of us did something. We slighted him terribly in some way, this small meek man with the rimless glasses and neat suit who used to smile so nicely at us all. We thought, I suppose, he was a bit of a fool and sometimes he was so quiet and grey that we ignored him, forgetting he was there at all.

When I was a boy I often stole apples from the trees at his house up in Mason's Lane. He often saw me. No, that's not correct. Let me say I often sensed that he saw me. I sensed him peering out from behind the lace curtains of his house. And I was not the only one. Many of us came to take his apples, alone and in groups, and it is possible that he chose to exact payment for all these apples in his own peculiar way.

Yet I am sure it wasn't the apples.

What has happened is that we all, all eight hundred of us, have come to remember small transgressions against Mr. Gleason who once lived amongst us.

My father, who has never borne malice against a single living creature, still believes that Gleason meant to do us well, that he loved the town more than any of us. My father says we have treated the town badly in our minds. We have used it, this little valley, as nothing more than a stopping place. Somewhere on the way to somewhere else. Even those of us who have been here many years have never taken the town seriously. Oh yes, the place is pretty. The hills are green and the woods thick. The stream is full of fish. But it is not where we would rather be.

For years we have watched the films at the Roxy and dreamed, if not of America, then at least of our capital city. For our own town, my father says, we have nothing but contempt. We have treated it badly, like a whore. We have cut down the giant shady trees in the main street to make doors for the school house and seats for the football pavilion. We have left big holes all over the countryside from which we have taken brown coal and given back nothing.

The commercial travellers who buy fish and chips at George the Greek's care for us more than we do, because we all have dreams of the big city, of wealth, of modern houses, of big motor cars: American dreams, my father has called them.

Although my father ran a petrol station he was also an inventor. He sat in his office all day drawing strange pieces of equipment on the back of delivery dockets. Every spare piece of paper in the house was covered with these little drawings and my mother would always be very careful about throwing away any piece of paper no matter how small. She would look on both sides of any piece of paper very carefully and always preserved any that had so much as a pencil mark.

I think it was because of this that my father felt that he understood Gleason. He never said as much, but he inferred that he understood Gleason because he, too, was concerned with similar problems. My father was working on plans for a giant gravel crusher, but occasionally he would become distracted and become interested in something else.

There was, for instance, the time when Dyer the butcher bought a new bicycle with gears, and for a while my father talked of nothing else but the gears. Often I would see him across the road squatting down beside Dyer's bicycle as if he were talking to it.

We all rode bicycles because we didn't have the money for anything better. My father did have an old Chev truck, but he rarely used it and it occurs to me now that it might have had some mechanical problem that was impossible to solve, or perhaps it was just that he was saving it, not wishing to wear it

American Dreams

out all at once. Normally, he went everywhere on his bicycle and, when I was younger, he carried me on the cross bar, both of us dismounting to trudge up the hills that led into and out of the main street. It was a common sight in our town to see people pushing bicycles. They were as much a burden as a means of transport.

Gleason also had his bicycle and every lunchtime he pushed and pedalled it home from the shire offices to his little weatherboard house out at Mason's Lane. It was a three-mile ride and people said that he went home for lunch because he was fussy and wouldn't eat either his wife's sandwiches or the hot meal available at Mrs. Lessing's cafe.

But while Gleason pedalled and pushed his bicycle to and from the shire offices everything in our town proceeded as normal. It was only when he retired that things began to go wrong.

Because it was then that Mr. Gleason started supervising the building of the wall around the two-acre plot up on Bald Hill. He paid too much for this land. He bought it from Johnny Weeks, who now, I am sure, believes the whole episode was his fault, firstly for cheating Gleason, secondly for selling him the land at all. But Gleason hired some Chinese and set to work to build his wall. It was then that we knew that we'd offended him. My father rode all the way out to Bald Hill and tried to talk Mr. Gleason out of his wall. He said there was no need for us to build walls. That no-one wished to spy on Mr. Gleason or whatever he wished to do on Bald Hill. He said no-one was in the least bit interested in Mr. Gleason. Mr. Gleason, neat in a new sportscoat, polished his glasses and smiled vaguely at his feet. Bicycling back, my father thought that he had gone too far. Of course we had an interest in Mr. Gleason. He pedalled back and asked him to attend a dance that was to be held on the next Friday, but Mr. Gleason said he didn't dance.

'Oh well,' my father said, 'any time, just drop over.'

Mr. Gleason went back to supervising his family of Chinese labourers on his wall.

Bald Hill towered high above the town and from my father's small filling station you could sit and watch the wall going up. It was an interesting sight. I watched it for two years, while I waited for customers who rarely came. After school and on

Saturdays I had all the time in the world to watch the agonising progress of Mr. Gleason's wall. It was as painful as a clock. Sometimes I could see the Chinese labourers running at a jog-trot carrying bricks on long wooden planks. The hill was bare, and on this bareness Mr. Gleason was, for some reason, building a wall.

In the beginning people thought it peculiar that someone would build such a big wall on Bald Hill. The only thing to recommend Bald Hill was the view of the town, and Mr. Gleason was building a wall that denied that view. The top soil was thin and bare clay showed through in places. Nothing would ever grow there. Everyone assumed that Gleason had simply gone mad and after the initial interest they accepted his madness as they accepted his wall and as they accepted Bald Hill itself.

Occasionally someone would pull in for petrol at my father's filling station and ask about the wall and my father would shrug and I would see, once more, the strangeness of it.

'A house?' the stranger would ask. 'Up on that hill?'

'No,' my father would say, 'chap named Gleason is building a wall.'

And the strangers would want to know why, and my father would shrug and look up at Bald Hill once more. 'Damned if I know,' he'd say.

Gleason still lived in his old house at Mason's Lane. It was a plain weatherboard house with a rose garden at the front, a vegetable garden down the side, and an orchard at the back.

At night we kids would sometimes ride out to Bald Hill on our bicycles. It was an agonising, muscle-twitching ride, the worst part of which was a steep, unmade road up which we finally pushed our bikes, our lungs rasping in the night air. When we arrived we found nothing but walls. Once we broke down some of the brickwork and another time we threw stones at the tents where the Chinese labourers slept. Thus we expressed our frustration at this inexplicable thing.

The wall must have been finished on the day before my twelfth birthday. I remember going on a picnic birthday party up to Eleven Mile Creek and we lit a fire and cooked chops at a bend in the river from where it was possible to see the walls on Bald Hill. I remember standing with a hot chop in my hand and someone saying, 'Look, they're leaving!'

American Dreams

We stood on the creek bed and watched the Chinese labourers walking their bicycles slowly down the hill. Someone said they were going to build a chimney up at the mine at A.1 and certainly there is a large brick chimney there now, so I suppose they built it.

When the word spread that the walls were finished most of the town went up to look. They walked around the four walls which were as interesting as any other brick walls. They stood in front of the big wooden gates and tried to peer through, but all they could see was a small blind wall that had obviously been constructed for this special purpose. The walls themselves were ten feet high and topped with broken glass and barbed wire. When it became obvious that we were not going to discover the contents of the enclosure, we all gave up and went home.

Mr. Gleason had long since stopped coming into town. His wife came instead, wheeling a pram down from Mason's Lane to Main Street and filling it with groceries and meat (they never bought vegetables, they grew their own) and wheeling it back to Mason's Lane. Sometimes you would see her standing with the pram halfway up the Gell Street hill. Just standing there, catching her breath. No-one asked her about the wall. They knew she wasn't responsible for the wall and they felt sorry for her, having to bear the burden of the pram and her husband's madness. Even when she began to visit Dixon's hardware and buy plaster of paris and tins of paint and waterproofing compound, no-one asked her what these things were for. She had a way of averting her eyes that indicated her terror of questions. Old Dixon carried the plaster of paris and the tins of paint out to her pram for her and watched her push them away. 'Poor woman,' he said, 'poor bloody woman.'

From the filling station where I sat dreaming in the sun, or from the enclosed office where I gazed mournfully at the rain, I would see, occasionally, Gleason entering or leaving his walled compound, a tiny figure way up on Bald Hill. And I'd think 'Gleason,' but not much more.

Occasionally strangers drove up there to see what was going on, often egged on by locals who told them it was a Chinese temple or some other silly thing. Once a group of Italians had a picnic outside the walls and took photographs of each other standing in front of the closed door. God knows what they

361

thought it was.

But for five years between my twelfth and seventeenth birthdays there was nothing to interest me in Gleason's walls. Those years seem lost to me now and I can remember very little of them. I developed a crush on Susy Markin and followed her back from the swimming pool on my bicycle. I sat behind her in the pictures and wandered past her house. Then her parents moved to another town and I sat in the sun and waited for them to come back.

We became very keen on modernisation. When coloured paints became available the whole town went berserk and brightly coloured houses blossomed overnight. But the paints were not of good quality and quickly faded and peeled, so that the town looked like a garden of dead flowers. Thinking of those years, the only real thing I recall is the soft hiss of bicycle tyres on the main street. When I think of it now it seems very peaceful, but I remember then that the sound induced in me a feeling of melancholy, a feeling somehow mixed with the early afternoons when the sun went down behind Bald Hill and the town felt as sad as an empty dance hall on a Sunday afternoon.

And then, during my seventeenth year, Mr. Gleason died. We found out when we saw Mrs. Gleason's pram parked out in front of Phonsey Joy's Funeral Parlour. It looked very sad, that pram, standing by itself in the windswept street. We came and looked at the pram and felt sad for Mrs. Gleason. She hadn't had much of a life.

Phonsey Joy carried old Mr. Gleason out to the cemetery by the Parwan Railway Station and Mrs. Gleason rode behind in a taxi. People watched the old hearse go by and thought, 'Gleason', but not much else.

And then, less than a month after Gleason had been buried out at the lonely cemetery by the Parwan Railway Station, the Chinese labourers came back. We saw them push their bicycles up the hill. I stood with my father and Phonsey Joy and wondered what was going on.

And then I saw Mrs. Gleason trudging up the hill. I nearly didn't recognise her, because she didn't have her pram. She carried a black umbrella and walked slowly up Bald Hill and it wasn't until she stopped for breath and leant forward that I recognised her.

American Dreams

'It's Mrs. Gleason,' I said, 'with the Chinese.'

But it wasn't until the next morning that it became obvious what was happening. People lined the main street in the way they do for a big funeral but, instead of gazing towards the Grant Street corner, they all looked up at Bald Hill.

All that day and all the next people gathered to watch the destruction of the walls. They saw the Chinese labourers darting to and fro, but it wasn't until they knocked down a large section of the wall facing the town that we realised there really was something inside. It was impossible to see what it was, but there was something there. People stood and wondered and pointed out Mrs. Gleason to each other as she went to and fro supervising the work.

And finally, in ones and twos, on bicycles and on foot, the whole town moved up to Bald Hill. Mr. Dyer closed up his butcher shop and my father got out the old Chev truck and we finally arrived up at Bald Hill with twenty people on board. They crowded into the back tray and hung onto the running boards and my father grimly steered his way through the crowds of bicycles and parked just where the dirt track gets really steep. We trudged up this last steep track, never for a moment suspecting what we would find at the top.

It was very quiet up there. The Chinese labourers worked diligently, removing the third and fourth walls and cleaning the bricks which they stacked neatly in big piles. Mrs. Gleason said nothing either. She stood in the only remaining corner of the walls and looked defiantly at the townspeople who stood open mouthed where another corner had been.

And between us and Mrs. Gleason was the most incredibly beautiful thing I had ever seen in my life. For one moment I didn't recognise it. I stood open mouthed, and breathed the surprising beauty of it. And then I realised it was our town. The buildings were two feet high and they were a little rough but very correct. I saw Mr. Dyer nudge my father and whisper that Gleason had got the faded 'U' in the BUTCHER sign of his shop.

I think at that moment everyone was overcome with a feeling of simple joy. I can't remember ever having felt so uplifted and happy. It was perhaps a childish emotion but I looked up at my father and saw a smile of such warmth spread across his face that

I knew he felt just as I did. Later he told me that he thought Gleason had built the model of our town just for this moment, to let us see the beauty of our own town, to make us proud of ourselves and to stop the American Dreams we were so prone to. For the rest, my father said, was not Gleason's plan and he could not have foreseen the things that happened afterwards.

I have come to think that this view of my father's is a little sentimental and also, perhaps, insulting to Gleason. I personally believe that he knew everything that would happen. One day the proof of my theory may be discovered. Certainly there are in existence some personal papers, and I firmly believe that these papers will show that Gleason knew exactly what would happen.

We had been so overcome by the model of the town that we hadn't noticed what was the most remarkable thing of all. Not only had Gleason built the houses and the shops of our town, he had also peopled it. As we tip-toed into the town we suddenly found ourselves. 'Look,' I said to Mr. Dyer, 'there you are.'

And there he was, standing in front of his shop in his apron. As I bent down to examine the tiny figure I was staggered by the look on its face. The modelling was crude, the paint work was sloppy, and the face a little too white, but the expression was absolutely perfect: those pursed, quizzical lips and the eyebrows lifted high. It was Mr. Dyer and no-one else on earth.

And there beside Mr. Dyer was my father, squatting on the footpath and gazing lovingly at Mr. Dyer's bicycle's gears, his face marked with grease and hope.

And there was I, back at the filling station, leaning against a petrol pump in an American pose and talking to Brian Sparrow who was amusing me with his clownish antics.

Phonsey Joy standing beside his hearse. Mr. Dixon sitting inside his hardware store. Everyone I knew was there in that tiny town. If they were not in the streets or in their backyards they were inside their houses, and it didn't take very long to discover that you could lift off the roofs and peer inside.

We tip-toed around the streets peeping into each other's windows, lifting off each other's roofs, admiring each other's gardens, and, while we did it, Mrs. Gleason slipped silently away down the hill towards Mason's Lane. She spoke to nobody and nobody spoke to her.

American Dreams

I confess that I was the one who took the roof from Cavanagh's house. So I was the one who found Mrs. Cavanagh in bed with young Craigie Evans.

I stood there for a long time, hardly knowing what I was seeing. I stared at the pair of them for a long, long time. And when I finally knew what I was seeing I felt such an incredible mixture of jealousy and guilt and wonder that I didn't know what to do with the roof.

Eventually it was Phonsey Joy who took the roof from my hands and placed it carefully back on the house, much, I imagine, as he would have placed the lid on a coffin. By then other people had seen what I had seen and the word passed around very quickly.

And then we all stood around in little groups and regarded the model town with what could only have been fear. If Gleason knew about Mrs. Cavanagh and Craigie Evans (and no-one else had), what other things might he know? Those who hadn't seen themselves yet in the town began to look a little nervous and were unsure of whether to look for themselves or not. We gazed silently at the roofs and felt mistrustful and guilty.

We all walked down the hill then, very quietly, the way people walk away from a funeral, listening only to the crunch of the gravel under our feet while the women had trouble with their high-heeled shoes.

The next day a special meeting of the shire council passed a motion calling on Mrs. Gleason to destroy the model town on the grounds that it contravened building regulations.

It is unfortunate that this order wasn't carried out before the city newspapers found out. Before another day had gone by the government had stepped in.

The model town and its model occupants were to be preserved. The minister for tourism came in a large black car and made a speech to us in the football pavilion. We sat on the high, tiered seats eating potato chips while he stood against the fence and talked to us. We couldn't hear him very well, but we heard enough. He called the model town a work of art and we stared at him grimly. He said it would be an invaluable tourist attraction. He said tourists would come from everywhere to see the model town. We would be famous. Our businesses would flourish. There would be work for guides and interpreters and caretakers and taxi drivers and people selling soft drinks and ice creams.

The Americans would come, he said. They would visit our town in buses and in cars and on the train. They would take photographs and bring wallets bulging with dollars. American dollars.

We looked at the minister mistrustfully, wondering if he knew about Mrs. Cavanagh, and he must have seen the look because he said that certain controversial items would be removed, had already been removed. We shifted in our seats, like you do when a particularly tense part of a film has come to its climax, and then we relaxed and listened to what the minister had to say. And we all began, once more, to dream our American dreams.

We saw our big smooth cars cruising through cities with bright lights. We entered expensive night clubs and danced till dawn. We made love to women like Kim Novak and men like Rock Hudson. We drank cocktails. We gazed lazily into refrigerators filled with food and prepared ourselves lavish midnight snacks which we ate while we watched huge television sets on which we would be able to see American movies free of charge and forever.

The minister, like someone from our American dreams, re-entered his large black car and cruised slowly from our humble sportsground, and the newspaper men arrived and swarmed over the pavilion with their cameras and note books. They took photographs of us and photographs of the models up on Bald Hill. And the next day we were all over the newspapers. The photographs of the model people side by side with photographs of the real people. And our names and ages and what we did were all printed there in black and white.

They interviewed Mrs. Gleason but she said nothing of interest. She said the model town had been her husband's hobby.

We all felt good now. It was very pleasant to have your photograph in the paper. And, once more, we changed our opinion of Gleason. The shire council held another meeting and named the dirt track up Bald Hill, 'Gleason Avenue'. Then we all went home and waited for the Americans we had been promised.

It didn't take long for them to come, although at the time it seemed an eternity, and we spent six long months doing nothing more with our lives than waiting for the Americans.

American Dreams

Well, they did come. And let me tell you how it has all worked out for us.

The Americans arrive every day in buses and cars and sometimes the younger ones come on the train. There is now a small airstrip out near the Parwan cemetery and they also arrive there, in small aeroplanes. Phonsey Joy drives them to the cemetery where they look at Gleason's grave and then up to Bald Hill and then down to the town. He is doing very well from it all. It is good to see someone doing well from it. Phonsey is becoming a big man in town and is on the shire council.

On Bald Hill there are half a dozen telescopes through which the Americans can spy on the town and reassure themselves that it is the same down there as it is on Bald Hill. Herb Gravney sells them ice creams and soft drinks and extra film for their cameras. He is another one who is doing well. He bought the whole model from Mrs. Gleason and charges five American dollars admission. Herb is on the council now too. He's doing very well for himself. He sells them the film so they can take photographs of the houses and the model people and so they can come down to the town with their special maps and hunt out the real people.

To tell the truth most of us are pretty sick of the game. They come looking for my father and ask him to stare at the gears of Dyer's bicycle. I watch my father cross the street slowly, his head hung low. He doesn't greet the Americans anymore. He doesn't ask them questions about colour television or Washington D.C. He kneels on the footpath in front of Dyer's bike. They stand around him. Often they remember the model incorrectly and try to get my father to pose in the wrong way. Originally he argued with them, but now he argues no more. He does what they ask. They push him this way and that and worry about the expression on his face which is no longer what it was.

Then I know they will come to find me. I am next on the map. I am very popular for some reason. They come in search of me and my petrol pump as they have done for four years now. I do not await them eagerly because I know, before they reach me, that they will be disappointed.

'But this is not the boy.'

'Yes,' says Phonsey, 'this is him alright.' And he gets me to show them my certificate.

They examine the certificate suspiciously, feeling the paper as if it might be a clever forgery. 'No,' they declare. (Americans are so confident.) 'No,' they shake their heads, 'this is not the real boy. The real boy is younger.'

'He's older now. He used to be younger.' Phonsey looks weary when he tells them. He can afford to look weary.

The Americans peer at my face closely. 'It's a different boy.'

But finally they get their cameras out. I stand sullenly and try to look amused as I did once. Gleason saw me looking amused but I can no longer remember how it felt. I was looking at Brian Sparrow. But Brian is also tired. He finds it difficult to do his clownish antics and to the Americans his little act isn't funny. They prefer the model. I watch him sadly, sorry that he must perform for such an unsympathetic audience.

The Americans pay one dollar for the right to take our photographs. Having paid the money they are worried about being cheated. They spend their time being disappointed and I spend my time feeling guilty, that I have somehow let them down by growing older and sadder.

Biographical Notes

CATHERINE HELEN SPENCE was born in Scotland in 1825, and brought to Australia by her family in 1839. She worked as a journalist in Adelaide and was an active and lifelong supporter of women's suffrage and other social causes. *Clara Morison* was the first-published and is today the best-known of her four novels. She died in 1910.

MARCUS CLARKE was born in London of English parents in 1846, and emigrated from there to Australia at the age of seventeen. Like most of the writers represented here, he worked chiefly as a journalist and published sketches, essays and stories as well as novels. He is best known for the classic 'convict novel', *For the Term of his Natural Life*. He died in 1881.

"PRICE WARUNG" (William Astley) was born in England in 1855 and brought to Australia as a child in 1859. His fiercely democratic views were shared and encouraged by the editors of the *Bulletin*, where most of the stories in his five published collections originally appeared. He died in 1911.

BARBARA BAYNTON was born in 1857 in the Hunter Valley district of New South Wales. Her fiction output was small — one collection of stories (*Bush Studies*, 1902), one novel (*Human Toll*, 1907), and a few later, uncollected stories — but her powerful, mostly grim stories of bush life have recently been attracting more and more attention. Critics have compared her work to that of Henry Lawson, her near-contemporary and fellow-protege of the *Bulletin*. She died in 1929.

HENRY LAWSON was born in 1867 in a tent on the Grenfell goldfield of New South Wales. His father was a Norwegian sailor who jumped ship in Melbourne to join the gold rush, and his mother was the woman who began the first Australian women's newspaper — a colourful figure in her own right. Like many of the writers represented here, Lawson was a radical whose writing is imbued with a political consciousness; the first piece he ever published, a poem which appeared in the *Bulletin* when he was twenty, was entitled 'Song of the Republic'. He became in his lifetime, and has remained after his death, one of Australia's best-known writers. He died in 1922.

"HENRY HANDEL RICHARDSON" (Ethel Florence Lindesay Richardson) was born in Melbourne in 1870; she was the daughter of an English mother and an Irish father who both emigrated to Australia in their youth. Her trilogy *The Fortunes of Richard Mahony* is one of the best-known works of Australian fiction; as well as this and several other novels, she published a collection of short stories and the autobiography *Myself When Young*. She lived abroad for most of her life and died in London in 1946.

KATHARINE SUSANNAH PRICHARD was born of Australian parents in Fiji in 1883. One of Australia's most politically active and committed writers, Prichard was a co-founder of the Australian Communist Party; and she is one of the few white Australian writers to have dealt in any detail in her work with the position and problems of Australian Aboriginals. She published poems, a play and an autobiography as well as the numerous short stories and novels for which she is best known. She died in 1969.

ETHEL ANDERSON was born in England in 1883 and brought as a child to Australia; she was educated in Sydney. Anderson published one volume of essays and three of poems as well as her two collections of short stories. Considering the charm and originality of her work, Anderson is an inexplicably neglected figure in Australian literature. She died in 1958.

FRANK DALBY DAVISON was born in Melbourne in 1893; apart from active service during the First World War he spent most of his life as a farmer. A novelist and short-story writer, Davison is best known for two of his novels: the unique *Man-Shy*, a book about animals which is neither an Orwellian fable nor a 'children's book', and his last, long-worked-at novel *The White Thorntree*. He died in 1970.

CHRISTINA STEAD was born in 1902 in Rockdale, New South Wales. Her magnificent imagination and inventiveness and her extraordinary prose style — described variously as 'rich' or 'turgid' according to the tastes of the commentator — make her a unique figure in Australian literature. Although contemporary with, and politically sympathetic to, the social realists, Stead is by no means one of them. She was a writer ahead of her time; *The Man Who Loved Children,* the novel regarded by many as her masterpiece, has — like the rest of her work — only had the critical attention it deserves comparatively recently. She died early in 1983.

ALAN MARSHALL was born in 1902, in the small Victorian town of Noorat. A writer of travel and history books as well as of novels and short stories, Marshall was best known for the autobiography *I Can Jump Puddles*. He died in 1984.

JOHN MORRISON was born in 1904 in Sunderland, on the heavily industrialised north-eastern coast of England, and came to Australia as a young man. Many of his stories deal with Australian life during the Great Depression; of the group of Australian writers loosely termed 'the social realists', Morrison has possibly the highest literary reputation. He has published two novels but is best known as a short-story writer.

E.O. SCHLUNKE was born in 1906 in Temora, New South Wales. He was a farmer all his life; his stories are frequently rural versions of Gavin Casey's or John Morrison's — variations on the social realist theme. He published three novels as well as the short stories for which he is best known. He died in 1960.

GAVIN CASEY was born in 1907 in the Western Australian city of Kalgoorlie; like much of Katharine Susannah Prichard's, Casey's fiction is largely concerned with the goldfields life there. Like many of the writers represented here, Casey earned his living chiefly as a journalist; his best-known work is the collection of short stories originally published under the title *It's Harder for Girls* and later retitled *Short Shift Saturday*. He died in 1964.

DAL STIVENS was born in Blayney, New South Wales, in 1911. He describes himself as 'a political animal'; an active conservationist and pacifist, Stivens was orginally considered to be one of the 'social realists', but much of his work — particularly his recent work — does not fit this category. A novelist and short-story writer, Stivens regards the comparatively recent and award-winning novel *A Horse of Air* — of which 'Warrigal' is a part, although published separately as a short story — as his best work.

HAL PORTER was born in Melbourne in 1911. One of the most highly regarded (and one of the most prolific) short-story writers in Australia, Porter also wrote novels, poems, plays and books of travel, fiction and autobiography. He died in 1984.

PATRICK WHITE was born in London of Australian parents in 1912. White had the widest national and international reputation of any Australian writer; he was awarded the Nobel Prize for Literature in 1973. As well as the eleven novels published since 1939, White wrote short stories and plays; and his autobiography *Flaws in The Glass* appeared in 1981. He died in 1991.

PETER COWAN was born in Perth in 1914. Cowan, a writer of substantial reputation in Australia, has published two novels as well as the four collections of short stories for which he is best known.

THELMA FORSHAW was born in Glebe Point, New South Wales, in 1923. Like many writers represented in this anthology, Forshaw has worked chiefly as a journalist and reviewer. Many of her stories have been published in journals and anthologies; her collection *An Affair of Clowns* appeared in 1967.

ELIZABETH JOLLEY was born into a half-English half-Viennese household in the England Midlands in 1923, and came to Australia in 1959. She is the author of short stories and radio plays as well as four novels; her most recent collection of stories, *Woman in a Lampshade*, appeared early in 1983. She teaches in the English Department at the Western Australian Institute of Technology.

ELIZABETH HARROWER was born in Sydney in 1928; she has worked in publishing, journalism and the Australian media. Like many Australian women writers, Harrower has received only in recent years the amount of critical attention merited by her work. She has published four novels.

FRANK MOORHOUSE was born on the South Coast of New South Wales in 1938. A leading figure in the recent Australian short story boom, Moorhouse has published six collections since 1969; he also wrote the screenplay of the Australian film *Between Wars*. Moorhouse, known in addition for his journalism, was widely regarded in the 1970's as a spokesman for his generation.

MORRIS LURIE was born in Melbourne in 1938; he has a diverse background in architecture, advertising and journalism. Like many of the writers represented here, Lurie lived and worked abroad for a number of years. His literary output includes novels, children's books and a screenplay as well as several collections of short stories.

MURRAY BAIL was born in Adelaide in 1941; he has lived in Bombay and in London, where he wrote for the *Times Literary Supplement* and published stories in the *Transatlantic Review*. His fiction is complex and sophisticated, concerning itself largely with the act of writing, the fact of language, and the limitations of both in representing reality. He has published one collection of stories (*Contemporary Portraits*, 1975), one novel — the award-winning *Homesickness* (1980) — and a study of the Australian artist Ian Fairweather.

MICHAEL WILDING was born in Worcester in 1942; he came to Australia after graduating from Oxford. Widely known as a reviewer, publisher, critic and colourful academic figure, Wilding has also published novels and several collections of short stories. He is a Reader in English at the University of Sydney.

PETER CAREY was born in Bacchus Marsh near Melbourne in 1943; he describes himself as 'a child of Menzies and General Motors'. His first collection of stories, *The Fat Man in History* (1974), drew much favourable critical attention; the next collection *War Crimes* (1979) and the award-winning novel *Bliss* (1981) have consolidated his reputation as a leading Australian exponent of the 'new fiction'.

ACKNOWLEDGEMENTS

The publishers acknowledge the following copyright holders for permission to reproduce material in this collection:
THE ADVENTURES OF CUFFY MAHONEY AND OTHER STORIES by 'Henry Handel Richardson' – 'Two Hanged Women', *Angus & Robertson*, Copyright Olga Roncoroni 1979; HAPPINESS by Katharine Susannah Prichard – 'Flight', *Angus & Robertson*, Copyright R.P. Throssell 1967; THE WOMAN AT THE MILL by Frank Dalby Davison, 'The Woman at the Mill', *Angus & Robertson*, Copyright Marie Davison 1940; STORIES OF THE RIVERINA by E.O. Schlunke – 'The Man Who Liked Music', *Angus & Robertson*, Copyright Estate E.O. Schlunke; SHORT SHIFT SATURDAY AND OTHER STORIES by Gavin Casey – 'The Last Night', *Angus & Robertson*, Copyright G.W. Casey; HAL PORTER: SELECTED STORIES by Hal Porter – 'Say to Me Ronald!', *Angus & Robertson*, Copyright Hal Porter; FREDO FUSS LOVE LIFE AND OTHER STORIES by Hal Porter – 'Brett', *Angus & Robertson*, Copyright Hal Porter; THE EMPTY STREET AND OTHER STORIES by Peter Cowan – 'The Voice', *Angus & Robertson*, Copyright Peter Cowan; THE AMERICANS BABY by Frank Moorhouse – 'A Person of Accomplishment', *Angus & Robertson*, Copyright Frank Moorhouse; THE EVERLASTING SECRET FAMILY by Frank Moorhouse – 'Audition for Male Voice', *Angus & Robertson*, Copyright Frank Moorhouse; AT PARRAMATTA by Ethel Anderson – 'Miss Aminta

Wirraway and the Sin of Lust'/'Juliet McCree is Accused of Gluttony', *Angus & Robertson*, Copyright Bethia Ogden 1956; THE SALZBURG TALES by Christina Stead – 'Sappho'/ 'Guest of the Redshields', *Angus & Robertson* – Laurence Pollinger Ltd., Copyright Estate of Christina Stead; 'The Three-Legged Bitch' by Alan Marshall, Curtis Brown (Aust) Pty. Ltd.; NORTH WIND by John Morrison – 'The Incense Burner', *Penguin*; 'Christ the Devil and the Lunatic' by John Morrison; SELECTED STORIES 1936-68 by Dal Stivens – 'Warrigal', *Angus & Robertson*, Curtis Brown (Aust) Pty Ltd.; 'Down at the Dump' by Patrick White, Barbara Mobbs; AN AFFAIR OF CLOWNS by Thelma Forshaw – 'On Our Safari', *Angus & Robertson*; FRICTIONS, 'Poppy Seed and Sesame Rings' by Elizabeth Jolley, Sybylla Press, Copyright Elizabeth Jolley; 'The Cost of Things' by Elizabeth Harrower; DIRTY FRIENDS by Morris Lurie – 'African Wall', *Penguin*; CONTEMPORARY PORTRAITS AND OTHER STORIES by Murray Bail – 'A,B,C,D,E,F . . .', *University of Queensland Press*; THE WEST MIDLAND UNDERGROUND by Michael Wilding – 'The Man of Slow Feeling', *University of Queensland Press*; THE FAT MAN IN HISTORY by Peter Carey – 'American Dreams', *University of Queensland Press.*